continued . . .

WINDFALL

BOOK FOUR OF THE WEATHER WARDEN SERIES

Rachel Caine

FIC
CAINE
2005
PBK

A ROC BOOK

ROC
Published by New American Library, a division of
Penguin Group (USA) Inc., 375 Hudson Street,
New York, New York 10014, USA
Penguin Group (Canada), 90 Eglinton Avenue East, Suite 700, Toronto,
Ontario M4P 2Y3, Canada (a division of Pearson Penguin Canada Inc.)
Penguin Books Ltd., 80 Strand, London WC2R 0RL, England
Penguin Ireland, 25 St. Stephen's Green, Dublin 2,
Ireland (a division of Penguin Books Ltd.)
Penguin Group (Australia), 250 Camberwell Road, Camberwell, Victoria 3124,
Australia (a division of Pearson Australia Group Pty. Ltd.)
Penguin Books India Pvt. Ltd., 11 Community Centre, Panchsheel Park,
New Delhi - 110 017, India
Penguin Group (NZ), 67 Apollo Drive, Rosedale, North Shore 0632,
New Zealand (a division of Pearson New Zealand Ltd.)
Penguin Books (South Africa) (Pty.) Ltd., 24 Sturdee Avenue,
Rosebank, Johannesburg 2196, South Africa

Penguin Books Ltd., Registered Offices:
80 Strand, London WC2R 0RL, England

First published by Roc, an imprint of New American Library,
a division of Penguin Group (USA) Inc.

First Printing, November 2005
10   9

Copyright © Roxanne Longstreet Conrad, 2005
All rights reserved

Ⓡ REGISTERED TRADEMARK—MARCA REGISTRADA

Printed in the United States of America

PUBLISHER'S NOTE
This is a work of fiction. Names, characters, places, and incidents either are the
product of the author's imagination or are used fictitiously, and any resemblance
to actual persons, living or dead, business establishments, events, or locales is
entirely coincidental.

The publisher does not have any control over and does not assume any responsibility for author or third-party Web sites or their content.

The following brave writers made their National Novel Writing Month goal and wrote fifty thousand words toward a book in November 2004. I salute their incredible dedication, and I was proud to sponsor the NaNoNov community for 2004.

Acknowledgments

The author wishes to thank
The Stormchasers, who encourage me in this madness.
(Hi, guys!)

JoMadge, without whom neither this book nor ANY
Weather Warden books would have been possible.

The Time Turners: Kel, Katy, Becky, Laurie,
Claire (haka, baby!), and Marla.

Rachel Sheer and Ter Matthies. They know why,
and it has to do with werewolves.

The greatest band in the world: Joe Bonamassa,
Eric Czar and Kenny Kramme!
www.jbonamassa.com
(and everyone who supports them)

America's Best Coffee in Arlington,
and whatever brilliant barista invented Caramel Mochas
that are served at 5:30 A.M.

. . . and, of course, Cat. Always.

PREVIOUSLY . . .

My name is Joanne Baldwin. I used to control the weather, but I've given that up. See, I've discovered that the Wardens—who are supposed to be protecting all of you from horrible deaths from fires, floods, earthquakes, storms, and other fun rides cooked up by a hostile Mother Nature—haven't been entirely on the up and up, and besides that, there's the whole question of the Djinn they use to help them in their work. I used to think it was okay to keep a magical being locked up in a bottle and subject to your will.

Not anymore, not since I fell in love with one.

Having given up my day job, I've found it necessary to put the tattered remnants of my normal life back together again . . . no easy task for a girl without many marketable skills outside of the supernatural realm. Plus, there's the whole issue of having been dead, once upon a time. Kind of makes going home difficult.

And that really fast car I love so much?

Could be getting me into trouble.

Or maybe that's just my natural state of existence.

INTERLUDE

It doesn't take much to destroy the world as humans know it.

Unseasonably hot sunshine beating down on a small patch of ocean off the coast of Africa.

The water warms up a few degrees. As it burns off into gray ghosts, rising up into the air, it could be just another thing, another day, another balancing of wind and water.

But it's not. The air is just a few degrees warmer than normal, and it rises faster, carrying the moisture as a hostage. Ghosts turn to shadows as mist condenses and takes on weight. It spirals up into the sky, where the air gets thin and cold. At this height, the water condenses from mist to drops, too heavy for the process to contain them, and start a plunge back for safety of the ocean.

But the air's too warm, and as the drops fall they hit another, stronger updraft that sends them up again, dizzyingly high. Drops eat each other like cannibals and grow fatter. Heavier. Head for the ocean again.

But they aren't going anywhere; the updraft keeps short-circuiting gravity. The cycle continues, driving moisture into the air and hoarding it, as thin white virga condense and form clouds. You can feel energy building as hot sun and warm sea continue a mating dance.

It's no different than what happens every day in the Cradle of Storms.

But it is, if you know what you're looking for.

If I'd been paying attention, none of this would have happened.

ONE

I kept trying to tell myself, *You've survived worse than this,* but it didn't seem to be working. Any second now, I was going to scream and kill somebody, not necessarily in that order. . . . *You've been through worse.* Yep. I had. It just didn't feel like it, right at the moment.

I stared blankly at the back wall of the studio and held my place under the hot, merciless lights. The news anchors, seated at the desk about ten feet away from me, were still doing happychat. *Morning* happychat, which is a whole yak-level higher than the annoying evening forced camaraderie. I was sweating under a yellow rain slicker and matching hat and stupid-looking rain boots. I looked like the Morton's Salt girl, only not as adorable.

The weather outside was clear, and there wasn't even a hope in hell of rain from the nice, stable system out there, but Marvelous Marvin McLarty, meteorologist extraordinaire, was about to pronounce a seventy percent chance of downpours in the next twenty-four hours. And this wasn't the first out-of-the-blue (no pun intended) prediction Marvin had pulled out of his . . . Doppler. Two nights ago, he'd been the only one to accurately predict landfall of a tropical storm up the coast, while everyone else including the National Oceanic and Atmospheric Administration—NOAA to the weather buffs—had put it two hundred miles to the south.

This should have made him good. It only made him even more obnoxious. Unlikely as that seemed.

Dear God in heaven, I never thought I'd miss being a Warden quite so much, but right now—and for some time, actually—I wanted my old job back so bad that I'd have crawled on broken glass for it.

I held onto my big, toothy smile as the red light lit up on the camera in front of me and Marvin, who was standing next to me. He was a big man, bulky, with implanted hair and big, overwhitened teeth, laser-corrected blue eyes, and a face made unnaturally smooth by dermabrasion and Botox. Okay, the Botox was just a guess, but he was holding on to his fleeing, screaming youth with both fists.

Camera Two lit up. Marvin sauntered around, quipped with the anchors, Janie and Kurt, and then turned to the weather map. He started talking about a cold front approaching from the southeast . . . only there wasn't one; there was a front stalled at the Georgia border that didn't have nearly enough zippity doo dah to make it across the state line anytime in the next, oh, year. Behind him, the Chyron graphics did all kinds of cool zooms and swoops, showing animations and time-lapsed satellite cloud movements, which meant zero to about ninety-five percent of the population tuning in.

Marvin was a certified professional meteorologist. A degreed climatologist.

Marvin knew dick about the weather, but he was damn lucky. At least so far as I could tell, and believe me, I could tell a *lot*.

He walked past the animated map, and the camera followed him and focused on me as he stopped in frame. I turned the smile on Marvin, wishing it was a really big cannon.

"Good morning, Joanne!" he boomed cheerfully. He'd snarled at me earlier, while pushing past me in the hallway on his way to makeup. "Ready to talk about what's coming up?"

"Sure, Marvin!" I bubbled right back, perky as a cheerleader on speed. *I used to have a real job. I used to protect people. Save lives. How the hell did I get here?*

He wasn't listening to my internal whining. "Great! Well, we know how rough the weather's been the past few days, especially for our friends up the coast. We already know today's going to be bright and sunny, but let's tell our viewers out there in the Sunshine State what it's going to be like for them outside tomorrow!"

The camera pulled focus. I was center stage.

I held on to my smile like it was a life preserver. "Well, Marvin, I'm sure tomorrow's going to be a beautiful day for going outside and soaking up some—"

Marvin had taken the required number of steps out of frame, and just as I said the word "soaking," the bored, cigar chomping stagehand standing off-camera to my left yanked a rope.

About twenty gallons of water dumped from buckets directly over my head, right on target. It hurt. The bastards had chilled it, or else it was a lot colder up in those rafters than down here on the stage; the stuff felt ice-cold as it splashed off the plastic rain hat, straight down the back of my neck, to splash down into the stupid yellow rain boots.

I was standing in a kiddie pool with yellow rubber duckies on it. Most of the water made it in. I gasped and looked surprised, which wasn't hard; even when you expect it, it's tough not to be surprised by the idea that someone will actually *do* a thing like this to you.

Or that you will not kill them for it.

The anchors and Marvin laughed like lunatics. I kept smiling, took my rain hat off, and said, "Well, that's the weather in Florida, folks, just when you least expect it . . ."

And they hit me with the last bucket. Which they *hadn't* warned me about.

"Oh, boy, sorry about that, Weather Girl!" Marvin whooped, and came back into frame as I shoved my dripping hair back and tried to keep on smiling. "Guess we're in for a few showers tomorrow, eh?"

"Seventy percent chance," I gritted out. It wasn't quite so perky as I'd planned.

"So, moms, pack those umbrellas and raincoats for the kids in the morning! Joanne, it's time for our weather lesson of the day: Can you tell our viewers the difference between weather and climate?"

A climate *is the* weather *in an area averaged over a long period of time, you moron.* I thought it. I didn't say it. I kept smiling blankly at him as I asked, "I don't know, Marvin, what *is* the difference?" Because I was, after all, the straight woman, and this was penance for some horrible crime I'd committed in a previous life. As Genghis Khan, apparently.

He looked straight into the camera with his most serious expression and said, "You can't *weather* a tree, but you can *climate*."

I stared at him for about two seconds too long for television etiquette, then turned my smile back on like a porch light and said to the camera, "We'll be back tomorrow morning with more fun weather facts, kids!"

Marvin waved. I waved. The red light went out. Kurt and Janie started doing more happychat; they were about to interview a golden retriever, for some bizarre reason. I gave Marvin the kind of look that would have gotten me fired if I'd given it on the air, and threw my wet hair over my shoulder to wring it out like a mop into the ducky pool.

He leaned over to me and, in a whisper, said, "Hey, do you know this one? How is snow white? . . . Pretty damn good, according to the seven dwarves. Ha!"

"Your mike is on," I said, and watched him do the panic dance. His mike really wasn't, but it was so nice to see him make that face. The golden retriever, confused, woofed at him and lunged; panic ensued, both on and off camera. I stepped out of the wading pool and squelched away, past the grinning stagehands who knew *exactly* what I'd done and wished they'd thought of it first. I stripped off the wet rain slicker, stuffed the hat in the pocket, and escaped from the set and out the sound-baffling door.

Free.

Hard to believe that less than a year ago I'd been a trusted agent of one of the most powerful organizations on Earth, entrusted with the lives and safety of a few million people on a daily basis. Even harder to believe that I'd thrown all that away without looking back, and actually thought that I wouldn't *miss* it.

Normal life? Sucked. I'd become a Warden out of high school, been trained by the elite, spent years mastering the techniques of controlling the physics of wind, water, and weather. I'd been taken care of and coddled and had everything I'd ever wanted, and I hadn't even known how good that was until I had to survive on a poverty-level income and figure out how to make a jar of peanut butter stretch from one payday to the next.

And then there was the magnificence that was my job.

I took a deep breath of recycled, refrigerated air, and went in search of a place to sit down. A couple of staffers were in the hall, chitchatting; they watched me with the kind of bemused expressions people get when they're imagining themselves in your place and thinking, *there but for the grace of God . . .*

I ignored them as I squished by in my big, yellow clown boots.

In the makeup room, some kind soul handed me a fluffy white towel. I rubbed vigorously at my soaked hair and sighed when I saw it was starting to curl—nice, rich, black curls. Ringlets. Ugh.

That never used to happen before I died. I'd been a *power*. And then I'd had a brief, wildly strange few days as a wish-granting Djinn, which was both a hell of a lot more and less fun than you'd imagine. And then, I'd been bumped back down to mere mortal.

But in the process my hair had gone from glossy-straight to mega-curly. All my power, and I couldn't even keep a decent hairstyle.

Maybe *power* was an overstatement these days, any-way. I'd turned in my proverbial badge and gun to the Wardens, quit and walked away; technically, that meant that even though I might have some raw ability—a lot of it—I was now a regular citizen. Granted, a regular citizen who could sense and manipulate weather. Not that I *did,* of course. But I *could.* For three months, I'd gone cold turkey, resisting the urge to meddle, and I was pretty proud of myself. Too bad they didn't have a twelve-step program for this sort of thing, and some kind of cool little milestone keychain thing.

The fact that I'd been told by my own former colleagues that if I so much as made one raindrop rub up against another they'd bring me in for a magical lobotomy *might* have had something to do with my amazing strength of will. Some people survived that process just fine, but with someone like me, who had such a high level of that kind of power, getting rid of it all was like radical surgery. There was a significant chance that things would go wrong, and instead of just coming out of it a normal, unmagical human being, I'd come out a drooling zombie, fed and diapered at the Wardens' expense.

They weren't likely to do that to me unless they had to, though. The Wardens needed people they could trust. The organization had taken a lot of hits, from within and without, and they couldn't afford to burn bridges, even as shaky and unreliable a bridge as I represented.

I sighed and rubbed moisture from my hair, eyes closed. There were days—more rather than fewer, now—when I really regretted giving in to the impulse to fling it in their faces and walk away. I was one speed-dial away from having my life back.

But there were reasons why that was a bad idea, principal among them that I would lose the one thing in my life that really *meant* something to me. I'd willingly live in a crappy apartment and wear secondhand clothes and knockoff shoes for David's sake, for as long as it took.

That had to be true and eternal love.

"Yo, Jo."

I looked up from vigorous toweling and found a steaming cup of coffee in front of my nose. My benefactor and personal deity was a petite little blonde who went by the name of Cherise, impossibly young and pretty, with a beach tan and limpid blue eyes and a fine sense of the inappropriate. I liked her, even though she was just too damn cute to live. Not *everybody* in my new life was a burden. Cherise made the days just a little bit brighter.

"Nice 'do," she said, poker-faced. "Is poodle-hair coming back in style?"

"Didn't you get the latest *Vogue*? Next big thing. Poofy hair. And Earth Shoes are making a huge comeback."

"I don't know, honey, you've got sort of a Bride of Frankenstein meets Shirley Temple look going on there. I'd page the emergency stylist on call."

She, of course, looked perfect. She was wearing a midriff-baring mesh knit top with big yellow smiley faces, and a Day-Glo orange camisole underneath. I envied the outfit, but not the pierced belly button. Low-rise hiphuggers showed off smooth, sculpted curves. The shoes were designer flip-flops with little orange-and-yellow jeweled bees for decoration. She smiled as I took inventory, lifted her arms, and did a perfect runway twirl. "Well? What's my fashion score of the day?"

I considered. "Nine," I said.

Cherise whipped back around, offended. "*Nine?* You're kidding!"

"I deducted for nonmatching nail polish." I pointed at her toes. Sure enough, she was wearing yesterday's Lime Glitter Surprise.

"Damn." She frowned down at her shapely toes, one of which had a little silver ring. "But I got points for the new tat, right?"

I'd missed it during the twirl. "Let me see."

She turned around and pointed at the small of her back. Just at the point where the hiphuggers met the curve, there was an indigo-fresh . . .

I blinked, because it was a big-eyed alien head. Space aliens.

"Nice," I said, tilting my head to study it. The skin was still flushed. "Hurt much?"

She shrugged, eyeing a woman in a conservative black

pantsuit who'd come in and given her one of those
blankly disapproving looks, the kind reserved for girls in
hiphuggers, tattoos, and belly button piercings. I saw the
demon spark in Cherise's eyes. She pitched her voice to
carry. "Well, you know, those tattoos kind of sting. So I
did a little coke to take the edge off."

The woman, who was reaching for a coffee mug, froze.
I watched her rigid, French-manicured hand slowly resume its forward motion.

"Smoked or snorted?" I asked. Still the straight
woman. Apparently, it was my new karmic path.

"Smoked," Cherise said blandly. "Best way to get my
high on, but then I got all, you know, nervous. So I
smoked a couple of spliffs to calm down."

The woman left, coffee mug clenched in white knuckles.

"HR?" I guessed.

"Yeah, drug testing. I'll be peeing in a cup within the
hour. So." Cherise dropped into the chair next to me as
I applied the towel to my feet. "I hear you have an
interview for the weekend forecast position."

"Yeah." I wiggled my damp toes and felt the drag of
clinging hose. "Not that I have a chance in hell, but . . ."
But it was more money, and would get me out of the
humiliation business, and I wouldn't miss being Joanne
Baldwin, Weather Warden quite so fiercely if I had
something else I could be proud of doing.

"Oh, bullshit, of course you have a chance. A good
one, too. You're credible on camera, honest, and the
guys just *love* you. You've seen the website, right?"

I gave her a blank look.

"Your page is going through the roof. Hits out the ass,
Jo. Seriously. Not only that, but you should read the
emails. Those guys out there think you're damn hot."

"Really?" Because I didn't think there was anything
hot about getting hit in the face with buckets of water.
Or standing around in walking shorts, an *I Love Florida!*
T-shirt, and oversized sunglasses with zinc oxide all over
my nose. Too much to ask that I appear in a decently

sexy bikini or anything. I had to look like a total dork, and do it on cheesy, cheap sets standing in rubber ducky pools or piles of play sand.

So not hot, I was.

"No, see, you don't get it. It's the theory of the magic glasses," she explained. Cherise had a lot of theories, most of them having to do with secret cabals and aliens among us, which made her both cute and kind of scary. I picked up a brush from the makeup table and started working on my hair; Genevieve, a burly Minnesota woman with a perpetual scowl, bowl-cut hair, and no makeup, took the brush away and began working on me with the tender care of a prison-camp-trained beautician. I winced and bit the inside of my lip to keep from complaining.

Cherise continued. "See, you know in the movies how the really hot girl can slip on a pair of horn-rims, and all of a sudden there's this entire silent agreement between all the people in the movie that she's ugly? And then there's the moment when she takes them off, and everybody gasps and says she's gorgeous? Magic glasses."

I stopped in the act of sipping coffee and braced myself as Genevieve tamed a tangle in my hair by the simple, brutally efficient method of yanking it out by the roots. I swallowed and repeated shakily, "Magic glasses."

"Like Clark Kent." Cherise beamed. "The outfits are your magic glasses, only instead of everybody being fooled, they're in on the joke. It's an open secret that you're totally hot under all that geek disguise. It's very meta."

"You're not originally from here, are you?" I asked.

"Florida?"

"The third planet from the sun."

She had a cute smile, one side lifting higher than the other and waking a dimple. I saw one of the office guys leaning in the door, mooning at her—not mooning her, mooning *at* her—but then there was always somebody doing that, and Cherise never seemed to notice, much less mind. Oddly, none of her admirers seemed capable of asking her out. Then again, maybe they knew something I didn't.

"How many hits?" I asked.

"Are we doing the drug talk again?"

I eyerolled. "To the web page, geek."

"Couple hundred thousand so far."

"You're kidding!"

"Um, not! The IT guys told me all about it." This was not surprising, because I was sure the IT guys tried to chat her up all the time. What was surprising was that Cherise had actually *listened*.

"What were you doing listening to IT guys?"

She raised an eyebrow. "We were talking about *The X-Files*. You know? Remember? The show with Mulder and Scully and . . ."

Oh, right. Alien invasions. Weird occurrences. This was, strangely, right up Cherise's alley. Hence the tattoo.

The coffee was decent, which was a surprise; generally it was rancid stuff, even early in the morning, because the station wasn't exactly upmarket. Maybe somebody had gotten disgusted and popped for Starbucks again. I consoled myself with sips as Genevieve continued to torture my hair. She was backcombing, or possibly weeding.

"So? You got the rest of the day off?" Cherise asked. I was unable to move my head to nod, so I flapped my hand in a vague *yes*. "Cool. I have to do some voice promo stuff tomorrow, but I'm outta here for the day. Want to go shopping? I figure we can hit the mall around ten."

It was seven A.M., but that was Cherise. She knew the opening schedule of every store in a tri-state area, and she planned ahead.

Genevieve picked up the hair dryer. My scalp cringed, anticipating third-degree burns. I'd have stopped her, but the weird thing was that at the end of all of this torture, I'd look great. That was Genevieve's special gift.

"I absolutely *need* to shop," I said. Shopping has a

deeply therapeutic effect when you're trapped in a less-than-ideal life situation.

Shopping with money would have been even better, but hell. Can't have everything.

Fort Lauderdale mornings are beautiful. Soft cerulean skies, layered with pink and gold. Smog is kept to a minimum by the fresh ocean breezes. When I stepped outside of the big concrete box of WXTV-38, I had to stop and appreciate it as only a Warden can.

I closed my eyes, lifted my face to the sun, and left my body to drift up to the aetheric level. It was a little hard to do, these days; I was tired, and out of practice, and it felt sometimes like I had more than my share of worries. Hard to get metaphysical when you're tied so closely to the real world.

Up there on the aetheric, once I'd achieve it, things were serene, too; glowing bands of brilliant color, swirling and moving together, everything lazy and calm. Out toward the sea there was energy, but it was carefully balanced, sea and sun and sky. No storms on the way at the moment, and no rain, regardless of Marvelous Marvin's bogus predictions. Poor Marv. Statistically, he should have been right about eighty-six percent of the time just by predicting sunny and warm in Florida, but no, he had to try to be dramatic about it . . .

Speaking of which, how exactly *did* he beat the odds? He shouldn't. I'd looked at him a dozen times up on the aetheric, though, and he was nothing but what he appeared: an obnoxious normal guy. Blessed with the luck of the entire nation of Ireland, apparently, but a regular human being, not a Warden, no matter how deep-cover. And certainly not a Djinn.

As I floated there, basking in the beauty, I felt something coming around to mess it up. Not weather. People. I blinked and focused and saw three bright centers of energy approaching me on foot across the parking lot. In aetheric-sight, you learn a lot about a person. The one in the center was male, tall, stooped, and comfortable with himself—he wasn't trying to make himself look bigger or better or scarier than anyone else. The other two, though . . . different story. One of the women saw herself as a warrior, all steel and armor that was designed more from a book cover than actual practical necessity—steel push-up bra and an impractical metal bikini bottom to match, a sword too big for someone her size to draw, much less swing.

The third was also a woman . . . elegant, wispy, a little unsettling.

I knew two out of three of them. Ghost-woman was a mystery.

I dropped down into my physical form as footsteps approached, and turned with a smile firmly in place. "John," I said. "It's really good to see you again."

"You, too," John Foster said. It was a friendly beginning, but really, there was no reason for my former Warden boss to show up this early wanting a word, especially flanked by muscle. In no way could this not be a bad sign.

John wasn't much different in the real world than he looked in the aetheric—tall, well dressed, a little professorial if such a thing could be considered a downside. He liked tweed. I regretted the tweed, but at least he'd gotten past the sweater vests of earlier years.

My eyes drifted over to the shorter, darker, punker woman standing next to him. Knew her, too, and the welcome wasn't so welcome-y. She was glaring at me through dark-rimmed eyes. Shirl was a Fire Warden, powerful, and the last I'd run into her she'd been assigned to Marion's Power Ranger squad, rounding up renegade Wardens for that ever-looming magical lobotomy. She wasn't exactly top of the list of people I'd wished would drop in. We hadn't bonded, back when she had been chasing me across the country.

She'd added some additional facial piercings since the last time I'd seen her, her dyed-black hair was tipped with magenta, and she'd taken up a close, personal friendship with leather. Not an improvement.

The third woman remained a mystery. We'd never met, and I couldn't tell what her specialty was; but if Shirl was here to cover fire, she was likely an Earth Warden.

"A little early for a social call," I said, trying to keep it pleasant.

John nodded and stuck his hands in his jacket pockets. Awkward with conflict, John. I wondered why they'd stuck him with the job. Maybe the more senior Wardens were busy. Or maybe they knew I had a soft spot for him and wouldn't be quite so difficult.

"You already know Shirl," he said, and gestured to her with an elbow, offhandedly, with a flat tone to his normally warm voice. Ah. He didn't like her either. Nice to know. "This is Maria Moore, she's come over from France to help us out."

Maria, the ghost-girl, was a wispy little thing in the real world, too. Older than she'd looked, up a level, but still a twig. I hoped she wasn't a Weather Warden; a good strong breeze might blow her out to sea. She looked more like a Djinn than most Djinn I'd ever met.

"Takes three of you to say good morning?" I asked.

"I need you to take a ride with me, Joanne," John said. He had an interesting voice, blurred with a North Carolina drawl; it always made him sound like he was in no particular hurry or distress. So I couldn't tell if this was a big deal, a little deal, or a consultation he thought I could help out with . . . or whether I was taking a ride that would end up with me dead or permanently disabled.

I decided I didn't really want to find out.

"Sorry," I said, not as if I in any way meant it. "I really need to get home. I have some appointments—"

"You're coming with us," Shirl said flatly. "Whether you like it or not. Get used to the idea."

I met her eyes. "Or what, Shirl? You'll get all skinhead on me?"

She'd been kind of hoping that would be my attitude, I could tell. Her hand cupped at her side, and a fireball ignited in her palm. "Or this is going to start loud and end badly."

I didn't want to fight. Really. Especially with John Foster in the middle, not to mention the French Ghost, who might or might not be someone I needed to piss off.

I glanced at John, who was stone-faced, and said, "Whoa, there, Sparky, I'm not picking a fight. I just would like a little warning if you're going to drop in and disrupt my day."

"Get in the car."

She wasn't taking any crap from me. That *might* have been because I'd kind of kicked her ass the first time around, and she was worried about a repeat; she needn't have been, as I'd been running on Demon-Mark Power then, and now it was just plain ol' me, and plain ol' me was tired and drained and really not up to a big, magical, hand-to-hand battle to the death.

Plus, I wasn't dressed for it. Stains would never come out of this top.

Maria Moore silently gestured me to a smoky silver Lexus, which I knew for a fact wasn't John's; Lexus wasn't his style. Must have been Maria's, and come with the ghostly self-image. She was probably aspiring to a Rolls-Royce Silver Shadow. After just enough hesitation to let them know that I wasn't always going to be so easily handled, I turned and walked to it, opened the back door and got inside. It was cramped, but then I had longer legs than most women. Maria got in the driver's seat. I got Shirl as my companion in the back. Joy.

"You want to tell me where we're going?" I asked.

Maria and John exchanged a glance. "It'll take us a while to get there," he said. "I'd suggest you call and cancel your appointments. You're going to be out most of the day."

It was a little late to bitch about it, now that the car was moving. I pulled out my cell phone and postponed Mall Day by twenty-four hours, much to Cherise's disappointment, and settled in for the long haul.

Which, in a Lexus, wasn't a bad thing.

It was a quiet drive. I dozed, part of the way, because I'd been up since four A.M. and besides, talking to Shirl the Human Pincushion didn't make for entertaining conversation. She had all the power of someone like Marion Bearheart, and absolutely none of the charm. I missed Marion and all her centered, Native American, Earth Mother attitude. At least she'd threatened me with style and class, and she had a clear moral center. Shirl . . . well, I wasn't so sure about any of that. Especially the style and class.

Maria the Ghost sporadically nattered on with John in bright, liquid French. John was multilingual, which surprised me for some reason. They seemed easy together. Old friends? Current lovers? Couldn't get a read. I made up dramatic scripts in my head, in which John flew over the Atlantic to sweep Maria off her feet in the shadow of the Eiffel Tower and the two of them ran around Europe getting into wacky, farcical mistaken-identity bedroom adventures.

Hey, I was bored.

Three and a half hours later, the Lexus made a right turn off the highway, and I started seeing signs of damage. We were entering the area where Tropical Storm Walter had blown in two nights ago. It had been a *really* bad hurricane season, and even though we were winding down, nobody felt very secure about it. The damage was mostly superficial, it looked like—shredded palm fronds, blown-down fences, the occasional busted sign or toppled billboard. Cleanup crews were out. Power had already been restored, for the most part. The beach looked clean and fresh, and the surf curled its toes in calm little foaming wavelets over the sand.

We drove about another fifteen minutes, and then John pointed off to the left. Maria slowed the Lexus, and we passed a partially downed sign with construction information on it. PARADISE COVE, it proclaimed, presented by Paradise Kingdom LLP. With a whole bunch of subcontractors, like the special effects cast of a big-budget movie. The artist's rendering on the sign was of a hotel about fifteen stories tall, avant-garde in shape.

It was a hell of a lot more avant-garde now, because

what lay behind the sign was a mass of twisted metal and slumping lumber. Looked like a war zone. Construction materials had been scattered around like Legos after playtime for the emotionally disturbed.

Maria put the Lexus in park.

All three of them looked at me.

"What?" I asked. I was honestly puzzled.

"Tell us what you know about this," John said.

"Well, I'm no expert, but I'd have to say that between this and the Motel 6 down the road, I'd have to choose the Motel 6 . . ."

"I'm serious."

"Hell, John, so am I! What do you want me to say? It looks trashed." I suddenly had a flash. It wasn't a pleasant one. "This is what they were talking about on the news. The freak damage from Tropical Storm Walter."

"This is it."

"Okay . . . and you think I know about it because . . . ?" They all exchanged looks, this time. Nobody spoke. I rolled my eyes and said it for them. "Because you think I did this. Grow up, guys. Why would I? The Wardens have made it really clear that if I screw around with the weather, somebody like good old Shirl here will come around and put me on Drool Patrol. I mean, I don't really like the architectural styling, but I don't feel that passionate about buildings."

Predictably, it was John who jumped in. "Right at the present time, there are fewer than ten Wardens in Florida," he said. "Somebody directed the storm. We recorded the shift."

"Well, talk to the hand, because it wasn't me."

Another significant look that didn't include me. John said, "Are you sure that's your answer, Jo?"

"Hell yes, I'm sure. And you're starting to piss me off with this crap, John. Why would I do a thing like this? Why would I risk it, first of all, and why would I pick on this particular section of coast?"

"It's close to where Bob Biringanine's home once stood," Maria the French Ghost observed.

"So, what, I have a grudge against a dead man? Don't be ridiculous."

I was starting to sweat. I mean, this wasn't usual behavior from Wardens. Suspected offenders got questioned, but usually by auditors, and rarely triple-teamed like this. I was starting to feel a little bit like some poor Mafioso taking a tour of the New Jersey dump, right before he joins the great cycle of composting.

"Look," I said. "What can I do to convince you? I had nothing to do with this." After a few seconds of silence, I asked, "Was anybody hurt?"

"Three people were killed," John said. "The night watchman had brought his two kids with him to work. The kids were asleep in the front when the tornado hit. He tried to get to them, but he'd lost a lot of blood. He died on the way to the hospital."

Silence. Outside, the insects were droning, and the sky was that clear, scrubbed blue you only get after a vicious storm. The few palm fronds surviving nodded in a fresh ocean breeze.

Storms were natural. We—the Wardens—didn't stop the cycle of nature, we just moderated it. Buffered it for the safety of the vulnerable people who lived in its path. But for a storm like this, we wouldn't have bothered. It wasn't that bad, and it was necessary to correct the ever-wobbling scales of Mother Earth. If somebody had messed with it, it was criminal, and intentional.

And murderous.

"It wasn't me," I said. "I'll take whatever oath you want, John. But I'm innocent."

He nodded slowly, and turned back to face front. "Let's get you back home," he said.

"That's it?" Shirl asked loudly. "Just like that? You buy it just because *she* says it?"

"No," Maria the French Ghost said, and turned her head slightly toward me. She had odd eyes, not quite any color, and they looked a little empty. "Not just because *she* says it."

Shirl opened her mouth, sensibly shut it, and scowled out the window. Maria started the car and reversed us back out to the highway.

It was a long, silent drive back, and I had a lot to think about.

I got home too late for any shopping, and way out of the mood anyway. I went home to my grubby little apartment, made chili from a can with some shredded cheese, and curled up on my secondhand couch with a warm blanket and a rented movie. The movie was one of those warmed-over schmaltzy romantic comedies with too much romance and not nearly enough comedy, but it didn't matter; I was too distracted to watch it anyway.

If somebody had been messing with Tropical Storm Walter, I should have known it. I've always been sensitive to those kinds of things. Of course, I could excuse it with the fact that John Foster's spider sense hadn't tingled, either, nor—apparently—had those of any of the eight other Wardens stationed in the state. So maybe I could forgive myself a little.

I couldn't shake the image of that father bringing his kids to work on a boring, safe job, and facing the nightmare of his life. Struggling to save his family in the face of someone else's malice.

Wardens screw up, that's a fact of life. Weather is difficult and tricky and it doesn't like to be tamed. It has a violence and vengeance all its own.

But this wasn't a screwup, didn't *feel* like a screwup, or a random event. It felt targeted, and it felt cold. No wonder the Wardens were sending out hit squads looking for an answer.

I did have to wonder why John Foster had accepted my word for my innocence. In his place, I'd have wanted proof. I wasn't sure that the fact he let me off so lightly was a good sign.

I did some internet research, made some phone calls to neutral parties—i.e., not Wardens—and put together a rough picture of what had happened. Tropical Storm Walter had turned vicious at the last second, gathering strength as it roared up on the coastline. It made a last-minute turn to the north instead of the south, and waded ashore with near-hurricane-force winds and a complement of tornados. So far as I knew, the only one that had touched down had leveled the hotel.

It might have been selfish, but I had to wonder why the investigation had focused on me. If they'd instantly focused suspicion on me, the obvious answer was that they didn't trust me—which, hey, they didn't but there must have been some connection I wasn't seeing. And not the hole in the ground that had once been Bad Bob Biringanine's house on the beach, either. Even the Wardens weren't shallow enough to buy the fact that I'd throw a meaningless tantrum and beat up a helpless coastline, unless they suspected me of going completely wacko.

Then again, I was dressing up like the Morton's Salt Girl on TV and getting water dumped on my head for money.

Maybe they had a point.

I felt alone. More alone than I had in quite some time, actually. I missed my friends. I missed the Wardens.

Boy kissed girl, and the music came up and tried to tell me that love would make everything all right with the world.

I missed David, oh *God* I missed David.

I curled up with my warm blanket and watched the rest of the movie, and fell asleep to the cold blue flicker.

The next morning's show went just about as badly as you might expect. No dumping of rain today; apparently Marvin was forecasting a good day for outside activities, so I got to pose in my stupid-looking walking shorts, oversized T-shirt, boonie hat, and zinc smeared white down my nose, while Cherise wore the cute little bikini and cheesecaked for the camera. One of us was happy. I got sand in my penny loafers, so it probably wasn't me.

But the worst was yet to come.

Cherise slipped into a thick terrycloth robe as soon as she stepped off camera—her usual habit on the set—and we were talking about doing the mall when I felt a thick, sweaty hand slide around my waist. A little too high to qualify as waist territory, actually—we were getting into oh-I-don't-think-so range. Cherise looked startled, then grim, as Marvin's other arm went around her. Luckily, her robe was belted the wrong way for him to slide his fingers inside.

"Girls," he said, and grinned, and squeezed. He'd definitely had his teeth whitened recently. They looked so white I was afraid they might glow in the dark. "Feel like a little breakfast? I'm buying!"

"Gee, boss, I have to fit into this bikini later," Cherise said. She wriggled free of his hold. "Thanks for the offer."

He didn't let go of me quite so easily. "Whaddaya say, Jo? Few pancakes might do you good! Sweeten you up a little! Come on, my dime!"

I blinked, torn between indignation that he didn't think I was sweet enough, and relief that he'd at least noticed my sour attitude. "Previous engagement," I said. "Thanks, though. Some other time." At least he wasn't trying to drag us out for drinks, although I was pretty sure that if it had been a little later in the day—like, say, noon—it would have been Mojitos all around at the Cuban bar, and an expectation of a three-way at his fabulous bachelor pad later.

Marvin managed to look both crushed and lecherous at the same time. "Okay, doll. You girls go get your beauty sleep. Not that you need it!"

He was up to something. I gave him the flinty eye as he walked away, whistling a jaunty tune. Cherise shook her head, and preceded me off the set and into the changing room. She had to shower off body makeup; I

just had to scrub off the zinc oxide and try to get my
hair to do something that didn't look as if I was trying
to take Best of Breed at the Purina Cup.

I finished first, and yelled into the showers, "Meet
you outside!"

"Fifteen minutes!" Cherise was deep into conditioning
territory. I navigated the tunnel-like hallways of the television station, avoiding harried interns and squinty-eyed
techs, hid from the news director, and managed to get
through the back door without being stopped to help out
with anything that wasn't my job.

I walked over to the tiny lunch area, complete with
palm trees, bolted-down picnic table, and overflowing
trash container nobody seemed to remember to empty.
Not exactly paradise, but it served, at times. I sat down
on the cool metal bench, rested my elbows on the table,
and watched the morning arrive.

Another lovely sunrise. Wispy clouds out to sea that
glowed orange and gold; the ocean glittered dark blue,
flecked with white foam. The sky shaded from turquoise
in the east to indigo in the west, and a few brave stars
were still glimmering through the dawn. A warm ocean
breeze that slid over my exposed skin like silk.

It was a lovely way to pass a few minutes. I didn't do
this nearly enough, just sitting, waiting, listening to the
whispers of the world.

As I drifted up there I began to feel something inside
me start to resonate. Liquid light. A cell-deep hum. A
deeply intimate feeling of coming home.

I had company again. The good kind, this time.

Down in the real world, warm fingers stroked my hair,
and up on the aetheric I saw a white, sparkling flare of
power, like a ghost.

The tense curls of my hair relaxed, and David's fingers
dragged slowly through it, straightening it into a glossy
black sheet of silk that fell heavily around my shoulders.

I turned. David was worth the resulting skipped heartbeat and raised pulse level on a visual level alone—
smooth golden skin, dark auburn hair that glittered with

red highlights in the sun, lickable lips, and eyes of an impossible bronze color behind a pair of gold-rimmed glasses. He was back in his usual uniform: blue jeans, a comfortably faded cotton shirt, an antique ankle-length olive coat.

David didn't look like a Djinn, most of the time. At least, not most people's idea of one, since that included pantaloons, loopy earrings, and bare, rippling chests. Not that his chest, when bare, didn't ripple satisfactorily. Far from it . . .

"I thought you were resting," I said, to get my mind off of the image of him, shirtless. I tried to make it sound stern, but he made it difficult when he leaned into my space. He slipped his fingers through my magically straightened hair, tilted my head back, and came *very* close to kissing me.

And, teasingly, didn't. Warm, soft lips just barely brushing mine.

"It's been too long," he said. "I want to stay with you for a while."

My pulse jumped into high gear. I knew he could hear it. Feel it through the brush of our mouths. I'd left him alone in the bottle for more than a month, hoping he'd be stronger for it, although I hadn't capped the bottle and sealed him inside. I just . . . couldn't bear to do that. It was too much like prison.

"You're sure?" I asked. My voice didn't sound too steady. It sounded breathless with excitement, actually.

"Just say the word."

"Which one?"

"The one you didn't learn from your mother." He made a low humming sound at the back of his throat, not quite a growl, not quite a laugh. I could almost forget how fragile he was at the moment. My body *wanted* to forget, but then, it had Attention Deficit Disorder, big-time.

"Are you—" I hated to ask it—it was like asking someone with cancer how the treatments were going.

"David, be straight with me. Really. Are you feeling better? Are you strong enough to—to do this?"

Because David had, since I'd met him, been through even more than I had. He'd fought demons and split himself in two to give me life when I died, and he'd allowed an Ifrit—a kind of Djinn vampire—to drain him nearly dry. He wasn't really healed from any of that.

Worse, I wasn't sure he *could* really heal. Jonathan, high muckety-muck of the Djinn world, hadn't been all that clear.

But today, he looked almost . . . normal. Maybe I'd been right. Maybe time healed all Djinn wounds.

He smiled. At close range, that was a deadly weapon. "Don't worry. I'm strong enough to spend a little time with you," he said. His eyebrows—fabulously expressive, those eyebrows—canted upward. "Unless, of course, you have a date?"

Right on cue, the back dock door banged open, and Cherise began flip-flopping down the steps to the parking lot. I looked over David's shoulder and expected him to mist away—like Djinn usually did—but he just turned to take a look as well. Which meant that he'd decided not to leave, but just to disguise himself with a minor use of his powers, a don't-see-me kind of magic that would direct Cherise's attention away from him . . .

"Whoa! Who's the hottie, Jo?" Cherise asked, focused directly on David. She came to a hard stop, wiggling her tanned toes in the designer flip-flops. Those bright blue eyes swept him head to toe, narrowed, and sparkled. "My, my, my. Holding out on me. Bad friend. No biscuit."

It was *possible* that David was just in the mood to be part of the human world for a while. He did that, sometimes; that was how I'd met him. It had taken me days to figure out that he wasn't entirely human, but in my defense, I was just a little distracted at the time with people trying to kill me.

What I was afraid of, though, was that David was visible to Cherise because he was too weak to magic himself out of being seen.

If that was the case, I couldn't see any sign of it in his body language. He looked relaxed, open, and friendly.

"Hi. My name's David," he said, and held out his hand. Cherise took it and made the handshake look way too intimate.

"*I* can be a friend. A really, really *close* friend." She pursed shiny, Maybelline-enhanced lips, and sent me a pleading look as she leaned into his personal space. "So, when you get tired of him, can I have him?"

"No."

"Trade you a date with Johnny Depp."

"Cherise, you don't *have* a date with Johnny Depp."

She sniffed. "Well, I *could*. If I wanted. So I suppose the arrival of Mr. Hottie means we're not going shopping."

"Would you go shopping if he showed up for you?"

"You're kidding, right? I would have shopping surgically removed from my system. And you *know* how much of a commitment that is for me." Cherise gave me a preoccupied kind of smile, tearing her attention away from David for about point oh two seconds, and finally heaved a theatrical sigh. "I suppose I'll just have to go abuse my credit rating all by myself. Although I plan to shop *heavily,* and it would be handy to have some nice, strong man to carry my—"

"Go," I said. She lifted an elegantly sculpted shoulder and flip-flopped off toward her red convertible, hips swaying, alien tattoo doing a funky hula to the motion. Yeah. She'd be carrying her own bags, sure. When hell opened a hockey rink.

"Did I interrupt something?" David asked, and moved back into kissing distance again. "I know how seriously you take a mall visit. Wouldn't want to stand in your way."

He was teasing me. I leaned in, too, brushed his lips

with mine, and stared deep into his burning bronze eyes. Teasing could go both ways.

His pupils widened and drank me in.

"The mall doesn't open until ten," I whispered into his parted lips. "Plenty of time."

His kiss took control and dissolved me into sparkles and tingles and a massive surge of heat. Damp, urgent, passionate lips, demanding my full attention. I felt myself collapsing against him, wanting badly to be horizontal somewhere with a lockable door. Jesus, he made my whole body shake.

"I missed you," he said, and his voice had gone low and rough, hiding in the back of his throat. His thumbs caressed my cheekbones, drawing lines of heat like tattoos.

"Show me."

"Right here?" He looked pointedly down at the gravel, asphalt, and thin grass. "Looks uncomfortable. Then again, I remember how much you like public displays of affection."

"Beast."

Those eyebrows went up again, dangerously high. His smile turned dark. "Oh, you really don't want to know how true that is."

I felt a tiny little tremor inside. Sometimes, David could be like a pet tiger—glorious and terrible. He wasn't just a sweet-natured, nice, agreeable guy, although he was certainly capable of being that. It was just that he was capable of anything. Everything. Djinn weren't fluffy little bunnies you kept as pets, they were *dangerous*. David was gentle with me, I knew that. But sometimes, occasionally, I would see the vast, dark depths underneath, and I'd get dizzy and breathless.

And hot. Dear God. Spontaneous-combustion hot.

He knew, of course. I saw it flash in his eyes.

I said, "I'm not afraid, you know."

His hands—everything about him—went still. Wind brushed over us with curious hands, ruffling my hair, belling his coat. It tasted of ocean. Palm trees rustled and shook out their fronds over our heads.

"Maybe you should be. You don't know enough about me."

Well, he was right. He'd live for eons. He'd seen human civilizations rise and fall. I barely knew a fraction of who David was, and what he was.

Sometimes I just forgot.

"Try me," I said. Cherise's glitter-bright flirting had reminded me, with a chill, that I wasn't some sweet young girl anymore, and next thing I knew I'd be buying in the Women's World section where dowdy clothes go to die. Reading *Modern Maturity*. Learning to tat lace and make scrapple. I wanted to *know* David. I wanted this to be something bigger and deeper and forever, or as far as my forever could go. "If we're going to stay together, then you can't just show me your good side, you know. And I mean it. I'm not afraid."

He looked uncommonly solemn, and he didn't blink. There was a hint of the tiger in those eyes again. "I don't think you understand what you're saying."

I heaved out a sigh. "Of *course* I don't understand. Everything about the Djinn is one big, dark, booga-booga secret, and just because I've *been* one doesn't mean I got the operating manual—"

He stilled my lips with his, in a damp, slow, breathless kiss. His hands slid up into my hair, stroking those achingly sensitive places behind my ears, at the nape of my neck . . . I lost my train of thought.

Which made me jump tracks to another one when he let me up for breath. "We need to get you home." What that really meant was, to put him back in his bottle—yes, Djinn really had bottles, glass ones; they had to be glass and they had to come with stoppers or a way to seal them, no exceptions. The worst case I'd ever seen had been a soap-bubble thin ornamental glass perfume bottle; it was stored in the Wardens Association vault in the U.N. Building in New York, because that thing would shatter if you so much as gave it a hard look.

David's was a somewhat sturdy ornamental kitchen bottle, the blue-glass fancy kind that store flavored oils and decorative grains. I kept it in a very safe place, right in my nightstand drawer next to oils, lotions, and other things I wouldn't want casual visitors to inventory.

Which inevitably led to thoughts of my bed, soft sheets, cool soft ocean breezes sighing over my skin . . .

"Yes. Let's go home." His hands slid over my shoulders, stroked down my arms, and lingered on my hands before letting me go. The heat from him stayed on my skin. Afterimages of light.

My car was parked over in the far corner of the lot, away from casual door dings. She was a midnight blue Dodge Viper, and I loved her dearly enough for her to qualify as my second-favorite-ever ride. The first-place winner had been a Mustang, also midnight blue, named Delilah, who had gotten scrapped around the time I met David, as if I had to give up one really lovely thing for another.

David took the shotgun seat, and I prowled Mona through the morning traffic toward my apartment. I'd been really, really lucky when I moved—had to move, thanks to the overzealous actions of some real estate people, who thought that just because I'd had a funeral I'd broken my lease—and I'd ended up with a beachfront second-floor sea view. All of my furniture was second-hand, and nothing matched, but the bed was comfortable and the balcony was to die for.

The bed was the only thing that mattered right now.

I must have parked, but that part was a blur. Then stairs, and then we were in the hall and I was hunting for my key. It was after morning commute time for most of my neighbors, and the place was nearly silent, except for the distant, muted hum of a TV somewhere down near the corner. Probably Mrs. Appel; she worked nights and liked to wind down to a little HBO before nap time.

David came up behind me and put his hands on my shoulders, then let them drift down my sides, stroking. Gentle, slow moves. Anyone watching wouldn't have found it terrifically sexual—we weren't exactly humping in the hall—but I had to brace my hands on the door and close my eyes. There was something magic about his hands, about the slow, deliberate way he used them. They followed the line of my shoulders, circled my arms, and moved all the way down to my wrists.

He moved closer until he pressed against me like a second skin. I tried to fit the key into the lock again. Missed. My hands were shaking.

"Jo?" His voice was velvet, with a slightly frayed edge that rasped like a purr. "Maybe you'd better let me do it."

I held the ring up. He took it from my fingers and leaned around me to fit the key in the lock and turn it.

Which shouldn't have seemed so suggestive, but maybe that was a combination of my boiling hormones and the heat of his body pressed against my back. Solid summer-warm flesh, hard in all the right places.

The door clicked open. I moved inside, flicked on soft, diffuse overhead lighting, and kicked off my shoes and dropped my purse.

He was behind me again, and this time there wasn't any holding back for the neighbors. His hands went right around my waist and pulled me against him, and I turned my head to look back at him.

Depthless black in his pupils, and the irises of his eyes were smoking-hot copper.

"I need you," he said, and moved my hair out of the way. His mouth found the side of my neck, licking and sucking, so fierce that it was right on the skin-thin border between pain and pleasure. His hands slid up to skim lightly over my breasts. "I need you."

"I—wait, David, I don't—are you sure you're—" *Feeling up to this* was a straight line waiting to happen. "—strong enough for—"

"You give me strength." His mouth was doing absurd things to my self-control. "You give me life." He murmured it against that incredibly sensitive spot just at the base of my ear. "You give me peace."

Which might have been the sexiest thing any man—or male Djinn—had ever said to me in my life.

"We going to talk all day?" I asked breathlessly, and felt him laugh. Not a nice laugh, and there wasn't much amusement in it, either. It was the kind of deep, rippling chuckle you might hear from the devil right before he let you see the fine print of your contract on that condo in Aruba, and dear God, it made my spine turn to water.

"That all depends on you," he said, and the hands reversed course, moved in and down. Demanding. Skimming up the thin fabric of my skirt in handfuls while he pulled me back hard against him in the same motion. "Are you in the mood to have a nice, long chat? Have some tea and cookies?"

It was *not* what I wanted to do with my mouth.

We fell onto the bed with a bouncing jolt. I didn't need to undress him; where my hands landed, his clothes just misted away to reveal an incredibly beautiful expanse of flawless golden skin. His eyes turned vague, half-lidded, as I stroked my fingers over his chest and down. His muscles tensed underneath them, corded cable.

He rolled us over, his weight balanced on top of me. I couldn't stop an involuntary arch in my back, and once I saw the answering glitter in his eyes I kept moving my hips. He moved back. Long, slow, hot torture.

"Yes," I whispered.

He kissed me. Not romantic, this time. Demanding. Driven by something I didn't fully understand. I'd never seen him like this before, full of a kind of frantic hunger, as if he wanted to consume me, possess me.

Own me.

This wasn't equal. It couldn't be equal, because I still held his bottle, and I'd claimed him. It was a master-slave relationship, no matter how nice the master, how willing the slave. It bothered me.

Just at this moment, I wondered if it bothered him, too.

He was too weak. If I set him free, he'd fade into smoke and hunger. Lose himself.

I couldn't let that happen. Right or wrong, I couldn't let it happen.

I lay awake, later, curled against his warmth as he drew lazy magical patterns on my back. They must have been magical. Every place his hand traveled left pools of pulsing silver light inside of me. Parts of my body ached. Other parts tingled and burned. There was a bright, sun-hot throb on my neck, and another several on the insides of my thighs, and I felt as if I'd been completely, breath-takingly destroyed. If that wasn't being totally possessed, I couldn't imagine how much more I could take without shattering.

His hand glided down to the small of my back and stayed there for a couple of beats, and I felt a very, very small stirring inside.

I turned my head and looked at him. He didn't meet my eyes.

"We need to talk," I said.

"I know."

"I don't understand how this is supposed to work." I rolled over, took his hand, and placed it over my womb.

And we both felt the stirring inside. His eyes flared, then went dark.

"It's been three months," I said. "Nothing's changed."

"You're not—" He stopped, shook his head, and those long, gorgeous fingers stroked gently over my skin. Caressing me, but caressing inside me, too. "It's hard to explain."

"But I'm *pregnant*. Right?"

"That's what's hard to explain. She won't—grow like a human child. She's like a seed, waiting for the sun. Just . . . waiting."

"For how long?"

He didn't answer that one. "I should have asked you first," he said, and his hand moved again, drawing silver.

"It would have been polite, yeah."

"I did it to protect you."

"I know." At the time, it had been the only way he had known to ensure I'd survive a trip to Las Vegas; and facing down the one Djinn he couldn't protect me from—his best friend, Jonathan. And it had worked, too. Jonathan hadn't killed me. He'd even shown some signs of thinking I was a little better than pond scum, which was a huge improvement. "Tell me how this is supposed to happen, then."

He shook his head again, David-speak for *I don't want to talk about it.* I waited him out, watching his face. He finally said, "It may not happen at all. Djinn children are rare. Even then, they're only born to two Djinn. A Djinn and a mortal . . . it's not   She exists inside you as a potential, but   she may never survive."

"Jonathan said she could only be born if you die."

His eyes slowly came up to meet mine. "That's . . . probably true. We come from death, not life."

Djinn were very hard to kill, but David was fragile. When he made me a Djinn, he'd fractured something vital inside of him into two pieces, one of which he'd given me to keep me alive. Even when I'd been granted the gift of humanity again, that root-deep fracture had remained. And then he'd gotten in the way of an Ifrit, who drained him nearly to death.

And now he was hanging onto the fragile thread between life and that kind of living death, of losing himself. If he stayed outside of his bottle for too long, or used too much power, he'd become an Ifrit, a thing of ice and shadow. A thing bent only on feeding on others.

As if he'd followed my thought, his hand on my back went still. I felt a shudder run through him, and his eyes dimmed just a little.

"David?" I sat up. He eased back on the bed and stared at the ceiling.

"I shouldn't have done this to you," he said. "I should never have done any of this to you. You deserve—"

"Don't do this to yourself. None of it is your fault."

He closed his eyes. He looked suddenly very, very tired. Human. "I didn't hurt you, did I?"

"No! God, no." I put my hand on his chest, then my head. My hair spilled dark over his skin. "Well, not any more than I wanted you to, anyway."

"I'm afraid I will," he said. His voice sounded distant, worn smooth by exhaustion. "No, I know I will; I can sense it." His eyes opened, and the last embers of copper flared in orange swirls. "You can't let me. I mean it, Jo. You have to have defenses against me. You have to learn . . ."

The fire was cooling under his skin, the light in him going out. "I have to go now," he said. "I love you."

I kissed him, quickly, lovingly, and said, "I love you, too. Go back in the bottle now."

I felt the sudden indrawn breath of his passing, sank suddenly down in the welter of disordered sheets, and when I opened my eyes again he was gone. Nothing left but an indentation in the pillows.

I turned over, slid open the nightstand drawer, and took his bottle out of its protective zippered case lined with gray foam.

I started to put the stopper in, but then hesitated. At some very deep level, he was still part of me, drawing on the magic I possessed; putting the stopper in the bottle meant cutting that connection, and although he hadn't said so, I suspected that the more I could give him, the better. I'd have opened my magical veins if it could have made him better. Hell, I wasn't in the Wardens anymore; I wasn't directing the weather or saving lives. I was just a poverty-level member of the vast, unwashed paid labor force.

I needed him for completely different reasons these days than making miracles happen for other people.

I sank back on the pillows with a sigh. I didn't actually know if he was recovering, or, if he was, how quickly; I'd need the opinion of another Djinn to find out, but then, none of the Djinn had been around to visit since I'd left the Wardens. They were staying clear. I figured Jonathan had something to do with it. The last thing he'd said to me, in a flat, angry monotone, had been, *You broke him, you fix him.* The unspoken *or else* had been daunting.

Jonathan hadn't dropped by since I'd returned to Florida, but with the kinds of powers he possessed, he hardly needed to. He was probably back in his house, watching me through his big plate-glass picture window and sipping magically imported beer.

Probably watching me right now.

I rolled over on my back, flipped the bird at the ceiling. "Hope you enjoyed the show," I said. "No encores."

No reaction. Which was no doubt for the best.

I fell asleep with the bottle beside me, to the steady, pounding whisper of the surf down on the beach.

I catapulted out of bed two hours later to a banging on the apartment door. I was halfway to the door before I realized I was stark naked. Back to the bedroom to throw on a floor-length silk robe, belted in front, and jam my feet into slippers.

"Coming!" I yelled, and hustled back as the knocking continued to thunder. I started to rip the door open, then hesitated and used the peephole.

It took me about ten seconds—long, full ones—to realize who I was looking at, because she didn't look like herself at all.

Oh. My. *God.*

I unlocked the dead bolt and flung the door wide. "Sarah?"

My sister was standing there. My sister from California, my married, nonmagical sister who, the last time I'd seen her, had been wearing the best of Rodeo Drive and sporting a designer haircut with fabulous highlights. Sarah had been one of those annoying girls who'd spent all her time scheming to catch a rich man, and . . . amazingly . . . had actually *done* it. I hadn't expected her to be happy, but I had expected her to hang on to her French millionaire husband with both hands and emotional superglue.

Lots had obviously changed. Sarah was wearing baggy,

wrinkled khaki shorts and an oversized Sunshine State T-shirt; the haircut had grown into an unkempt shag, and the remaining, faded highlights looked cheap as tinsel. No makeup. And no socks with her battered running shoes.

"Let me in," she said. She sounded tired. With no will of my own I stepped back, and she came in, dragging a suitcase behind her.

The suitcase—battered, ugly, and bargain-basement—gave me a bad, bad feeling.

"I thought you were in LA," I said slowly. The door was still open, and I reluctantly shut and locked it. There went my last chance for a decent escape. I tried for a pleasant interpretation. "Missed me, huh?"

She plumped down on my secondhand couch in an uncoordinated sprawl, staring down at her limp hands, which hadn't seen a manicure in weeks. My sister was a good-looking woman—walnut brown hair, blue eyes, fine, soft skin she'd worked hard to keep supple—but just now she looked her age. Wrinkles. My God. Sarah had *wrinkles*. And she hadn't been to a plastic surgeon and Botoxed them out of existence? *Who are you and what have you done with my evil sibling?*

"Chrêtien left me," she said. "He left me for a *personal trainer!*"

I felt behind me, found a chair, and sank into it, staring at her.

"He divorced me," she said. Her already-tense voice was rising like a flood tide. "And he enforced the prenup. Jo, he took the *Jag!*"

That came out as a true, raw wail of grief.

My sister—who'd always made me look like a piker when it came to composure, style, and taking care of herself—blubbered like a little girl. I jumped up and found some Kleenex, which she promptly used with enthusiasm, and fetched a trash can from the bathroom to catch the soggy remains. I was *not* picking those up.

Finally, she was blotched, swollen, red-nosed, and done crying—for a while—and gave me the rest of the tired, familiar story. Chrêtien and personal trainer Heather (Heather? Really?), meeting every Tuesday for a *really* intense private session. Sarah getting suspicious because his workout clothes never seemed overly worked out. Hiring a private eye to follow them. Dirty pictures. Screaming confrontation. Chrêtien invoking the dire terms of the prenup, which had taken her house, her car, her bank account, and left her with her *second* car, an old Chrysler she'd let the maid use for errands.

And no place to live.

My once-rich sister was homeless.

And she was sitting on my couch with a suitcase, blubbering, looking at me with pleading, swollen eyes.

I silently returned the look, remembering all those childhood grievances. Sarah, yanking my hair when Mom wasn't looking. Sarah, telling all my friends and enemies about my crush on Jimmy Paglisi. Sarah, stealing my first steady boyfriend out from under my nose. We weren't close. We'd never been close. For one thing, we weren't anything like the same. Sarah had been a professional woman . . . emphasis on the woman, not the professional. She'd set out to snare herself a millionaire, which she'd done, and to live the life she'd always wanted, and damn whoever had to suffer to get her there. She'd signed the prenup because, at the time, she'd thought she had Chrêtien completely beguiled and could get him to tear it up with enough honeyed compliments and blow jobs.

I could have told her—hell, I *had* told her—that Chrêtien was way too French for that to work.

Sarah was stranded on my couch: sniffling, humiliated, practically penniless. No marketable skills to speak of. No friends, because the kinds of country club friends Sarah had made all her life didn't stick around after the platinum American Express got revoked.

She had nobody else. Nowhere to go.

There was nothing else I could say but, "Don't worry. You can stay with me."

Later, I would remember that and pound my head

against the wall. It was the flickering warning light on a road where the bridge was out and, like an idiot, I just kept on driving.

Right into the storm.

I set about getting Sarah settled in my tiny spare room. She'd been weeping with gratitude right up until I heaved her suitcase onto the twin bed, but she stopped when she took a look around.

"Yes?" I asked sweetly, because I could see the words *Where's the rest of it?* on the tip of her tongue.

She swallowed them—it must have choked her—and forced a trembling smile. "It's great. Thanks."

"You're welcome." I looked around, seeing it through her eyes. Her utility closet in California hadn't been this small, I was certain. The furniture wasn't exactly *au courant*—a rickety '50s nightstand in grubby off-white French Provincial with a cockeyed drawer, a campus castoff bed too hard and lumpy for even college students. A scarred, ugly dresser of no particular pedigree, with missing drawer pulls and a cracked mirror, salvaged out of a Dumpster with the help of two semipro football players.

A real do-it-yourself nightmare.

I sighed. "Sorry about this. I had to move when—"

"—when we thought you were dead," she said. "By the time they'd tracked me down to give me the news, your friends already knew you were all right and let me know, thank God, or I'd have just gone crazy."

Which gave me a little bit of a warm, sisterly glow, until she continued.

"After all, I'd just found out about Chrêtien and Heather. I swear, if I'd had one more thing to think about, I don't think even the therapy would have helped."

I stopped feeling bad about the furniture. "Glad I didn't set you back on the road to recovery."

"Oh! No, I didn't mean—"

I sat down on the bed next to her suitcase. The frame

creaked and groaned like an exasperated geezer. "Look, Sarah, let's not kid each other, okay? We're not best buddies; we never were. I'm not judging you, I'm just saying you're here because I'm all you've got. Right? So you don't have to pretend to like me."

She looked just like me, in that second—wide-eyed with surprise, and a little frown crinkling her forehead. Except for the hair. Even my current poodle-hair curls were better than the badly grown-out shag she was sporting.

She said, slowly, "All right, I admit it. I didn't like you when you were younger. You were a bratty kid, and then you grew up into somebody I barely even know. And you're weird, you know. And Mom liked you best."

No arguing with that one. Mom really had.

But Sarah kept going. "That doesn't mean I don't love you, Jo. I always have loved you. I hope you still love me. I know I'm a bitch, and I'm shallow, but we're still, you know, sisters."

It would have been a warm, tender moment if I'd jumped up and thrown my arms around her and burst into tears. We weren't that kind of Hallmark Card family.

I thought it over and said, "I don't really know you, Sarah. But I'm willing to get to know you."

She smiled. Slow, but real.

"That sounds . . . fair."

We shook hands on it. I stood up and watched as Sarah unzipped the suitcase and started unpacking. It was a pitifully short affair. She'd left most of the good stuff behind, and what good stuff she had left was horribly wrinkled. We made a dry-clean pile, a "burn this" pile, a Goodwill pile, and a keeper stack. That one was short. It filled exactly one drawer of the dresser.

"Makeup?" I asked. She pointed to a tiny plastic case that couldn't have held more than lipstick, mascara, and maybe an eyebrow pencil. "Shoes?"

She pointed to the battered running shoes and held up a pair of black, squarish pumps, something suitable for a grandmother, so long as Grandma didn't care much about appearances. I winced. "The bastard didn't even let you keep your *shoes*?"

"He cleaned out the house and gave everything to the Salvation Army," she said. "All my clothes. Everything."

"Jesus." I had a sudden flare of suspicion. "Um, look, Sarah, not that I'm doubting you or anything, but wasn't Chrêtien the, um, guilty party . . . ?"

She had the good grace to look just a *little* ashamed. "He found out about Carl."

"Carl?"

"You know."

"Nope. Really don't."

She rolled her eyes. "Fine, if you're going to force me to say it . . . I wasn't exactly guiltless. There. I admit it. I was having an affair with his business partner."

"Jesus."

"And the donkey he rode in on," she finished, just the way she'd always done it when we'd been in school. "But he didn't have to get so *personal* about all of it. He cheated on me, after all. You'd think he'd at least understand that it was . . . well . . ."

"Recreational?" I supplied dryly.

"Yes! Exactly!"

"Should have joined the bridge club, Sarah."

She gave me a helpless, angry look. "I'm not saying I was guiltless, but . . . he gave me a couple of hundred dollars and told me to buy replacements. *In my new price range.* God, Jo, I didn't even know where to *shop*!"

I took a deep breath and said, "Tell you what? I was going to the mall anyway with a friend, so if you want to get ready—"

"I'm ready," my sister said instantly.

I picked up the phone and called Cherise.

Cherise had, of course, changed clothes in the interim. She'd gone to a magenta see-through mesh shirt with lime green tie-dyed patterns, over a lime green camisole.

It all matched the lime glitter toenail polish, which evidently she liked enough to accessorize to.

"Ten," I said instantly when she got out of her red convertible. "Maybe a ten point five. You blind me with your magnificence."

"But of course. Man, Jo, I knew you were a saint, but you gave up your hottie for your *sister*? Damn. I'd have blown off taking my grandma to dialysis for that man!"

Sarah came out of the apartment behind me, wearing her wrinkled khaki walking shorts and badly fitting button-down shirt. Cherise's perfectly made-up eyes widened into something usually seen only in Japanese animation.

"Oh my *God*," she said, and looked at me in horror. "You told me it was bad, but damn, this is a seven point five on the fashion disaster scale. And what's with her *hair*?"

"Cherise," I said. "I know it's hard for you, but please. Sarah's had a bad time. Be kind."

"I *was* being kind. That is way worse than a seven point five."

Sarah said, "Jo? Did she just say you have a boyfriend?"

Trust Sarah, of course, to blow past Cherise's fluff to get to the potentially disastrous part of the conversation.

"Not *just* a boyfriend," Cherise said. "Boyfriends are Ken dolls. Boyfriends are safe. Her guy is the kind of hottie who needs to keep a fire extinguisher around, just to hose down any passing women who spontaneously combust."

I stared at her, amazed. For Cherise, this was, well, poetic.

Sarah was, meanwhile, frowning at me. "And you didn't tell me about him?"

I didn't want to bring up David yet. That was going to be a strange and difficult conversation, with somebody as earthbound-normal as Sarah, and I couldn't really mislead her too far. Trying to keep him secret would only lead to low comedy and farce. Not to mention put a serious cramp in my love life.

"He had to leave," I said. Not a lie. "I'll see him later."

"I should have known you'd have a boyfriend," Sarah said. She sounded bitter. "What was I thinking? When do you not?"

"Kind of a 'ho, isn't she?" Cherise asked. Sarah nodded wisely.

"Hey!" I said sharply. "Watch it!"

"Oh, come on, Jo. Your libido isn't exactly on the low end of the curve. I've seen you checking out the boys at work," Cherise said. "Even, you know, Kurt. The anchor."

"I would *never*! That man is made of plastic!"

"Oh, the plastic ones are the best," she said, and gave me a wicked look. "They come with D-cell batteries, off switches, and you never have to meet their folks."

Cherise worried me sometimes. "Please tell me you haven't—not with *Kurt*—"

"Please. I have standards," she said. "He may be an anchor, but he's a *morning* anchor. Hardly worth the investment."

"Now *who's* your boyfriend?" Sarah began again. I hustled her toward the car. Cherise broke ranks, rushed back, and flipped switches in her convertible. The canvas top whirred up and locked in place.

"Marvin says it's going to rain," she said.

"Marvin doesn't know his—" I bit my tongue to keep from saying something that might get back to him. "His meteorology from a rain dance."

Cherise looked up at the cloudless blue sky, shrugged, and slid on her dark glasses. "Yeah, well, easy for you to say. You don't have to wet-vac. And you know all about the Percentage."

Yes. They liked to use that in advertising: Trust the Percentage. Because Marvelous Marvin really did have the best percentage of forecast accuracy in our area. Not that it was anything but blind luck. I'd asked him to walk

me through the calculations for his rainy-day forecast
two days ago, and he'd happily brought out the charts,
the National Weather Service models, the radar images,
all the good stuff . . . and proceeded to come to exactly
the wrong conclusion.

But he was 91% percent accurate over the last two years.

Hard to argue with that, but I lived in hopes that
today, at least, would be the beginning of the end of
Marvin's reign of meteorological omniscience.

We piled into the Viper and headed for Shopping Nir-
vana, otherwise known as the Galleria—150 shops, with
everything from Sak's to Neiman Marcus. I both loved
and hated living so close to it. It was like a diabetic with
a sweet tooth living next door to the fudge factory. We
cruised along, drawing envious stares from teenagers in
gleaming low-riders, faded Yuppies in Volvos, soccer
moms in enormous SUVs. Mona *was* a sexy car. I still
pined for my beloved Mustang, but I had to admit, the
throbbing growl of power from the Viper was seductive.

Even doing something as tame as crawling from one
red light to another on this cloudless suburban day.

We'd only gone about three blocks when Sarah suddenly said, "Did you know you're being followed?"

We were heading down East Sunshine, and the traffic
wasn't exactly light; I looked at her in the rearview (she'd
been relegated to the back) and studied her carefully.
"Okay, you've been living in California *way* too long.
This is Florida. We don't get tailed in Florida."

She didn't look behind her as she said, "Chrêtien had
me followed for six months; I know what I'm talking
about. There's a white van with dark-tinted windows and
a magnetic sign that says it's from a flower shop. It pulled
out of the apartment parking lot when you did. It's three
cars back."

I blinked and focused on the traffic. She was right,
there was a white van back there. I couldn't see anything
about the sides, but the windows were dark-tinted.

"So? He dropped off some roses. Unfortunately, not
to me." And I so deserved it, for putting up with Sarah.

"Change lanes," she said. "Watch him."

Couldn't hurt. I spotted an opening and did one of those sports-car levitation glides laterally from one lane to another, no signal, and then sped up and whipped back over two lanes. Cherise yelped and grabbed for a handhold; Sarah turned to look back, just a quick glance.

"He's following, but he's trying to look casual about it," she said. I nodded. It wasn't easy to do in traffic, but I split my attention and sent part of myself up into Oversight, to see what was going on in the aetheric.

It wasn't a Warden behind us, at least. Nothing but normal human stuff happening, not even the faint smear I'd come to recognize as a Djinn who didn't want to be spotted. I dropped back into my body, put my foot down, and felt Mona respond with a fast, eager purr. "Hang on," I said, and whipped the wheel over hard at the next light. Cherise yelped again, higher-pitched; Sarah grabbed for a handhold and tilted without making a sound.

"Hey!" Cherise blurted. "This isn't the way to the mall!" She was much more panicked about the idea of missing her shopping appointment than any sinister, faceless stalker we might have picked up.

Hey, I never said she was deep. Just fun to be around.

"Back entrance," I said. The van turned the corner, a block behind me, and accelerated. I eased back down to a regular street speed, mindful of any cops that might be lurking and itching for a chance to ticket a Viper, and made another turn, to the left.

I took the turn into the Galleria parking lot. It was a typical day, which meant busy; I cruised around for a while, watching for the white van. It was still back there. When I pulled into a space, so did it, several rows away.

All very sinister, suddenly. I didn't like it at all.

"Cherise, you take Sarah and go on to Ann Taylor," I said, and popped my door open. "I'll be right behind you. Sarah, you've got my Mastercard. Just—don't buy big ticket without me." I realized that Sarah's standards of big ticket might vary from mine. "Um . . . that means anything over a hundred dollars."

She looked briefly shocked, probably at the low-limit amount. Both of them started to argue, but I slammed the door and kept walking, fast and purposefully, heading for the white van that was parked and motionless several hundred yards away. I made sure to stay blocked from it as much as possible by giant SUVs—who the hell *needs* a Hummer the color of a yield sign, anyway?—and the ubiquitous Gran-and-Gramps-do-Florida RVs, and came at it from the passenger side.

I knocked on the dark-tinted window. After a few silent seconds, a motor whirred and the glass glided down. I didn't recognize the man in the driver's seat. He was Hispanic, older—forty, forty-five maybe—and he had graying hair, fierce, dead dark eyes, and a windburned complexion.

Looked damn intimidating.

"Hi," I said, and gave him my best, most confident smile. "Want to tell me why you're following me? If this is about Sarah, tell Chrêtien that he can stick it up his French . . ."

"You're Joanne Baldwin," he interrupted me. No trace of an accent.

"In the flesh." Scars and all, which had fortunately faded with a little help from silicone patches and the tanning salon.

"Get in the van," he said.

"Oh, I really don't think—"

He produced a gun and aimed it at my head. "No, I really do." I wasn't good with guns, especially not identifying them, but this one looked big and serious about its job. "In the van. Now, please."

I felt an overwhelming impulse to do *exactly* what he said, but I also knew better than to climb into some stranger's van. Especially in Florida. I tried to focus past the gun and hold his stare. "It's broad daylight in a mall parking lot. You're not going to shoot me, and I'm not getting in your damn van, either. Next subject."

I surprised him. It passed over his face in a flash. Blink and you'd miss it, but it was definitely present. He cocked one eyebrow just a millimeter higher. "Why exactly do you think I wouldn't shoot you?"

"Security cameras everywhere, pal, and my sister and my friend both have really good memories for license plate numbers. You wouldn't get back to the main road before the cops cut you off." I forced myself to smile again. "Besides, you don't want me dead, or you'd have shot me already and been out of here, and we wouldn't be having this lovely conversation."

For a long, long second, he debated it. I held my breath, and let it slowly out when he shrugged and holstered the gun again, with a move so deft it might as well have been a magic trick.

"You know my name," I said. "Want to tell me yours?"

"Armando Rodriguez," he replied, which took *me* by surprise; I hadn't expected a guy who'd just pulled a weapon to introduce himself so readily. "Detective Armando Rodriguez, Las Vegas Police Department."

Oh, dear. I felt goosebumps shiver up the back of my arms.

"I'd like to ask you a few questions about the disappearance of Detective Thomas Quinn," he said. Which I'd already figured out.

Too bad I knew *exactly* what had happened to Detective Thomas Quinn. And there was no way on earth I could talk to this guy about it.

"Thomas Quinn?" I didn't want to out-and-out lie, but the truth was a nonstarter. "Sorry, I don't think I know the name."

Rodriguez opened up a folder stuck in the side pocket of his driver's side door and slid out a collection of photos—grainy, obviously off of surveillance cameras. Me, in a black miniskirt, being escorted by Detective Thomas Quinn.

"Want to try that one again?" he asked.

"I hear everybody has a double," I said. "Maybe you've got the wrong girl."

"Oh, I don't think so."

"Prove it."

"You drive a blue Dodge Viper. Funny thing—we had a report of a blue Dodge Viper driving away from an area in the desert where Quinn's SUV was found burned." His dark eyes kept their level stare on me. "His truck was destroyed, like somebody had loaded it up with dynamite, but we didn't find any trace of explosives."

I lifted one shoulder, let it fall, and just looked at him. He looked back. After a moment, he let one corner of his mouth lift in a slow, predatory smile. It didn't soften the harsh, hard eyes.

Quinn had managed to look coplike and friendly at the same time. Rodriguez just looked coplike, and didn't bother with any warm-and-fuzzy bullshit to make me feel better.

"Quinn was a friend of mine," he said softly. "I intend to find out what happened to him. If anybody did him harm, I'm going to see that that person suffers for it. You understand me?"

"Oh, I understand," I said. "Good luck with that."

Any friend of Quinn's was *definitely* not going to be a friend of mine.

I pushed off from the car and walked away, heels clicking, hair ruffling in the breeze. It was hot and turning sticky, but that wasn't what was making the sweat run cold down my back.

In retrospect, becoming a television personality probably hadn't been the best career choice I ever made, when a cop was missing and presumed dead, and I'd been the last one to be seen with him. Guess I should've thought of that. I'd spent too much time in the Wardens, where things got taken care of, and frictions with the rest of the mortal world were smoothed over with influence and cash and—sometimes—judicious use of Djinn.

Shit. I wondered about the Viper now. Since I'd actually stolen it off of a car lot in Oklahoma. Was it listed as hot? Or had Rahel, my friendly neighborhood free-range Djinn, taken care of erasing it from the records? She hadn't bothered to mention it. I wasn't sure how important she'd have found that, in the great scheme of things.

Hell, she'd probably think it was kind of funny if I got arrested. Djinn humor. Very low.

I needed to take care of that, soon. I had the bad feeling that Armando Rodriguez wasn't going to just go away, and if there was anything he could find as leverage, he'd start pushing. Hard.

Just as I started to think my day couldn't get much worse, I heard a rumble from overhead, and saw that a thick bank of clouds had glided over the top of the mall while I was worrying about how not to get myself thrown in the slammer.

I stretched out a hand. A fat, wet drop hit my skin. It was as chilly as the water that the stagehands had dumped on me in the studio.

"No way," I said, and looked up into the clouds. "You can't be happening."

It peppered me with a couple of drops more for evidence. Marvelous Marvin had been right after all. Somebody—somebody other than me, most certainly—had made damn *sure* he was right. Looking up on the aetheric, I could see the subtle signs of tampering, and the imbalance echoing through the entire Broward County system. Worse than that, though, was the fact that as far as I could tell, there weren't any other Wardens anywhere around. Just me. Me, who wasn't supposed to be doing any kind of weather manipulation at all, under penalty of having my powers cut out of me with a dull knife.

I was *so* going to get blamed for this.

And, dammit, I didn't even *like* Marvin.

INTERLUDE

A storm is never just one thing. Too much sun on the water by itself can't cause a storm. Storms are equations, and the math of wind and water and luck has to be just right for it to grow.

This storm, young and fragile, runs the risk of being killed by a capricious shift in winds coming off the pole, or a high-pressure front pushing through from east to west. Like all babies, this storm's nothing but potential and soft underbelly, and it will take almost nothing to rip it apart. Even as at-tuned as I am, I don't really notice. It's nothing, yet.

But the weather keeps cooking up rising temperatures and the winds stay stable, and the clouds grow thick and heavy. The constant friction of drops churning in the clouds creates energy, and energy creates heat. The storm gets fed from above, by the sun, and from below, by blood-warm water, and a generator starts turning over somewhere in the middle, hidden in the mist. With the right conditions, a storm system can sustain itself for days, living off its own combustion, an engine of friction and mass.

It's just a few days old, at this point. It won't live more than a few weeks, but it can either go out with a whimper, or with a bang.

This one can go either way.

It moves in a wide, slow sweep over the water. A wall of white cloud, drifting gray veils. No rain makes it to the ocean below; the engine sucks it back up, recycling and growing.

As the moisture condenses inside the clouds, conditions get strange. Intense energy sends water into jittering frenzies, producing even more power. The clouds darken as they grow denser. As they crawl across open water they are getting fatter, spreading, spawning, and that engine at the heart of the storm stores up power for leaner times.

And still, it's really nothing. A summer squall. An annoyance.

But now it's starting to know that it's alive.

Two

By the time we broke up the Great Mall Trek of 2004 for lunch, Sarah, Cherise, and I had enough shopping bags to outfit an Everest expedition, if the climbers were planning to look really, really adorable and hang out extensively at the beach.

Sarah had always been a natural-born clotheshorse. Not as curvy as me, and with the kind of perfect angular proportions that sparked envy and were held up as examples by plastic surgeons to keep them in the lipo and sculpting business. Life with the French Kiss-Off (as I decided to title Chrêtien) hadn't ruined her, except that she had some lines around her eyes, a good haircut gone bad, ugly shoes, and a generally sour attitude about men. A nice toning lotion took care of the lines. Toni & Guy bravely addressed the hair issues. Prada was very willing to practice some accessory therapy. I didn't think anything could possibly help her with the attitude, except massive applications of chocolate, which with her figure she wouldn't accept. After half a day of it, I was ready to send Sarah to the Bitter Ex-wives Club for an extra session of getting in touch with her whiny inner bitch.

"He was a lousy lover," she declared, as she was trying on shoes. She had perfect feet, too. Long, narrow, elegant—the kind of feet men liked to think about rubbing. Even the salesman, who surely must have had his fill of stinky, sweaty toes, was looking tempted as he held her by the heel and slipped her into a strappy little pointy-toed number. Personal service. It only happened at the best stores these days, but then, he *was* trying to sell her shoes worth more than your average television set.

"Who?" Cherise asked, inspecting a pair of kitten-heeled pumps. She must have missed the entire ongoing monologue about the flaws of Chrêtien. I stared gloomily at the ruby red pair of sandals I'd been saving up for, which were likely to go out of style and come back again three generations from now before I could actually afford them again, at the rate Sarah was shopping.

Not that I hadn't asked for it. And it was in a good cause. But I *really* needed to introduce her to the concept of outlet malls.

"The ex, of course," Sarah replied, and tilted her foot to one side to admire the effect of the shoe. It was, I had to admit, very nice. "He had this terrible habit; he'd do this thing with his tongue—"

Okay, that was *too much information*. I shot to my feet.

"I really don't think I'm ready for this level of sister-bonding. I'm going to get a mocha. You guys—shop."

Sarah smiled and waved. As well she should. She had my Mastercard in her purse, and I had exactly ten dollars and change in mine.

Being the younger sister *sucked*.

As I walked away, Sarah was amusing the shoe sales-man and Cherise with an account of something having to do with her husband, a Spider-Man costume, Silly String, and Velcro sheets.

I walked faster.

Outside, the mall was starting to buzz. It was packed with moms, squealing kids, harassed-looking singles clutching shopping bags, and a grim flying squadron of gray-haired mall walkers in heather gray sweats. Some had canes. I had to hug the wall to avoid a rumbling wagon trail of mothers with strollers, and then a flock of businesswomen with scarves and briefcases.

Men, apparently, no longer malled. Or at least, not

alone. Every one that I saw had a female solidly by his side, like a human shield.

The coffee shop was busy, but efficient, and I walked away with mocha gold. As I sipped I window-shopped, and I was admiring a dress that was very, very me—and very, very not my budget—when I caught sight of someone in the mirror-reflection of the glass, watching.

I turned and looked. LVPD Detective Armando Rodriguez smiled slightly, leaned against a convenient neon-wrapped pillar, and sipped on his own cup. Smaller than mine. Probably black coffee. He looked like an uncomplicated sort of man, in terms of his caffeine tastes.

I walked right up to him with fast, impatient clicks of my heels.

"Look," I said, "I thought we were sort of done."

"Did you?"

"You need to leave me alone."

"Do I?" He sipped coffee, watching me. Big eyes with warm flecks of wood brown in an iris nearly as dark as his pupil. He was wearing a jacket, and I wondered if he'd worn the gun inside—a pretty big risk, these days—or had stashed it in his van. Not that I thought he'd particularly need it. Even his casual moves seemed graceful and martial arts–precise. He'd probably have me on the ground and handcuffed inside of five seconds, if he were given the least excuse. In the harsher light of the mall, he had rough skin and a pockmarked face. Not a pretty man, but an intense one. Those eyes didn't blink.

"If you keep following me, I'm going to have to call the cops," I said, and was instantly sorry I had when he smiled.

"Yes, do that. All I have to do is flash my badge and ask for professional courtesy. Or I might possibly show them the surveillance photos, and request their assistance. I'm sure they'd be happy to help me out in questioning a suspect." He shrugged slightly, never taking his eyes off me. "I'm a good cop. Nobody's going to believe I've driven all the way here to stalk you. And a word of advice: I don't think a drowning person really ought to be flailing around in the water. Could draw some sharks."

I didn't say anything for a few seconds too long. A runaway five-year-old darted between the two of us, brushing my legs; I took a step back as the mom charged after and veered around us, yelling out the kid's name. Both Rodriguez and I watched as she caught up to the escapee and marched him back toward the Food Court, where evidently a firing squad of fast food awaited.

Rodriguez said, still looking away from mother and child, "Quinn was my partner. He was my responsibility. Do you understand?"

I didn't like what I was understanding.

"I'm not going, sweetheart. *Mira,* you and I are going to get very, very friendly until you tell me what I want to know." He finally turned his gaze back on me. Dead-eyed and intense.

"Don't you have a job? Family? Someplace to be?" I was used to handling difficult situations, difficult people, but he kept throwing me off my stride. "Come *on,* this is ridiculous. You can't just—"

"Quinn had a wife," he cut in. Those eyes were glittering now. "Nice woman. You know what it's like, living with that kind of uncertainty? Knowing he's *probably* dead, but you just can't move on because you can't really know? You can't sell the house, you can't get rid of his clothes, you can't do anything, because what if he's not dead? His insurance won't pay out. His pension's locked up. And what if he comes walking in the door and there you are, in a brand-new life you made without him?"

"I can't help you," I said around a sudden lump in my throat. "Please leave me alone."

"Can't do it."

And I couldn't give in to him, even if he'd hit me hard and in a vulnerable place. "Fine. Prepare to admire my ass for an extended period of time, because it's all of me you're going to see," I said. "This is our last conversation."

He didn't bother to debate. I took off so fast I splashed mocha on my fingers. As I sucked it off, I looked back.

He was still leaning against the pillar, watching me. Impassive and impartial as a hanging judge.

I met Cherise and Sarah coming out of Prada with a fresh bag. I winced to think what kind of bar tab this latest binge had run up, but smiled gamely and stepped back to admire the effect. Sarah was now dressed in a peachskin sundress in splashes of tangerine and gold, with lavender trim; her makeover at the Sak's counter, like the wave of a fairy godmother's wand, had returned her gleaming skin and butter-smooth sophistication. The shoes added just the right touch of sassy cool.

Of course, she was still broke. But she *looked* damn good.

And now *I* was broke. The karmic circle of life continued.

"So," I said. "Lunch?" I walked them through the neon gates of Calorie Paradise. About thirty culinary choices, everything from Greek salad to Diner Dogs.

"I'm starving," Sarah admitted. "I could murder a prime rib. I haven't had a prime rib in *ages*."

"It's the mall, honey. I don't think the Food Court does prime rib."

"We could go to Jackson's," Cherise piped up cheerfully. She was loaded up with bags, too, mostly having to do with hiphuggers and shiny belts. "They have prime rib. And steaks to die for."

"Do you know what it costs to eat at Jackson's?" I said. She gave me a blank look, because, well, of course she didn't. Cherise wasn't the kind of girl who picked up her own check. "Think pocket change, people." I steered them toward the choices I could—barely—still afford. The ones with a bright-primary-color decorating sensibility.

Eyeroll. "Fine." Cherise marched—how one marched in jeweled flip-flops, I have no idea—up to join the overweight queue standing in line at McDonald's. "I am *not* eating anything fried. I have a weigh-in coming up, you know. . . . Do they have anything organic?"

"It's *food*," I pointed out. "It digests. By definition, organic."

We bickered companionably about the usual food-related topics, which had to do with all-natural and bug-munched versus pesticided and bug-free, as the line wandered up toward the counter. The three sulky teens in front of me giggled and whispered. Two of them had tattoos. I was trying to imagine what would have happened if I'd gone home with a tattoo at their age, and decided I had enough nightmares in my life and besides, it made me feel old. Even Cherise had a tattoo. I was starting to think that I'd missed an important fashion trend.

Someone joined the line behind Sarah. I glanced back at her and caught an impression of a tall, lean man with slightly shaggy caramel-colored hair, and the kind of beard and mustache that always makes men seem to be faintly up to no good even while giving them a debonair kind of mystery. It looked good on him. He was scanning the menu and smiling gently, as if he thought the whole McDonald's experience was about to be very amusing.

"Sarah?" I asked. "Anything look good?"

"I don't know," she said. "What about the cheeseburger? Oh, no, wait . . . salad . . . they have so many kinds!" My sister, the decisive one. This, I remembered from childhood. She sounded on the verge of panic. Salad choices apparently unnerved her. "I don't know what to get."

"Well, I wouldn't recommend the caviar," the guy behind her said in a warm voice—not to me; to Sarah. He had bent slightly forward, not quite intruding. "I have it on good authority that it's not really Beluga." Definitely *not* a Florida accent . . . British. Not upper-class British, more of a comfortable working-class sound to him.

Sarah turned to look at him. "Were you talking to me?"

He snapped upright and out of her space, eyes going

wide. They looked blue or gray, but it was tough to be
sure—a changeable kind of color. Depended on the light.
"Er . . . yes, actually. Sorry. I just meant—" He shook
his head. "Never mind. Sorry. I meant no disrespect."
He took two steps back, clasped his hands together, and
tried hard to look as if he'd never opened his mouth.

Cherise had turned around at the sound of his voice.
She grabbed my wrist and squeezed, dragged me close,
and hissed, "Jesus, what's your sister doing?"

"Confronting," I said. "She's in a mood."

"Is she *nuts*? Look at him! Cute British guy! Hello!"

"She's on the rebound."

"Well, get her ass off the court and let me play!" All
of this delivered in a fast, rapid fire hiss that wouldn't
carry even as far as Sarah's ears, much less those of Cute
British Guy, who was looking increasingly uncomfortable
as Sarah continued to stare at him.

"Oh, you get enough court time, believe me. Go
order," I said, and nudged Cherise toward the tired-
looking order-taker at the register, who mumbled something about being welcome to McDonald's. Cherise gave
me a theatrically harassed look and made a production
of ordering a salad, interrogating the pedigree of every
tomato and carrot while she was at it.

Cherise's performance was distracting enough that I
missed the historic moment of détente, when Sarah over-
came her bitter hatred of men. When I looked back,
she was extending her hand to Cute British Guy. "Sarah
Dubois," she said, and I saw a tremor go right through
her. I could just hear her thinking, *Oh, Jesus, not Dubois,
you idiot, that's Chrêtien's name, your name is* Baldwin!
Unfortunately, it was a little late to backtrack on the
surname. At best, it would sound loopy. She covered
with an especially glittering smile, greatly enhanced by
the new Clinique lipstick we'd bought for her earlier.

Cute British Guy folded his fingers over hers in a
friendly grip, and wow, those were some long fingers.
About twice as long as my own. Concert pianist hands,
well manicured and soft and graceful. "Eamon," he said,

and gave her a slightly shy smile and an inclined head that was like a hint of a bow. "Lovely to meet you, Sarah."

She glowed like a sun at the attention. I mean, honestly. This, from a woman who was bitching half an hour before about how she'd rip the liver out of any man who tried to buy her a drink. She might have just set a new land speed record for rebounding.

Cherise grabbed my shoulder and yanked me off balance. I tottered on my high heels, caught my balance, and turned as she shoved me up to the order window. "Get something fattening," she said. "If you're forcing me to eat here, I want to see you suffer."

Just for sheer perversity, I went with the Quarter Pounder with Cheese. And fries.

Sarah, locked deep in conversation with Eamon, ended up snacking on a side salad and bottled water at another table, and forgot all about us.

I half expected Sarah to run off into the sunset, drop me a postcard from London thanking me for the use of my now-devastated Fairy Godmother Card, and live happily ever after until her next marital emergency, but no. The nice lunch with Eamon ended on a handshake parting that looked like no handshake *I* ever got from a lunch date, all eyes and smiles and long, beautiful fingers wrapping all the way to her wrist.

And then she was back with us. Glowing and smiling like the Madonna after a visitation.

"I'm done here," she announced. Cherise, who was clearly not enjoying her salad, glared, but hell, at least she'd bought herself some nice hiphugger capri pants and matching shoes. Except for coffee and Mickey D's, I hadn't spent a dime on myself.

But then, my shopping enthusiasm was somewhat dampened by the dark, relaxed figure of Armando Rodriguez, who had taken up a seat at a table about twenty feet away, sipping even more coffee. Apparently, he intended to never, ever sleep again. Or leave me alone.

"Fine. Let's go home," I said, and piled trash on my tray. The place was giving me a headache, anyway. Too many people, too much noise, too many flashing, blinking, spinning lights.

By the time we were out of the mall, the rain was over, but the parking lot shone in slick black puddles that rippled and shuddered in the wake of passing cars. Humidity was murder, closing warmly around me like a saturated, microwaved blanket. I herded Cherise and Sarah and the profusion of bags to the car; by the time we were getting inside, our preferred, close-in space was being scouted by an eagle-eyed old vulture in a shiny Mercedes and a determined-looking teenybopper with the ink still wet on her learner's permit. I pulled out and fled before the combat could get up to ramming speed. A few sullen raindrops spattered the windshield. Overhead, the sky was lead gray and utterly wrong; the patterns were definitely wonky. There was wobbling all up and down the aetheric, and little sparks of power as some other Warden made slight corrections. Nobody seemed too exercised about it, at least not yet; it was obviously not developing into the storm of the century. What was worrying to me about it was that I was supposed to be the only free-range talent out here. And *somebody* had messed with the weather to make this happen.

Thunder rumbled on cue. Resentfully.

"His name is *Eamon*!" Sarah said, leaning forward over the seats as I made my way toward the road. "Did you hear his *accent*? Isn't it adorable?" Sarah always had been a sucker for a foreign accent. Hence, the whole French Kiss-Off debacle.

"Yeah. That's Manchester, by the way, not West End London," Cherise said, and inspected her fingernails in the sunlight to admire the glitter effect. "Probably hasn't got a dime, Sarah." Never mind that she was tripping all over herself to get his attention before Sarah had captured the English flag. "I wouldn't get my hopes up if I were you. He's pretty, but he's probably . . . you know."

"What? Gay?"

"Nah, didn't feel gay to me. Kinky. Most English guys are."

"You think so?" She sounded interested, not alarmed, but then Sarah, I remembered belatedly, had stories about Spider-Man costumes and Velcro sheets. Oh dear God. Top of the list of things I didn't need to know about my sister . . .

I felt compelled to run the train off the tracks. "Oh, c'mon, he was just being friendly," I said.

"Who are you kidding? He was jaw-droppingly cute," Cherise said. "Cute guys are *never* just being friendly when they throw out pickups in the fast-food line."

True. Cherise was heartless, gorgeous, and *very* perceptive. "It wasn't like he *kissed* her or anything. It was a handshake." I shrugged. "I'll bet he didn't even give her his phone number."

"Actually . . ." Sarah said. I looked in the rearview mirror. She was dangling what looked like a crisp, white business card.

"Oh, kill me now," Cherise sighed, and slumped down in the passenger seat. "I schlepped around the mall all day carrying another woman's packages and what do I get? Dissed by a Brit. Man, I may just have to go seduce Kurt to restore my self-image."

"Set yourself a challenge, at least," I said. "Go for Marvin."

"Ewwwww. Please. I need to *have* a self-image at the end of it. That's just gross. *You* go for Marvin. He's hot for you, you know."

Sarah was reading over the business card. I distracted myself with that, to drive away the image of Marvin in his skivvies, leering at me. "So what does he do, your knight in shining tweed?"

"And don't tell us he's got some kind of title and a castle, or I really will commit suicide by Marvin," Cherise said.

"He's a venture capitalist. He's got his own company. Drake, Willoughby and Smythe." Sarah ran her newly manicured finger over the card type. "Raised printing.

He didn't just run it off on a laser printer or anything."
She frowned. "Although I guess he *could* be broke. Did
he seem broke to you, Jo?"

"Hey, he could have lifted the card off of some guy
he murdered at the airport," Cherise said. "And then he
stashed his body in a steamer trunk and checked it
through to Istanbul. He's probably a serial killer."

We gave a moment of silent homage to the fact that
Cherise's mind actually worked that way. At least she'd
steered away from any explanation involving aliens and
body-switching.

I felt duty-bound to try a defense, even though I barely
knew the guy. "First, Cherise? Way too many scary movies; second, Sarah, it might be a little early in the relationship to run a full Dun and Bradstreet on the poor
man," I said. "So? Are you going to call him?"

"Maybe." That secret little smile again. "Probably."

I couldn't be too unhappy with that. If Sarah was dat-
ing, she wouldn't be looking to hang with me quite so
much, and her stay in my guest room would be very
limited. Nothing like potential romance to get a woman
motivated to be independent.

"Hey, Jo? That van's still following you," Sarah said.
She was looking out the back window again, frowning.
"I thought you said it was no big deal."

"It's not."

Cherise piped up, "Then why's he following you?
Don't tell me you have a stalker. You already have a
boyfriend; it's not fair you have a stalker, too. You're
not *that* cute."

I eyed the van in the rearview. It was weaving in and
out of traffic fluidly, not drawing attention but staying
glued to my tail. Detective Rodriguez wasn't worried
about anonymity; he wanted me to know he was watching. A little psychological warfare.

He'd have to step up some to equal the stress of squir-
ing around both Cherise and my sister.

"He's not a stalker," I said grimly. "He's a cop."

There was a short silence, and then Cherise said, "Cool.

You're two-timing the cute boy with a cop? Man, Jo, that beats Cute English Serial Killer Guy. I didn't know you had it in you."

The clouds cut loose with a vengeance, torrential curtains of silver rain shimmering like silk and pounding like hail against the windshield. I flipped the wipers into grumpy motion and slowed down; Mona didn't like the rain, and I didn't like the idea of controlling a skid in these conditions. Or repairs to a Viper, perish the thought. Paying off Sarah's binge would take the rest of my working life as it was.

Behind me, the white van ghosted out of the rain and kept pace. I felt a snap of energy up in the aetheric, and a lightning bolt tore the sky with a sound like ripping silk, followed by vibrating thunder. I also felt the Wardens responding, this time with more force. *It's not me, not me* . . . How exactly was I supposed to make myself look innocent? Actually *being* innocent wasn't going to do it. I knew the Wardens far, far too well. They were already out for blood.

Cherise said, "I'm glad I put the top up on the car. You know, Marvin's percentage keeps holding. I mean, no doubt he's a total tool, and a real pervert, but he knows his weather."

I bit my tongue. Hard.

I was going to have to look into Marvin, and the Percentage.

Cherise took off for parts unknown upon arrival at her car, walking the five steps to her convertible under the protection of an umbrella big enough to shelter an entire football team. No way was she going to get so much as a drop on her flawless shell. Sarah and I divided up the packages and ran for the apartment door, breathless and soaked to the skin in about five seconds flat. The rain was hard-driving and cold, and it stung with the force of tiny, hard pellets. Shimmering silver curtains of it flared and billowed in the glow of streetlights. It was dark

enough to be twilight, but it was—I checked my watch—
only a little after two in the afternoon.

There was nothing currently brewing up out in the
open waters off the coast of Africa . . . even if I hadn't
had a vested interest in the weather, as a Warden, I
would still have known what was on the radar. Floridians
follow hurricane season with at least as much attention
as they give to professional sports. There weren't any
tropical storms out there, at least none big enough to
register at this point, though there was a low-pressure
system hanging out there, waiting.

But this storm didn't make sense. It shouldn't have
been here, and it didn't look like it had any intention of
moving on. And I couldn't seem to really get a decent
look at it, either. I was sluggish on the aetheric. Slow.

Maybe I really *was* tired. It had been kind of a full
half day.

We made it to the apartment, dumped packages and
wet shoes, and I squelched back to grab towels for us.
Sarah's hair fluffed out to look gleaming and fabulous.
Mine just looked frizzy. I glared at it in the bathroom
mirror and decided on a hot bath and something tasty
for dinner.

As I was laying out tomatoes and onions, the better
to make some homemade Mexican food, the doorbell
rang. I put the chopping knife down and tapped Sarah
on the shoulder. She was sitting at the small kitchen table
next to the water-rippled patio door, cutting tags off of
her precious new acquisitions.

"Chop now," I said. "Clothes maintenance later."

She gave me an absolutely childish pout, but got to it.
Sarah had taken culinary classes; it was one of those
things you do in California when you're rich and bored.
I paused on the way to the door to watch her take my
knife and start a rapid-fire slice-and-dice of the tomato,
as competent as any sushi chef.

The bell rang again. I sighed and pushed my curling
hair back from my face. Still damp. I used a tiny spark

of power to evaporate the moisture, was rewarded with dry hair and a white-blue static discharge from my fingers to the doorknob when I reached to touch it.

"Who is it?" I yelled, and pressed my eye to the peephole.

My heart did that funny little thumpy thing at the sight of the tall, brown-haired man standing out in the hall, hands jammed in the pockets of his blue jeans. I unzipped the chain and swung the door wide with a genuine smile. "Lewis!"

"Hi," he said, and came forward to fold me in a hug. He had to stoop a little to do it, and I wasn't all that short; where he touched me I got that familiar sensation of vibration, of energy feeding and building up between us. Lewis was, without any doubt, the single most powerful Warden I'd ever known. A friend. More than a friend, that would be fair to say . . . if it hadn't been for David, probably a lot more. He fascinated me, and frightened me, too. He'd saved me and betrayed me and saved me again . . . complicated, that was my boy Lewis.

"What the hell happened to you?" I asked.

"What?" He stepped back, blinking.

"Last time I saw you, you looked like warmed-over death," I said, and studied him more carefully. He actually looked as if he'd gotten some sun and discovered food again. "Remember? Lobby of the hotel in Nevada? You were still—"

"Shaky," he supplied, and nodded. "I'm better."

"How?"

He gave me one of those smiles. "Earth Warden." He shrugged. "Rahel helped it along. I heal pretty quickly when I need to."

"I'm glad. I was worried," I said, and couldn't quite keep the smile from my face. He just had that effect on me. "Oh, try not to say anything, you know, confidential. I have company."

Lewis cocked an eyebrow toward the ceiling as he shut the door. "Male company?"

"Female. As in, sisterly."

"I forgot you had a sister."

"I spent most of my life trying to forget, too. But she's family, and she needs a little— help. So I'm helping. You said something about Rahel helping you. Is she—are you—um —"

"She's fine," he said, which wasn't an answer, and he knew it. Lewis wasn't one to talk about his personal life, even to me. "David?" Equal parts genuine concern and irony. He and David liked each other well enough, but Lewis and I had history, and David knew it. "Doing better?"

I cut my eyes toward the kitchen, where the sound of chopping went on, opened my mouth to reply, and was interrupted by Sarah yelling, "Jo! Is that Eamon?"

Which stopped me in my tracks for a second. I held up one finger to Lewis and backtracked a couple of steps to look around the corner at Sarah, who was finishing up chopping the tomato and sliding the mathematically perfect cubes into a bowl. "Excuse me?" I asked. "Why would it be Eamon at the door, exactly?"

She glanced up, then set the bowl aside and made herself busy rinsing off the cutting board of tomato blood before putting the onion on the chopping block.

"Did you tell Eamon where I live?" I pressed.

"Well, you know, I gave him my phone number and—"

"Did you tell Eamon where I live?"

She pulled her lovely, ripe lips into a stubborn line and started attacking the onion. "I live here, too," she said defensively.

"Wrong. You're *staying* here, and Jesus, Sarah, you barely unpacked and you're already giving out my home address to guys you meet at the mall . . . !"

I felt warmth behind me, and Lewis's hand fell on my shoulder. "Sorry. Just thought I'd say 'hi,' and sorry, I'm not Eamon . . . Who's Eamon?"

"Sarah's mall pickup." I sighed. "Sarah, meet Lewis. Old friend from college."

She'd stopped chopping, instantly, and I could see her

snapshotting him. *Cute,* she was probably thinking. *But way too flannel.* And she was right. Lewis was all about the old blue jeans and worn checked shirts. His hair was getting too long again, curling halfway down his neck, and there were smile lines around his eyes and mouth. I knew for certain that he'd never in his life owned a suit, and never would. He'd never have a hefty bank balance, either. Not Sarah's type.

She smiled impartially at him. Sarah's version of *Hi, how are you, now go away.* I could see she was disappointed that Eamon hadn't come calling to whisk her off to an evening of prime rib and a selection of stout British ales.

"We're making Mexican food," I said. "You're staying, right?"

"Sure." Lewis looked around. "Nice place, Jo. Different."

"Thrift store," I said, straight-faced. "Kind of like my life right now."

"Could be worse." Didn't I know it. His gaze brushed mine, warm and full of concern. "I need to talk to you for a few minutes. Somewhere private?"

Which made all of my warm fuzzies curl up and die. I nodded silently and led the way out into the living room, then hesitated and took him into the bedroom and closed the door. The bed was still unmade. In normal times, Lewis might have made a sly little joke out of it, but he just sat down on the edge of the bed, looking at me, hands clasped loosely between his knees. He was a lanky thing, all awkward angles that somehow always looked weirdly graceful.

It made me feel . . . well. I'd missed him.

"Where's David?" he asked.

"Let's change the subject," I answered. Not angrily, just with finality. The last time we'd had dealings, he'd been in a scheme to separate me from David, and I wasn't having any of that, ever again. Lewis was probably the only Warden who knew I still had him, and that made me a little bit wary of the whole reunion vibe.

"You don't want to talk about it, fine. I respect that."
Lewis rubbed the pads of his thumbs together and looked
down at the carpet. "I'm only asking because I want to
be sure you have . . . protection. People are asking questions about you."

"People?"

"The wrong people. There's a big discussion going on,
and a pretty sizeable number are yelling about how you
shouldn't have been let out of the Association without—"
He didn't say the words *being neutered,* but that was
pretty much what we both knew he meant. "—making
sure you don't continue to use your powers. They're
pointing to some anomalies down here as proof you're
still playing Warden without a license."

That . . . wasn't good. And it explained my visit from
the Three Amigos yesterday morning. "Have you told
them I'm not? That I'm abiding by the agreement?"

"I'm not telling them anything." Lewis shook his head
slowly. "Look, I'm in the Wardens now, but I'm not
really . . . *in* the Wardens. You know what I mean. Whatever I have to say, it's not likely to help you. They respect me. They don't like me, and trust doesn't enter
into it."

I did know. Lewis had spent a lot of years on the
outside, making himself thoroughly lost from the Wardens, including me. A substantial number of Wardens
probably didn't want him around at all, and an even
greater number thought he was useful but didn't trust a
thing he had to say.

"Then what's Paul saying?" Paul Giancarlo, current
acting National Warden, was a friend, too. But Paul had
a streak of ruthlessness about a mile wide, and friendship
wasn't going to alter that one bit. Our friendship had
taken some pretty good hits in the past few months, too.
I wasn't sure I could ever really forgive him for what
he'd done to me in Nevada.

It's one thing to put me in danger. It was quite another
to blackmail me with the life of my lover. Not a thing
friends did.

"He's been trying to keep things reasonable." Lewis looked up at me with those warm, compassionate eyes. "I'm just guessing on some of this, but from the level of conversation going on, somebody has information, and it may not be in your favor. It might be smart for you to lose yourself for a while. Just take David and go someplace new."

"Just pick up and go?"

He nodded. He'd abandoned the Wardens early, and it had taken them years to find him. Actually, it wasn't so much *them* finding him as *me* finding him, and he'd let himself be talked into staying. More or less. I suspected some days a lot less. "I think it would be a good idea for you to not present them with such an easy target right now. There's too much going wrong, and nobody to blame for it. Too few Djinn, the Wardens are falling apart after that screwup at the UN Building—it's a mess. Paul's doing everything he can to hold things together, but honestly, Jo, I think they're starting to look for people to scapegoat. You're an obvious choice."

"I haven't done a damn thing."

"I know. I've been watching."

"What?" I took a couple of steps toward him, then stopped. "Want to rephrase that in some way that doesn't sound, oh, creepy and stalkerish?"

"I wish I could, but it is what it is. Paul sent me. He wanted to be sure there was no truth to what was being said about you."

"I haven't been manipulating the weather!"

He nodded. "I know that. But somebody around here has been. Subtle, mostly, but that Tropical Storm Walter thing was a big screwup. You must have noticed—" He gestured at the windows, where rain lashed and lightning flashed. "I'm just saying that in the absence of a suspect, you're looking awfully tempting. Whatever I say."

"But you'll tell them—"

"Yes. And do you really think they'll care, in the end? Jo, I'm not exactly the fair-haired boy around there anymore. Besides, we have . . . history. It's not a secret."

He had a point. A kind of scary one, actually. "So what do I do?"

"Like I said, leave," he said. "Or join the Ma'at. They can protect you." The Ma'at were his own creation, a kind of low-wattage version of the Wardens—there weren't any true powers in it, except for Lewis himself, and one or two others. Its strength had to do with its ability to *negate* power, not generate it. It was designed to restore balances that the Wardens—wittingly or unwittingly—had knocked out of whack.

Useful suggestions. However, I wasn't generally fond of them, either. Wardens, Ma'at . . . none of them had gone out of their way to make sure I was taken care of, in the end.

Everybody had their own agendas. I'd quit because I was sick of being at the mercy of everyone else's priorities but my own.

Speaking of that, Lewis was right. I should just go my own way. I should toss stuff in a suitcase, leave Sarah the keys to the apartment, and head out of town, David in the passenger seat and the road in front of me. But *God*, how long had I been doing that? Since the night that Bad Bob and I had fought, and I'd started running, I hadn't had a home or a place in the world, and I was *tired*. I wanted . . . I wanted to rest.

I wanted to belong again, and to be part of the world.

"I'm staying," I said softly. "I'll be careful, okay? But I'm staying. I don't want to live like that for the rest of my life, looking over my shoulder."

Lewis reached out and took my hand in his. Big hands, scarred and a little rough in places. Strong fingers and a tight grip. "I'm your friend," he said. "I'll do what I can for you, you know that. But Jo, if it comes down to it, you have to be prepared to run. I don't want to see you destroyed, but I don't want to have to choose which side I'm on."

I leaned forward and put a kiss on his forehead. "You won't have to." He was still holding my hand. His grip tightened, just a bit, and I felt that power humming between us again. We had a kind of complementary vibration to our talents, something that built in waves. Powerful. Dangerous. Kind of sexy, too. It had always drawn us together, and at the same time, driven us apart. We'd had exactly one truly intimate encounter, and that had been pretty much earth-shattering, in a literal sense.

Lewis wasn't a safe date, even if my heart didn't already belong to David.

Sarah knocked on the bedroom door. "Hey! Don't do anything I wouldn't do in there!" she yelled. "And the tomatoes and onions are chopped already. Do you want me to brown the meat?"

"Yes!" I yelled back, and rolled my eyes as I stepped back.

Lewis let go of my hand, stood up, and said, "You know, your sister reminds me a lot of you."

I gave him a dirty look.

"What?"

"Nothing."

I opened the bedroom door and went out to help make dinner.

It turned out to be okay, really. Lewis was pleasant company, Sarah more or less behaved herself, apart from grilling him mercilessly about the nature of my relationship with him, and going on and on about David, whom she hadn't actually met, which sort of set my teeth on edge.

Lewis kissed me good night chastely on the cheek and strolled off into the night air, hands in his pockets, looking as if he might be planning on kicking back at the beach and doing nothing much. In reality, he was probably off to save the world. That was Lewis. False advertising in battered hiking boots. I wondered what Rahel and the Ma'at were up to.

Decided firmly that it was none of my business.

Sarah didn't do dishes. Apparently they didn't teach that particular skill in snobby culinary classes for bored, rich housewives. I did the dirty work and got to bed at about my normal time, set the alarm, and settled in for a short night's sleep. I tossed and turned and missed David, missed him a *lot*. Hugged my pillow. Reached in the drawer, took out his bottle, and ran slow fingers over it.

But I didn't call him back, and in the end I fell asleep touching the cool glass, imagining he could feel my hands on him.

Which led to a very nice dream. Which was cut short by the ringing of the telephone. I rolled over in bed, flailing, knocking over small, knockable things—luckily *not* the bottle still lying on the sheets next to me—and squinted at the red digital numbers on the bedside clock after combing the mess of tangled hair out of my eyes.

Three thirty in the morning.

It took six rings to remember where the phone was and fumble it to my ear; when I finally did, I heard a conversation already in progress.

". . . a good day, then?" A velvety-smooth British voice, spiced with a lilt. Liquid and fast and a little spiked with adrenaline. "Sorry to be calling so late. I promise not to call you at this ungodly hour again; I was just on the phone with New Zealand and I forgot what time it was here. Will you forgive me?"

It took my sleep-fuzzed brain a minute to figure out why that voice was familiar. Oh, yeah. Eamon. I started to tell him to call back at some hour when people were actually *awake,* but Sarah's voice interrupted me in midbreath.

She sounded languid and relaxed and very glad to hear from him. "No, not at all. I wasn't really asleep." Liar, liar, panties on fire.

My inner Miss Manners, who was barely awake and bitchy as hell, told me to hang up the phone before I heard something personal. Which I was going to do. Any second.

"Did you enjoy your day out with your sister?"

"Jo? Oh, yeah. She can be sweet, you know?" That was surprising. It threw me off track for a second, until she continued, "Well, when she wants to be. She's been a total bitch to me most of our lives, though."

Well, fine. Then I felt no guilt in listening, and besides, who the hell did Mr. Sexy English Guy think he was, calling up my sister at oh-dammit in the morning? I had to get up in an hour! And it was *my apartment!*

Miss Manners woke up a little more and reminded me that I'd be pretty damn pissed if she'd picked up the phone and listened in on, oh, say, me and David having intimate moments. I debated about it long enough to hear Eamon say, "No more trouble from the ex, though? Not got anyone else looking for you, has he?" He sounded genuinely concerned. "I just worry, you and your sister all alone. It's a dangerous town, for two beautiful women on their own."

Trouble? What trouble? There'd been trouble with Chrêtien? From the version Sarah had given me, the trouble had been with the lawyers. Nothing about physical danger.

But then Sarah sometimes omitted facts. Such as the initial significant detail about two-timing Chrêtien with his business partner. That hadn't exactly been up-front information.

"You're sweet," Sarah said, in that half-asleep, breathless tone. I heard sheets rustling. If I could hear them, Eamon was hearing it, too. Sarah always had known how to work the flirt better than anyone I'd ever met. "No, I think he's given that up. He just calls me, when he can find me. And says . . . cruel things."

"I'm sorry."

"At least he isn't actually *doing* the cruel things anymore. Just talking about them."

Chrêtien? Cruel? New idea to me. I mean, he'd always been shallow and supercilious; I just couldn't see him as abusive. And she'd have told me, right? Even if I was a total bitch. My sister would have told me if she'd been married to someone who hurt her.

Right?

"Sarah, he has money and a grudge," Eamon said. "Bad combination. Does he know where you went?"

"He can guess. I haven't got a lot of family."

"Still worried, then?"

She sighed. "A little. About Jo. She's—she doesn't know when to quit, sometimes. I'm afraid if he does send someone, she might get hurt."

"It may sound forward, but . . . you know that you can call me. Any time. Day or night. I'll come right over," Eamon said, and it was delivered in a half whisper, low in his throat. And yeah, I had to admit, my instant answer might have been *Oh, yes, please, come on over right now, baby.* But that would have been my silent internal answer. Right before I calmly told him no, thank you, right out loud.

Right, I reminded myself from the lofty moral high ground. *Because you've never done anything like that.* Hell, I'd picked up David as a hitchhiker on the side of the road. The lofty moral high ground and I were the proverbial slippery slope.

Sarah gave a low-voiced laugh. "You're an awful flirt."

"Not at all," he said. "I'm an honorable man. I'd sleep on the couch, love. Completely platonic. Pure as the driven snow." His voice dropped even lower. "Sarah. I know all of this is really sudden—but I like you. And I want to get to know you better. I hope you don't think that's inappropriate."

"No."

"Good." I could almost hear the smile through the phone. "Then you don't mind if I call again? Or see you in person?"

"Not at all," she purred.

Not at all, I mocked silently, making a face at the phone. And held my breath as I slid it into the cradle and hung up, finally convinced that maybe I was a *little* out of line.

As I did, warm lips touched my shoulder, and David said, "What are you doing?"

I yelped—loudly—and twisted around in the sheets, ending up wrapped like a mummy, and saw him up on one elbow, stretched out in the moonlight. Gorgeous as a midnight dream, with those eyes burning like low-banked fire. "What are *you* doing?" I demanded breathlessly. "Hey! You should be—"

He put two fingers on my lips to hush me. "I should be here," he said, and replaced fingers with his mouth, a warm, liquidly intimate kiss that melted me into butter-warm contentment from the inside out. There was tongue, and hands sliding under the sheets, and oh my God, it was nice. My sleepy nerve endings came awake with an electric hum.

Outside, the rain was still falling, a steady whisper against the glass, and it reminded me that I had an hour before I had to shower and drive to the studio to be humiliated again by Marvelous Marvin and his horse's-ass predictions that seemed way too lucky to be true.

"I have to get up soon," I said, and worked my way down his bare chest with slow, damp circles of my lips and tongue, over the trembling, velvet-warm planes of his stomach. . . .

I heard the breath come out of him in a slow, moaning rush.

"Then we should hurry," he whispered, and stroked the curls from my hair.

In the morning—well, the predawn darkness—the rain finally stopped just in time for me to pull into the parking lot. My carefully straightened hair looked glossy and gorgeous when I checked it in the mirror; I did makeup fast, forbade Genevieve to backcomb *anything* on me, and then got a look at the outfit she had hanging on the rack next to the door.

"You've got to be kidding," I said. She shrugged massive, muscular shoulders. "Oh, God, I'll pay you *money* if you say you're kidding."

"You can't afford me, darling," she said, and lit up a Marlboro. There was no smoking in here. She never had cared. I held my breath and got out of the chair to take my costume off the hanger, and held it up to the light.

Apparently, Marvin's prediction was going to be sunny and warm. I was going to be wearing a huge, clownish, foam rubber yellow sun, with a hole cut in it just big enough for my face. Armholes and legholes, and yellow tights.

"No," I said. "I'm not wearing this. Tell Marvin—"

"Tell me what?" Marvin walked up and threw a heavy arm around my shoulders, leaned in, and looked down my shirt. He smelled like bad cologne and breath mints and a sour aftertaste of alcohol left over from the night before. His hair implants still looked like seedlings, but he'd cover them up with the toupee before going on the air, Visine the reddened eyes, and do a quick white-up on his teeth. Marvin knew television the way other, better meteorologists knew their way around a satellite graphic. "What's wrong? Don't like the outfit? Should have come to breakfast with me yesterday, heh heh."

I forced a smile and reminded myself that I needed a job, and this one paid better than working the register at the 7-Eleven, with a slightly smaller chance of being robbed. "I'd rather not wear it," I said. And tried to sound professional about it. "How about something else? Something less—"

"Kids *love* Sunny," he said, and squeezed the foam rubber, right about where my chest would be. "She's just so huggable. C'mon, Jo. Be a sport."

The jovial tone wasn't fooling me; his eyes were mean and bright, and he wasn't taking no for an answer. The news director, a harried young guy by the name of Michael, wasn't going to be taking any moral stand against foam rubber, and so far as I knew, there was no Weathergirl Union to protect me from this crime against fashion.

"Fine," I said, and forced a smile. "No problem."

He winked, swear to God. He did.

I had to sincerely fight the impulse to channel a lightning bolt.

*   *   *

The segment went about as badly as I could ever hope. My lines were stupid, the foam rubber sun suit was hot, Marvin was obnoxious, and Cherise was notoriously absent from the moral support trenches. They threw more water on me, this time to warn of some unusually big waves. One of the stagehands giggled.

As I was stripping off the sticky, sweaty tights, Genevieve took time off from her smoke break to toss me a towel and say, "You know, you're better than he deserves. You actually make him look good. Me, I'd forget my lines and throw up on him." She raised an overplucked eyebrow significantly and flicked her Bic on a fresh cancer stick.

I dropped the damp tights into the laundry basket—three points—and wriggled my toes in the ecstasy of freedom. "Would that work?" I asked.

"Sure," she said. "Worked for the last two girls. Well, okay, one of them went postal and beat him with a rubber fish. But actually, ratings went up, so maybe it's not such a good idea to go that direction, especially with the fish. Hey, you know what? Your hair looks good. You ought to take a beach day. It's supposed to be sunny."

We both laughed, and I smacked palms with her and left her to backcomb the noon anchorwoman into submission.

The weather was clearing in the east, but as I stood and felt the wind, I knew that it wouldn't stay that way; another wave of damp, cool air was moving in over the ocean, and the collision with the existing high-pressure system was going to drive more clouds. Rain today. Rain tomorrow, probably. Sunshine, my ass. Marvin *had* to be wrong, or else he had a Warden in his back pocket. But who? Not me, obviously. And since the local office here was run by John Foster, one of the few truly honest Wardens I'd ever known, I couldn't see it. But John had a flaw. He trusted people, until they let him down.

I wondered if I should start seriously looking around for the culprit. In self-defense.

You have power, I reminded myself. *You can call*

*storms and lightning and water. You can kick ass if neces-
sary.* Yeah, and get my ass dragged in for a magical
lobotomy for my troubles. Not a good situation. I was
too aware of what Lewis had said. I hadn't used my
powers at all, and even so, the Wardens were turning
against me. If I used them now, even in self-defense . . .

As I rounded the corner heading for my car, I spotted
a depressingly familiar white van. It was sequined with
leftover rain that glittered orange in the rising sun.

Dammit.

Rodriguez was sitting in the driver's seat, eating the
last crumbs of a Danish. He had a tiny little LCD television plugged into the lighter on the dashboard, tuned to
WXTV. He'd been watching—and no doubt enjoying—
my morning's humiliation as Sunny the Wonder Idiot.

Somehow, that didn't make me feel any better.

"Having a good time?" I asked him. He wiped Danish
from his mouth with a napkin, licked his lips, and sipped
coffee. "Because this is getting old. Go home. I can't tell
you anything."

"Sure you can," he said. "Hop in. Explain to me how
you knew Tommy Quinn, and what happened to him.
Confession is good for the soul."

"This is a waste of time. Yours and mine both."

"Well, I'm on extended leave, so my time is my own,"
he said. "And about your time, I don't particularly give
a shit. You *are* going to talk to me. Sooner or later."

I was tired, pissed off, and felt violated by the morning
in general; nothing like being the foam rubber butt of
bad jokes to put you in a great mood to start the day.
But even more than that, I was just *tired.* I felt . . . heavy.
Exhausted. Gray.

And maybe that was why I made the snap decision to
shoot my mouth off.

"Fine," I snapped. "Thomas Quinn was not a nice
man, and if he was your friend, I'm sorry, but believe
me, you're better off without him. He'd have stuck a
knife in your back in a second if he'd thought it was
worth the trouble. And I don't mean figuratively."

Rodriguez had gone still and very, very cold, watching me. Cop-cold, with a human fury burning somewhere underneath.

"Tommy was a good man," he said with deliberate calm. "A good cop. Good husband, and a good father." The fury underneath burned its way to the surface. "I saw him pull a six-month-old baby out of a burning building and puke his guts out when it died in his arms. You don't know a fucking thing. He was a *good man*."

I remembered Quinn, all those facets and impressions I'd had of him. I'd liked him. I'd feared him. I'd hated him. I hadn't known him at all, and neither had Armando Rodriguez, regardless of what he might think. People like Quinn weren't really knowable. They never showed you their true faces.

"He was also a murderer and a torturer and a rapist," I said. "But you know, nobody's ever just one thing."

I was walking away, digging for my car keys, when Rodriguez said from behind me, "Hold up. You said *was*. Past tense."

I kept walking, cold settling in between my shoulder blades. I heard the creak of metal, heavy footsteps on wet pavement behind me, and I had time to think *oh, shit* just before he grabbed hold and shoved me forward into the wet, slick finish of the Viper's passenger-side door. The breath puffed out of me; partly shock, partly the impact, and before I could even think about resisting he had both my arms behind my back, gripped in one huge hand, and the other hand holding my head down, pressed painfully against the roof of the car. My hair had fallen in a black curtain over my face, and it puffed in and out with my fast, scared breathing. I was off balance and shocked and my arms felt like they were about to be ripped right out of my sockets.

I felt myself reflexively reach for the air and water around me, and forced myself to let go of it. I had bigger problems than Detective Rodriguez.

"Settle down," he growled at my ear. Another jerk on my arms. *"Settle."*

I wasn't even aware I'd been fighting, and it damn sure didn't matter anyway; there was no way I was breaking free. I had no leverage at all. I forced myself to relax, and the pain in my arms reduced to a dull throb. I couldn't fight with supernatural means. For all I knew, the Wardens were parked across the street, monitoring my every move.

"You'd better listen to me," Rodriguez said. "I'm not playing with you. You know what happened to Tommy; you'd better tell me *right now* or I swear, I'm going to toss you in the back of that van and we're going to go someplace we can talk in private a really, really long time. You got me? I can make you hurt. Believe it."

"Okay," I whispered. Metal felt cold against my cheek, the raindrops as warm as tears. "You don't want to know this. I'm not kidding you, you really don't. Let him be who you think he was. Let his family remember him that way. I can't do anything to make it any better—ah!"

That last was a sharp cry, just short of a scream, ripped out of me when he wrenched up on my wrists and dug a knee into my ass to grind me harder against the car. Nothing sexual about this; it was all pain. He didn't care that I was a woman. I was just a suspect, and I had something he wanted.

Just then, a car turned the corner and slowed down to pull into the parking lot. Not one I recognized. Not Cherise's flashy little chickmobile; this was a conservative black sedan, with rental plates. Two people in it, that was all I could make out through the veil of my hair and the tears in my eyes.

It screeched to an abrupt halt, and the driver's side door flew open.

I felt a sudden, visceral rush of relief as Armando Rodriguez let go of me. I collapsed against Mona's sleek finish, knees wobbling, and clawed hair out of my eyes to look over my shoulder.

The cop walked quickly but without panic back to his white van, got in, and gunned the engine. He'd picked the premium getaway spot, I noticed. It was a slick exit.

He turned right and disappeared into traffic within seconds.

A strong pair of hands gently closed around my waist and helped me steady myself. I smelled expensive cologne. "All right?" a low, liquid voice asked. I managed to nod. "Do you know that man?"

I looked up to see my rescuer, and for a panicked second I didn't recognize him. Then all the pieces clicked together. Slightly shaggy brown hair, beard, mustache. Warm British voice.

Eamon.

I didn't have either the breath or the time to answer his question. "Oh my *God*! Jo, are you all right?" Sarah's shrill voice ratcheted a couple of octaves higher with fright. She hit me in a flying rush, hugging me, and I winced when I felt strained muscles creak.

And then I hugged her back, grateful for the unquestioning love and concern in her embrace.

Eamon stepped away and watched the two of us, blue-gray eyes bright in the morning light. After a moment, he put a hand on Sarah's shoulder.

"It's all right, she's safe now," he said in a steadying voice. "Joanne? Are you hurt?"

I shook my head and pulled back from Sarah's hug. "No, no, I'm all right. Thank you."

"We were coming to see if you wanted to go to breakfast," Sarah blurted. "Oh my God, Jo, that man—that was the same van! He was—was he trying to abduct you? Did he—"

"I'm okay," I interrupted. "Really, Sarah, I'm okay. He was just trying to scare me."

Eamon, apparently reassured that I wasn't bleeding profusely or otherwise horribly injured, took a step away and looked at the street where Rodriguez's van had disappeared. His eyelids dropped slightly, hooding the hard light in his eyes. "Looked like more than a scare to me, love," he said. "Looked like he was really trying to hurt you."

"As big as he is, if he'd wanted to hurt me, I'd be

hurt," I said, which was pure wishful thinking; actually, I *was* hurt. My arm ached like a son of a bitch. I didn't want to move it much. "Besides, he's –" *A cop.* I don't know why I didn't say it. Years of concealing things. Old habit. "—He's gone."

"And what if he comes back?" Eamon asked, reasonably enough. "Seems persistent."

"I can take care of myself."

He turned that look full on me, and I felt something inside both shudder and jump at the force of it. "Can you?"

I straightened and nodded.

"Well, then," he said. "I suppose I'll have to take your word for it."

"But—" Sarah frowned.

Eamon took her hand in his, and she went quiet. Well, I would've, too. There was something gentle and persuasive in the way he did it, not a *shut up* kind of gesture, but something reassuring. Comforting. "Let's talk over breakfast," he said, and led her back to the rental car. Handed her into the open passenger side door with an old-fashioned grace, then turned to me as he shut it. He was wearing a dark shirt today, top two buttons undone, and a freshly pressed pair of dark pants. Long, thin shoes— I was no expert on men's couture, but the shoes looked vaguely like Bruno Magli. Expensive. Maybe even custom.

He sure didn't *look* poor. Not at all.

"Coming?" he asked me, and quirked his eyebrows.

I took a deep breath. "Sure."

He opened the back door and held it for me like a gentleman while I slid inside.

INTERLUDE

For something so powerful, a storm is oddly vulnerable. This one—born out of the heat of water and a whim of air—is no different. All it will take is a powerful west wind from the middle latitudes to cut the top off its clouds, stall it in place to starve and die. Or maybe it avoids the west winds, but it moves into cooler waters, which would slow it down. It might find drier air that would leave it tired and weak, blown apart by the first little challenge.

But none of that happens.

It advances at the rate of about ten miles an hour, sometimes slower as it encounters small patches of cooler water; it captures the cooler air it finds and wraps it around— insulates itself, keeping its energy-producing warmer air inside. Clouds find resistance at higher elevations, and pile up like soldiers storming a wall. The fluffy, blunt-headed anvil thunderheads are its war flags.

As it pushes forward—an army on the march—inside the huge, thick mass of clouds there are bright blue-white pops of energy as the generator bleeds off excess. Just small flares. It isn't ready yet.

But it's getting there fast.

THREE

Eamon had exquisite table manners. For some reason, that fascinated me. The neat, precise movements of his hands, the elegance in the tiny adjustments of his knife and fork. Elbows off the table at all times. He didn't talk with his mouth full. In fact, he didn't say much at all, just listened politely as Sarah rambled on. And on. And on.

"I just can't *believe* that happened in broad daylight!" my sister said for about the twentieth time. I took a bite of French toast, made sure it was liberally dosed with maple syrup, and savored the sugar rush. "Don't those people you work for have any security? It's awful! . . . There should be security lights in that parking lot!"

"Well, I don't believe it would have helped, Sarah. It *was* broad daylight," Eamon pointed out reasonably. Bless him, he sounded more amused than irritated. "Do you have much trouble with such things around here? Criminal trespass, assault . . . ?"

"Couple of car break-ins," I said, and washed down the sugar with coffee. Which accounted for two of the major food groups. "Nothing serious. Kids, probably."

"And am I to think he was just another hooligan?" He ate a neat mouthful of eggs and arched his eyebrows at me.

"Not him," I admitted.

"Sarah said you were being followed," he continued after a polite pause to chew and swallow. "The same kind of van."

"The *same* van," Sarah insisted, and turned her big eyes to me. "Was it the guy? The one from the mall?"

No point in lying about it. "Yes. But—it's all right, really. I'll handle it."

"Are you certain that's the right thing to do? You might want to go to the police," Eamon asked. He sounded neutral about it. Around us, other diners clinked silverware on plates and went about their daily lives, which probably didn't involve getting stalked by out-of-state cops. I shook my head. "Ah, I see. Any particular reason why not . . . ?"

"I know him, sort of," I said. "I'll handle it."

Eamon gave me a long, considering look, then put down his fork and dug his wallet from his back pocket. I've always thought you could tell a lot about a man from the state of his wallet; Eamon's was slick, black, and expensive. He pulled a business card from it and handed it over.

"Cell phone," he said, and tapped the corner of the thick paper. Sarah was right, the cards weren't lightweights—creamy paper, raised type, a match in price range for the wallet that held them. "Look, I know you hardly know me, and I'm sure ladies like you have no shortage of men waiting to squire you around, but best to be safe."

I nodded. He put the wallet away.

"I don't care if you know him, Joanne. It's the ones you *do* know that hurt you."

I looked up from the card into his eyes. Large, gentle eyes that somehow mitigated the harsher angles of his face.

"No offense," I said, "and I don't want you to think I'm not grateful for the rescue this morning, but are you sure you really want to get into this? The two of us together could be a whole lot of trouble. You're just an innocent bystander. And if we hardly know you, well, you hardly know *us*. What if we're—"

"Villains?" Eamon sounded vastly amused by that. "Oh, love, I hardly think so. Keep the card, though. I've no duties just now, waiting for a deal to come through; there's no reason I can't help if you need it. Even if it's just the occasional walk to and from your car, which, by the by, is *quite* the looker. Your car, I mean. What model is she?"

Firmer territory. We talked autos. Eamon had a startling breadth of knowledge about British race cars, and had a taste for Formula One, and ten minutes later I noticed that Sarah was looking more than a little put out by the whole conversation. Oh yeah. He was *Sarah's* date, not mine. I suppose having animated, extended chatters probably was the wrong side of friendly.

I mopped my lips and excused myself to the ladies' room, and took my time with the hand-washing and the application of vanilla cream lotion and refreshment of lipstick. My hair wasn't too badly damaged from the wrestling match with Detective Rodriguez. In fact, I looked pretty good, for a change.

I felt a tug of longing so strong I had to grab the counter with both hands. I wanted David. I wanted to call him out of the bottle and have him sit across from me and smile and talk, as if there were something approaching a normal life for us, somewhere.

I found my hand slipping down to press flat over my stomach. There was still that unsettling flutter, deep down. The promise of life. I didn't know how to feel about that . . . hopeful? Terrified? Angry, that he'd committed me to a responsibility so huge it made my Warden job look easy?

I wanted to have a normal life with the one I loved. *Ones.* What was vibrating so gently under my fingertips was the possibility, however small, of . . . family.

But I knew normal life was a fantasy, and not just because of the oddness of loving a Djinn. This morning, I'd felt him getting weaker before he'd gone back in the bottle. He hadn't been out that long.

He wasn't getting better, as I'd convinced myself he was.

David was dying.

The despair of that just went on and on, when I let myself look at it straight on. *There's a way to fix this. There's got to be a way. I just have to . . . find it.*

"Jonathan," I said. "If you can hear me, please. I'm asking you. For David's sake. Help me."

No answer. Not that Jonathan was particularly omniscient, of course. I didn't flatter myself to think that he had me on constant observation; hell, I probably didn't even rate a speed dial. Time passed differently, to Djinn. He'd probably forget all about me until I was eighty and pushing my walker around the retirement home.

That was an oddly cheering thought, actually.

I took a deep breath, practiced a smile in the mirror, and went back out into the restaurant. As I weaved around tables and kicking children and a man who just *happened* to have his hand at butt level, waiting for me to squeeze by, I saw that Eamon and Sarah were deep in conversation. I slowed down to study the body language, and liked what I saw; he was leaning forward across the table, taking in every word, eyes fixed on her face. She was animated and vivid and luminous in the morning light.

The silent language of attraction.

As I watched, she dropped her hand down on the table, leaning forward into him, and his long, elegant fingers moved to cover hers. Just a brush, but enough that I saw the tremor go through her.

I almost hated to interrupt. Almost. But then, that was a younger sister's place, to screw up the good times.

I slid back into my chair and they immediately sat back, aside from giving each other little secret smiles. "So," I said to Eamon. "What are your plans for the day?"

"Actually, I'm at loose ends." He was still watching Sarah, eyes half-closed. "I was thinking of taking in the sights. I'm not well acquainted with Fort Lauderdale. What can you recommend?"

He was including me, but not really; I got the clue memo. I politely bowed out. "Wow, that would be great, but I've got a thing today. To do. So why don't you and Sarah go have some fun? It looks like it's going to be—" Without even thinking about it, I felt for the weather.

And fumbled the effort.

I froze, blank, coffee cup half to my lips, and concentrated harder. I felt horribly clumsy. The delicate sensitivity I'd always had to the balance of things, the breathing of the world, it felt . . . muffled. Indistinct.

"Jo?" Sarah asked, and looked over her shoulder, toward the wall I was staring a hole in.

I blinked, forced a smile. "—it's going to be beautiful," I finished. "Warm and sunny. Or so says Marvelous Marvin, anyway. So you might want to take in the beach. I think Sarah picked up a killer swimsuit yesterday, right, Sarah?"

My sister turned a rapt smile back to Eamon, who was watching me with a little frown grooved between his eyebrows. I sent him a silent *I'm okay,* and Sarah distracted him with a question about England, and they went back to living in a two-person world.

I closed my eyes for a second, concentrated, and drifted up toward the aetheric. Moving between dimensions was something so automatic that it was like breathing for me; I lived half my life there, connected to the world, seeing its layers and levels.

It felt like swimming through syrup, today. And once I was there, the colors looked dim and indistinct, the patterns muddy and confusing. There was something happening to me, but I couldn't think what; I didn't *feel* bad. I just felt . . . disconnected.

"Jo?"

Sarah was saying something, and from her tone of voice, she'd been saying it more than once. I opened my eyes and looked at her, saw her impatient frown. Eamon was measuring me again.

"Are you all right?" he asked.

"Fine," I said. "Sure. A bit of a headache, I guess. Listen, I'm really—I'm just really tired. I think I'm going to go home and lie down for a while before I have to do—the thing I have to do. Why don't you guys go have fun?"

They didn't seem too unhappy about that, although Eamon insisted on paying for breakfast and taking me back to the studio for my car, and tailing me home, and even went so far as to escort me upstairs and do a quick tour of the apartment. (I wished I'd cleaned up better.) When he was satisfied that I wasn't going to be jumped on by a crazed stalker hiding in the overstuffed closet, he and Sarah took off. I waved at them from the patio balcony, and stood outside for a few minutes, watching as his car made its way out onto the street again, heading for a glorious day of sun and fun.

A white van turned a corner, glided into the lot, and parked. I could see a shadow in the driver's seat.

"Hope you're comfy," I said grimly, and looked up at the sky. It was clearing. The humidity was down, and the cool ocean breeze whispered over my skin and rustled palm trees down at ground level.

There was absolutely nothing I could think of to do that would make a damn bit of difference, except wait and pretend to be completely comfortable with Detective Rodriguez's continuing campaign of intimidation.

I went back inside the apartment, changed into a turquoise blue bikini, grabbed a towel and a folding chaise lounge, and made myself a pitcher of margaritas. My arm still throbbed, but it didn't look as if it was badly damaged. I had shadowy bruises forming on my wrists to match the far-sweeter marks of David's lovemaking from earlier in the morning.

Party on the patio, Detective. Intimidate this.

I slid on my sunglasses, oiled up, and saluted him with a drink as I soaked in the morning rays.

What's the cardinal rule of sunbathing? Oh, yeah. Don't fall asleep.

Well, I did. I was lying on my stomach, sun massaging all the tension out of me, and I was thinking about David and hot-bronze eyes and golden skin, and getting that pleasant liquid ache that made me want to call his name, and somewhere around there I slipped into dreamland. It was a nice place. I stayed.

When I woke up, I knew immediately that I was as burned as if I'd stuck myself under the oven broiler. My back felt puffy and numb, and I'd sweated so much I'd soaked through the bikini *and* the towel. I sat bolt upright, grabbed the rest of my warm margarita and bolted it down, and hastily decamped from the patio into the apartment.

The white van was still downstairs, sitting innocently in a legal parking space. No sign of Rodriguez I couldn't tell if there was still a shadow in the driver's seat or not, but right at the moment, I had another problem.

I dumped the chair, oil, pitcher and towel, and hurried into the bathroom. My front looked fine. I bit my lip and began to turn, very slowly. Tan . . . tan . . . redder . . . red . . . scarlet . . .

Oh *man*. I peeled down the back of my bikini bottoms and found the contrast to be just a little bit more than a barber pole's stripes. This was *really* going to hurt.

I stripped off the bikini and got in the shower; that was a mistake. The numbness wore off fast, replaced by a nice selection of agony and pain, depending on where I directed the spray; I gingerly patted myself dry and slathered as much of myself with burn cream as I could reach. And suffered.

When the phone rang, I was in a high temper, ready to bite a telemarketer's head right off. "What?" I barked, and clutched the towel looser around my aching back.

"Damn, girlfriend, I knew you'd be in a bitchy mood after the Sunny costume," Cherise giggled on the other end of the line. "But you looked so *cute* and cheerful!"

"Oh, please, Cherise. At my age, *cute*? Not really what I'm going for." I tried sitting down. My thighs and back lodged a violent protest. I paced instead, went to the patio doors and pulled the curtains shut, then dropped the towel on the pile of Things I Had To Pick Up Later and continued pacing around naked. "That was Marvin's little joke, right? Because I one-upped him yesterday?"

"Sorta," she agreed. I could practically see her checking her fingernail polish. "Hey, there's been somebody asking questions about you down at the station. Tall guy, Hispanic, real polite? Sound familiar?"

Except for the polite part, it matched the description of Mr. White Van downstairs. "What does he want to know?"

"How long you've been here, where you were before, past history, how long we've known you, shit like that. Hey, are you in trouble? And is it, you know, serious?" She didn't sound worried. She sounded breathless with excitement.

"No, and no."

"Is he your stalker-guy? Because usually they don't interrogate your close personal friends. They're more of the scary watching-from-a-distance kind of weirdos. Oooh, is he from the FBI?"

"No. Cher—"

"Did you see the UFO over the ocean last night?"

"Did I—what?"

"The UFO." She sounded triumphant. "I'll bet they're tracking down everybody who saw it. There was a thing on the 'net about it; the IT guys told me over breakfast. Don't open the door if guys in black suits and buzz cuts show up."

"Cherise."

"Call me if Mulder drops by. Oh, speaking of that, look, could you do me a favor? I, ah, lost Cute British Guy's phone number . . ."

"You never *had* his phone number."

"Yeah, but your sister had it and she was going to give it to me only—"

"I'm not giving you Eamon's phone number."

"Oh, so now it's *Eamon*," she said. "Fine. Be that way. Break my heart, since you won't share Hot Boy David either."

"Bye, Cherise."

"See you at three?" We had some promo commercial thing. I checked the clock. Still four hours to go. "I'll pick you up."

"Yeah. See you then."

I hung up and kept walking. The air-conditioning kicked on and felt like ice on my back, which was good. Maybe I could find something light to wear—gauze would be just barely acceptable. Anything heavier would be torture.

The phone rang again before I could put it down. It was Cherise again. "I forgot to tell you: Marvin said you were supposed to wear the Sunny costume for the promo. Don't worry, I stuck it in the car. I'll bring it." She hung up fast.

Before I could scream.

"Wow," Cherise said, when she saw me in the halter top and shorts and flip-flops. "You've really mastered this business casual thing."

I threw her a dirty look and tried to ease myself gently into the passenger side of her convertible. Gasped when my burned back touched the leather. Cherise exclaimed and grabbed me by the shoulder to inspect the damage.

"Oh, man, that's bad," she said, and clucked her tongue, just like my grandmother. "You can't wear the Sunny suit like that. I mean, jeez, you'll die. Foam rubber on a burn?"

Like I had a choice. I sent her a miserable look.

"You're *so* gonna owe me, girlfriend." She slammed the convertible into reverse, peeled out, and shifted like a Grand Prix champion on her way out of the parking lot. The white van flashed by in a blur. I saw tail lights flare as it started up. "I may have to blow Marvin to get you out of this, you know. Hell, we may both have to blow Marvin. Oh, don't worry, we'll figure it out. He can't ask you to put on the damn suit like this; it's got to be against some government OSHA rule or cruel-and-unusual punishment or something."

I groaned. "Yeah, that Marvin, he's all about the work rules."

She knew I had a point, and frowned at the traffic as she merged onto the street. A Lincoln Continental seemed to have personally offended her, from the scowl she threw the driver. "So maybe you had an accident. I could drop you off somewhere. Like the hospital. You could even have a bill to back it up."

"Much though I'd like to pay a thousand dollars to have some teenage barely-out-of-medical-school intern diagnose a sunburn . . ."

She was already moving on from the idea. She looked at me with the utmost gravity, the kind of look you'd get from a close personal friend if they'd decided to donate a life-saving organ to you. "I'll wear the Sunny costume. You be Beach Girl today."

Which was quite a sacrifice. Cherise was *always* Beach Girl; that was her thing. Tiny bikinis and a perfect smile. Except for being too short, she was a *Sports Illustrated* swimsuit model. And she *never* did costumes. I think it might have been against her religion. She'd have to say ten Donna Karans and one Tommy Hilfiger to make up for it later.

Tempting as it was, I honestly couldn't see Marvin going for it, not when he had such a golden opportunity to make my life miserable. "He'll never agree," I said morosely. "And besides, Burned Beach Girl? What kind of message does that send? This is supposed to be a spot *talking about* the dangers of the sun, remember?"

"Oh, come on, they'll only shoot your front, anyway. And hey, baby, if your back isn't a cautionary tale, I don't know what is . . ."

I gave her a wan smile and held back my hair as I turned to look over my shoulder. I wasn't all that shocked to see the white van turning out of the parking lot in pursuit—well, not really pursuit. He wasn't in any big hurry to catch me.

"Something wrong?" Cherise asked, and checked the

rearview. "Oh, shit, you've got to be kidding me. Is that the same guy from the mall?"

"Yeah." I turned back to face front, slid on sunglasses, and leaned my head against the seat. "Don't worry about him. He's just—"

"Obsessed?" Cherise put in, when I didn't. "Yeah. I totally get that. You know, I've got at least three fanboys who send me letters every week wanting me to—well, you don't really need to know that. Anyway, it comes with the territory. We come into people's lives, and they want to keep us."

Cherise merged onto the freeway, blew her horn at a trucker who made a kissy face, and whipped around traffic with a speed and ease that would have impressed a NASCAR crew chief. Her Mustang—which I coveted, badly—was a new model, gorgeously maintained, and Cherise had never been one to keep her light under a bushel, so to speak. She was dolled up in a denim mini-skirt that rode three-quarters up her tanned, toned thighs, a tight, midriff-baring little top, and a Victoria's Secret bra that gave the top a little lifting and smooshing action. Her hair streamed out like a silk flag in the wind. She was one of those women who would arrive at her destination, after thirty minutes of sixty-mile-per-hour hair abuse, and look salon-fresh with a pass of her brush and a quick, careless flick of her head.

I used to have that. I missed that. My hair was curling again. Not that it would matter under the Sunny Suit.

"So," she said. "Tell me all about him."

"Stalker guy?"

"No, idiot. David." Cherise weaved in and out of steady traffic, keeping us in the shade of big trucks. She waved at a cop car as she passed it. The cop winked and waved back. "How'd you meet him?"

"Taking a cross-country trip," I said. Which was true. "He was on his way west. I gave him a ride."

She let out a high-pitched squeal. "Oh my *God,* was he hitching? 'Cause all the guys I see hitching are three weeks out of safe-hygiene zone, not to mention all skanky-haired and not cute."

"I gave him a ride," I continued, with wounded dignity, "and he helped me out with some trouble. We just sort of—clicked."

"I'll bet it wasn't so much a click as a bump . . . never mind. So where's he from? What does he do? I mean, I'm assuming he's not a homeless guy wandering the streets . . ."

"No, he's—" Man, how had I gotten into this conversation? "He's a musician." That was nearly always safe. No visible means of support, odd hours, weird habits. Ergo, musician. "He plays gigs here and there. So he's in and out. He's not always around."

"Bummer. Then again, it's tough to get tired of them when they're not hanging around farting on the couch and complaining about the Lifetime channel. Is he hot in bed? I'll bet he's hot."

"Cher—"

"Yeah, I know, I know. But still. Hot. Right? C'mon, Jo, throw me a fantasy bone, here. You *know* half the fun of having a hottie boyfriend is bragging."

I smiled. "I'm not complaining."

"And look, I die. Thank you very much." Cherise suddenly eased off the gas. I opened my eyes and looked at the road; traffic was slowing up ahead. "Oh, dammit. Wouldn't you know? Two miles to go, and what the hell is this . . . ?"

Traffic was stopped heading up onto the overpass. As in, *stopped,* all lanes screeching rubber. Cherise came to a halt, put the car in park, and eased herself up in the seat to try to catch a look. People were bailing from their cars to point.

I popped the door and got out to stand and gawk like everybody else.

There was a guy standing on the railing of the bridge, clearly about to go over to his death and splash on the concrete below. Okay, that was clearly bad.

But it really was way, way worse than anyone else could

possibly know. I realized almost instantly that nobody else there was seeing what I was seeing.

There were Djinn fighting over him.

There were two of them, facing off against each other. One of them was instantly recognizable to me—little pinafore-wearing, blond-haired, straight-out-of-the-storybooks Alice, who'd done me a few favors back in Oklahoma. She looked sweet and innocent, except for the nuclear fire in her blue eyes. Regardless of appearances—which in Djinn were notoriously unreliable—she was right up there in the don't-mess-with-me rankings. I liked her, and so far as I know she didn't dislike me, but that didn't make her a friend, exactly. You don't make friends with the top predator when you're below her on the food chain. You just enjoy not being on the menu.

Alice was standing between the stopped cars and the side of the bridge, staring up. The poor bastard on the railing—who in my view was looking less like a suicidal maniac than a pawn in a high-stakes card game—was teetering *on* the narrow rail itself and, to most eyes, he probably looked as if he was precariously balanced in mid-air; in actuality, his arm was being held in a viselike grip by another Djinn who was standing up there with him.

I recognized her, too—I'd nicknamed her Prada, once upon a time, because she had a pretty sharp fashion sense, but she was looking a little the worse for wear right now. The fine designer jacket was torn, the crisp white shirt stained, and whatever jewelry she'd been affecting was long gone. The look was, well, feral would be one word for it. She was glaring at Alice, who by contrast looked unruffled and altogether too clean to have been in a grudge match, although that was obviously what was going on.

I'd arrived just in time for Act III of an ongoing drama. And possibly a tragedy.

Even if the cops arrived, they weren't going to be able to handle this.

"Um . . . stay here," I said to Cherise, and moved around the stopped cars, heading for Alice.

"Hey! What are you doing?" She bailed out on the driver's side. "Do you know that guy?"

"Just stay here!" I barked, and I guess the ring of command must have come through; Cherise stopped where she was, watching me as I moved carefully toward the railing.

Something she said made me think. The guy up there did look vaguely familiar, but no, I wasn't sure I knew him. But there was something . . .

He fixed on me. Like recognizing like. He stopped flailing with his free right hand for balance and held it out to me. Palm exposed.

And I saw the swift, silver glitter of a glyph.

He was a Warden.

Prada, balanced on the railing with the ease of a hawk on a high wire, shook him violently for moving without permission. His feet scrabbled for purchase on the slick metal and he yelped, face gone pale and blank with strain.

Alice suddenly flicked that nuclear-hot stare in my direction, and there was nothing childlike in those eyes.

"You shouldn't be here," she said to me.

"Tell me about it," I said. "I'm not thrilled about it either."

"*This* is what you bring as reinforcements?" That was Prada, indulging in a sneer while Alice's attention was elsewhere. I wouldn't have, if I'd been her, but then, I wouldn't have been stupid enough to get into the fight in the first place. Alice was definitely not a power you wanted to mess with. "This *human*?"

Prada had killed me once. Well, temporarily. And to be fair, she'd been under orders to do it, since she was enslaved to a master—speaking of which, no sign of her hit man Warden boss. Which made me both happy and nervous.

Alice didn't so much as look at Prada, just shifted her weight slightly in the other Djinn's direction, and I felt the aetheric swirling in new, scary ways. Oh, this was way ugly, and bound to get worse. Wardens having at it with their powers was bad for humanity at large; Djinn had the potential to be far, far worse.

Why were they fighting? And more importantly, what were they fighting over?

And wait . . . *reinforcements*? That sounded bad. That sounded like Prada might have help coming. Did Free Djinn fight in public like this? I'd never heard of it happening before.

Especially not with a Warden as the chew-toy between two attack dogs. *That,* I would have heard of.

"I didn't call for help," Alice said, in that sweet little-girl voice. "I don't need any. One last chance. Let him go."

Prada gave her a mocking little laugh and jerked the Warden off balance again. All she had to do was open her hand. It was a good long ways down to an ugly, bone-crunching impact on the busy freeway below. Alice didn't move; it was possible, given the power balance, that there was nothing she could do that wouldn't kill the hostage caught in the middle.

"Alice, what's going on?" I asked.

"Who's Alice?" Cherise asked, craning her neck. She'd ventured over to stand next to me. "That guy's named Alice? Hope it's his last name."

"Shut up and go back to the car!" I practically yelled it at her. She winced and danced backward, holding up her hands in surrender.

This was out of control, and it was very, very dangerous. Prada and Alice couldn't unleash anything like a full-scale Djinn war here; there were way too many innocent people in range. They could bring down this whole bridge. There was no way I could protect against that.

"This isn't your fight," Alice said to me. Her attention was riveted on Prada, on the man Prada was holding. "Leave. You'll draw their attention if you interfere."

"Me? Wait . . . *their* attention? Who are you talking about? Alice, talk to me! What the hell's happening?"

I could feel Cherise looking at me strangely, since I was apparently having a conversation with thin air. I couldn't worry about that right now.

"Go!" Alice said sharply, and I felt a sudden push on the aetheric. She meant business. "I can't protect you. Stay away from us."

I was liking the sound of this less and less. "Not until I know what's going on with you guys."

She made a growling sound. It was *really* unsettling, because so far as I'd ever noticed, Alice in Wonderland hadn't been big on growling like a rabid animal.

The growl broke off as if somebody had pulled the switch on it, and she swiveled away from me to survey the general area. "Too late," she said. "They're here."

As I turned, I saw the *other* Djinn. Four of them, misting into visibility at strategic points in the crowd. She was outnumbered. Probably not outclassed, but still.

"You have to stop," Alice said, turning back to Prada. "He'll forgive you for what you've done, but you must stop now. No more."

Prada sank her flawlessly polished talons deeper into the Warden's left arm, and pulled him off balance again. He teetered desperately, struggling to stay alive. I could hear his gasps even over the shouts of the onlookers, trying to talk him down. They, of course, were operating under the assumption that he was crazy, and could choose to do something on his own. Could save himself.

I knew better.

Around me, the four new Djinn were closing in. Slowly. They seemed to be either cautious about Alice's abilities, or enjoying themselves. Maybe both.

This didn't make any sense. Djinn didn't bring their fights into the human world like this, not so publicly. And a Warden trapped in the middle, a tender morsel between tigers . . . no, this wasn't good at all. Things were shifting. I could feel that, even if I didn't know why it was happening.

Prada was aiming a cold, hard, inhuman smile at Alice.

"You should run, little one," she purred. "I promise not to chase you."

"I'm not running," Alice said. "You started the fight. You should be prepared to carry it all the way."

"I am."

"Then leave the man out of it. He doesn't matter."

"Of course he matters!" Prada gave her a contemptuous look. The Warden's feet slipped, and he flailed for balance, anchored by Prada's ruthless grip. The crowd of spectators who'd gathered gasped. A trucker leaned out the door of his semi, open-mouthed.

I didn't have a lot of time. I could hear the wail of sirens approaching; the cops would be here soon, and God only knew what that would mean.

Alice folded her hands together and watched. Wind ruffled her cornsilk-smooth hair, fluttered the sky blue dress and white pinafore. She was straight out of Lewis Carroll, but when I focused on the adult strength in that child's face, I could see something older, stronger, and far scarier than anything out of the Looking Glass.

Prada had made her angry. That was probably a really, really stupid move.

"That guy's gonna jump," Cherise murmured softly from behind me. "Oh my God. Oh my God . . ."

The four other Djinn—had to be allies of Prada—were stalking closer. Alice suddenly made her move, lashing out with an explosive flare of power. It hit Prada, looped around her, and attempted to jerk her and her hostage off of the railing and onto the relative safety of the bridge, but it backfired. Prada, straining to counter it, nearly went over instead. Alice immediately dropped the attack when the Warden screamed in panic.

With all the power she had, she was helpless to do anything without endangering innocent lives. She needed help.

I had no idea whether Alice was on the right or wrong side in this, but at least she wasn't the one holding a guy over a three-story drop.

I considered my options, and decided on something relatively risky. Djinn are, essentially, vapor in their atomic structure; they can increase their weight and give themselves the corresponding mass, but just now I figured that Prada was more interested in keeping her balance than having true human form. A human appearance was doing the job, for her purposes. She didn't need the actual reality.

All I needed to do was hit her from behind with a powerful wind gust, enough to break her grip on the guy she was holding, and at the same time tip him backward and encourage him to hop down onto the concrete again.

Simple. Relatively elegant. And a hell of a lot better than waiting for the Djinn Deathmatch to turn up a winner.

I closed my eyes, took a fast, deep breath, and reached out for control of the air around me.

And missed.

I gasped and reached farther, stretched. Felt a faint stirring come to me. A stiff breeze. Nothing nearly strong enough. *Oh my God* . . . I felt clumsy, drugged, imprecise. Horribly impaired. I fought my way up onto the aetheric, feeling like I was swimming against a flood tide, and when I arrived everything was gray, dimmed, distant. Gray as ash.

It was like what had happened to me over breakfast with Sarah and Eamon, only far worse.

I buckled down and went deep, all the way deep, into reserves I hadn't called on since I'd survived the Demon Mark. Pulled energy out of my cells to fire the furnace of power inside. Pulled every scrap of power I had and threw it into the mix . . .

And it wasn't enough. I could bring the wind but I couldn't control it. It would be worse than useless, it would hit with the force of a tornado and swirl uncontrollably, throw the man's fragile human body onto the concrete and that would *be my fault* . . .

Prada sensed I was doing something. She snarled and extended her free hand toward me, talons outstretched and gleaming, and it was déjà vu all over again. I could *feel* her reaching into my chest to take hold of my pounding heart. She wouldn't even have to work hard to kill me; it would be a simple matter of disrupting the electrical impulses running through nerves, just a quick jolt . . .

"David!" I yelped. I didn't mean to; I knew better, dammit, but I was scared and there was a Warden who was going to die because I wasn't strong enough . . .

"David? Where?" Cherise, distracted from the drama for a second, stared at me. "Who, the guy up on the rail? That's not David, is—"

I felt the warm surge of power, flaring to a white-hot snap, and David came from out of nowhere between parked cars, olive drab coat belling around him in the wind. Auburn and gold and fire in flesh. Moving faster than human flesh could manage. Nobody standing around watching the action even glanced at him. To their eyes, he didn't even exist.

The other four Djinn in the crowd froze, staring. And as one, took a step backward.

Prada hissed and instantly transferred her attack to him, which was a mistake; it brought him to a stop, all right, but only because he wanted to get a good, hard look at her. He looked tired, so horribly tired, but he dismissed whatever she was trying to do to him with a negligent shake of his head. He looked at the man on the railing, then the cops. Took it in, in a single comprehensive glance. I wondered, not for the first time, what Djinn saw when they studied a scene like that. The surface? The glowing furious tangle of human emotions? The energies we exerted, even unconsciously, on the world around us?

Whatever it was, it couldn't have been pretty. I saw faint lines groove themselves around his mouth and eyes.

His eyes turned to hot, molten metal, and his skin took on a hard shine. Getting ready for battle. He looked at Prada, who returned the glance with level calm.

"Why are you doing this?" he asked.

"I don't answer to you," she replied. "You betrayed us. Turned your back on us."

David turned to Alice, who raised pale eyebrows. "It's begun," she said. "It's spreading like a disease. A Free Djinn kills a master, sets loose a slave, who frees another, who frees another."

He looked appalled. "Jonathan ordered this?"

"Of course not." Alice's cornflower blue eyes fixed on Prada again, unblinking. "Ashan killed her master for her, in return for her loyalty."

Prada echoed, sarcastically, "My *master*." It was a curse, loaded with acid and venom. "He didn't deserve to lick my shoes. I broke no laws. I never touched him."

"What about him?" David said, and nodded at the Warden she was jerking around on the railing. "What has he done to you to deserve this?"

Prada's elegant lips compressed into a hard line. "They all deserve this."

"Oh, that's where we differ," he said. "They don't. Let him go. If you do, I swear that I'll protect you if Alice makes a move against you."

"David," Alice said, and there was a warning in it. "I'm here on Jonathan's orders." He ignored it.

"I'll protect you," he repeated. "Let him go."

Prada bared perfectly white, shark-sharp teeth. She looked, if possible, even more feverish. "You're Jonathan's creature," she said. "You always have been. He and his creatures don't command me, not anymore."

David looked—well, shocked. As if she'd just told him the Earth was a pancake carried on the back of a turtle. "What do you mean?"

"I follow the one who knows that humans are our enemies," Prada said. "The one who understands that our enslavement must end, regardless of the cost. I follow Ashan."

Oh, shit.

I was looking at a civil war. Playing out right here, messily, in the human world—Djinn Lord Jonathan and his second lieutenant (now that David was incapacitated) Ashan had had some kind of falling out. The Djinn were splitting into sides. Ashan hated humans—I knew, I'd met him, back when I'd been a Djinn. Jonathan didn't *hate* humans, but he didn't love us, either. We were just an annoyance and, at best, he wouldn't actively extermi- nate us. Allowing us to die was another thing entirely.

David was the only Djinn I'd ever met who seemed to really care one way or another about the fate of hu- manity as a whole, and David was nowhere near power- ful enough to be in the middle of this. Not these days. If the other Djinn were wary of him, it was only because they knew him from the old days.

They couldn't yet see the damage that had been done to him.

He didn't *look* impaired, though, not at the moment. The wind ruffled his bronze-struck hair, and the light in his eyes was like an open flame. More Djinn than I'd seen him in a long time. Less human.

He turned slightly and shifted his gaze to me, and I felt that connection between us pull as tight as a belaying rope. I was his support, his rock. And he was in free fall now, burning through his fragile resources at a terrify- ing pace.

I have to try to stop this, I felt him say across that silent, secret link. *Hold on. This may hurt.*

He wasn't kidding. Suddenly the drain between us— the one-way flow cascading from me into him—opened up to become a torrent, and damn, it didn't just hurt, it felt as if my guts were being ripped out and scrubbed with steel wool. I must have looked like hell, because Cherise called my name and I felt her grab me by the shoulders. I couldn't pull my eyes away from what was happening in the Bermuda triangle of the three Djinn standing in front of me, and the four moving into posi- tion to attack David from behind.

Whatever was about to happen, it was going to hap- pen *now*.

David started walking forward. Prada's eyes—burning ruby red now—followed him, but she didn't move. Still caught in her iron-hard grip, the Warden watched tensely, too. Helpless to affect any outcome. He wasn't a Weather Warden, I could sense that much, and I doubted he was an Earth power. Probably Fire, which wouldn't do him a damn bit of good right now.

Poor bastard. He'd spent his life thinking that he was a pinnacle of power in the world, and he was getting a hard lesson about where he really stood in the great scheme of things.

David reached the railing. Prada didn't make a move. David considered the metal for a second, then hopped up with a fluid, catlike movement, and began walking the thin, slick curve. He was smooth and careless about it, as if it were solid ground. No hesitation. No human awkwardness. It was as if gravity was just another rule to break for him. Even the gusts of wind didn't have any effect except to whip the tail of his coat out to the side as he covered the rest of the distance toward Prada and the Warden.

It was the single most inhuman thing I'd ever seen him do.

David was still two or three steps away when Prada let out a high-pitched shriek like ripping metal, and let go of her hostage. David lunged forward, but he was too late. The man windmilled for a fraction of a second, and then his head and shoulders leaned back, and his battered cross-trainers slipped off the slick metal of the railing.

And then he was gone. Heading for a fast, ugly death.

"David! Do something!" I screamed. Everybody else was screaming, too, but David heard me; he turned his head, and even at this distance I saw the hot orange flare of his eyes. As alien as the perfect balance he demonstrated up there on the railing. I saw the doubt in his face, but he didn't argue, and he didn't hesitate. Without a sound, he spread his arms and jumped off the overpass. Graceful as a plummeting angel.

At the same moment, Alice moved forward in a blur, launched herself up and out, and took Prada in a flying tackle out into space. The other four Djinn launched after her like a pack of wolves. They were a snarling, snapping, furious bundle of power, and I heard Prada howl in fury and pain a second before they all disappeared with a snap so loud it was like a thunderclap. Gone.

I lunged forward, gasping, and if there were people in my way I didn't care. They moved, or I moved them. I banged hard into the railing, hot metal digging into my stomach, both hands reaching down as if I could somehow grab hold, do *something*.

Anything.

"David!" I screamed.

I didn't see anyone down below. The cops had arrived on the street below, a sea of flashing lights and upturned faces. No sign of David. No sign of the Warden.

Movement in the deep shadows of the overpass drew my frantic eyes. They were hanging in midair. David had hold of the man. The two of them were suspended, turning slowly and eerily in the wind. A silent ballet.

Nobody else could see them, I realized. Just me.

I felt sick and cold and terribly, terribly weak, and realized that the flow of energy from me to David had gotten bigger. Wider. Deeper. As if we'd broken open some dam between us, and there was no stopping the torrent until the reservoir was dry.

"Oh God," I whispered. I could literally feel my life running out.

He looked up, and I was struck by the white pallor of his face, the bitter darkness of his eyes. "I can't," he said. I could hear him, even across the distance, as if he were speaking right next to me. "Jo, I'm killing you."

"Put him down first."

He tried. I felt him start to move but then he lost control, and it was free fall. He managed to brake, but it wasn't going to hold, and then he was going to plummet. I had about three seconds to act.

I wasn't a magician, able to suspend the laws of gravity at will. I had power, yes, but it was best used on the massive scale if I had to move fast, turning forces that measured in the millions of volts. Power that could destroy, but rarely heal. To grab the Warden required pin-point control of very treacherous forces, precisely balanced winds from at least three quarters, and an exact command of how much force was being exerted on frag-ile human flesh at any given instant.

David was a bright spark, fading. Between us was a black bridge, a fast-flowing river of energy going out of me, into him. Being devoured.

I stretched my arms and reached out until I felt I might unravel and break and be swept away. I tasted blood and felt my body starving for air and dying inside as its energy poured out onto the wind, screaming. I tried to do what I'd done a thousand times before, and alter the temperature of the air at the subatomic level, creating friction and lift and heat and wind.

For the first time . . . I failed.

I felt David break first with a bright, hot, shattering *pop,* and the black drag on my power fell away. The rebound slammed into me with stunning force, knocking me backward, and then I lunged for the railing again and saw David let go of the Warden.

Who fell, screaming, to his death.

There was nothing I could do. Nothing.

I screamed and covered my eyes from the sickening sight of his body crushing on pavement, his blood splat-tering in an arc as his skull shattered.

I felt his life snap like his bones.

David froze in midair, fixed in place, eyes dark and strange, body transforming from the fire of the Djinn to the black coal shadows of the Ifrit.

"Oh God . . ." It wasn't stopping. I felt every bit of energy being sucked out of me; the life, the heat, the *baby oh God not the baby you can't David . . .*

I felt everything around just . . . *suspend.* In some odd way, I kept on . . . outside of time, of life, of breath. It felt like being a Djinn, or at least what I remembered of it. Except I could feel some core of me screaming and coming apart under the strain. I wasn't healed.

Time had stopped. Pain hadn't.

Someone had intervened.

I heard the scrape of shoes on the asphalt behind me.

I turned and looked, gasping for breath, and saw Jonathan walking toward me through a flash-frozen world. People were locked in midstep, midword, midgasp. He and I were the only things moving.

Unlike most Djinn, Jonathan—the most powerful of them all—looked human. Middle-aged, with graying short hair. A runner's build, all angles and strength. Black eyes, and a face that could be friendly or impassive or cruel, depending on the mood and the light. Just another guy.

And yet, he was so far from human he made David look like the boy next door.

"You have to help me," I began. I should have known that the sound of my voice would piss him off.

He walked right up to me, grabbed me by the throat, and shoved me against the rail so hard that my back bent painfully over open air.

"You're lucky," he said in a whiskey-rough growl, "that I'm in a good mood."

And then he looked over my shoulder at the frozen, twisted shape of David, stopped in midtransformation. The shocking ruin of the Warden's body on the pavement below. Jonathan's face lost all semblance of humanity, all expression. There was a sense, even more than before, of some vast and terrible power stirring around him.

Even the wind was utterly silent, as if afraid to draw his attention.

"Jonathan—" I began hoarsely.

"Joanne," he interrupted, and it was a low purr, full of darkness and menace, "you just don't seem to *listen*. I told you to fix David. Doesn't look fixed to me. In fact . . ." His hand tightened convulsively around my throat and rattled me for emphasis. I gagged for breath. "In *fact*, he looks one hell of a lot worse than the last time I saw him. Not surprising that I'm very *disappointed*."

There was absolutely no mistaking the fury in him, even though it was cloaked behind a good-looking face and eyes that had all of the charm and warmth of black holes.

"I don't have time for this crap," he said, and turned those eyes back to meet mine. And oh, God, the rage simmered, red flashing points in black. Ready to break free. Ready to rip apart me, this bridge, the city, the world. He was that powerful. I could feel it rising off of him like heat from a lava flow. "I let you have your stupid little games and your stupid little romance, and it's destroying him. I don't have time for this. *I need him back. Right now.* This isn't some goddamn game I'm playing, do you understand that?"

Because he was in the middle of a war. I did understand. The battling Djinn had disappeared, but the aftereffects of their battle lingered like burned cordite on the raw air. If this was happening all over the world . . .

"I don't know how to help him," I croaked. "I've tried. I just don't understand how to do it."

I felt his grip on my throat tighten again. He pressed right against me, his thighs against mine, bent over me in a parody of a dance.

"Well, then, you're no good to me, are you?"

"Wait . . ." I tried to swallow. Pretty much useless. This was going to hurt so, so badly, if I survived it. "You—you must be able to—"

"If I could fix him, don't you think I already would have? Do you think this is some kind of game for me, watching him suffer?" No, I didn't think that. I could see the furious pain in Jonathan's eyes. "He's your *slave.* I can't touch him until you set him free."

David. The bottle. Jonathan couldn't interfere. Those were the rules. I could only imagine how much he hated that, hated *me* for being in his way.

I tried to swallow, but his grip was too tight. I could barely choke out the words around the burning pain in my throat. "*I can't.* You know as well as I do that if I let him go now—"

He knew. David would be beyond anyone's control once I released him from the bottle. Jonathan *might* be able to help him, but first he'd have to catch him, and that might not be possible.

"Help me help him," I whispered.

Oh, he didn't like that idea, not at all. I'd never scored high on the list of Jonathan's favorite people, for a lot of reasons—first, I was human, which was not a selling point; second, my relationship with David, and David's tenacious commitment to me, had upset the long-standing order of Jonathan's universe. And as Jonathan was, in Djinn terms, well-nigh as powerful as a god, that wasn't really a good thing.

It was also very hard to mistake the fact that Jonathan cared for David. A lot. In deep and eternal ways that stretched back to the days of their making. It didn't make for a comfortable three-sided relationship.

"Help you?" he repeated. "Oh, I think I've helped you just about as much as you deserve, sweetheart. As in, you're still breathing."

"Not very well," I croaked, and flailed a helpless hand toward my aching throat.

Which made his lips twitch in something that wasn't quite a smile. He let go of me, but he didn't step back. I slowly braced my hands on the railing and pushed myself back upright, careful to make no sudden movements—not that I could in any way hurt him, of course—and we ended up pressed together, chest to chest. He didn't care about my personal space.

He stared at me from that very intimate distance. Seen close, those eyes were terrifying indeed . . . black, shot through with sparks like stars, galaxies burning and dying and being born. Once upon a time, far in the past, he'd been human and a Warden, with the three powers of Earth, Fire, and Weather . . . like those Lewis possessed these days. I didn't know much about his human life, only his death; it had caused the Earth herself to wake and grieve. Jonathan had been made a Djinn by the force of that mourning. David, who'd been dragged along with him through those fires of creation, had come out sublimely powerful. Jonathan had come out a whole order of magnitude greater than that, perilously close to godhood.

He was losing that, to Ashan. How in the hell Ashan had the big brass ones to decide he could win in a toe-to-toe dogfight with Jonathan was beyond me, but the fact was, even if Jonathan kicked the crap out of him and all his Djinn followers, it was a war to make the Earth tremble. Nobody would be safe.

Nothing would be sacred.

Jonathan looked into me. It hurt, and I flinched and trembled and wanted desperately to hide in some dark corner, but there was no hiding from this. No defending against it, either. His hands came up and rested on my shoulders, slid up to cup my face between them with burning warmth. The heat of his skin on mine confused me, made me feel odd and disembodied. I wanted to pull away but I had nowhere to go, and besides, I wasn't sure my body would even listen to any such command.

"Feeling weak?" he asked me, and bent closer. His eyes swallowed the world. "Feeling sick? A little *off* these days?"

My lips parted. He was very, very close. So close that if he'd been human, we'd have been engaged.

He turned my head to a slight angle, tilted his own, and put his lips next to my ear. "He's killing you," Jonathan whispered. "Can't you feel it? It's been going on for a while, a little at a time. He's eating you from the inside. You don't think that's been killing him, too? Destroying him?"

I remembered all of the signs. The weakness. The clumsiness I felt when reaching for power. The gray indistinctness of the aetheric. The overwhelming drag when I tried to call the wind.

"Human power can't sustain him anymore. He'll suck you dry. He's an Ifrit; never mind how he looks when he's gorged himself on your energy. He can't help it. He'll kill you, and once he does that, even if I can get him back, he'll be a wreck. He'll recover, but it'll take too fucking long."

I felt tears burn hot in my eyes, break free, slide cold down my cheeks. He moved back just an inch, and turned my head again in those large, strong hands to look at me again. His thumbs smoothed the wetness from my skin.

"I don't care about you," he continued with soft intensity. "Make no mistake; I'll rip you apart if I have to, if it comes down to a choice of you or him. But I can't let him kill you. He'll be useless to me."

I flinched. He held me in place. "I don't know how to fix this," I said. "I swear, Jonathan. *I don't know!*"

"Simple. Go home, get that fucking bottle, smash it, and survive the rest of your pathetic life like everybody else in the human world. You have to let him go. He's already dead to you."

"Liar," I whispered.

And got an evil, beautiful smile in return. "Yeah? If I'm a liar, why can't you save him now? Why couldn't you save that sad bastard down there from falling to his death? All in a day's work for a Warden like you, right? You don't need me. Go on. Be a hero."

He let go of me and stepped back, and it was like going from the baking heat of the desert to Antarctica. My body cried out for his warmth, as if he were a drug and I'd developed a lightning-fast addiction. Bastard. He'd done it deliberately.

David was a wonderful, lyric poet of a lover. Jonathan, if he'd ever stoop to anything so intimate with a human, would be a pirate, taking what he fancied and forcing his partner to want it too. All cruel, casual grace and absolute dominance.

I grabbed the rail on either side and sucked in deep, calming breaths. Jonathan folded his arms and watched me as the energy drained away. Spiraled out into the black hole of David's need.

"Help me," I said, and God, defeat tasted bitter as poison. "Show me how to stop this."

"Say the magic word."

"Please."

"That's not the one I was looking for, but I'll take it." He reached out and put his hand flat against my chest. Heat spilled into me, intrusive as a stranger's hands, and I went rigid against the invasion. Not that it mattered. Jonathan could do anything he wanted.

But it was life he was giving me, and I didn't have the strength to refuse it anyway.

Jonathan watched me surrender to him with those hidden, dark eyes, and gave me a tiny thin slice of a smile. It was almost human. Not kind, but human.

"All right. What I've done is create a reservoir of power inside of you. It won't last long. You need to let him go or you'll die."

"If I do, how do you know you can stop him from coming after *you*?" Because David would be drawn to power, sure as a Demon.

"I can take care of myself," he said offhandedly. "We're done. Might want to hold on to something."

He let his hand fall back to his side.

Behind me, power exploded. The flash burned through me like a shock wave, and wind came in its wake, raging and furious at being held back; it nearly knocked me over, and Jonathan reached out to steady me as my hair blew straight toward him, long and tattered as a battle flag. Through the waving curtain of my blowing hair, I saw Jonathan give me another very small, cynical smile.

And then he looked past me and I saw pain in his expression. He said something, but it wasn't in human language; it was the bright and singing tongue of Djinn. A prayer, a curse, a lament . . .

I sensed a black presence behind me in the air.

David was transforming into something terrible, something with cutting edges and hunger for a heart.

When I tried to turn around to see, Jonathan held me in place and shook his head. "Don't look."

It was bad enough seeing the devastation in his eyes. I was watching the end of a friendship that wasn't supposed to have an ending . . . something time itself was supposed to respect. *I did this. No,* we *did this, David and I, together.*

Love, I was starting to realize, was beautiful, but it was also ruthlessly selfish.

I touched Jonathan and felt fire, not flesh; it burned me with wild and intimate fury, but I didn't let go. "Jonathan . . ."

"I have to go," he said, and I heard that edge of grief in his voice again, liquid and molten with pain. "He'll kill me if I stay here. Or worse. I'll kill him. He's too hungry right now. Remember what I said. You don't have much time—just *get it done.*"

He let go of my arm and stepped back. My hair obscured my vision again, and I reached up to shove it out of the way as I whirled to see what he was looking at.

David was gone. In his place was a black, twisted shadow of a thing, angles and glittering edges and nothing remotely human to it. An Ifrit.

It touched down on the bridge's surface and stalked toward us, fixed on power.

Fixed on Jonathan.

"No!" I screamed, and threw myself in David's path, but he went through me as if I were smoke, lunged with diamond-bright claws outstretched . . .

And Jonathan vanished before they could touch him.

David misted out a few seconds later. Chasing after that bright, shining ghost.

I was alone.

Well, except for the onlookers who were suddenly coming to realize that *something* weird had happened. But not exactly what, or who was responsible.

The cops arrived. I was hustled off to stand beside a police cruiser. Nobody knew what to ask, because no one understood what had just happened; all I had to do was be just as clueless. Pretty easy, actually. I wasn't faking the shock and trauma. The questions they tried to frame were just as vague as my answers, so in the end the cops just gave it up and accepted the whole thing as a suicide.

I wished I could see it that way, but I couldn't stop crying. I couldn't help but replay the terror in the Warden's eyes as he'd reached out to me, or the scream that had ripped out of him when David let him go.

My fault.

I'd never even found out his name.

Eventually, the cops remanded me to the custody of Cherise, who had been standing at the barricades looking anxious and dumbstruck and more than a little freaked out for some time. She didn't say a word. She grabbed my hand and towed me off toward the Mustang, this time pulled over to the breakdown lane, and got me well out of the way before turning on me.

"What the fuck was that?" she yelled over the resumed din of traffic, honking horns, and the wind. "Joanne! What in the hell did you think you were doing?"

I couldn't answer. I didn't have the strength. I just looked at her, walked around to the passenger side and got in the car. Cherise continued to berate me and pepper me with questions, which made no more sense than the ones the cops had managed to put together. I ignored her.

David was gone. I couldn't feel him anymore. I shut my eyes and remembered that back in Las Vegas, when I'd held the bottle of another Djinn turned Ifrit, I hadn't been able to sense any connection to her either . . . but she'd obeyed my commands. At least, the most important one.

Without opening my eyes, I whispered, "David. Get back in the bottle, *now*."

I had no way of knowing if he had. Hopefully it would give Jonathan some space. Maybe David would even recover a bit. Maybe, maybe, maybe . . . everything was so screwed up. I pressed the heels of my palms into my eyes until I saw stars.

The warmth in me felt foreign, like artificial life support. Jonathan had warned me it wouldn't last. How long did I have to find an answer, one that wouldn't destroy David in the process?

Cherise was saying something about us being so fired; we were the better part of an hour overdue for the shoot, of course, not that I cared. I just wanted to go home. I felt the thrum of the engine as she started up the Mustang, but then she slammed it back into park and reached over and grabbed me by the shoulder.

I looked at her. She was the picture of astonishment, from her raised shaped eyebrows to the shiny, lip-glossed *O* of her mouth.

"What?" I asked.

For answer, she shoved me forward and put her hand on my naked back.

"Hey!"

"Joanne," she said, and slapped me lightly there, several times. "Your burn. It's gone."

A parting gift from Jonathan. For completely different reasons than her subsequent declaration of a miracle, I found that more unbelievable than anything else.

I wanted to go home. Cherise flatly refused to turn the car around, since we were so close to our destination. "If I'm going to get my ass fired, I want them to do it to my face," she said grimly, and hit the gas to power us around the fast-moving traffic and down the off-ramp.

The shoot was being staged in a used-car lot. Of course. Some sort of promo tie-in with the local junker dealership. Cherise shrieked the Mustang to a sliding stop in a convenient space and eyed the salespeople mistrustfully as they appeared like—well, like magic.

"Nobody touches my car," she said to the Alpha Marketer, a big ex-football-type guy with a flattop haircut and that I'll-make-you-a-great-deal gleam in his eye. He grinned and gave her the thumbs-up. "And save it, gorgeous, I'm not in the market." Maybe not for a car, but her eyes skimmed him up and down, giving him the Male Blue Book rating. It must have come out a *ka-ching*, because Cherise came out with one of her famous smiles. "Watch it for me?"

"Absolutely," he said, and handed her his card. "Anything you need, you come straight to me."

She slipped it in her back pocket with a wink, and hustled me up to the cluster of people near the main building. I went, barely aware of moving. I just wanted to collapse in a heap and cry.

Marvelous Marvin was *not* in a good mood. He was pacing, face flushed under the pancake, snapping off orders to some poor intern who looked anemic, asexual, and on the verge of giving notice—or possibly expiring of an asthmatic fit. Marvin still had his makeup napkin tucked into his collar. It was not a humorous sight.

The camera crew was lolling around, looking happy as clams. As well they should be, at fifty bucks an hour or more each. One was catching a light nap in a portable chair with a sunshade.

"You!" Marvin bit off as he caught sight of us. "You are *fired*, get me? *Fired!* Both of you!"

I mustered up some sense of responsibility. "It's not Cherise's fault," I said dully. No, it was my fault. I kept replaying the Warden's fall, his impact on the concrete. He'd been young. Too young to die like that, caught in the middle of something he couldn't understand.

"I wasn't talking to her, and anyway, I don't give a shit whose fault it was, you're both fired! Look, I can get pretty girls twelve to a dollar out there on a beach; I don't need you two with your prima donna attitudes. . . ."

"Hold up," said the director, who was watching a portable TV in the shadow of a minivan with the channel logo painted on the side. "Come here, Jo."

I came. Cherise came with.

The director—Rob—pointed at the screen as he took a bite of his cheese sandwich. "Is that you?" He looked up at me as his finger touched a tiny, foreshortened figure on the screen.

"Yeah, that's her," Cherise jumped in when I stayed quiet. On the screen, the Djinn didn't show up—just us humans. The Warden on the railing fought for his life, flailing against the air. "God, Rob, she tried to save that guy. She really did."

He turned his attention back to the footage. I closed my eyes when I saw the Warden's feet slip off the railing for the fatal plunge, but not before I saw myself lunge forward. Didn't seem like I'd reacted all that quickly, but there it was, in grainy news footage. It looked as if I'd been trying to grab his hands or something.

"Jesus," Rob said quietly. "Joanne, I'm sorry. This is terrible." He thought about it for a few seconds, then raised his voice. "Yo! Doug! Change of plans! Let's get back to the station right now. Get on the phone to—what channel is this?—Channel Four—and get whatever raw footage they have. Feature story. Get Joanne and Cherise on camera with—who's up?—yeah, Flint, and do the standup with them on the bridge, if you can. If not, studio. We need to get this now."

Marvin had followed us. He ripped the makeup napkin theatrically out of his collar. "What are you talking about?" he thundered.

Rob glanced up at him, then back down at the screen. "Sorry, Marvin. I'm scrubbing the promo."

"You can't do that!"

Rob tapped his baseball cap. It was dark blue, and it said in big, white, embroidered letters, NEWS DIRECTOR. "I believe I can, actually."

Marvin turned and stalked away, tossing the balled-up napkin at his intern, who fumbled it and had to chase it under a freshly polished Toyota.

"You want me to get into the Sunny Suit for the interview?" I asked bitterly. Rob looked up and met my eyes. His were gray, sharply intelligent, and utterly calculating.

"From now on, you don't wear the Sunny Suit. Somebody else does," he said. "Maybe Marvin."

In spite of everything—even the crushing uncertainty

and grief of not knowing where David was, what was happening to him, the guilt and shock and horror—that made me smile.

Cherise cocked an eyebrow. "What about me?" she asked. Rob gave her a more guarded look. "I'm not fired, right? So, are you going to need me today?"

"Just for the interview, Cherise. But you'll get the full appearance fee for the promo."

She nodded soberly, took a long look at me, and reached behind Rob and took his navy blue windbreaker off the back of his chair to drape it around my shoulders. I was shivering. Delayed shock. Outright fear.

I needed to get home.

The interview took hours.

By the time I staggered in, it was late afternoon, and I was absolutely exhausted. No sign of Sarah, which was lucky; the last thing I wanted to do was put up with my sister's cheery enthusiasm about her new beau right now.

I shed purse and shoes and stripped off clothes as soon as I'd slammed the bedroom door shut, threw on my warmest and most comfortable bathrobe, and curled up on my bed, pillow in my lap.

I opened the bedside drawer and took David's bottle from its case. It gleamed blue and solid and cold to the touch, but it was just a bottle, no sense of him in it or around it. I didn't know if he was in there. Didn't know if he was suffering. Didn't know if he even remembered who I was.

I took hold of it and thought about how easy it would be, really. A quick, hard swing at the wooden nightstand.

I'd promised Jonathan that I'd set David free, but if I did that, it was like giving up hope. Giving up everything. I didn't think Jonathan could save him, and while I might not be able to either, at least David wouldn't get any worse inside the bottle. If I did set him free, he might complete the transformation to Ifrit. He'd almost certainly start preying on the most powerful source around—and that meant Jonathan.

But most importantly, I might lose him for good this time.

Jonathan's artificial life support was still going strong. I had time left.

I couldn't do it. Not yet.

I curled up with his bottle held close and cried until I fell into an exhausted gray twilight sleep.

Dreaming.

The mountaintop was familiar. I'd been here before . . . a small, flat space of empty rock, surrounded by the sky. Far below, canyons cut deep into the earth. Dry, for the moment, but I knew how fast they could fill and flood. Water was the most treacherous of the elements.

I was sitting cross-legged, warmed by the sun, wearing something white and sheer that barely qualified as fabric, much less cover . . . ceremonial more than functional.

There was no sound in my dream but the dull whispering rush of the wind. The breathing of the world.

I felt a warm hand touch my hair and fingers sink deep into the soft mass. Where they touched, curls straightened and fell into silk-smooth order.

"Don't turn around," David's voice whispered in my ear. I shivered and felt him hot against my back, hard muscle and soft flesh. As real and honest and desirable as anything I'd ever known. "You have to be careful now, Jo. I can't protect you—"

"Just stay with me," I said. "You can do that, can't you? Just stay."

His hands moved down to my shoulders and bunched gauze-thin fabric, then slid it free to drift away from my skin. "If I do that, you'll die."

"I'll find a way."

His kiss burned hot on the side of my neck. "I know you'll try. But you have to promise me that when the time comes, you'll make the right choice. You'll let go."

I had a nightmarishly slow vision of David's hands opening, of the Warden sliding loose and falling to his death. Only this time it was me falling, screaming, reaching out.

I was toppling over the edge of the mountain, toward the currents below.

David grabbed me around the waist and held on.

"Don't let me hurt you," he whispered, and his voice was shaking with strain, vulnerable with need. "Stop me. Please, Jo, you have to stop me, I can't do it myself . . ."

I looked down to where his arms were around me, his hands touching me.

Black, twisted Ifrit hands. Angles and claws and hunger.

"Please," he whispered against my skin, and he sounded so desperate, so lost. "Please, Jo. Let me go."

"I can't," I said numbly.

"Let me go or let me have what I need! I can't—I can't—" He exploded into a black, oily mist, howling, and was gone.

I collapsed forward, the white gauze drifting over me in the relentless, murmuring wind, and screamed out loud, until I woke up.

My sister was home. I could hear her moving around out there in the living room, humming something bright and happy. Probably something classical; Sarah always had been more cultured than I was, from the early days when she'd looked forward to piano lessons and I'd cut them to go chase baseballs out on the corner lot. I didn't hear Eamon's voice. I realized I was still holding David's bottle in a death grip, in both hands, and put it back in the padded case in the nightstand.

You promised, a little voice whispered in the back of my mind.

I had. But I wasn't ready.

I closed the nightstand drawer, shuffled into the bathroom, and winced at the glare of the bright, unflattering Hollywood lighting. I looked like crap . . . swollen eyes and bedhead. I struggled through combing the tangles out, got my hair more or less straight, and decided to leave the eyes as is, except for a quick application of Visine. I tossed on a crop top and tight low-rise jeans (artfully, though not intentionally, bleached in a random pattern, thanks to an accident with the Clorox Fairy) and walked out barefooted into the rest of my world.

Which was in surprisingly good order.

Sarah was cooking. She had fresh, bright vegetables laid out on the kitchen counter and was whaling away with a gleaming oversized knife. Behind her, a pan simmered with a pool of oil. She looked up at me and froze in midaria, then forced a smile and went on with her chopping.

"Hey," I said, and sat at the kitchen table, staring at my hands.

"Hey, yourself." She did something in my peripheral vision, and then a glass of wine appeared on the table in front of me. White wine, silvering the outside of the glass with chill. "Will that help?"

"Help what?" I sipped the wine. It was good, light and fruity with a kick at the end. Dry finish.

"Whatever the problem is."

I sighed. "It's more of a rotgut-whiskey-out-of-a-paper-bag problem than a fine pinot grigio problem."

"Oh." She retreated to her vegetables again. "You've been dead to the world all day, you know. Eamon's coming over for dinner; I hope that's all right. I was hoping your, ah, friend could join us. David. The musician."

Oh, God, it hurt. I took another gulp of wine to dull the knife-sharp pain. "He's touring."

"Oh. Too bad." She shrugged and kept on with food prep. "Well, there's plenty. I'm making chicken primavera. I hope you like it."

As I had no opinion, I didn't answer, just sipped wine and stared out the patio doors. The ocean rolled in from the horizon, and it was a beautiful twilight out there. We didn't face the sunset, but the faint orange tinge was in the air and reflected off the sheer, glassy points of the waves. The sky had turned a rich, endless blue, edging toward black.

I'd been asleep a while, but it felt as if I hadn't rested in days. Everything felt sharp and fragile and not quite right.

I let it fade into white noise as Sarah scraped meticulously dismembered vegetables from cutting board to bowl. She left the veggies and checked a stock pot on the stove, which sent out an aroma of chicken and herbs when she lifted the lid. I didn't remember owning a stock pot. It looked new. Like the gleaming chef-quality knives. I couldn't remember if I'd gotten my credit card back. That worried me, in a distant sort of other-worldly way.

She kept talking about my neighbors, whom I guess she'd spent the morning chatting up. I failed to follow, but it didn't really matter; she was babbling with an edge of nervousness, the standard Sarah tactic when she was trying not to think about something else. I remembered her doing this in high school, getting ready for dates with Really Cute Boys. She was nervous about Eamon.

". . . don't you think?" she finished, and began draining the chicken. She saved the stock, I noticed. The better to boil the pasta.

"Absolutely," I said. I had no idea what the question was, but she beamed happily at the answer.

"I thought so. Hey, give me a hand with this, would you?" She was struggling with the weight of the stock pot. I got up and grabbed one of the side handles, and a hot pad—those were new, too—and helped out. She flashed me a grin that faded when I didn't grin back. We drained the chicken in silence. The stock pot, refurnished with broth, went back on the burner and got a new load of pasta. Sarah dumped chicken and veggies into the oil-prepped pan to sauté.

"Is it David?" she asked as she expertly stirred and adjusted the heat. I blinked and looked at her. "Did you have a fight?"

"No." There was no easy answer. She took it for the avoidance it was and concentrated on her cooking.

I'd turned off the phone before collapsing on the bed

this afternoon; I wandered over to the wireless base and saw that there were messages. I picked up the cordless and punched buttons.

"Would you like to own your own home? Rates today are . . ." Erase.

"Hot singles are looking for *you*!" Erase.

A brief moment of silence, and then the recording said, "Be on your balcony in thirty seconds. I'll be waiting."

I knew the rich, ever-so-slightly inhuman female voice. And that *wasn't* a recording. Not exactly.

I put the phone down, walked over to the plate-glass window and looked out. No one out there. But I knew better than to think I could avoid this, even if I wanted to; the Djinn Rahel wasn't the kind of girl you could avoid for long. I opened the sliding glass door and stepped out into the cooling breeze. As I rumbled the door shut again, I felt . . . something. A little stirring inside, a slight chill on the back of my neck.

When I turned around, Rahel was seated at my wrought-iron café table, legs crossed, inspecting her taloned fingernails. They were bright gold. The pantsuit she was wearing matched, and under it she wore a purple shirt the color of old royalty. Her skin gleamed dark and sleek in the failing light, and as she turned her head to look at me I saw the hawk-bright flash of her golden eyes.

"Snow White," she greeted me, and clicked her fingernails together lightly. They made a metallic chime. "Miss me?"

I sat down in the other delicate little café chair and folded my hands on the warm wrought iron table. "Like the bubonic plague."

She folded a graceful, deadly hand over where her heart would be if she'd actually had one. "I'm devastated. My happiness is shattered."

"To what do I owe this pleasure?"

"Ah, is it one?"

"Just say whatever you've come to say." I said it in a flat tone, tired of the banter already and just wanting to crawl back in bed and avoid reality for another few hours. Avoid the choice I knew I had to make. Which wasn't even really a choice.

Rahel leaned forward and rested her elbows on the wrought iron. Those alien, bird-bright eyes studied me without any trace of mercy or humor.

"You're dying," she said. "Broken inside. I see that Jonathan has given you time, but you'd best not waste it, sistah. Things are happening too quickly."

"David's an Ifrit," I said suddenly. I remembered seeing it happen to Rahel—who, so far as I knew, was the first Djinn to ever recover from it. And she'd done it by sapping the power of the second-most-powerful Djinn in the world . . . David . . . and by a unique confluence of events that included human death and intervention by the Ma'at in an extraordinary cooperation of human and Djinn.

"I need the Ma'at," I said. "I need them to fix David."

Rahel was regarding me with those steady, predatory eyes. In the dying daylight, they looked surreally brilliant, powered by something other than reflected energy. She drummed her long, sharp fingernails on iron, and the chime woke a shiver up and down my spine.

"The Ma'at won't come. The Free Djinn have affairs of their own to attend to, and even if we did come, we would not be enough. David is too powerful. He'd drain the life from all of us, and it would accomplish nothing."

"Jonathan wants me to—"

She held up her hand. "I don't care what Jonathan wants."

This was new. And unsettling. Rahel had always been fanatically in the Jonathan camp; I understood there were cults of personality within the Djinn world, if not outright political parties, but I'd never thought of her as changeable in her allegiances. She was for Jonathan. Period.

She continued, "If you let David free now, he will hunt, and he will destroy. I was dangerous, when I was an Ifrit. *He* will be deadly, and if he goes after Jonathan, Jonathan will not act to stop him as he should. Do you understand?"

I did, I thought. I'd felt the voracious hunger in David, the need to survive. I knew he'd have died rather than even consider feeding on Jonathan, in saner days, but what was happening to him had no relation to sanity. Not as I understood it.

"If you keep him in the bottle, he'll drain you dry," Rahel whispered softly. "But it will end there. He will be trapped in the glass."

"But he's not draining me now!"

She merely looked at me for so long I felt a sick gravitational shift inside my stomach.

"He is?"

"Ifrits can feed on humans," she said. "But only on Wardens. And there is something within you that is not human that attracts him as well."

The baby. Oh, God, the baby.

"You want me to *voluntarily* let him kill me," I said. "Me and the baby. To save Jonathan."

"You must," Rahel said. "You know what's happening; you feel it already. Djinn are fighting. Killing. Dying. Madness is taking us, and there will be no safety without Jonathan. No sanity in anything, including the human world. Do you understand this?"

I shook my head. Not so much from ignorance as exhaustion. "You're asking me to sacrifice my life and my *child.* Don't you understand what that does to him if he's left standing after that?"

"Yes. Even so, even if it destroys him forever, it must be so. There has not been a war among the Djinn for thousands of years, but this—it's coming. We can't stop it. Some want to pull away from humans, from the world. Some want to stay. Some feel it is our duty, however distasteful, to save humanity from itself."

"Gee," I said. "Don't put yourselves out."

She gave me a cool look. "There have been blows

exchanged that cannot be taken back. I fear for us. And you. This is darkness, my friend. And I never thought I would see it again."

"Jonathan knows that if I don't break the bottle, there's no bringing David back."

Rahel didn't answer, exactly. She etched sharp lines into the metal of the table, eyes hooded and unreadable. "He thinks he knows the outcome of things," she said. "I think he sees what he wishes to see. He believes he can master David, even as an Ifrit. I don't believe he can. But as much as he wishes to save David, he is thinking of your child, as well. He wishes to save all of you, if he can."

"And you don't. You want us to die for the sake of damage control. What am I supposed to say to that, Rahel?"

Rahel opened her elegantly glossed lips to reply, but before she could I felt a sudden hard surge of power up on the aetheric, and a male voice from behind me said, "I can solve all of your problems. Give David to me."

Ashan. Tall, broad-shouldered, a sharp face that tended toward the brutal even while it was elegantly sculpted. He was a study in grays . . . silvered hair, a gray suit, a teal-colored tie that matched his eyes. Rahel's fashion sense was neon-bright; he was like moonlight to her sun. Cold and contained and rigid, and nothing of humanity about him at all, despite appearances.

Rahel threw back her chair in a shriek of metal on concrete and hissed at him, eyes flaring gold. Ashan just stared at her. He looked breathtakingly violent, one second from murder, even though all he did was stand there.

I was looking at the embodiment of the war Rahel had been talking about, and I was the chosen battleground.

"Still campaigning for your master?" he asked. Not directed at me; I didn't matter to him at all. I was human, expendable meat. "Time's up, Rahel. Are you staying with him? The old guard's changing. You don't want to be stupid about this. I've got a place for you at my side."

She didn't answer. Didn't need to. Her defensive crouch was answer enough.

"It's a small army you've put together," Ashan said. "Small, and weak. You stink of humans, Rahel. Don't you want to wash yourself clean of them? Them and all of the filth that we've wallowed in these thousands of years while Jonathan watched his plans rot and die?"

"I'm clean enough," she said, "and I don't answer to *you*."

"Not yet," he agreed, and turned those eerie eyes on me. "I don't know why Jonathan hasn't killed you, human, but if you get in my way, I won't hesitate. You know that."

I dug my fingernails into my palms and slowly nodded.

"Now be a good girl and go get the bottle for me," he said. "I want David. *Now*."

INTERLUDE

As the storm nears its first brush with land, it's almost unrecognizable from the soft, pale breeze born off the coast of Africa. It stretches hundreds of miles across, thickly armored in electric gray arcs of clouds. It carries inside of it the energy of the sun, stored in the form of tightly packed moisture that continues to rise and fall, condense and shred, and every transfer bleeds more fury into the system.

Dangerous, but not lethal. When it breaks, it will dump torrential rains and heavy winds, but it's still just a storm.

But as it nears the first of several islands in its way, a one-in-a-billion confluence of events comes together, as an ocean current winding its way north to south is warmed by just the right angle of the sun. Its temperature rises by four degrees.

Just four.

Just at the right time.

The storm passes over the current, and bumps into the sudden warm wall of rising moisture. Something alchemical happens, deep within the clouds; a certain critical mass of moisture and temperature and energy, and the storm begins its relentless suicidal course.

The last small variable in the equation is a random brisk wind spinning off the Cape. It collides with the storm's far perimeter and slides along, and because it is cooler it drags the storm with it.

The storm begins to turn. The storm has rotation. It has

mass. It has a gigantic energy source, self-sustaining. It has taken a huge leap, grown explosively and deepened in its menace, and it is no longer a child.

It is now a full-fledged hurricane; and it is still growing.

FOUR

In retrospect, snarling, "Over my dead body!" probably wasn't the smartest thing to say to a Djinn willing to take on Jonathan in a straight-up dogfight for control of the Djinn world.

I never said I was smart. But at least you can't call me a coward.

Ashan reached out to grab me, but his hand never reached me; Rahel lunged past me in a flash of neon gold and flung herself on him like a tiger, ripping and snarling. Ashan, taken by surprise, fell back a few steps . . .

. . . off the balcony.

He didn't fall. He floated, looking surprised and annoyed and a little bit pissed-off, and yanked a handful of Rahel's cornrowed hair to get her off of him. His strength was incredible. I knew how tough Rahel was, and the ease with which he slung her around and threw her in a violent, swinging arc that ended in a crushing impact with the ground thirty feet below, and with at least four rows of cars on her way into the parking lot. Rahel hit the ground, rolled, and came up fluidly to her hands and knees, looking for all the world like one of those clawed raptors from the dinosaur movies.

She vaulted up to the roof of the white van, where Detective Rodriguez might have noticed a slight weight displacement but wouldn't have seen a thing even if he'd looked out. She ran the length of it, then planted her

feet and arced gracefully up into the air, heading straight
for Ashan . . .

. . . who knocked her out of the air as easily as Babe
Ruth swinging for the bleachers.

I could feel the disordered currents of energy in the
air around me. The Djinn were causing instability, and
dammit, there was nothing I could do about it. Whatever
damage had been done to my powers when I'd overex-
tended and David had . . . changed . . . wasn't fixing
itself, and the energy Jonathan had thrust into me wasn't
made for weather work.

Rahel flew bonelessly through the air, crashed to the
pavement of the parking lot, and rolled about fifteen
feet, arms and legs flopping.

And then she vanished into mist.

Poof.

Ashan turned his attention back to me.

I gulped and stood up, backing away. Not a lot of
escape opportunities on the balcony.

"You know what I want," Ashan said, and held out
his hand. His fingernails gleamed a kind of opal-silver in
the twilight, and his eyes were as bright as moons. He
might have been wearing a designer suit, but he was no
kind of human. "Get the bottle."

"You can't even touch the bottle," I said. I meant it
to come out cool and logical, but it sounded shaky.
"Djinn can't—"

"Little girl, don't presume to tell me what Djinn can
or can't do," he interrupted in a voice so low and cold
that I felt ice form along my backbone. "I said *get it.*"

"Or?"

"You don't want to test me." He took a measured
step forward. I felt the ozone crackling in the air, felt
the menace in the clouds overhead. Wispy things, but
firming up as the disruptions in the aetheric mirrored
themselves into the physical world . . . whipping, uncontrolled winds in the mesosphere; cold spots; a streak of
heat from Ashan that cut through weather patterns like
a spearhead. I could feel the electricity in the air trying

to find a way to ground itself. He could fry me right here on the patio, and with my powers currently registering somewhere from zero to dead, I couldn't even defend myself. "David is fond of humans. I'm not. I don't care if I level this entire building to make my point."

"Djinn," I said, and forced a grin. "No sense of proportion."

I didn't see him move, but I felt the blow—hard enough to temporarily white out my nervous system and send me reeling to slam back against stucco and brick. I'd missed the plate-glass doors, at least. That was a relief. When sensation came flooding back, it brought with it a tide of stinging-hot ache along the side of my face. It had been an open-handed slap, but damn, he hadn't pulled it. I put my hand to my cheek and felt heat. My eyes were watering.

Ashan took another step forward. "I'm not interested in how clever you imagine yourself to be, and if you think your human body interests me, you're deluded," he said. "I only find it interesting in how many creative ways I might be able to take it apart. Now, go and get the bottle."

He couldn't touch the bottle. He couldn't take it away from me. Even Jonathan hadn't been able to do that. Was it a bluff? Or did he just want to know where it was?

I slipped open the sliding glass door and backed inside, then slammed it shut. For all the good it would do, of course. Outside, Ashan stood silhouetted against the failing twilight, gray as a dead man, with those eyes swirling cold and silver.

"Hey," Sarah said. She was still deep in her culinary trance, doing something now involving bread and the oven. The kitchen smelled like rosemary and olive oil and roasting chicken. Heaven. I wished I could appreciate it; I was shaking, shaken, and scared. I watched her slide the tray into the slot and close the oven door, then strip off oven mitts and turn toward me with a smile. "It's nice out there, isn't it? Kind of peaceful. Maybe we can have dinner out there . . ."

"Yeah," I said. "Great. Okay." What a horrible idea. I started to move past her to the bedroom.

She reached out and grabbed my arms, pulling me to a stop. Her frown creased into faint lines. "Jo? What happened to your face?"

"Um . . ." I was drawing a blank. "I tripped."

"Tripped?"

"It's nothing, Sarah." I tried to pull free. My sister was stronger than she looked.

"Bullshit, nothing. You look spooked, Jo. Is it that guy? That van guy?" Now she looked angry as well. "Dammit . . . I'm calling the police. Right now."

"No! No, look, it's nothing like that—" This was all getting way too complicated. I yanked free of her grip. She lunged for the phone. I grabbed it away from her and slammed it down hard on the table. "*Sarah!* It's my business, all right? And the guy in the van *is* a cop!"

She stared at me, astonished. "He's *what*?"

"A cop." I had trouble controlling my breathing. Panic was getting the better of me. "I had some trouble in Las Vegas a couple of months ago. It's temporary."

"Jesus *Christ*, what did you do? Kill somebody?"

"Do I look like a murderer to you? You're my *sister*! You're supposed to believe in me!"

I hadn't answered the question, but luckily I'd hit the right guilt buttons. "Jo . . ." Sarah flapped her manicured hands helplessly. "Fine. All right. I believe you. But why is he following you?"

"He thinks I know something about a crime that happened while I was—before you ask, no. I didn't." She opened her mouth to fire off another question, and I hastily searched for an excuse to escape. "Sorry. I have to use the bathroom."

Even persistent people don't want to argue with full bladders. She let me go. I hurried through the doorway into the living room, heading for my closed private space, and . . . the doorbell rang.

JESUS! "Get that!" I yelled over my shoulder, and kept moving. I ran into the bedroom, slid open the bedside table, and grabbed David's blue glass bottle. My heart was hammering. I was about to take a huge gamble, and it was likely to get me hurt or killed in the process. I went back out into the living room, passing Sarah on her way to answer the doorbell, frowning at me; she'd taken the time to remove her apron and fluff her hair.

I slid the sliding glass door open and stepped out onto the patio. Ashan turned from contemplation of the ocean to stare at me. His eyes flicked toward the bottle in my hand.

"At least you take direction properly," he said. "Call him."

"You don't want me to do that," I said.

Ashan's eyes went stormcloud-dark, tinged with lightning blue. "I won't tell you again."

"You want to kill him."

Ashan smiled. Not nicely.

I closed my eyes, opened them, and said, "David, come out of the bottle."

For a long second I was sure that I'd made a terrible mistake, that he'd never gone back in the bottle at all, and then a shadow detached itself from the corner and stood, swaying and angular, at my side. It wasn't David. It wasn't . . . anything I could recognize. But it answered to the name, and evidently I still had some control over it.

Ashan took a step *back*. That predatory smile went south, fast.

"What's wrong?" I asked him, and this time, my voice stayed steady and cool. "You wanted David. Here he is."

"Ifrit."

"Oh, now that's just mean. You shouldn't judge a Djinn by the color of his . . ." Before I could finish what was admittedly a very weak joke, I lost whatever control of the situation I had, as the Ifrit formerly known as David lunged, fastened himself around Ashan, and began to *feed*.

Ashan screamed, backed up, hit the railing, and began raking the Ifrit—I couldn't think of him as David—with

silver claws. Ashan's form changed, flowed, became
something larger and only barely human in form. Gray
and vague and shot through with vivid streaks of white.

The two of them misted through the railing and
plunged down, twisting, falling. The Ifrit had two mis-
shapen, angular limbs plunged deep into the Djinn's
chest, and the silver essence flowed in spirals up coal
black, glittering arms, disappearing into the black hole—
mouth?—in the center of that twisting shadow.

He's in pain. Not Ashan, David . . . I could feel it. I
could feel his agony, and it made me stagger and grab
for the railing and bite back a scream. The connection
between us was coming back, and oh *God* it hurt. Like
a gallon of bleach poured into my guts. I held onto the
railing in a death grip, staring down at the two battling
figures as they hit the parking lot—like Rahel before
them—and rolled, ripping at each other like wild tigers.

And then, suddenly, just when the pain was about to
drive me to my knees, it stopped. There was a floating
sensation, an overwhelming burst of peace, and I saw the
Ifrit change.

Twist.

Take on color and shape and form.

David was crouched on top of a prone Ashan, hands
sunk to the wrist into the other Djinn's chest. He was
dressed in jeans and nothing else—bare-chested, gleaming and bronze and shimmering with what looked like
sweat. His shoulders heaved, although he didn't need to
breathe, unless he'd really taken on human form.

He yanked his hands free of Ashan's chest. They were
smeared with silvery residue. Ashan, for his part, lay
there motionless, staring up at the darkening, cloud-
littered sky.

Lightning jumped from one cloud to another, a hot,
white flare that I felt along my nerve endings. Thunder
slammed through the air and buffeted my chest, such a
physical presence that it set off car alarms.

David looked up at me, and his eyes glowed hot
bronze. Alien. Familiar. Haunted.

He pulled himself away from Ashan, staggered to his feet, and braced himself against a convenient Volkswagen Bug. The car's alarm went off. He absently shushed it with a tap of his fingers against the fender, got control of himself with a visible effort, and formed a blue checked shirt out of thin air. He put it on, but didn't bother with buttoning it. I don't think he had the strength.

He looked so *weak*.

"David," I whispered. I was gripping the rail so hard I thought I might have to have it surgically removed from my fingers.

He looked up again, and I got a faint, ghostly smile.

And he misted out.

I gasped and leaned over, looking for him, but he was gone, gone . . .

Warm hands slid over me. I bit my lip, tasted tears I didn't know I'd shed, and leaned back into his embrace.

"Shhh," David whispered against my ear. His breath stirred my hair. "Not much time. I couldn't take enough from him to stay in this form, and I won't kill him. Not even him."

"I know," I said, and turned to face him. He looked *normal*. Healthy and sane and perfectly all right, and that was the torture of it, that it was temporary. That he'd have to feed again and again to maintain this illusion of normality.

I kissed him breathlessly. Hard. He returned it with interest, trying to pour emotion into the briefest span of time possible, and reached up to cup my head in his large hands, holding me in place while his warm, silk-smooth lips devoured mine.

When we parted, it was like losing a limb. I could feel him again, inside—the connection was strong, humming with potential. But I could already feel the drain. I had little energy left, and something in him was siphoning it off. It was like trying to fill up a black hole.

"Put me back in the bottle," David said. "You have to. Do it now."

I nodded. He stroked hands through my hair, smoothing curls, making it silky straight the way he knew I liked it.

"I love you," he said. And that hurt, oh God. Because I knew he meant it, despite everything.

I said the words, and he was gone, back into the blue glass bottle I'd dropped, forgotten, on the wrought-iron table. I hadn't even remembered putting it down. I picked it up again, shocked by the several-degrees-too-cold chill of the container, and remembered to look back down at Ashan.

He wasn't dead. In fact, he was moving. Rolling up to his knees, with one hand bracing himself on the pavement. He looked like he'd had the shit kicked out of him, but I had absolutely no doubt that he was completely, utterly pissed off, and looking for payback and something more than a pound of flesh.

I couldn't use David to protect me. Not when he was barely clinging to his sanity and identity.

I stood there, looking down at him, as Ashan made it to his feet. He passed an absentminded hand over his suit, and the rips and dirt disappeared. He was once again a Brooks Brothers ad, except that his expression wouldn't effectively sell anything but firearms or funeral arrangements.

He didn't move, just stared at me with that burning threat in his eyes, and waited.

I said, "If you come back at me, I'm going to make you an all-you-can-eat Ifrit buffet."

He said something in that liquid-silver Djinn language, the one I could almost understand. I doubted it was complimentary.

"I mean it," I said. "Get out. If you come back, I won't be the one getting bitch-slapped."

Behind me, the sliding glass door rumbled open, and I heard Sarah say, "Jo? Eamon's here. I'm getting ready to serve the pasta. And I'm serious about the police. You really should call them. I don't care if that man is a cop; he still can't do this to you. It's not legal."

I didn't move. Down on the pavement, Ashan didn't, either. We stared for a good thirty seconds. Wind whipped at my clothes, my hair, going west, then south. Random winds, confused by the boiling disturbances in the aetheric. God, the weather was so screwed up. The Wardens were going to go insane.

Which reminded me of what had happened on the bridge. I had no idea of how much all this was affecting the Wardens, but I knew for certain there'd already been one human casualty. I needed to report it.

"Jo?" Sarah sounded concerned. "Are you all right?" The patio door slid farther open, and she stepped out next to me, enveloping me in an ever-so-slightly over-done cloud of Bulgari's Omnia, which was—she'd assured me—a bargain at $75 for two ounces. The wind ruffled her highlighted hair, and she frowned out at the parking lot, focusing on the white van. Her breath exploded in an exasperated sigh. "That's it. I'm calling the cops. At the very least, they can make him stop parking down there and staring at us all the time."

Down in the parking lot, Ashan's intense eyes—swirling from silver back toward teal blue—suddenly shifted away from me to focus on my sister. And he smiled. It was a dark prince's smile, something chill and amused and terrifying. I felt an answering righteous surge of fury. *Don't you dare, you bastard. Don't you dare look at my sister like that.*

Whether he sensed that or not, he misted away without another sound or word.

Gone, except for that lingering, unspecified threat.

I sucked in a deep breath, turned, and laid a hand on Sarah's bare shoulder. Her skin felt creamy-soft under my cold, shaking fingers.

"It's okay," I said, and smiled. "Everything's okay now. Let's just have a nice, peaceful dinner."

Yeah. That was likely.

While I'd been playing Juliet to Ashan's homicidal Romeo out on the balcony, Sarah had transformed my dining room table—another secondhand special—from its usual distressed state into something that might have made an interior designer reach for a camera. I recognized the tablecloth, which was something of Mom's that she'd left me—a gigantic crocheted ecru thing, big enough to use as a car cover—but Sarah had dressed it up with an accenting silk-tasseled runner, candles, a bowl of fresh flowers floating in water. The dishes—all matching—looked suspiciously new. Also mod and oddly shaped and matte black, which I knew had not been in my meal-serving arsenal last night. In fact, my china collection mostly consisted of secondhand Melmac, with the occasional chipped Corningware.

The kitchen looked spotless. There were three glasses of chilled white wine sitting next to the plates, glimmering delicately in candlelight.

Eamon was standing next to the table, his back to us, watching something playing silently on our (still crappy) television set. Financial news, apparently. At the sound of the closing patio door he turned, and I have to admit, he looked good. Like Sarah, he'd gotten the "let's dress to impress" memo I'd missed. His pants were some kind of dark, rough-textured silk, his shirt a deliciously pettable peachskin, open just enough to demonstrate how casual he was, yet nowhere approaching the sleazy postmodern disco look so currently in vogue. He looked hand-tailored, and still just the slightest bit forgetful about it.

Class without effort.

He extended his hand to me. I reflexively accepted and watched his smile go dim, a frown of concern take its place.

"Joanne," he said. "You're cold. Everything all right?"

"Yes," I said. "Thanks. I'm fine."

His long fingers—long enough to span my wrist and wrap over by at least three inches—slid up to touch a bruise on my arm left over from this morning. "You're sure?" He sounded doubtful. "You don't want to see a doctor? No problem with the arm?"

"I'm fine." I tried to put some conviction into it. "Glad you could make it. Sarah's been cooking for—hours." Which might have been true. I had no idea.

Eamon let go and accepted the conversational detour. "Yes, it smells delicious. And your apartment looks lovely, by the way."

I shot Sarah a look that she accepted with raised eyebrows. "Yeah, apparently. Much to my surprise." I looked significantly at the new plates. Eamon's eyes darted from me to Sarah, then back again.

"I hope you don't mind," he said. "She said you were short on a few of the essentials, so I took her shopping. We got a few things."

In my world, fancy black foo-foo plates and new wine glasses and silk table runners didn't really constitute *essentials,* but I was willing to go with it. "I don't mind, but really, if you bought them, I'll pay you back." Then again, those plates looked like they might be worth more than my entire shoe collection.

"No need." He shrugged it off. "As it happens, a freelance payment came through today. I don't mind contributing a bit, since you're being so kind as to invite me as your guest."

"Most dinner guests just provide a bottle of wine, not the whole place setting. Well, anyway, it's nice to hear good news for a change."

He smiled slowly. "I don't know if it's good news for everyone; money that comes to me does have to come out of someone else's pocket, at someone else's expense . . . ah, well. Life does turn in interesting ways." His eyes flicked toward David's bottle. I was still holding it in my left hand. "May I put that in the kitchen for you?"

I immediately flinched backward. "This? No, it's—skin cream." Which might have been the dumbest explanation I'd ever come up with, but I was rattled. Too much, happening too fast. And I obviously couldn't let Eamon touch the bottle, or he'd have ownership of David. At least temporarily. "It's empty." I turned it upside down to demonstrate. "I'm just putting it back. To refill it."

I slipped past him and went to my room. Stood there in the dark for a few moments, sliding my fingertips slowly over the glass, thinking about David, about how *good* he'd looked. Could he have been . . . cured? Maybe he was fine now. Maybe . . .

Yeah, I told myself. *Maybe you could call up your Djinn boyfriend and bring him out to dinner and explain how your musician boyfriend was living in your closet when you said he was on the road.* Now was not the time to experiment. I slid the drawer open, kissed the glass, and slipped the bottle into its padded case. After a hesitation, I zipped the case shut. If I needed to grab things in a hurry, seconds might count, and with Ashan on the warpath, flight might be the best defense.

Since Sarah and Eamon looked so nice, I threw on a blue dress—nothing too suggestive, since he wasn't supposed to be looking at me, after all—and stepped into a decent pair of secondhand Jimmy Choo kitten-heeled pumps. Lipstick, some mascara—it was a fast makeover, but at the end I looked decent. The mirror showed a brightness in my eyes that hadn't been there before, and a flush in my cheeks.

My hair was glossy and straight from the touch of David's stroking hands.

I thought about the Djinn, fighting among themselves. I thought about Wardens taking killing falls from bridges.

I thought all that for about thirty seconds, then sat down on the bed and picked up the telephone. Dialed a number from memory.

"Yo," said a rough, Italian-spiced voice on the other end; I could tell he hadn't yet looked at Caller ID. There was a short, fumbling pause, and then a much warmer, "Jo! Nice to know you still remember the number."

"Paul, how could I forget?" I sat back and crossed my legs, and smiled; I knew he could hear it in my tone. "I just thought I'd better let you know that there's something going on with the Djinn. It's bad, Paul. Really bad."

Sometimes, being proactive with your ex-boss is a good idea, especially when said ex-boss has the power to haul your ass into a special clinic and give you a lobotomy. Forcibly. For not much of any reason at all, actually. And I wanted Paul to hear things from me before he started getting the reports in from Florida of wacky things happening around me up on the aetheric.

He sighed. "What's going on?"

"I personally witnessed a Warden get killed." I wrapped a hand slowly in the bedsheets. "Paul . . . the Djinn meant for it to happen. It was deliberate."

Silence, for a long moment, and then I heard his chair creak as he readjusted his weight. "He's not the first."

I'd been afraid of it. "How many?"

"I can't tell you that. But if I didn't know better, I'd go join some cult and start preaching about the Apocalypse, because all this is . . . it's bad, Jo. And it's making no sense to me. You got any information I can use?"

I chewed my lip for a few seconds. "It looks like the Djinn are splitting into sides. It's a power struggle of some kind. We're just . . . caught in the middle."

"Great."

"Look, I know it's probably nothing at this point, considering everything that's going on, but . . . I got taken for a ride by three Wardens the other day. They seemed to think I was still in the weather manipulation business. Is that coming from you?"

Silence.

"Paul?"

"I can't discuss this, Jo."

Dammit. It was coming from him. "I need to know. Look, I'm not running, I just . . . there's so much happening. I can't afford to be caught off guard by Wardens right now."

"Cards on the table?" he asked. "I've got a dozen senior Wardens yelling for your blood. Their point is that whatever's going on, you're in the middle of it, and besides, you haven't been straight with us, not about much of anything. And I *know* that part's true. So. Where does that leave us?"

"Standoff, I guess. Because if you send them back to take me in, there's going to be a fight. And it won't be pretty. You can't afford the losses."

"That I know. But babe, make no mistake. It can be done. There'll be some collateral damage, and that would be on you, right? You can't win. Too many of us, and even if we're not at full strength, you're all alone. So don't start the fight. I got too many other fucking problems. If they want to take you in, you let them take you in."

That was about what I'd expected. And from Paul Giancarlo, who really didn't have a lot of latitude to work with, that was a gift.

"So where am I?" I asked. "In? Out? Under house arrest?"

A long, long silence, and then Paul said, "Don't fuck up. That's all I'm sayin'."

"Okay." I sucked in a breath and brought out the question I'd really called to ask. "Do you know how to get hold of Lewis these days?"

"Lewis? Yeah. Why?" He sounded guarded.

I tried for casual. "I wanted to tell him something, that's all. Got a cell number?"

He did, and he read it off. I scribbled it down and committed it to memory at the same time. We chatted on some neutral topics, lied to each other some more, and hung up two minutes later.

I called Lewis, who answered on the first ring.

"I need you," I said. "Where are you?"

"Up the coast."

"Doing . . . ?"

"Disney World," he said. Which might have been the truth. With Lewis you could never really tell. "What's wrong?"

"Apart from the Djinn fighting in the streets and Ashan himself coming to kick my ass? Well, I have a time clock running on my life, and Jonathan wants me to break the bottle and free David, but if I do that we'll never be able to heal him, and besides, he'll probably kill Jonathan and win the war for Ashan. I got sunburned and my boss tries to feel me up every day. Also, my sister asked a date over for dinner, and David's an Ifrit."

Stunned silence. And then he said, carefully, "Have you been drinking?"

"Not yet, and not nearly enough, believe me. I need you. Get your ass down here as soon as you can. Get Rahel to fly you in express if you can."

"No, I'll drive. I'll send Rahel to you. At least she can keep you out of trouble until I can get there."

Curious, that Rahel evidently hadn't informed Lewis about her conversation with me, and the ass-kicking she'd received from Ashan. But then he was a mere mortal, and she was a Djinn, and hey, even the nicest of them didn't exactly regard us as equals. He wasn't her master, and she wasn't anyone's slave.

"Jo?" he asked. I felt a rush of power and heard a quiet pop of noise, like a champagne cork letting go. When I looked up, Rahel was standing on the other side of the bed. Unsmiling. Watching me with lambent gold-flaring eyes, and the kind of clinical interest you might see in your better class of death row guards.

"How long will it take you to get here?" I asked.

"Two hours," he said. "Watch your ass. It hasn't been all happy puppies around here, either." *Click.* He was gone.

I hung up and let the phone slide down to the bedspread, cautiously stood up, and faced the Djinn, who crossed her arms and stood hipshot and elegantly neon, looking me over. Her head tilted to one side, cornrows rustling like silk.

"Huh," she said. "Ashan is slipping. I thought he'd hurt you much worse than this."

I glared at her. "If he shows up again, are you going to defend me?"

"No."

"How about Jonathan? Would you keep him off of me?"

"Don't be ridiculous."

"Right. So you're just here to observe while they beat the crap out of me. Hey, thanks for your help."

"I am doing a favor for Lewis. That doesn't mean that I am doing *you* a favor." She inspected her nails, and must have decided they weren't sharp enough; the tips glinted knife-bright. Her eyes, flicking to me, were almost as unsettling. "For someone in your position, you show remarkably little gratitude."

"Gratitude for what? For provoking a fight and then bugging out and leaving me to face Ashan?" I felt a late-breaking surge of panic and my old friend, anger. "Here's a tip: Help me less. It's better for everybody."

"I don't come here at your request," she pointed out, and made herself at home on my bed, testing the mattress. "Go on about your business, Snow White. I need no watching. You're the one who requires nursemaids. However, I will tell you that if Lewis needs me, I will drop you without hesitation. Do you understand?"

I understood, all right. There really wasn't much I could do to stop her if she decided to hang around in my bedroom trying on my clothes and generally making a pest of herself, or if she decided to bug out in the middle of a fight. She was not the most supportive support I'd ever had.

I gathered the tattered shreds of my dignity closer around me, and decided that I really was kind of hungry, after all, and staring at Eamon and Sarah would be better than enduring the sardonic, unearthly stare of a Djinn for a couple of hours.

"Don't let anything happen to David," I warned her, and glanced toward the nightstand.

Her face went very still. "Oh, believe me," she said, "I will not."

I went out to eat some dinner off the new plates.

Sarah hadn't waited for me; she and Eamon were already sitting at the table, facing each other, with candles glowing between them. She'd switched off the overhead lights, and it was like a little island of romance in a sea of darkness. Very sweet.

I bumped into a corner of the couch, cursed, and ruined the mood. Sarah gave me a long-suffering look and paused, fork halfway to her perfectly rouged lips, as I sank into a chair next to Eamon and unfolded my napkin. It was in some origamilike complication of a swan. Another Martha Stewart-esque thing that few working mortals had the time to learn how to do.

The wine was pleasantly cool and tart, and the salad crisp, and she'd whipped up some kind of vinaigrette that for the life of me I hadn't realized could come out of a noncommercial kitchen. Sarah should have become a chef, not a trophy wife.

"Were you talking to David?" Sarah asked. I nearly fumbled my fork. "On the phone."

"Oh." I stabbed a tomato wedge. The silverware felt strange and heavy, and when I looked it over, it was as unfamiliar as the plates. My total of debts to repay, whether karmic or Mastercard, was getting pretty hefty. "Yes. He was a little sick, but he's feeling better."

"Sarah told me that he's a musician?" Eamon asked, and applied a little black pepper to his salad. Which was not at all a bad idea. I followed suit.

"A singer," I said. Which would explain, should it ever come up, the lack of gear to haul around. "He's with a band."

"Have I heard of them?"

"Probably not."

Eamon was too polite to try to work around that roadblock; he turned his attention back to Sarah, who practically combusted under the force of it. He did have a lovely smile, I had to admit. "I did enjoy the day, Sarah. I had no idea Fort Lauderdale had so much to offer."

"It was educational," she said, but there was color high in her cheeks, and a sparkle in her eyes, and I wondered if the wonders of Fort Lauderdale had been the standard tourist attractions or something a good deal less family-friendly that featured a tour of the backseat of Eamon's rental car. "Thank you for everything. It was lovely, really. Dinner was the least I could do."

"Careful," Eamon said, and his voice had dropped into a range I could really only classify as a purr. "You feed me like this, I might never leave." His eyes were luminous, watching her. As if she were the only thing in the world.

She winked at him.

I began to remember how I'd felt back in high school, watching my accomplished, polished older sister devastate the boys with a flick of her perfectly manicured fingers. Oh, yeah, this was that feeling. Like being the dumpy training wheels on the bicycle of love. I wondered if I should take my salad and go eat it in my room, with Rahel, who would make me feel like a particularly nasty insect but at least wasn't going to be beating me on social graces.

"Get a room," I said, and shoveled in a mouthful of greens. Sarah sent me a shocked look. Yep, we were right back to high school. Sarah the martyr, Jo the brat, poor Eamon caught in the middle.

Except Eamon was no hormonally overbalanced teenager, and he just smiled and reached across the table to pour my sister another half glass of wine.

"Actually," he said, "I like this room perfectly well."

The salad course mercifully ended before I could make more of an ass out of myself, and Sarah served pasta. She and Eamon flirted. I tried to look as if I didn't notice. It was uncomfortable. My sister's chicken primavera was unbelievably delicious, but I shoveled it in with reckless disregard for either manners or culinary appreciation. Sarah, naturally, ate about a third of her plate and pronounced herself full. Eamon came around to help her clear the table, shirtsleeves rolled up to reveal elegantly long-boned forearms, and brushed past her close enough to qualify as courtship in quite a few parts of the world. As they were standing at the sink together, I watched their body language. His was . . . comfortable. Proprietary. In her space, drawn to her by gravity. Over the rushing water, I caught snatches of their conversation. I sipped wine and watched him lean closer, put his face close to her neck, and draw in a deep breath. It was amazingly sensuous.

"Bulgari's Omnia," he said, in that lovely voice, so precise and warm.

"You know perfumes?" Sarah asked, startled, and turned her head to look at him. He was over her shoulder, close enough to kiss. Neither of them moved away.

"A bit," he said. "I had some training in chemistry; perfumes were always interesting to me. Omnia has a black pepper base, you know."

"Really?" She dried her hands on a towel and turned to face him. "What else?"

"Is there any dessert?"

She blinked at the change of subject, but moved aside and uncovered a pan of perfect little tarts, pale with a browned crust on top. Crème brûlée. Dear God. I didn't even *own* one of those fancy little blowtorches, did I? Well, apparently, I did now. Along with a double boiler.

Eamon made a sound in the back of his throat that I swear I'd only heard during particularly intimate moments, took one of the tarts, and bit into it, watching my sister. "Delicious," he mumbled.

"No talking with your mouth full."

Which looked like a private joke, from the intensity of their smiles at one another. He offered her the tart. She bit a neat piece out of it, never taking her eyes from his.

"What do you know about that perfume?" he asked her.

"Tell me."

His smile widened into something that was both angelic and liable to melt women into butter. "Perfumes have a base, heart notes, and bottom notes. Omnia's base is black pepper. Its heart notes are tea, cinnamon, nutmeg, and Indian almond. Very exotic. It suits you."

Sarah looked fascinated. "And there are bottom notes?"

He took another bite of tart. "Indian wood, sandal-wood, and chocolate." He made chocolate sound inde-cent. "Practically edible, that scent."

"And how do you know it isn't edible?"

"Is that an invitation . . . ?"

I rolled my eyes, got up, and said, "I'll be in my room."

They didn't even notice. I closed and locked my door, flumped down on the bed, and realized my heart was racing. Contact high from the flirting. Those two were Olympic champions at foreplay.

Although I suspected they might have blown past it earlier and gone right to the main event. Probably more than once. The hormones were definitely running at high tide.

I looked around the room. No sign of Rahel. I wasn't surprised. She was probably in a don't-see-me mode, or else she'd already decided to check in on Lewis again. I ignored her—or her absence—and stripped off my dinner clothes, threw on sloppy sweat pants that rode low on my hips and a crop top, and slid open my window to get a taste of fresh ocean breeze. It felt cool and dark on my face. I wanted to get out of here, suddenly; I felt trapped. I checked the clock. Thirty minutes until I was supposed to meet Lewis.

I figured I'd better not wait too long, and it would save time if I met him outside; we couldn't exactly have a heart-to-heart with my sister and Eamon getting to know each other better, in the Biblical sense, in the next room. I slipped running shoes on my feet, laced them tight, and unlocked the bedroom door to take a cautious peek outside.

Eamon was kissing Sarah in the kitchen. They were backed up against the refrigerator; his hands were cup-ping her head and combing through her hair, her arms were around his neck, and *damn,* they looked good together.

I blinked, thought about announcing that I was going for a run, then decided it might be a mood-killer and besides, they couldn't possibly have cared less. I grabbed keys, ID, and cell phone, stuffed them into the zip pocket on my sweats, and headed out.

I was halfway down the steps when my pants rang. I dug my cell phone out and flipped it open; before I could answer, I got a blistering burst of static that made me stumble on the stairs and yank the phone back from my ear.

But I clearly heard somebody yell my name on the other end.

I pressed the phone back to my ear and said, "Who is this?"

"Lewis!" His voice sounded raw, almost drowned by static, and then the noise evened out to a dull roar. Traffic, maybe? Only if he was driving in the Indy 500. "Change of plans. Meet me on the beach across from your apartment."

"Any particular place?"

"We'll find you."

He hung up. I tried redial, got no answer, and decided it was a good thing I'd decided to wear jogging clothes. Gave me a chance to do covert meetings *and* get some exercise in.

I bounced down the last set of steps and stretched a little, and as I did, I saw that Detective Rodriguez's white van was still parked facing my apartment, watching the show. No lights. Well, screw him. If he wanted to come after me, he was going to get hurt. I wasn't in a mood to pull punches.

I put my right foot up on the steps and began stretches. I touched my toe, bent the foot back toward me, and while I was about it sneaked a look up at my apartment window. All I could see was shadows, but that was enough. I was pretty sure Eamon was taking off Sarah's dress.

"Draw the curtains, idiots," I said under my breath, but hey, who was I to judge? I was the one who'd had my first really great sexual experience with a Djinn in a hot tub in the middle of a hotel lobby. Maybe exhibitionism ran in the family.

I concentrated on stretches. The rubber-band burn in my muscles had a nice focusing effect.

Once I was decently warmed up, I picked my way through the parking lot, dodging cars, watching for tail lights, jogged in place at the street light as passing motorists whizzed by.

I stiffened up when I felt a presence arrive next to me. Detective Rodriguez wasn't jogging in place, just standing. He didn't believe in keeping the heart rate up, I gathered. I could respect that.

"Going somewhere?" he asked.

"Yeah. I'm planning to swim to England, steal the crown jewels, hide them in the Titanic, and hire James Cameron to pick them up for me. Do you mind? I'm on a timetable." I kept jogging. Anger pulsed with my heartbeat. *Damn him.* I really, really didn't need this right now. "Look, I'll be back, okay? I'm just going for a run. People do it. Well, people who don't live in a van and stalk other people do it, anyway."

He smiled slightly. He'd changed clothes, or he'd been dressed for exercise anyway; he was wearing dark blue cop-colored sweat pants with official-looking white reflective stripes, and a hooded sweatshirt that had LVPD in big yellow letters on the back. "I wouldn't dream of interrupting your workout," he said blandly. "I need the exercise."

I kept moving, ready for the green, and when it clicked on I hurried across the street and onto the beach proper. Rodriguez, of course, followed.

"You should have stayed back there!" I said over my shoulder. "I'm not slowing down for you!" And I put on the speed. Sand, soft and uncertain under my feet. There was a fresh, warm breeze blowing in from the ocean, smelling of twilight and the sea. Always people out, even at this time of day—couples taking romantic walks near the surf, posing for pictures. Kids sneaking beers, or if they weren't that brave, sipping on Coca-Cola cans liberally jazzed up with booze. The night shift would come in soon—the older kids, the harder ones, the ones looking for sandy sex and mischief. The night surfers, who always baffled me. Why take a dangerous sport and make it even more dangerous?

I looked behind me. I didn't have to look far. Detective Rodriguez, though older and burdened with all that stakeout food, was keeping up just fine. He moved with a loose, easy stride, shortened to match mine. I hadn't noticed it before, but he was kind of pumped. Not obviously, not like the muscle hunks and steroid addicts you saw every day at the beach, but he was strong and agile.

I knew about the strong. I had the bruises to prove it. Oddly, I found I didn't hold it against him.

"Nice form," he said.

"Bite me," I replied.

And that was about the extent of our conversation, for a while. I pushed it. He kept up. I got tired of pushing it and settled into a comfortable, loping rhythm, racking my brains for a way to get rid of him.

About ten minutes in, we passed an SUV pulled up illegally, three teens sitting on the open tailgate and looking like young, rabid wolves. Rodriguez gave them a coplike stare. They straightened up and pretended not to have noticed us.

"Storm's coming in," Rodriguez said.

Well, the Djinn fights had screwed up the aetheric, but I could feel—distantly and muffled—that they had put the patterns back together again. Humpty Dumpty wasn't quite broken beyond repair, not yet. "No, I think it's clearing."

For answer, he nodded out at the sea. I glanced in that direction and saw a dark layer of cloud, way out near the water, almost invisible in the growing night. I reflexively went up into the aetheric, or tried to, and immediately felt the drag that meant I wasn't strong enough to do this. I managed to make it and took a look around in Oversight while my body continued to do the simple, repetitive work of putting one foot in front of the other.

Not that I could make much sense out of it. For one thing, my aetheric vision was clouded, indistinct. Like I needed a laser corrective procedure for my inner eye. For another, my range of perception had gone from nearly infinite to something frustratingly human. I could barely see the horizon, much less make out what was happening there. Energy, yeah, but what kind? A naturally occurring storm? One cooked up inadvertently by the Djinn Smackdown that had occurred back at my apartment, and that the Wardens had failed to fix? All too possible, unfortunately. I couldn't even get a sense of whether or not it was dangerous. Maybe it was just a squall, bringing nothing but a quick rain shower and some disappointed tourists.

I dropped back into my body. Not by my choice, more as if my aetheric strength had just failed. *Wham,* and I was falling back down so fast I might have been a missile fired from on high. I hit flesh so hard I staggered, tripped, and went down. I came up spitting sand, disoriented, and angry.

Detective Rodriguez, who'd drawn to a stop, didn't offer me a hand.

"Dammit," I muttered, and dusted myself off. He didn't say anything, just waited until I moved on. The beach glimmered white, sparks of quartz reflecting the last light of day. Surf pounded the sand in muscular, flexing rolls, broke into foam and retreated. I felt my frustration erupt in a white burst of fury, and rounded on him, fists clenched. "Look, would you *leave me alone?* I just want to be alone, okay? I'm not running away!"

"You don't leave my sight," he said flatly. "Not until you tell me what I want to know about Quinn."

Just run, I told myself. *Just run and forget everything.* Nice advice. I wished I could follow it, but my brain wouldn't shut down, and it was seriously compromising my endorphin rush. I wanted Lewis to show up. And now I was starting to think that seriously hurting Detective Nosy might not be a bad idea, because he was really starting to piss me the hell off.

Can I take him? I looked over at Rodriguez, who was continuing to jog effortlessly at my side. He had that kind of mechanical, thoughtless motion that meant he probably trained a hell of a lot harder than me, and could run me into the ground without breaking a sweat. He glanced over at me, dead-eyed, and I was honest enough to answer my question with a solid *No*. At least, not without using Warden powers, and I didn't have those. Not enough to matter, and not enough to burn gratuitously.

"Why didn't you call the cops?" he asked. "After what happened at the TV station?"

"Oh, you mean the unprovoked assault?"

He had the grace to look grim about it. "You made me angry."

"Don't sweat it, you're not the first guy who's gotten physical with me." I grinned when I said it, but it didn't hold a lot of humor. "Your partner got there long before you did."

"All I want is the truth."

"No, you don't. You want to believe that Quinn was some kind of fallen hero, and buddy, I can't help you."

Silence. We ran, wind tossing my hair in its neat ponytail, surf crashing like the heartbeat of the world. Sweat was forming along my back and under my breasts, trickling and wicking up into the jog bra. My Achilles tendons were already screaming. Way out of practice. I told them to shut the hell up and pressed harder. Night was falling like a thick, humid blanket, and it would have felt suffocating if not for the continuing ocean breeze. By my inner alarm clock, it had been over thirty minutes. No sign of Lewis, but it had sounded like he was in trouble, and maybe he was running late. *He'll call.* If he was conscious. If he wasn't fighting for his life.

"What did Quinn do to you?" Rodriguez asked.

I took a ragged breath. "I told you."

"You said he was a rapist and a murderer."

"There you go."

"You're still alive. So the murder part, that didn't happen to you."

That didn't require an answer. I kept going in silence until Rodriguez suddenly reached over, grabbed my wrist, and dragged me to a stumbling halt in the sand. Surf roared and crashed, stinging us with spray.

I couldn't see his expression. I pulled myself up into the aetheric again, feeling like I was pulling the weight of the world, and saw him as a dim orange smudge. Whatever he was feeling, I no longer had the capacity to read it, but then the auras and patterns of regular humans had never been all that clear, even on my best days.

I could only trust my gut, which said that Detective Rodriguez might be a hard bastard, but that he wasn't a killer, and he wasn't blind to the truth.

"Tom hurt you," he said.

"Yes."

"Got any proof to back this up?" he asked.

"No."

"Then why should I believe you?"

I studied what I could see of him in the dark. "Because you already know something that you didn't want to believe. Right? You know he wasn't the sunshine-and-light guy you thought he was all these years. You say you just want the truth from me, Detective. Well, I'm giving you the truth. Right here, right now. And you can take it or leave it. Do you want to listen?"

"It's why I came out here," he said. "I'll listen."

So I told him. Not about the Ma'at, not about the Djinn, which was a bit of a problem, narrative-wise, but the high points. I'd gone to Las Vegas to help a friend, run into Quinn, and fallen into a nightmare out of my past. And Quinn had tried to stop me from revealing the truth.

When I was done, Rodriguez cocked his head, unblinking, and asked, "Is he really dead?"

"Yes. I was there, and I saw it. But you'll never bring anyone to trial for this, and if you keep trying, you can only hurt the very people you want to help. I don't know anything about Quinn's wife, but if she's a good person, it can't help her to know that her husband wasn't. Just let it go."

Rodriguez looked impassive. Unreadable. "I can haul you in as an accessory to the murder of a police officer."

"So you've said. I don't see any hauling on the horizon, Detective." I backed off a step. "I'm sorry about Quinn. I liked him, too, and you have no idea how profoundly that bothers me, all things considered."

He let me go. I turned back the way we'd come and kicked it up a notch, running from my memories, legs pumping, heart pounding. The red pulse of effort dissolved the anxiety inside me, washed away doubt and fear and anguish. I was healthy, I was alive, and just for this moment, I was in control.

If Rodriguez had been straight about what he wanted from me, he'd go back to his van. Think over what I'd told him. Probably get on a laptop and match up dates and times from his own records, find out if Quinn had alibis for anything.

He'd find I was being straight. And then he'd go away and leave me with the humpty-dozen other life-threatening crises I had going on.

I was feeling cautiously good about that when the sand suddenly went soft and liquid under my feet, and I disappeared under the surface so fast that I might as well have vanished in a puff of smoke.

INTERLUDE

As the storm approaches the islands, it picks up speed, traveling at fifteen miles per hour, but by now it's so huge that the increase in speed means little. Anything trapped in its path is in for the worst. Winds at the outer wall whip ahead at pulverizing speeds, and their forces are so great that they actually press down the waves, creating greasy-smooth swells that hump in huge shudders toward the horizon, a slow-motion shock wave that is an indicator of just how massive that explosion in the clouds really is.

There is no force in nature so huge, so unstoppable, and so intelligent as a hurricane.

Rain begins to fall on a massive scale. On the ocean, there's no way to measure how much water is plummeting from the lead-thick sky, but anything on the surface that disappears into the shimmering black curtain of the storm will never be seen again. The force kills fish under the surface of the sea. There's no wreckage in its wake; it churns everything in its path to pieces, digests it, and feeds on the pain. The sea left behind the storm is glassy-smooth, shocked into silence. The water is forgiving. Its wounds heal quickly.

The shore won't be so lucky.

Those curiously ribbonlike swells roll toward land, traveling impossibly fast—flat humps that reach shallow water and roar into explosive life. The waves shatter with stunning force against rock, sand, flesh. The smashing force *comes in wave after ever-building wave, monsters fleeing a greater terror behind.*

As the winds increase, trees rip free of ground that has held them safe for a hundred years or more.

As the storm approaches the first large island, the storm swell raises ocean level by more than twenty feet, and many parts of the land are already sinking into the sea.

Nothing can survive this one.

It is not lethal.

It is legend.

FIVE

I dropped straight down, sliding through slippery, frictionless sand, arriving on a solid surface with a bone-jarring thump that transmitted through my legs, up my spine, and exploded in my skull like a grenade. I pitched forward and reached out blindly, felt something like stone under my hands. Bedrock. I'd fallen a long way. Lucky I hadn't broken anything.

Hands grabbed my shoulders, jerked me backward, off balance. I flailed and screamed, caught myself, and whirled around, striking blind. I connected with flesh hard enough to get another shock wave up through bone. The hands holding me let go, accompanied by the sound-track of a grunt.

It was black as pitch in this hole under the ground. Not good for me. I'd had bad things happen in a cave; I wasn't comfortable in caves, and I could feel the tense freakout potential in my guts.

Calm. I had to stay calm.

I was facing someone with Earth powers, that much was obvious; it took a pretty special talent to suck some-one through the beach and into a cave, especially since Fort Lauderdale wasn't exactly known for caves in the first place.

I felt like a powdered doughnut. I'd been nicely sweated from my beachside run, and the fine-textured sand coated me in a gritty layer that wasn't going to come off without benefit of a shower and a washcloth.

Oh, someone was going to pay.

First things first: I wasn't about to do this in the dark. I needed light, and I was flashlight-free. However, even though I wasn't a Fire Warden, the basic principle of making fire wasn't beyond my powers; I'd created hard-shelled little bubbles of oxygen before and ignited them. A shake-n-bake lamp.

When I reached to do that very simple thing—disengaging the O_2 molecules from the long chemical chain of breathable atmosphere and segregating them together inside a vacuum—it was like trying to do micro-surgery with oven mitts. Under anesthesia. I fumbled it, felt the air go wrong and stale around me.

Yeah. I wasn't up to doing even the simple things. Great news. I decided I'd better stick to feeling my way through the problem.

Said problem was large, human, and coming at me again. I felt something brush me and instinctively ducked; fingernails grazed my cheek. Not talons, so this wasn't a Djinn—not that I'd really thought it was; they weren't usually so sneaky or so subtle. And they didn't smell like fear and sweat.

I moved back, got a wall against my back, and swept my foot out in a roundhouse kick. It connected solidly with someone who *oofed* and tumbled. Bull's-eye.

I was feeling nicely ferocious when blinding light suddenly erupted, and I had to flinch backward with my eyes covered.

"For God's sake, Jo, stop!"

The voice was Lewis's. I peeked through my fingers and saw that the dazzle was a plain old garden-variety flashlight. He tilted it slightly, and the backwash of light gave me the long, tanned features of Lewis's face—only not relaxed and gentle as I was used to seeing. He looked seriously tense.

And there was blood on his cheek. Fresh blood. More splattering his shirt.

"What the hell is going on?" I asked. "Are you okay?"

"It isn't my blood," he said. "I need your help. Come on."

"With what?" Because it wasn't going to be easy explaining to Lewis that my help would be strictly of the moral-support variety, at the moment.

"Kevin," he said, and turned away, already moving to focus the flashlight on . . . Kevin Prentiss's thin, acne-bubbled face. The kid who had once been the bane of my existence, not to mention my master when I was a Djinn, hadn't changed much—still greasy, still dressed in floppy, oversized jeans with too many pockets and chains, and a black, sloppy T-shirt that needed at least one more spin cycle. He'd taken on a decidedly goth look since last I'd seen him in Nevada; the nose piercing was new, and so was the pentagram around his neck. He still looked like a wannabe badass. Only with Kevin, it was a mistake to underestimate him. He had the capacity to be a genuinely scary badass, and I'd seen him do it. I didn't want to witness it in close quarters, underground.

And then I realized that Kevin wasn't sitting on the ground, back to the wall, because he was being a sulky little bastard, although that wasn't beyond him; he was pale, leaning, and breathing in shallow gasps.

Hard to tell against the black, but it looked as if the front of his shirt was wet. I didn't think he'd taken a splash in the surf.

"They came after us," Lewis said. "Wardens. I got us hidden, but I didn't know the boy had been hit until we were already down here. I can't leave him."

"Why?" It was mean, but hell, Kevin deserved it. "All right, fine. He needs medical help, I get it. Let's get him out of here."

"I can't."

"Why?"

He sent me a look, then nodded at the cave around us. I realized—belatedly—that the hard-packed walls were really just packed, sculpted sand. Sand being held together by his willpower. Yep, Lewis had hollowed himself a secret hideout, which was pretty damn cool, but the idea that the whole thing could collapse in on us at any moment didn't exactly make me glow with confidence.

"I need your help," he said. "Actually, I need David's help. I can't do everything at once. He can hold back the sand while I treat the wound . . ."

Oh, shit. "Um . . . I can't do that."

Lewis's expression turned even more tense, which really wasn't good. "Jo, I just need to borrow him. I won't keep him."

"I can't."

"I *need him*."

"He's not—he's not well, Lewis. He's—"

"Jo! The kid's going to die!"

I sucked in a deep breath. "I'm not calling David. What's Plan B?"

For a second I saw sheer fury erupt in him, which was pretty frightening, considering he was the human equivalent of what Jonathan was in the Djinn world—a near-perfect repository of power—but it wasn't like Lewis to lash out with it. He pulled it all back inside and closed his eyes for a second, and when his voice came, it was low and quiet. "Plan B consists of me watching him slowly bleed to death," he said. "I don't like Plan B. Look, Jo, healing is the hardest of everything I do. I can't do it and hold this place together at the same time. It takes precision. I need help."

"Fine. Just lift me back up, I call an ambulance, we get him out of here. Regular, mundane medical treatment. It does work, you know."

Lewis shook his head, watching Kevin's shuddering breaths. Kevin seemed to not be hearing us. "He's got a torn artery," he said. "I'm holding it shut, but between that and keeping this cave open I'm at the limit. You'll need to get yourself out."

Something occurred to me. "Where's Rahel? Why isn't Rahel helping you do this?"

Another flare of anger in his face. He didn't bother to

hide the edge in his voice. "Rahel doesn't think he's worth saving," he said. "She also thinks she has better things to do. She left. Jo, I wasn't kidding. I need David. Please."

Cell phone. I dug it out and checked for reception.

Uh-oh. A couple of dozen feet of sand resulted in a flashing NO SIGNAL. "Um . . . the answer's still no. Look, if I call wind down here—"

"You'll kill us."

"Right. Bad idea. Water . . . right, will kill us. Lewis, you called the wrong girl. I've got nothing."

"You've got a *Djinn*!"

"No I don't!" I yelled back. "I've got an *Ifrit*, dammit, and I'm *not fucking calling him,* so you need to get your head together! Tell me what I can do!"

"Nothing," Lewis snapped. "Thanks for dropping in."

"Guess I'm fucked, then," Kevin whispered, and opened his eyes. Not by much. They were vague and unfocused; I guessed that Lewis was also doing some kind of pain blocking. I crouched down next to the kid, feeling a strain in my knees. Nothing like landing flat-footed after a ten-foot fall to really limber up the joints.

"How do you feel?" I asked.

"Like you'd care," Kevin shot back. It was half reflex, I could see that. His heart really wasn't in the whole dystopian thing today, and he looked scared. Really, really scared. "You dropped me like a bag of trash when you got what you wanted. Went back to your nice life. Hey, Jo, how's that going for you?"

I didn't want to debate how playing Stupid Weather Girl on an off-brand TV station could constitute *nice life.* "If you were trying to get attention, there were easier ways of doing it," I said. He flipped me off. Clumsily. It was actually kind of cute. He had funky shadows on his cheeks, and I realized two things: one, he was wearing black liner—definitely gone to the goth side—and two, it had smeared down his face.

Kevin had been crying.

I felt my heart, which had started to take a clue to

ease up on the pounding, start thumping faster again. Kevin was short of breath, and his lips looked slightly blue. "Damn, Lewis, I'm all screwed up inside. It feels—"

"Easy," Lewis murmured, and got down on one knee beside him to move up the hem of his none-too-clean long-sleeved T-shirt. It advertised some undead band with an umlaut in its name and a zombie graphic, but the real horror was underneath—a long, deep slice in his side, gaping wide and welling a constant, slow pulse of blood. He'd lost a lot of the stuff, and most of it was smeared and spotted on his skin in damp, tie-dyed patterns.

Lewis put his fingers around the wound in a rough circle, bent his head, and concentrated. Kevin shuddered and grabbed convulsively for my hand; I let him have it without protest. He was strong, but not as strong as he should have been.

The bleeding slowed to a trickle again. Kevin choked, coughed, and swallowed convulsively. Trying not to throw up, I guessed.

"What happened?" I asked.

"I don't know." Kevin's hand was shaking, and so was his voice. "We were asking around about the Djinn, and Lewis was teaching me stuff. Everybody was kinda— cool, you know? They didn't hate me or anything. The old guys, the Ma'at, they even said I could help people. I—I was trying—"

"Kevin, *what happened*?"

"Somebody tried to kill us."

"You and Lewis?"

"Yeah." He wiped his face with his free hand, smearing his eyeliner into a sad-clown mask. On his other side, Lewis was a frozen statue, unmoving, doing whatever it was that Earth Wardens do when they fight for a life in jeopardy. I had no doubt it was a terrible strain on both of them; Kevin would rather have died than let me see him weak like this. "Fucking assholes. We weren't hurting anybody."

I had a really bad feeling. "Was it the Wardens?"
He nodded.
"Anybody I know?"
He tried to shrug, one of those liquid up-and-down expressions of boredom that teenagers must have invented in the dawn of evolution. He only managed a weak imitation, though. He became even more pale from the effort, and glanced down at the exposed mess of the wound in his side.

It was bleeding again. Not much, but a steady trickle. As I watched, the trickle ran a little bit faster.

"Kevin," I said to distract him. Kevin's panic couldn't do anything but make Lewis's job harder. "You said it was the Wardens. Tell me what they looked like."

"You know some bitch with punk piercings and some guy looks like a lumberjack?"

"Maybe." I thought fast. It could be Shirl and Erik, who had come after me during my first hellride across the country, when I'd been heading for what I thought was a safe haven, and Star. They were on Marion Bearheart's staff, but I couldn't see Marion authorizing a hit squad for Kevin, not now. Not after what had happened in Las Vegas. "Where did this happen? Vegas?"

"No, here. Me and Lewis were up the coast, checking out some ruined hotel where we heard some Djinn were fighting. They came at us—" He stopped and gulped. "Oh, shit. I'm gonna die, right?"

I wanted to reach over and put my arms around him. It was manifestly a bad idea for so, so many reasons.

"You're not going to die," I promised him. I risked a look down at the wound, and Jesus, was I wrong? Was it bleeding more, not less? Lewis was locked in silence, concentrating. Trying to heal, or at least keep things at a rough status quo.

He wasn't going to be able to lift me out of here, and he couldn't do this alone. The wound was too deep, and he was having to split too much of his power off to keep the cave intact.

None of which I could help with.

"Oh, damn," Kevin whispered. His breath hissed in, caught, and I saw his face grow paler. "You know, this is actually a lot worse than it looks." He was trying to joke about it. That broke my heart. He was too young for this. Too young for a lot of the things that had been done to him during his short life, and way too young for some of what he'd done to others. Kevin was a freak and a killer and a surly little bastard, but he hadn't exactly been born lucky.

"I'm not glad to hear that, because it looks pretty damn bad," I said. "But you've got Lewis. And nobody can do this better."

It occurred to me that there actually was something I could do, albeit not on a mystical level. I took a look at what I was wearing—nothing I could use to wad up without revealing a hell of a lot more than was really PC. "Lewis. Lewis! I need your shirt."

I tugged on his shoulder, dragging the fabric half off; he shifted to accommodate me, letting me pull the blood-spattered flannel off of him to reveal a bare chest, lean arms, and abs that, if we'd been in better circumstances, I'd have taken the time to admire the washboardiness of.

"Dear Penthouse," Kevin whispered. "I never thought this would happen to me . . ."

"Shut *up,* already." I folded Lewis's shirt up into a clumsy pad, and pressed it hard against the open wound, or as much of it as I could reach around Lewis's hand. That got a gasp and a shudder, and a parchment pallor I didn't like very much.

Kevin slipped into unconsciousness.

"Lewis. *Lewis!* How bad is it? Really?"

His tired brown eyes opened and focused slowly on me. "Fatal if I don't keep on it. There's a major artery severed. I'm doing what I can to keep it clamped, but . . ."

But he couldn't keep it up forever. That kind of thing took a hell of a lot of concentration. "Can you heal him?"

"No. Too much damage."

"What do you want me to do?" I asked, as calmly as possible.

He didn't answer. His eyes drifted closed.

"Lewis?"

No response. I reached over and tapped his face lightly, got a flicker of his eyelids and then a slow return. I repeated the question.

"Get help," he said. "Find a way. If you don't . . ."

He didn't go on. He wasn't unconscious—if he'd passed out, Kevin would have bled out in thick, pumping bursts. Instead, the bleeding slowed to a warm trickle against my hands and the already-soaked pad of the shirt. Lewis had gone deeper into trance to try to keep things locked down.

I took Lewis's hand and moved it to press down on the bandage. He took over the pressure.

"Hey," Kevin whispered. Awake again. He stared at me with wide, bloodshot eyes. He smelled strongly of stale, unwashed clothes, and faintly of the green, earthy aroma of pot. *Lewis,* I thought, *you suck as a guardian.* Not that I'd have been any better. "What are you going to do?"

"Can you make fire?" It was Kevin's native power, and he'd always been strong in it. Plus, fire was one of the easiest of the states of energy to manipulate, so long as it didn't get large enough to develop any kind of sentience.

He nodded. "Stupid, though. No ventilation. Kill us all. Lewis said there's a limited supply of air in here."

"Trust me. I'll get us air."

He made a weak, theatrical, one-handed gesture at the sand behind me, and *presto,* a fire exploded into red-yellow-orange glory. Burning up the limited oxygen we had available.

My turn. *Concentrate,* I ordered myself, and shut my eyes.

Air molecules, turning and burning and twisting apart. Being destroyed and reformed. Heat shimmering as the air column rose toward the sand ceiling. I could still see the pale smear overhead where the sand itself was partly porous—the trap door where Lewis had pulled me down. It was gradually trickling down and sagging in on itself. I could see glimpses of black sky overhead. The heat would help speed that process, open the hole further. Widen the air molecules between the grains of sand.

You can do this. You have to do this.

I'd done it before. It was a party trick, something Wardens did to amuse each other during boring patches. Fire and air, interacting. I could do it in my sleep.

Usually.

I took a deep breath and threw everything I had into the effort, and stepped up on top of the fire.

The air cushion felt squishy and unsteady, like a waterbed. Not at all the firm platform it should have been. And it was *warm*. Verging on, well, *hot*. And these were not shoes I wanted melted.

I exerted pressure on the hardened layer of air under my feet to pull it tighter together. This would never work unless the heat could push against it . . .

I started rising. Slowly. I opened my eyes and gasped as the fire's energy started cooking through my running shoes, blinked away tears, and bit my lip. *Hang on.*

Up. Slowly. *Dammit, a year ago I'd have done this in five seconds flat.*

The heat was intense now, and I was sure my shoes were melting. I smelled burning rubber. Maybe something else, something worth panicking over.

The sky crawled slowly closer, the walls of the sand pit shifting and sagging around me. The thing was starting to lose its coherence. If I didn't do this right, if I didn't get help, Kevin and Lewis were going to be buried alive. . . .

I realized I was panting, partly from the relentless pressure of the heat, partly from the pain that was quickly turning to agony. It felt as if flames were licking the backs of my calves. The air under my feet softened like pudding, threatening to drop me the seven feet I'd traveled back down into the flames.

I sank my teeth into my lip, raised my hands to the sky, and chilled the air above me. Blew the molecules far apart, slowed their movement, dropped the temperature at least twenty degrees. Easy stuff. Child's play. I could barely manage it, and when I did, it felt as if I were seconds from an aneurysm. Intense pain in my head, shortness of breath. I tasted blood in the back of my throat.

I rose faster. Faster.

I didn't dare look down because I knew my feet were burning now, dear God, it felt as if the flesh was already roasted off and now the muscles were cooking, but if that were true then I wouldn't feel anything once the nerves died. . . .

Hang on. Hang on. Hang on.

I clung to the vision of Kevin's parchment-pale face, of the blood pouring out of his side, and then, suddenly, my face was passing ground level and I was *out*.

I pitched forward, pushed with the last of my strength, rolled and kept on rolling until I splashed into a shockingly cold surf. A wave curled over me and I heard a hiss as my smoking shoes hit water.

I breathed liquid, coughed, choked, tasted salt and decay, and rested my face on cold, wet sand with a relief so intense it felt like orgasm.

"Son of a bitch!" A pair of hands rolled me over on my back, and I blinked and focused on the barely visible glimmer of Armando Rodriguez's face. For the first time, he had an easily readable expression: shocked. "What the hell was *that*?"

Like I could explain. I coughed salt, gagged water, and croaked, "Two people down there in the hole; one's hurt bad. Get help, *now*."

He had a gun in his hand, which wasn't useful. He put it away and came up with a cell phone, dialed, and gave the rescue bulletin.

"Get an ambulance," I added. He nodded and kept talking.

I squirmed up to a sitting position and peeled my melted jogging shoes off of my feet. They were pink and tender, but not Cajun-fried.

God, that was going to hurt tomorrow.

"We can't wait," I said. "Find some rope, blankets we can tie together, anything. Run!"

He raced back the way we'd come, heading for the glow of headlights that marked the three kids tailgating on some unlucky parent's SUV. I squirmed back over to the hole. It was widening.

"Kevin!" I yelled. "Help's on the way!"

No answer. I scrambled back from the hole and looked around. Rodriguez was MIA. I couldn't see anybody else on the murky stretch of beach. Time was running out.

Call David, my worst angels whispered in my ear. *Call him. You fixed him before. You can fix him again. Ashan wasn't even hurt all that badly.* Was this how it had started for Patrick and his Ifrit love? One little concession at a time, until he was killing his own kind to give her one more small slice of life? Until she was willing to settle for that kind of existence, just to stay with him?

No. No, no, no, never, and David wouldn't stand for it.

"Rahel!" I screamed it at the top of my lungs. "Rahel, where the hell are you? Get your ass back here, I need you *now*!"

A flash of lightning illuminated the beach, a long blue-white streak that raced across the sky and shattered into forks that stretched across half the horizon. Spectacular.

Those clouds hugging the ocean looked larger.

In the next hyperactinic flash, I saw someone coming out of the water. Tall, perfect carriage, dark skin glistening with water drops. Rahel was as magnificent as a sea goddess, and her eyes were burning so brightly they were like suns.

She came out of the curl of a wave and collapsed to her hands and knees on wet sand. Her body was solid to the knees, swirling fog below. Barely coherent. She looked like shit—beaten, exhausted, ripped, and blood-ied. The blood was metaphorical for her. She hadn't be-

come human; she'd just become unable to repair damage
to a physical avatar.

Rahel hadn't flounced off in a fit of pique and stayed
away deliberately; she'd probably meant to come back
and help. But the dramatic gesture got interrupted along
the way by a serious fight. The kind you came out of
injured, or dead.

Rahel was as tough as any of the Djinn. She'd lose in
a dogfight with Ashan, Jonathan, or David, but she
should have held her own against anyone else. Unless . . .
unless it *was* Ashan she'd gone up against.

Or Jonathan.

Either way, not good news right now.

I crawled toward her. She looked up, expression turning hard, and I stopped.

"They're coming," she said. "I couldn't hold them
back. Be ready."

"Who?"

Too late to matter. I could sense it coming in the real
world, in the aetheric, even blinded and weak as I was.
A gigantic disturbance, headed this way.

Out in the darkness, I saw shapes moving. Indistinct,
but definite.

"Joanne Baldwin," one of them said. "Stand up."

Sounded human. With a gigantic effort—and I wasn't
sure how many more of those I could even stand to
attempt—I went up into Oversight and saw at least ten
flares of power gathering around me and Rahel. Wardens. Holy shit. How many had Paul sent to put me into
custody? How hard did he really think I could fight?

"They don't want you," Rahel said. "They're after
him. Lewis."

On the grand, sliding scale of things, that wasn't the
best news I'd ever heard. "Who am I talking to?" I asked
hoarsely, and managed to get to my feet. Ow. Ow ow
ow. I wanted to dance around in pain, but stillness was
required right now. Stillness, and a really good poker
face.

Someone summoned fire, a brilliant orange bonfire

that hovered over her palm. In its reflected light I saw
Shirl. Goth black, sloppily cut hair, too many piercings
in awkward places. Tattoos crawling her bare arms. She
didn't look any happier to see me now than she had
driving along the coast to accuse me of weather-related
murder.

"What the hell is going on?" I asked her.

"None of your business," Shirl snapped back. "You're
not even a Warden anymore. Stay out of it."

Rahel wasn't getting up to her feet, but she pulled into
a crouch next to me. Intimidating. I approved. From the
uneasy glance Shirl gave her, it worked.

"By order of the Wardens, I'm here to take Lewis
Levander Orwell into custody," Shirl said. "And you
need to get the hell out of the way, Joanne. You're on
shaky enough ground as it is. You really don't want to
give us more reason to come after you, too."

Which might have been meant to be funny, considering
the sandpit I'd been trapped in. If so, Shirl's sense of
humor needed work. "I have no idea what you're talking
about," I said. "Lewis isn't here. You're going to want
to move along, guys. I'm here with a cop, and he's kind
of grumpy, if you know what I mean. So, unless you
want to do your intimidating from the inside of a jail—"

She threw the fire at me. I mean, fastball-speed. It
hissed past my face and out into the ocean, where it
impacted a building wave and instantly vaporized the top
half into superheated steam. "I'm not playing with you,
bitch," Shirl said. "That's where everybody else goes
wrong. They let you talk. You have one chance to tell
me where he is, or I swear the next one burns right
through your stomach."

My plan to scare her into leaving wasn't going quite
as well as I'd hoped.

"I want to talk to Marion," I said, and was surprised
my voice stayed steady.

"Denied. Marion's busy." Shirl sounded way too smug
about that. Marion was probably under house arrest after

protesting too much, or flat-out refusing the order. "Last chance. Produce Lewis, or we'll go through you."

"Then let me talk to Paul!"

Her smile was utterly sinister. "Talk all you want. Paul's irrelevant. We're on the front lines out here, and we're going to defend ourselves, with or without permission."

"Defend yourselves against what?"

She must have remembered that she didn't want to talk, because her arm drew back, and plasma burned toward me. I dodged. It followed. Not as fast as the previous pitch, but then, I didn't think she meant it to be; she was playing with me. The plasma moved in mirror jerks with me, tagging me and cutting me off at every turn. I was tired and weak and clumsy with pain, and when I finally overbalanced on the soft sand and fell backward, the burning, incandescent globe dipped toward me and hovered just inches above my heaving chest. Hot enough to give me third-degree burns and make my jog bra start to char.

I dug my fingers into the sand and grabbed handfuls, trying to resist the sick urge to destroy David to save my own life.

Rahel lunged forward with a snarl, reached out with one taloned hand, and batted the fireball away. Right back at Shirl, who ducked. It hit someone else, who screamed in high-voiced agony, and Shirl turned to put out the resulting fiery chaos. Rahel grabbed my arm.

"Run," she ordered roughly. "They'll kill you. They've already killed others."

She launched herself up in a graceful, feline leap and landed on Shirl, who screamed. Fire erupted. I saw Rahel's neon yellow clothes burst into flame.

I flipped over and crawled to the hole. I felt the sand under my knees shift. *Oh God.* Lewis was losing it. The tunnel was collapsing. Sand was falling in on them.

There was nothing I could do.

Another flash of lightning streaked overhead, reflecting white on waves, showing a freeze-frame of the other Wardens converging around Shirl and Rahel. Rahel was going to lose. She didn't have the wattage necessary to stop all of them, not alone, not as a Free-range Djinn.

"Hey!" A deep-voiced yell from a couple of sand dunes over. "What's going on over there? You kids stop that!"

"Help!" I screamed. "Get help!"

The pompous jerk—and I was never so happy to hear one in my life—sounded even more self-righteous. And a little alarmed. "I tell you, I'm calling the cops! You clear out of here while you've still got the chance!"

"Yes, you idiot, *call the cops*! And the paramedics! *Help!*"

I was dimly aware of Detective Rodriguez racing back along the beach, some kind of rope slung over his shoulder, but I felt it in my bones, it was too late. All too late.

Rahel and Shirl were a bonfire rolling on the sand. Fire and blood and fury.

The sand heaved and collapsed in on itself, dropping me suddenly a good five feet. I slid down an instantly made dune.

The cave had collapsed.

Lewis was dying down there. "No!" I screamed, and started digging. It was useless. It'd take hours to move all this sand; no way they could survive down there.

I only had one option. Just one.

"David!" I yelled. "David, I need you!"

I felt the connection snap taut between us. Waiting for the command. One precious heartbeat went by. Two.

"David—"

Rodriguez skidded to a stop next to me and slapped the rope down on the sand. "Where's the hole?"

"Collapsed," I gasped. "Oh, God—David, get them out, get Lewis and Kevin out of there—"

I felt the draw of power dig deep into me, sucking out what little I had left, and the pull was agonizing. I moaned and wrapped my arms around my stomach. It felt as if my guts might literally be ripped out and dragged through the sand like some biological lifeline.

Rodriguez abandoned the effort at rescue and turned toward the Wardens, and the struggle. His gun came out of its holster under his hooded jacket.

"Police," he yelled. "Everybody freeze *now*."

Most of them did, realizing that they weren't exactly operating undercover; Rahel vanished in a wisp of smoke, and Shirl was left lying on the sand, whimpering. Alive, but battered and scorched. One of the other Wardens knelt down next to her and put a hand on her arm to still her—Earth Warden, I had no doubt. I felt the surge go through the aetheric as he pumped healing power into her body.

The connection between me and David stretched thinner, thinner, cutting like razor wire. I held back a cry, squeezed my eyes shut and ratcheted in wet, painful breaths.

"Did you get them?" I whispered.

I felt something hum along the connection, something powerful and intense. Affirmation and love, condensed emotion that was too deep and powerful to grasp all at once. As if he'd sent me everything he felt in a frantic, desperate burst, like a submarine going down and transmitting one last, despairing SOS as it went into the dark.

A hand broke out of the sand on the beach, clawed and flailing. I yelled wordlessly and grabbed for it, dragged until my muscles popped.

Lewis slid free of the clinging sand. His face broke the surface with a gasp, and he started coughing, choking, spitting.

He was holding on to Kevin. As soon as he was free I let go of him and lunged forward to grab Kevin's wrist as Lewis hauled. The boy's arm slowly slid free, then the curve of his shoulder. Sand fell in a thick cascade from his bent head.

He didn't gasp for breath, because he wasn't breathing.

I choked back a curse and got behind him, grabbed him under the armpits, and pulled like a stevedore, every muscle in my body straining. He finally pulled free. Sand clotted thickly around the open wound on his side, but it wasn't gushing blood anymore. I wasn't sure if that was good news, or just the worst possible news. Because you don't bleed when you're dead; you leak.

In the white-hot light of another lightning strike I saw that Kevin's eyes were shut, his face still.

He definitely wasn't breathing.

Lewis joined me in pulling, and we put the boy down on his back. I bent over him and put my ear to his mouth and nose, listening.

Nothing. Not a single whisper.

"You're not dying on me, you jerk," I told him, and pulled down on his chin to open his mouth. When I fitted my lips over his, I tasted grit and fear. I breathed into him. I didn't have anything left in the way of power, or I'd have superoxygenated his lungs, but simple human methods were all I had left.

I pressed my ear to his chest and heard a faint, fluttering heartbeat.

Breathed for him again. Waited. Breathed. Waited. Saw stars and felt like I might pass out from the exertion.

I felt his chest suddenly convulse under my hand and grab in a breath on its own.

"Dammit!" Lewis rasped, and I looked up to see that the wound in Kevin's side had begun pumping out blood in high-velocity jets. I clamped my hands down on it. Lewis put his hands over mine, and I felt the power cascade in. Hot and burning and pure as liquid gold . . . and not enough. Not for an injury of this magnitude.

"I need another healer!" I yelled at the knot of people standing with their hands up, under Rodriguez's attention. "One of you, get over here! Now!"

None of them moved. *None of them.* I looked up, desperate, and in the next flash of lightning I saw something terrible on their faces. My friends and colleagues, my fellow guardians of the human race.

They just didn't give a crap.

Two forms appeared out of the darkness next to me.

David, his long coat swirling in the ocean wind, his eyes blazing. Face pale and focused, as if he were holding to this form with his last strength.

Rahel, battered and ragged and bloody, limping. Holding David's shoulder for support.

"Help me," I said.

David collapsed to his knees opposite me, on the other side of Kevin's limp form, and put his hand over mine. His skin was burning hot, enough to make me wince, and his eyes met mine for a long second.

He smiled. It was a terribly weary smile, sweet and defeated and full of indescribable pain.

"Don't forget me," David said, and I felt the spark travel through his hand, into mine, into Lewis. Everything he had left. Everything he'd taken from Ashan, and from me. A needle-bright surge of pure healing power, drawn not from me but from that last, tightly defended core of what made David who he was.

Like the spark of life he'd put inside of me, our child, formed of the union of our power.

I heard Rahel's protest rip the night in half, a high, wailing shriek like the grieving of angels.

The wound in Kevin's side stopped bleeding.

David distorted, blackened, turned Ifrit. Rahel, closest to him, stumbled backward as the creature's blunt, razor-angled face turned toward her, like a lion scenting prey. She was too weak. He'd destroy her.

As if he knew that—*could* he know that?—he whirled and lunged for a Djinn barely visible as mist in the darkness. One of the Wardens' personal stash. It gave out a high, thin shriek of panic as the Ifrit latched on and began to feed.

Rahel, reprieved, lost no time in vanishing.

I moved my hand, carefully. No spurting blood, though I was pretty much soaking in it. There was a massive open wound, and it would make a huge scar that would be a great conversation starter from now on, but Kevin wasn't in danger of dying.

At least, not from that.

The Wardens weren't reacting to the Ifrit in their midst, and I finally remembered that they couldn't actually see him. Only Djinn—or someone like me, with Djinn Emeritus status—could see what was happening. David—the Ifrit—had the Djinn down on the sand, and his black talons were deep into its chest, sucking out power and life.

I might *want* that to happen, but I couldn't *let* it happen. Not if I wanted to sleep nights.

"David, get back in the bottle," I said, and watched as he misted away into a black, howling whisper.

The moon slid free of the cloud layer on the horizon and gilded everything silver.

"Okay, again: What the *fuck* is going on?" Detective Rodriguez demanded. He was saying it in a loud voice, as if he'd been asking it for a while. I stared at him, then at Lewis, who maintained pressure on Kevin's wound and gave me a vintage don't-look-at-me shrug. "Who are these people?"

"Trouble," I said. "Shoot anybody who comes near this guy. They're trying to kill him."

That, he could understand. "Do I want to know why?"

"Not—exactly. Look, I'll tell you. Just not now, okay?"

Rodriguez settled in next to Kevin, who was breathing more steadily now, color returning to his face. I stood up and walked toward the Wardens, who were regrouping from their confusion in various stages of defiance.

Shirl was still down. I stared at the Earth Warden who was next to her. Didn't recognize him, but he looked earnest and well scrubbed, in a Fortune 500 kind of way.

"You come after him again, you deal with me," I said flatly. "Lewis and Kevin are under my protection. And I swear, next time, I won't call off my Djinn. If you want to make this war, fine. I'm ready. Better bring along body bags."

He opened his mouth, then shut it. Jerked his head at two of the others standing there, and they got Shirl up and into a fireman's carry over the bulkiest Warden's shoulder.

"What about him?" the Earth Warden asked. He had

a nice voice, vaguely Canadian, and there was an off-kilter tilt to one of his eyes that made him seem sly. He nodded at Detective Rodriguez.

"What about him?"

"We shouldn't leave a witness."

I was dumbfounded. Was he actually saying . . . ?

Yes. He actually was.

"Over my dead body," I said flatly. I must have looked like it would be tough to achieve, because he took a step backward. "Get it straight, assholes. *Wardens don't kill people.*"

Some of them looked away. Some didn't. I felt a familiar prickle along my spine. If I could see the Ifrit, I wondered, could I see Demon Marks? Humans couldn't, generally, but if I could, I could check out these guys and see if they were under the evil influence. Not that any of these guys, male or female, were likely to bare any chests if I asked.

Lewis joined me, standing at my side. No words. Just a hell of a lot of strength, unmistakable, shivering the air like a quiver of heat. He looked grim and exhausted and haunted, but *not* weak. Not at all.

And then, unexpectedly, Kevin woke up.

"Yeah," he croaked faintly. "You want a fight, bring it on, buttwipes." He accompanied all that with the kind of inept theatrical gesture associated with bad magicians, kind of an awkward, limp-wristed wave. I winced.

"Yeah, thanks, kid," I said. "Just rest, okay? . . . Anyway. Hit the road, all of you. You're done here."

Detective Rodriguez stood up and joined me on the other side. The sound of his gun slide ratcheting was very loud, even over the continuous roar of the surf.

They might have decided I was no threat, that they could take Kevin, that an unpowered cop with a handgun was chicken feed. But up on the coast highway, flashing lights began to paint the sky, and sirens howled.

Cavalry on the way, and they didn't seem to have the appetite for a full-scale battle that involved the rest of the non-Warden world.

The Earth Warden held my eyes and said, "You'll see us again."

"Count on it."

They turned as a unit and walked away, into the darkness.

Silence, and the rising shriek of ambulance and rescue on the way. I became aware of just how much my feet hurt—as if I'd taken a five-mile firewalk—and that there was a glassy ache in my knees, and my head hurt.

And I wanted, desperately, to cry because I had blood all over me and David was gone. As if he'd never even existed. And I didn't think he was coming back this time.

This had turned out to be one hell of a jog.

It was a long night. Kevin went to the Emergency Room, who diagnosed anemia and said he was running a quart low on blood despite the healing David and Lewis had put into him. We spent most of the wee hours watching blood drip from a bag into his veins. Rodriguez kept his mouth shut about the whole standoff issue, mostly because he couldn't understand what had happened enough to try to explain it, and none of us were talking. Lewis stayed close to me, whether looking for protection or offering me his own was not clear.

We managed, somehow, to avoid the press, who were scurrying all over the story of sinkholes on the beach. IS YOUR CHILD SAFE? Film at eleven . . . by the time we made it back to my apartment, I realized that my life was well and truly out of control. Bad enough there was the whole job situation, but now there was Sarah and her boyfriend, and Lewis, and Kevin, and the Djinn War, and a cop from Las Vegas who was turning out to be kind of cool, actually.

And my feet hurt like hell.

Rodriguez insisted on coming in and checking out the apartment. Eamon and Sarah were not in immediate view, but her bedroom door was closed. I didn't, ah, inquire.

"Right," I said, and looked at my little flock. "Kevin, Lewis—sit down before you fall down."

Lewis was already lowering himself to the couch, but he shot me a grateful look. Rodriguez leaned against the door, arms folded, and frowned at me. Kevin, who should have been out on his feet from the painkillers, shuffled around the apartment, ragged black jean hems dragging the carpet, and fondled my stuff. Ah, yes. I remembered his great respect for personal boundaries. Even his brush with death hadn't dampened his enthusiasm for that.

I sucked in a pained breath as I put my feet up on a battered hassock and let myself relax, just a little, for the first time in hours. "I don't suppose you have anyplace to go," I said to Lewis. Who shook his head. "Fine. You're staying here. Kevin, you too. Um . . ."

Detective Rodriguez arched his eyebrows. "I have accommodations." Yeah, the White Van Hilton.

"Thank you," I said.

"For leaving?" He sounded amused.

"For staying when you didn't have to. When things didn't make any sense."

He shrugged and gave me a wintry smile. "I'm just saving my interrogation for later. Tonight, I'm just having a drink and trying not to think about it."

"Good plan," Lewis said. "I could use a beer."

I took the hint, went into the kitchen, and popped two Michelob Lights, carried them out along with a Coca-Cola, which I handed to Kevin. Who gave me a filthy look.

"Underage," I said. "And way too unpredictable to give beer to, anyway. And do we need to talk about painkillers and alcohol?"

He kept glaring.

"Take it as a compliment that I don't still want you dead."

He didn't, but he drank the Coke anyway. I held up another Michelob for Rodriguez's inspection; he accepted without a word. I went for a glass of white wine. Sarah had left a bottle chilling in the fridge.

"So," I said, and sat down on the floor to mournfully consider my aching, pink feet. "How screwed are we, exactly?"

Lewis tipped back the beer bottle. His throat worked. He considered everything carefully before he said, "If we were any more screwed, we'd be having a cigarette and enjoying the afterglow."

Rodriguez choked on his beer. Nice to know he had a sense of humor. I'd been starting to wonder.

"Why are they after you? No, wait, back up. *Who* are they?"

"Wardens."

"Yeah, obviously. But . . . ?" Lewis pressed the cold bottle to his forehead and cast a quick look at Rodriguez. I shrugged. "Don't worry about it. I'm telling him everything. No way around it at this point; besides, he's Quinn's old partner. He should know the truth."

"The whole truth?"

"Yep."

Lewis shook his head, obviously not convinced of my sanity, but let it go. Got back on the subject. "The Wardens are breaking apart. I knew it was coming; they just don't have enough structure left to keep it in place. They're breaking into factions. This one caught the rumors about the Djinn turning on their masters, and most of them sealed their Djinn bottles and stuck them in vaults, safety deposit boxes, whatever was convenient. And then they came after me."

"Why the hell would they come after *you*?"

"They've been told that I'm on a crusade to free all the Djinn."

I looked at him for a second. "Hmmm. Are you?"

"Separate issue." Oh, boy.

"Lewis—"

"Drop it, Jo."

"Okay, fine, so you've been preaching freedom for all Djinn, the Djinn suddenly start turning on their masters, the Wardens start coming after you." It made an un-

leasant amount of sense. "It's Ashan's group that's be-
ind this."

"Yep."

"And I think some of those Wardens may be . . ."

"Demon-marked? Makes sense, they're certainly pow-
rful enough. Rahel's been trying to keep them off my
ack, but they're like wolves. I can't shake them for long.
t's going to come down to killing, sooner or later." He
eemed depressed by that.

"One of them—Shirl—she was a protégée of Mari-
n's," I said. "I'll call Paul, find out if Marion still has
ome kind of control over things . . ."

"Marion's in the hospital," Lewis said flatly. "She was
urt. Car accident. I just heard from Paul an hour ago."

I stopped worrying about my feet. "They're targeting
s. This isn't random."

"They're going after the most powerful senior War-
ens. That leaves gaps to fill. It's a coup, or at least they
hink it is. From Ashan's perspective, he's just disman-
ling the Wardens altogether."

"What about Paul?"

He shook his head. I tried to stand up and felt my
nee give a sharp enough twinge that I had to stay down.
looked over at Kevin, who was fondling my minuscule
DVD collection. "Hey. Walking wounded. Put Mel Gib-
on down and step away."

"*Lethal Weapon* rocks."

"Yes, it does. Go get me the phone."

"Get it yourself, b—"

"Kevin," Lewis said softly. "Look at her feet. She can
arely walk. Shut up and get the damn phone."

Kevin flushed—unattractively—and glared at him, but
ucked his head and put the DVD back on the shelf.
"Where is it?"

I nodded toward the kitchen. Kevin shuffled off in that
irection. Lewis's eyes followed him. "He's not a terrible
id," he said. "But he needs somebody to tell him when
e's a fuckup."

"He should be lying down."

"Trust me, he will. Right now, he's scared half to death. Let him walk it off." I was afraid that the light in Lewis's eyes might be fondness. As if he was seeing something of himself in Kevin. Which was ridiculous, of course. Lewis had never been anything like Kevin, in any way.

"Lewis—he's a sociopath," I said, "and don't you forget it, or you'll end up with a knife between those nice broad shoulders, and I'll be very sad."

Rodriguez finished off his beer in one long, expert gulp, and said, "Okay, that's it for me. Entertaining as this little fairy tale is, I'm going to get some rest. Don't you do anything stupid. I'll know."

I had no doubt. He probably had motion sensors or something set up, or maybe had hired a second line of private eyes to keep track while he was catching shuteye. He was the thorough type.

"I won't go anywhere," I told him. "Oh, except to work. I'm due at the studio at six." Which made it barely worth trying to go to bed, at this point.

"Tomorrow," he said, "you and me, we're going to sit down. And you're going to explain this. Right?"

I saw no way around it, really. "Right."

He nodded, glanced at Lewis by way of a cop's goodbye, and let himself out. Tapped the door significantly. Lewis got up to click the dead bolts—both of them—shut. Not that they'd do much good against the Wardens or the Djinn, of course, but they were symbolic. And hey, there were still mere mortal bad guys out there, too. It would be really embarrassing to be engaged in a battle for the fate of the world and get killed by somebody wanting my crappy little stereo.

Kevin wandered back in with the phone, tossed it to me, and said, "Can I get some food?"

"Sure," I said. He disappeared so fast he might have been Djinn. "No beer or wine!" I yelled after him. Like he'd care what I said.

Lewis turned and sat down on the floor across from

ne, Indian-style. He reached out and took my foot in
his large, warm hands. I sucked in a warning breath.

"Relax," he said. "Trust me."

He guided it to his lap, and began to stroke his fingers
over the swollen skin. Where he touched, the hot skin—
which had been screaming in agony for hours—began to
cool and regain its shape. It was deliciously, amazingly
wonderful.

"You should open a spa," I said, and leaned my head
back against the cushions of a chair. He smiled down at
my foot as he stroked his fingers across the skin.

"For you, I should open a hospital," he said. "Jo
somebody helped us down there, in the sand. We were
dying, and somebody came."

I didn't answer.

"Was it David?"

I felt tears start to burn, and wiped them away with
shaking hands. His caress on my burned skin stopped for
a second, then resumed.

"I thought I could save him," I said. "I really
thought—"

I couldn't think about this, couldn't feel this, couldn't
handle anything right now. The tears were uncontrolla-
ble. They *hurt*. Lewis continued to stroke the burn out
of my foot, pressing just hard enough on the instep to
work out the ache along the way. Undemanding and unassuming, as ever.

"You're not losing him," Lewis said. "You'll never
lose him until he's dead. Or you are."

My left foot felt cool and soothed and sated. He gently
put it back on the carpet and took my right one. I closed
my eyes and concentrated on the sheer animal comfort
he was offering me.

"Then it's already over," I said softly. "I think he is
dead. I think what's left . . . oh God, Lewis. You don't
know what they're like. The Ifrit. You can see who they
were, and sometimes they *know* who they were . . ."

"Shhhh," he whispered. "Close your eyes. Don't
think."

I fell asleep with his fingers slowly, methodically taking away the pain.

When I woke up, I was in bed. Somebody—probably Lewis—had carried me in. I checked: still dressed in the jogging clothes. I felt sand in every fold of skin. I itched all over, and whatever sleep I'd gotten wasn't nearly enough.

I sat up and pulled David's bottle out of the nightstand. It was silent and inert, and there was no connection to it. No sense of his presence at all. It was just a container, fragile and limited. Like a human body.

Was that what a Djinn really was? A soul, unhoused? Then what was an Ifrit? What was a Demon? The classes at Warden U. hadn't exactly prepared me for the big questions. It was a technical school. Philosophy wasn't considered important to the curriculum.

But now I was starting to wonder if philosophy was what the Wardens were missing, and had been missing all along. The Ma'at might be a bunch of upright assholes, but at least they understood what they were doing, and why. All we did was react. React to this disaster, that crisis. We were the world's paramedics, and maybe we were spreading as much disease as we were curing.

"I love you," I whispered to the bottle, and pressed my warm cheek against it. "God, David, I do, I do, I do. Please believe me."

I fell asleep again with the bottle in my hands, still dressed in my gritty jogging clothes, and dreamed that a dark, jagged shape in the corner, like a broken nightmare, watched me the rest of the night.

INTERLUDE

The storm drives clear skies ahead of it. Warm weather, soft breezes. There is no sense of danger coming, no hint of the chaos moving on the horizon like an invading, destroying army.

The island nation in the way is fat, prosperous, and complacent about its safety. In all of its recorded history, which stretches back a thousand years, it has never been conquered. It is a paradise, a center of trade and culture and learning for half the human world. Its harbors are vast and constantly busy.

It doesn't matter. Humans have more energy than smaller animals, and the storm craves it.

The storm changes its course, unfurling its killing tentacles toward them.

First warning is the unnaturally clear sky, wrong for the season. Towards evening, the first breezes begin to arrive, and waves come faster, hit harder. A constant roar of surf crashes on high cliffs in explosions of white foam.

In the morning, people gather in the morning's soft, green-tinted light and find the sea itself boiling in distress where it meets the land. Out toward the far horizon, the storm shows itself in a black line stretching across the curve of the sky. The ocean humps toward them in long, rolling swells, each higher than the last.

The beaches go first, swallowed by wave after wave after wave. There is no alarm, at first. They have seen flooding before. Those living in the valleys and by the sea gather *their families and possessions and start a trek inland, whether they will shelter with families or friends.*

But the sea keeps rising, and as the storm's breath begins to blow, they realize that this is no ordinary rain coming to their fair and quiet land.

By the time they ring alarm bells, drawing the people to the temples, to the highest hills, the wind is slashing apart trees and the surge is bringing down everything in its path. They hope for divine intervention, but the wise among them already know the end of the story.

SIX

Two hours? Not enough sleep. Oh, no.

I stumbled up and into the shower, where I finally washed away the blood and sand of the night's adventures, and realized halfway through that I was still wearing my pull-on jog bra. Ever tried to get one of those off when it's wet? Not a pretty picture.

I stumbled comatose out of my bedroom, barely remembering to belt my bathrobe along the way, and started coffee. The asthmatic *chug-hiss-chug* of the machine echoed through the predawn stillness. Lewis was sprawled out on the floor, wrapped in a blanket. Kevin looked boneless and well rested on the couch. He slept open-mouthed.

War refugees. I felt a prickle along my spine, a dizzying sense that all this was just prelude to something a whole lot worse. I hoped I was wrong.

Not a sound from Sarah's bedroom. I tapped gently on the closed door, then eased it open.

The two of them were asleep, wrapped tightly around each other. Eamon, in sleep, looked younger and almost angelic, that sharp intelligence missing and a kind of gentleness in its place. His arms were around Sarah. Her back was pressed against his front, and his forehead rested on the disordered silk of her hair.

It looked . . . sweet. And definitely postcoital.

I shut the door without waking them and went back

to stare blankly at the coffeemaker as it peed into the carafe.

A hand on my shoulder made me jump. It was Lewis, yawning, all lean and shirtless and tousled, hair sticking in a dozen directions, eyes heavy-lidded.

"Hey," I said, and moved away from him. "I made a big pot."

"I'm going to need a syringe to inject it directly into my bloodstream."

"IV kit, third cabinet. Rinse it out when you're done. I'll need it later," I said. My hair was still wet. I leaned over the sink and twisted it into a rope, drizzling out a stream of silver water. Lewis busied himself with coffee cup retrieval, sorted through the thrift-store assortment, and handed me a GOT COFFEE? mug with a pop-eyed, jittery Too Much Coffee Man on it. He took Garfield.

"Did you sleep?" he asked me.

"A little." I'd dreamed, too. Not good dreams. "I'm sorry I got weepy on you. Bad night."

"I understand." He poured himself a cup, mutely offered the same to me, and I nodded. "David doesn't love you."

I nearly fumbled the cup he was holding out. "What?"

"David doesn't love you," he repeated patiently. "He lives for you. I don't think you understand the difference. Djinn don't just *love*. It isn't a game to them, and it isn't something they fall out of when it gets old. That's why the Wardens have rules about these things. Not just because compelling a Djinn against his or her will is— unsavory—"

I thought of Yvette Prentiss, and her use and abuse of her Djinn. And David. "It's rape," I said. "Might as well call it what it is."

He nodded, sipped coffee, and continued. "Sex, yes. But I'm talking about love. The rules are there to protect Djinn from their own instincts, as well as from anything humans might force them into. Because when they fall in love, it's . . . not on a human scale. And people get hurt. I'm worried, Jo. You and David—I know you love him. But the thing is, it's the kind of love that can destroy both of you. So be careful."

If he was trying to scare me, he was doing a good job. "David would never hurt me."

"He *has* hurt you." Steam blurred his expression. "Listen, last night you warned me about Kevin. I have to do the same. I like David, and I respect him, but you have to know who and what he is. His instincts won't always run in your favor. Just . . . be careful, will you?"

I intended to be. "I have to go to the studio. Will you guys be here when I get back?"

"I don't know. We really should get on the road, try to get lost. I don't want to put you and your sister in danger. Well, any more danger than you already seem to have attracted, anyway."

"You're too tired to hit the road," I said reasonably. "If you're going to flee for your life, at least stay long enough to get some decent meals and rest. Sarah's a hell of a cook. You can take my bed while I'm gone."

There's nothing like the first swallow of coffee after a night of exhaustion; it was like a cattle prod to the spine, a fierce jolt of reality. I savored it and held his stare. "So," I said. "Are you and Rahel together?"

"What makes you think I'll answer that?"

"Cold light of day. You're warning me about falling in love with a Djinn. I'm just curious."

His expression clearly reflected skepticism of that. "Rahel and I understand each other."

"Which means, what? You play chess? You give each other backrubs?"

"I don't think it's any of your business." Well, well. Lewis had developed a prim streak. For a guy who hadn't hesitated to get wild with me on the floor of a college lab, that was a bit hilarious.

"I'm just pointing out that there may be a pot/kettle issue on the table here regarding sleeping with the Djinn."

"Funny, I didn't invite you into my private life."

"Did too."

"Did not."

"Pot."

"Kettle."

"Bite me, Lewis."

"Very mature."

"Bite me *hard*!"

"Grow up."

"You first!"

We stopped, staring at each other, and for no apparent reason, burst into laughter. Flagrant, stupid giggles. Stress and near-death will do that to you. I had to set my coffee down for fear of acquiring more burns he'd have to heal.

When we settled down again—which took a while—I said, "Okay, I've thought about it. I'm not going to work today."

I picked up the phone. Lewis reached over and took it away from me. Our fingers brushed, and he was very close to me.

"You are," he said. "I don't think you should stay here."

"But—"

His fingers twined with mine. "I'm not blind and deaf, Jo. You think I don't know? You think I can't feel it?"

I felt horribly off balance. Were we flirting? Had we been flirting? Was he coming on to me? I'd thought he understood . . .

Lewis said, "No buzz."

I blinked. "Excuse me?"

He raised our clasped hands. "No buzz. No resonance. No feedback. Jo, you can't hide it from me. Your power is gone."

He wasn't talking about flirting. He was talking about my Warden abilities . . . and he was almost right. My power wasn't *completely* gone, but it was definitely operating at such a low voltage that he wasn't drawing a spark from it anymore. Lewis, who'd always drawn fire and power out of me, couldn't even feel a tingle anymore.

That wasn't seduction in his eyes. It was pity.

"Jo—" He let go of my hand and moved damp hair back from my face. "Go to work. I don't want you here in case things get ugly. You'd get hurt."

"Sarah—Eamon—"

"I can keep them safe; nobody's gunning for them. *You*, however, don't have enough sense to stay out of the line of fire, and you'll be a target. Go. Do whatever it is you do." He winked at me. *Winked*. "And besides, I love watching you on TV."

Mona was running a little rough. In-town driving really didn't agree with her, of course; she needed open road and high RPMs and curves to conquer. Her heart just wasn't in the few miles to the studio. I patted her console and promised her a weekend in the country soon, not to mention a nice detailing.

Cherise's convertible was parked in its accustomed space when I arrived. Top up. I scanned the horizon. Yep, the clouds were crawling closer. Rain later today, for certain.

I checked in with Genevieve, who laconically pointed out my costume hanging on the rack. I did a double take. "What . . . ?"

Genevieve, who had for some reason added some white streaks to her hair during the night, as well as a raspberry stripe from front to back, sucked on her cigarette and shrugged. She had a new tattoo as well. I'd never actually seen a woman with a naked woman tattoo before. It seemed recursive.

"You've got a new gig, sweetheart," she said in that tobacco-stained voice. "Want my advice? Avoid the Fruit." She meant Cherise, whom Genevieve had nick-named Cherry back in the early days. Hence, the Fruit.

The costume hanging on the rack was an aqua-blue bikini.

I gulped and held it up. Not enough fabric to it to make a blindfold. It would be different if I was strutting it on the beach, or—better yet—wearing it for David, but for an audience in the hundreds of thousands . . . I felt faintly violated.

"Um, do I have a—"

"Choice?" Genevieve's laugh sawed the air. "You're funny, kiddo."

I tried a smile, went behind the screen, and changed.

It was worse than I'd thought. I'd had the perfect bikini—in fact, I still had it in a drawer at home—and this wasn't it. It was way too *Penthouse* for public view, and it was designed for someone of Cherise's build, not mine. I felt like I was modeling fabric swatches. The thick bathrobe was a relief. I came out to give Genevieve a miserable look, and she raised one overplucked eyebrow in commiseration.

And then proceeded to torture my hair with hot irons until she was satisfied.

Thirty minutes later, I was walking onto the set, feeling like I was on my way to the electric chair. Clutching my bathrobe in a death grip. Cherise was sitting in a chair over to the side, looking like a thundercloud. I don't mean frowning, although she was doing that, of course. No, she looked like a *thundercloud*. As in, blue foam cloud suit, with little drops of silvery rain glittering all over it and hanging by wires. Her legs were covered in thick black tights.

I clapped my hands over my mouth in outright horror. She frowned harder.

"I did *not* ask for this," I blurted. "God, Cher—"

"I know," she interrupted. "It's not your fault."

"This is *awful*."

"Are you wearing my bikini under there?"

"We can quit."

Cherise managed to look mutinous and defeated at the same time. "And do what? Flip burgers? Internet modeling? I've got my pride, you know. I'm a *professional*."

Her little, silver suspended raindrops were shivering with indignation.

I swallowed a bubble of laughter and nodded. "Let's just get through this, okay?"

"I will if you will," she said, and looked around at the stagehands, who were all staring at us. Probably waiting for me to drop the bathrobe. "You! Assholes! *Nobody* drops water on me today unless you want to cash in on that pension, you got me?"

For a little thing, she was ferocious. Nobody answered.

Marvelous Marvin strolled onto the set, toothy as a land shark, and patted his stiff hair. "How do I look, girls?"

"Clark Gable and Valentino all rolled into one," Cherise said. He beamed at her and moved into his camera position. She glared after him. "They're dead, asshole."

"Let me guess. Marvin's behind this?" I asked.

"Oh, yeah. Marvin wants to ogle your ass for a while. And besides, he's pissed at me because I wouldn't put out."

Usually, that would have been a joke, but the way she said it . . . "Seriously?"

She just looked at me.

"You're going to report him, right?"

"Oh, yeah, right. Like Bikini Girl is going to get any traction on a sexual-harassment issue. Plus, there's the whole issue of me having tormented the hell out of every HR person to the point where they run when they see me coming." She eyed me speculatively. "But you, on the other hand . . ."

"Me?"

"If he snaps your bikini, you'd report him, right?"

"No," I said flatly. "I'd kill him." Especially today. *So* not in the mood for this. I wanted to do this, grab my paycheck—which would be the last one, as I planned to be fleeing soon—and get the hell out.

Whatever Cherise was about to say was cut off by the command for silence on the set, and we stood in silence, waiting for our cues.

Hers came first. I watched her lumber out into public view in her thick, lumpy cloud costume. Watched Marvin deliver his lame-ass jokes at her expense. I'd never really looked at it from this side of the camera before. Damn, I had a really pathetic job.

Marvin had set up a water-drop joke. The stagehand didn't pull the bucket. Cherise was just that scary, and besides, the stagehands were union. They didn't give a shit. When Marvin gave the signal, the stagehand up there just grinned, shrugged, and chomped gum.

Cherise gave him a behind-the-back thumbs-up.

Commercial break. The anchors sniped at each other over who had stepped on whose leads. One of them was rewriting an intro for the next piece. Badly.

Marvin speared me with a look and gave me the toothy grin of death.

"Joanne," he said. "Let's flash some skin. You're up."

I took a deep breath and slid the bathrobe off of my shoulders, then folded it neatly on a chair. The air felt ice-cold on my all-too-exposed skin. I walked over onto the tiny ocean set, which had glittering white sand, a blue-sky backdrop, and an oversized beach ball. Marvin came over to join me. Close up, his tan looked a shade of orange that earthly sun didn't produce, and the professionally even smile didn't really disguise the ruthlessness in his eyes.

"Okay, this is the standard beach setup, right? So look pretty and nod." He gave me an analytical once-over. "Turn around."

"What?"

"Turn around."

I didn't want to, but I did it, a fast circle. When I was halfway around, he reached out and stopped me.

"Your tag's showing," he said, and slipped his fingers into the back of my bikini bottom.

And snapped it.

And burst out laughing.

I spun, with perfect timing, and yanked his toupee off his head just as the camera operator finished his silent three-two-one countdown. The thing felt damp and dead-animal in my hand. I tossed it offstage, to where Cherise was standing. She fielded it neatly, waved it like a battle flag, and grinned at me.

Marvin was *not* amused. The red light went on, and

he was still glaring at me for a full two seconds before he pulled himself together enough to bare his teeth at the audience and start the shtick. His hair plugs looked naked and sickeningly experimental under the harsh lights, and some of them were standing up stiff as cornstalks from where I'd pulled the toupee off. We were talking about the possibilities for fun and sun in the next three days, I gathered. Marvin talked in totally unscientific generalities about updrafts and warm fronts, and gave us the assurance that we were over the worst so far as hurricane season went. "And I can personally guarantee that the next weekend is going to be spectacular!"

I stood hipshot in my best cover-model pose, waving and smiling. Presenting myself mostly in profile, because it seemed slightly less revealing than standing full-on or (God forbid) facing away.

Marvin turned to me and gave me the most furiously charming smile I'd ever seen. I smiled back. Give us pistols at ten paces, and we'd be the picture of friendship.

"Why don't you read the forecast for the next week, Joanne?" he asked. Which gave me a pleasant little shock of surprise.

"Sure," I said warmly, and caught, too late, Cherise frantically making a no-go gesture with both hands. Damn. Whatever was coming, I'd just walked right into it.

"It's on the beach ball," he said.

The beach ball was behind me.

I froze, stared at him for a second, and then recovered my smile. "Would you get it for me, Marvin?"

He kept smiling. "Sorry. I'm busy."

The whole point was, of course, to get me to turn my nearly naked ass to the camera. I bit the inside of my cheek and decided to just go for it. "Actually, Marvin, I'd like to give it a shot without the notes."

Which wasn't what he expected or wanted to hear. He shot a look at the director, who made a bored keep-moving motion. "Sure." He rolled his eyes for the benefit of the viewers.

"Well, Marvin, from the radar imaging you showed us earlier, it's pretty obvious that we have a warming trend moving in from the southwest, moving northeast. I'd say from the satellite time-lapse that we can expect to see some clouds later today with a strong possibility of afternoon showers, and by tomorrow, lows in the mid-eighties and highs topping out around ninety-two degrees. The dew point will be around seventy-four, with humidity of about eighty-four percent, rising through the weekend. We can expect to see some thunderstorms by tomorrow evening, about a seventy-three percent chance. So let's be careful out there. There should be some major electrical activity associated with these storms, as well as the possibility of rising winds."

I finished it with a wide smile.

There was a stunned silence. The two anchors and the sports guy looked at each other in open-mouthed amazement; I guess they didn't think a girl in a bikini could so much as string together a sentence, much less deliver a coherent, scientific analysis.

I hadn't used even a little bit of Oversight to do it, either. I didn't think I was capable of that, at the moment. I'd done it all from my own observations last night, and the maps, and the same data Marvin had available at his disposal.

And I knew I was right. One hundred percent right.

Marvin looked like a gaffed fish. He must have realized it, because he flushed under the pancake makeup and forced a labored smile in return. "Ha! That's very funny, Joanne. You've been watching a little too much Weather Channel." He broadly mugged for the camera. "Sorry, folks, but Joanne's forecast is completely wrong. There's not going to be any rain. I've already guaranteed it."

"Want to bet?" I asked.

"Oh, we don't encourage gambling on our show," Marvin shot back, with a quick, frantic glance at the director. Who was looking enraptured with the sudden tension on the set, and gave him a go-ahead nod. "But I suppose a friendly wager, in the interest of science . . ."

"If it rains, Marvin, I think you should have to wear the Sunny Suit," I said sweetly.

The anchors laughed, off camera. Cherise had her fist stuffed in her mouth. All her silver, suspended raindrops were glittering as she shook.

Marvin sputtered and twisted, but after all, he'd given his personal guarantee. "Well," he finally said, "I'll take that bet. Because Marvelous Marvin stands by his predictions!"

The anchors clapped. So did the stagehands, who were all giving me—not Marvin—a big, double thumbs-up.

Marvin did a *back-to-you*, and the newscast resumed. They were about to interview a 110-year-old man from Coral Gables who had a pet tortoise nearly his own age.

The red camera light flicked off, and Marvin lunged at me. I danced back through the sand, stepped off the narrow ledge onto the cold floor of the studio, and mouthed at him, *Want to see my ass?*

And then I turned, pointed to it, and walked away, head held high. Put my arm around the squishy mass of Cherise's costume, and walked her toward the door. I tossed the bathrobe over my shoulder on the way out and made sure that I was doing a full model's sashay, the entire time.

When I looked over my shoulder, Marvin was doing a silent dance of fury, right in the director's face. The stagehands were convulsed with silent laughter.

So endeth my career as Weather Girl. Sad, really. I was just getting to like it, in a perverse, kinky kind of way.

It occurred to me, on the drive back, that I had a lot to worry about. Jonathan's threat was still in force, and although he'd temporarily forgotten about me, he was almost certainly going to come reinforce his point anytime now. And whatever wistful hopes I had to repair the damage to David were now officially dead, buried, and had grass growing on their graves.

David was an Ifrit, and I didn't know how to get him back without human blood and the Ma'at. I was dangerously willing to get the human blood. The Ma'at, however, were notoriously not easy to convince, and with the Djinn in the middle of political warfare, that wasn't even vaguely an option.

When Jonathan showed up, I'd have to do what he said. I wouldn't have any choices left.

I felt such a crashing wave of anguish that it left me breathless, tears cold on my cheeks, and I pulled into a strip mall parking lot to let it pass.

It didn't pass. The waves kept coming, battering me, releasing more and more pain. It was as though a dam had broken inside of me, and I couldn't stop the flood.

I found myself hunched over, head against the steering wheel, hands over my stomach. Protecting my unborn child, my child who was just an idea, a possibility, a spark.

David was already gone, but he wasn't dead. He'd told me he had to die for the child to live. Probably.

I tried to sense something, anything, from her, but like the bottle that contained David in thick, obscuring glass, my own body refused to grant me a connection. Was she still there?

Please, I thought to her. *Don't go.*

It took me an hour to dry my tears and feel up to facing what was waiting for me at home.

When I arrived, Lewis and Kevin were gone. That wasn't totally a surprise; Lewis never had liked hanging around waiting for trouble, and he'd be thinking of Kevin, too. I wondered why the Ma'at weren't rallying to protect him. Yet another thing I should have found the time to ask.

I wished I hadn't missed Lewis, but at the same time, I was relieved. He'd have taken one look at my reddened eyes and known what I'd been crying about, and I wasn't really sure I could stand the sympathy just now.

When I closed the door, I heard Sarah banging around in the kitchen. By *banging* I mean cooking, with punctuation. I saw Eamon standing in the living room, sipping coffee, and raised my eyebrows; he raised his back and nodded toward the source of the noise.

"I think she's a bit unhappy," he said. "Considering that she walked out of the bedroom thinking she'd be alone in the house and, well, she wasn't."

I blinked. "That was a problem?"

"It was the way she walked out of the bedroom."

"You mean she was . . . ?"

"Naked as the day she was born," he said with careful gravity. "I think the resulting shriek woke half your neighbors."

I was going to hell for the fact that this actually *cheered me up*. I tried to be a dutiful sister. Tried very, very hard. "I'm sorry. I should have warned you, but you guys were asleep—"

"Oh, believe me, it's not me you have to convince. I thought it was a lot funnier than she did," he said. "By the way, your friend—Lewis?—said to tell you that you looked great this morning."

Eamon's tone had just a bit of a question in it. I felt a blush coming on again.

"On television," I clarified. "He said he was going to watch me on television. Not like rolling over in bed and saying I looked great or anything."

"Ah." Eyebrows up and down. "Of course."

Hurricane Sarah was making omelets, apparently, with lots of agitated chopping of mushrooms and onions and peppers. Ham had already suffered the same fate. When I came into the room, she pointed the chef's knife at me and said, *"You."*

"I surrender. I throw myself on your mercy. Please don't mince me," I said, and sat down at the table. There was a pitcher of orange juice out, so I helped myself to a glass. Tart and pulpy, just the way I liked it. I sipped liquid sunshine and waited for the storm to break as Sarah went back to her chopping.

And waited. And waited. She just kept chopping. Finally, I ventured, "So you're mad, then."

"Oh, you think?"

"Look, Lewis needed a place to stay for the night. It was late. I didn't want to wake you—"

"Yes, all very logical, but you're not the one who wandered out here *naked* and got ogled by that—lecher!"

"Lewis?" I blinked in surprise. Not that Lewis *wouldn't* ogle—he was a guy, after all, and highly aware of women—but he was usually a lot more subtle about it.

"No, not him. The other one. The kid."

Oh. Kevin. Of course. "Um, right. Sorry about that. Don't take it personally. He's a teenager. He's constitutionally lecherous." I edited out the response that began, *If you weren't so focused on shagging Cute British Guy, you might have thrown on a robe, and damn, I'll bet it was funny. . . .* "Are you really mad?"

The chopping paused for three long seconds, then resumed at a slower pace. "No," she admitted. "I'm embarrassed. First of all, Eamon and I—well, we got carried away. I mean, it was rude of us to stay here, in your home, and—do—what we did. I don't know what came over me. I'm usually a lot more reserved than that."

"Hey, I wasn't even here. Unless you got carried away and had incredible sex in my bed or something. . . ." Oh, *man,* I didn't like that silence. "Sarah? Tell me it wasn't in my bed?"

"Just the once," she murmured.

I'd thought it looked more than usually rumpled when I came back, but I'd been exhausted and traumatized and distracted.

"I think that makes it a dead heat on insensitivity," I said. "Speaking of which, thanks for asking me how work went. I got fired this morning. No more Weather Girl."

"What?" she blurted. "But—how are we going to pay the bills?"

Typical Sarah. Not, *Oh my God, that's awful, are you okay?* I eyed the feast she was cooking up. "Well, I did get a decent severance check, mostly because they were afraid I'd sue, given the bikini-snapping by a senior staff member. But I think we'll have to economize on the haute cuisine. And the couture is right out. Also, anything else with French derivations."

A quiet cough from the door. Eamon was standing there, looking sober and remarkably self-possessed for a guy who'd appropriated my bed for illicit purposes. "I know you don't want charity, but I'd be more than willing to offer a loan. Purely to tide you over until you find something else. No strings attached."

Sarah's face lit up. Eamon, however, was watching me. Very wise of him.

"No," I said. "Thanks. It's a nice offer, but honestly, I can't accept it. We'll just figure it out for ourselves." I didn't want Sarah to jump from being taken care of by Chrêtien to being taken care of by Eamon. Especially since she barely knew him, for God's sake. Not that I disliked him—in fact, I thought he was pretty cool—but the pattern bugged me. "Okay, Sarah?"

More agitated chopping. No answer. I sighed and sipped orange juice.

"Were you fired because you were right and that idiot with the hair problem was wrong?" Eamon asked.

"No," I said. "I was fired because I was right while I was on camera. Plus, I wouldn't let him snap my swimsuit with impunity."

Sarah laughed. Eamon didn't. He just watched me with those cool, quiet eyes, as if he understood everything.

"Good for you," he said. "You deserve better than that. I heard you give the forecast. It was very clear you deserved his job, at the very least. I doubt they could ever afford your talents, if they understood what you were worth."

He wasn't delivering that in a tone of flattery, or admiration—just a dry, brisk, undramatic statement of fact.

I exchanged a look with my sister. She smiled.

"See?" she asked.

I did. I approved. Not that I'd ever admit it, of course. I was, after all, the bratty one.

"So," I said. "What's on your schedules for this morning, beyond the best breakfast of our lives?"

"I have some work to do," Eamon said. "However, after that, I thought I might take you lovely ladies out for a bite of dinner. Would that be acceptable? Someplace nice. Help you forget your troubles for a bit. It's really the least I can do, after . . . imposing on your hospitality."

Sarah got that smile. That secret, glowing smile of Really Good Sex. She gave him a smoking look from under lowered lashes, and I controlled a weary flash of petty jealousy, because I wanted David, I needed him, and I was grieving for him, all at the same time. Sarah might be living her idyll. Mine had crashed headlong into the real world, flamed out, and was plummeting toward earth at Mach One.

I got lost in those waves of sadness again. Luckily, they'd lost a little of their force, and I only got a little hot prickle in the corners of my eyes instead of the full, embarrassing breakdown.

"Jo?" Sarah prodded. "Are you staying here today?"

It was a very good question. I wanted to sit and grieve, but sitting and waiting for all of my dizzying array of enemies to come and take their shots sounded really, really dumb. Much as I wanted to hang out and pretend to have a normal life, that possibility had gone out the window last night on the beach. "I've got some things to take care of, too. Will you be all right on your own for a while?"

"Sure." She gave Eamon another one of those little looks that promised to drag him off to the bedroom. "I've been thinking of cleaning up around here. As a thank-you to you, Jo. If that's all right."

As long as it kept her busy and preferably not spending any of my dwindling bank account . . . "Okay. But

I want you to keep the phone close, okay? That friend of mine, Lewis, he had some trouble. There may be people looking for him. They wouldn't hurt you, but it doesn't hurt to be careful. Don't answer the door if somebody shows up asking for him, and if you get in trouble, call me." Eamon made that quiet coughing noise again. "Or, okay, call Eamon. Right?"

"Sure." Sarah abandoned the chopping and turned to the beating of eggs, which she did with amazing skill. "I can take care of myself."

I knew she believed that. I'd just never seen any real evidence of it.

But she did make one hell of an omelet.

The first stop on my list of things to do was to have that heart-to-heart conversation with Detective Rodriguez, whose van was still conveniently located downstairs. Avoiding him wasn't going to get it done. I'd rather finish the conversation, amen, and at least have one fewer potential gun aimed at my head.

It wasn't quite as hot as it had been, although it was way too muggy—the clouds overhead, which had started out thin and cirrus, sliding like white veils over the sky, were thickening to cotton clumps. Cumulonimbus. I couldn't feel the tingle of the energy building, but I could read the sky about as well as anyone, and there was definitely rain on the way. The wind had shifted.

I knocked on the van's window, waited, and finally got a sliding door opened in the back for answer.

I don't know what I expected from the Good Ship Surveillance, but it was clean. Really, really clean. There was a neat little bed, made up so crisply it probably would have passed a drill sergeant's inspection. No food wrappers or loose papers or detritus of a normal life. Near the back was a closed metal locker that probably held necessities like toothpaste and changes of clothes and spare ammunition.

He had video running. Video of all of the entrances

to my building, plus a pretty good view through the patio window into the apartment. Some kind of wireless cameras. Good God.

"Good morning," Rodriguez said, and nodded me to a chair. It was bolted down to the floor, but it swiveled. Kinda comfy, too. I settled in as he slid the door closed behind me. "Coffee?"

"I'm already soaking in it," I said, and held out a cup I'd brought with me. "Here. Fresh orange juice. My sister got enthusiastic and pulped half the state's cash crop for breakfast."

"I know," he said, and gestured toward the monitor that showed the view through the patio door. Sarah was at the sink, washing dishes. Eamon was rinsing and drying. They were so much in each others' spaces it was like watching something a whole lot more intimate, with a whole lot fewer clothes.

"Remind me to pull the shades later," I said. He leaned over and took the OJ, but he didn't drink, just set it aside. "What? You think it's poisoned?"

"I'm careful," he said. "No offense."

"Fine. Your loss. Are you taping all of this? The video?"

"Yes."

"Is there anything embarrassing I can use on my sister?"

I got a very faint smile that didn't reach those impartial eyes. "Privileged."

Banter was over. Silence fell, hot and oppressive, and he studied me with wary eyes. Waiting.

I caved. "Look, Detective, what can I do? What is it going to take to make you, you know . . ."

"Go away?" he supplied, and eased down into a chair across from me. Not as comfy as mine, I noted. "Answers. I need you to tell me everything, start to finish. Nothing left out."

"That's why I'm here. I'll give you the whole story, but honestly, it won't do you any good. And there's not a shred of proof, one way or the other, so you'd better give up on having any peace of mind. All you'll have is my word, and I have the impression that isn't going to carry a lot of weight with you."

He sat back, watching me, and finally picked up the orange juice and sniffed it, then took a sip. "Actually, I revised my opinion a little," he said. "Last night. On the beach."

"Why?"

He didn't answer. He swiveled his chair instead and looked at the screen, where my sister and her new boyfriend were scrubbing dishes and laughing.

"What's his story?" he asked. "Your new friend."

"Sarah met him at the mall. Same day I met you, as a matter of fact. Though you and I haven't hit it off quite so well."

He sent me one of those looks. "You live an interesting life."

"You have no idea. What made you change your mind on the beach?"

He drank more of the OJ. "Two things. One of them has nothing to do with the beach itself: You were pissed off, not scared, when you confronted me the first time. Guilty people get scared, or they get smooth. You're different."

Well, that was a nice compliment. "And the other thing?"

"Guilty people don't save lives in the dark. Murderers can save lives, if it suits them. They can run into burning buildings and grab babies out of cribs at risk of their own skins. They can even feel sorry about it if it doesn't work out. But if there's a *choice,* and if there's no percentage and no witnesses, they won't put themselves out for it. If a guy's bleeding to death in an alley and all they have to do is make a 911 call, they won't unless there's a reason—unless somebody sees them and expects them to do it, or there's some profit in it. Get my point? It's all about the way it looks, not the life they're saving; they really don't give a shit about that." He shrugged and tilted the glass to drain the orange juice to a thin film of gold. "You do. All you had to do was walk away and let that hole collapse on those poor bastards, and nobody would have known."

"Nobody but me."

"Yes. That's my point."

Something he said rang a bell. "You said, a murderer can run into a burning building and grab a baby . . . you were thinking of Quinn, weren't you?"

He was silent for a moment, reluctant to say it out loud. "There was something about the way he did it. Standing there in the street, calculating the angles. There was a crowd, there was a mother begging him for help, but it was like some little computer inside of him was adding up benefits. Look, I wasn't lying to you. Quinn was a good guy. I liked him. But being a good guy doesn't mean you're not a bad man."

"Detective, if you're not careful, you might start sounding deep."

He gave me a faint, strange smile. "No chance of that. I'm a good cop. If I can't see it, feel it, taste it, explain it to the jury, I don't believe it. Quinn, he was intuitive. Mind like a jumping bean. It was all like a game to him. A contest; see who's the smartest guy in the room." His hands were clasped now, his thumbs rubbing slow circles on each other. He bent his head and watched them at work. "Can I believe he was a wrong guy? Yeah. I can believe it. I didn't want to, but I've been thinking about it, and I've been watching you. You don't change when nobody's looking. You say what you mean, and you say it to anybody who'll listen."

"Are you saying I'm not subtle?"

"You're about as subtle as a brick. But you can take that as a compliment. Hero-types generally aren't that subtle."

Hero-types? "Anything else?"

"Yeah," he said. "The greasy-looking kid who was in your apartment last night ripped off some cash from the flour jar in your kitchen. And the guy you were talking to before you left for work made him put it back."

Kevin and Lewis, each acting according to their na-
tures. It made me smile.

"Also," Rodriguez finished, "you looked totally hot
on TV, and your sister looks pretty good naked. Now.
Tell me about what really happened with Quinn."

I realized, about two sentences into it, that I couldn't
not tell him about the Wardens, and especially the Djinn.
He had to understand what we were dealing with, and
the stakes we played for. He had to understand that
Quinn was doing something far beyond the capacity of
the justice system to punish.

It took a long time. When my voice ran hoarse, Rodriguez got me a cold bottled water, and when I started
trembling from nerves, he switched me to cold beer. The
air conditioner kicked in with a dry rattle at some point,
drying the sweat trickling down into the neckline of my
white tank top.

It was a strangely quiet interrogation. He just listened,
except for those small acts of kindness. Occasionally,
he'd ask for a clarification if I wasn't getting something
across, but he never disputed, never doubted, never accused me of being a lunatic straight off the funny farm.

Which I would have, if I'd been in the less-comfy chair
hearing someone spout the same explanation.

When I got to the part that talked about his partner's
death, I saw his eyes go cool and hooded, but his expression stayed neutral. Then it was over, and I was clutching
an empty brown bottle in my hands, and all I heard was
the steady whisper of the A/C fighting the Florida heat.

"You know how that sounds," he said.

"Of course I know. Why do you think I didn't tell you
all this up front?"

He got up, as if he wanted to pace, but the van was
too small and besides, I thought what he really wanted
to do was put his fist through something yielding. Like
me. There was that kind of sharp angle to the way he
moved.

And still, nothing in his expression. The anger was

burning, but it was somewhere miles down and sealed off with a steel hatch.

"You say there's nobody to back up this version."

"Well, there is," I said. "The guy that was here last night. The kid. And you saw some of it yourself last night on the beach. Hell, you could call my boss in New York if you wanted. He'd tell you it was true—well, maybe he wouldn't, come to think of it; he's got a hell of a lot of problems of his own. But the point is, none of these people would be credible to you. They don't have real jobs and real identities you can check out with independent sources. They're ciphers. Like me. So I think you've got to go with your gut on this one, Detective. Do you believe me or not?"

He stopped and put his hand on a leather strap hanging from the wall—the better to grab onto if the van had to move into gear, I realized. This was quite a mobile cop shop he had.

"Tell you what," he said after a moment. "I'll believe it if you show me something."

"What?"

"Anything. Anything, you know, magic."

"It's not *magic*," I said, exasperated. "It's science. And—well, okay, the Djinn, maybe that's magic, but really, it can all be explained if you go far enough with the physics, and—"

"You do stuff other people can't do, and you make things happen with the power of your mind?"

"Well—um—"

"Magic," he said, and shrugged. "So show me something."

Truth was, I didn't have enough power to show him much of anything. I stared at him blankly for a moment, and then said, "Okay." I had enough energy left inside for a tiny little demonstration. Maybe.

I held out my palm and concentrated.

It should have been easy, doing this; it was a trick I'd been practicing since I'd first joined the Wardens. Nothing to it—anybody with more than a spark of talent could pull it off; the trick was controlling it and doing it with grace and elegance.

I closed my eyes, let out a slow breath, and built a tiny little rainstorm over my hand. Pulled moisture out of the surrounding air and carefully crowded it together, cooled the vibrations of the molecules just enough to make them sticky. When I opened my eyes, a faint, pale fog was forming above my palm. It was ragged and not very well established and, all in all, the crappiest demonstration I'd ever seen, but I held on and continued to draw the moisture together into a genuine little cloud.

A tiny blue spark zipped from one side to another inside of it, illuminating it like a tiny bulb, and Rodriguez drew closer, staring.

I made it rain, a tiny patter of full-size drops on my hand—they had to be full-sized, because it had to do with gravity, not scale. I only squeezed out two or three, because of the size of the source material, but enough to get the point across. The friction of molecules sparked another baby lightning bolt; this one zapped me like a static charge. I winced.

Rodriguez dragged a hand through the cloud, and stared at his damp fingers in fascination.

"Real enough for you?" I asked him, and let it go. It broke apart into fog, which rapidly evaporated into nothing in the dry, air-conditioned environment of the van. I wiped my wet palm on my leg.

He didn't answer for a long moment, and then he reached over and picked up the empty orange juice glass. Handed it back to me.

"We're done," he said. "Watch your step when you get out."

That was it. He slid the door open. The glare of sunlight startled me, as did the humidity rolling in the door. I looked at Rodriguez, who stared back, and finally stepped out and onto the hot pavement.

"That's all?" I asked him.

"Yeah," he replied. "That's all." He started to slide the door shut, then hesitated. "Two pieces of advice; take them or leave them. First, get rid of the car. It's a sweet ride, and it's also hot and it attracts too much attention. Somebody's going to figure it out."

I nodded. Poor Mona. Well, I was really more of a Mustang girl, anyway. . . .

"Second," he said, "if what you told me about Quinn is true, he was in business with somebody, and he had a shipment to deliver. You might want to think about the possibility that somebody might be looking to collect, and why they wanted it so bad in the first place."

I felt the skin tighten on the back of my neck. "You mean, collect from me?"

"You're the visible link, Joanne. I found you. Somebody else could do the same thing. Watch your ass."

I nodded slowly. "So this is good-bye?"

"You see me again, it's because I found out you were lying to me, and believe me, that *would* be good-bye."

He slid the van door shut. I stepped back. He slid into the driver's side seat in the front, and the van started up with a shiver and a roar. He rolled down the window, gave me a little salute, and backed out of the parking spot.

I watched him drive away. Except for a small patch of oil on the asphalt where he'd been parked, my cop stalker was gone as if he'd never been there.

One problem down. About a million to go.

Overhead, the clouds piled thicker, darker, and more imminently threatening.

I wished I knew what to do next. If Lewis hadn't bugged out, at least I could have mined him for information—I knew he had a lot more than he was saying—but of course holding on to Lewis was like trying to hold on to a wave in motion. And without access to the aetheric, trying to find *anyone* was trouble. The Djinn were—at least for now—leaving me alone, probably too preoccupied with their own battles and problems. Jonathan, despite his threats, hadn't come knocking for his pound of flesh. Ashan was proving the once-bitten, twice-shy cliché. I didn't know whether that was a good sign, or bad, but at least it gave me a little more time to do whatever it was I proposed to do.

Which was . . . what?

I was in the middle of dithering about it when my cell phone rang, and it was Paul Giancarlo, calling from the Warden offices at the U.N. Building in New York.

"Good morning," I said. "Before you forget to ask, thanks, I'm fine."

"I wasn't going to," he grunted. "Lewis was with you last night?"

He had good sources, but then, he was the Head Honcho. At least for now. "Yeah. He needed someplace to stay and recover. Look, you've got rogue Wardens running in packs out here. Lewis has a bull's-eye painted on his back. You need to do something, fast."

"Would if I could. I've got a problem. I need your help."

"Does the word *no* ring any bells with you? Because I've said it before."

"Joanne, I'm not fucking around here. When I say *problem* to someone like you, what do you think it means?"

"Disaster," I said briskly. "From what I've seen, there's plenty of that going around, and I'm sorry about it, but I can't help."

"Yes, you can."

"Seriously, I can't."

His voice went very quiet. Gravelly. "Did you hear me ask you a question? Short declarative statements, sweetheart. Not negotiable. This is serious business, and you're going to get in line or I promise you, your powers get yanked. Clear?"

Fuck. Frankly, Paul sending Marion's team after me to rip out my powers was far down my waiting list of panic attacks, but it wasn't worth risking, either. "Clear," I said. "What do you need?"

"Get over to John Foster's office. Nobody's answering over there. I got nobody on the ground I can trust right now. Just make sure everything's okay."

That gave me a quiet moment of worry. "Paul? Is it that bad?"

His sigh rattled the speaker of my cell phone. "However bad you think it's gotten, it's worse than that. And I don't think it's anywhere near hitting bottom yet. Get over there, but watch your back. I'd send you cover if I could."

"I know. Are you all right there?"

"So far. Nobody wants to uncork a Djinn around here, though. Six Wardens reported dead in the Northeast, and word is their own Djinn stood by and let it happen."

I remembered Prada on the bridge, her defiant anger. "And once they're free of their masters, they go after others to free them," I said. "Packs of them."

"Yeah. It's a mess. Swear to God, Jo, I don't know if we're going to survive it. We're warded halfway to hell around here, so I think this building's secure, and I gave my Djinn a preemptive that her job was to protect my life from all comers until I said otherwise. I passed that along to everybody in the system; don't know if it'll do any good. You know how expert they are in getting around orders when they want to."

"Yeah," I agreed softly. "I know. Listen—be careful. I'll call you when I know something."

"Thanks. I can't afford to leave the Florida stations unmanned."

I knew. Key areas had seasonal posts of enormous responsibility. California was important all year long. Tornado-prone states like Kansas, Missouri, Oklahoma, and Texas got extra staffing for the spring and summer.

Florida, in hurricane season, was a key weather post, and if John was missing . . .

We were in big trouble.

I signed off and headed for my car.

The Warden Regional Office was located not far from the National Weather Service offices in Coral Gables, conveniently enough; we'd sometimes used them for conferences and research. But the Warden offices were unassuming, located in a seven-story building with standard-issue brown marble and sleek glass. There was no sign on the building itself, just a street number etched in brass. Security on the entrance. I didn't have a card key, so I sat in the car and waited until someone else pulled into the parking lot and wheeled a laptop toward the front door. I didn't recognize her—she probably didn't work in the Warden offices, of course, because they only had a couple of small offices out of seven floors, and the others were all occupied.

I moved in behind the woman, smiled when she smiled, and she carded me into the building and took off for the stairs. I, feeling lazy, went for the elevator. The lobby was quiet and dimly lit, going for soothing and achieving a state of restfulness usually reserved for dropping into a nap. The elevators were slow—it was a general rule of the universe that the shorter the building, the slower the elevators—and I killed time by trying to imagine what the hell I was going to do if I got up there and found a major fight in progress. I wasn't going to be of any help, that much was sure.

I was hoping like hell that it was a downed-phone-line problem. Weak, but sometimes optimism is the only drug that works.

But it's sadly temporary in its effects.

The front door of the Warden offices looked like somebody had taken a sledgehammer to it—splintered in half, raw wood shining naked under the sleek brown finish. The lock was shattered, pieces of it scattered for ten feet down the carpeted hallway. The windows on either side were gaping, glassless holes, and I felt the crunch of broken pieces under my shoes as I walked carefully toward the destruction.

I was half afraid I was going to find everybody dead, given the state of the door, but I heard voices almost immediately. I recognized the slow, Carolina-honey voice of my ex-boss.

The tension in me let go with a rush of relief. John Foster was still alive, and I was off the hook.

I knocked on the shell of a door and leaned over to look through the opening.

John—still in a shirt and tie, which was his version of business casual—was standing, arms folded. With him was Ella, his right-hand assistant; she was a dumpy, motherly Warden with moderately weak weather skills but a stellar ability to keep John's stubborn, independent group working together.

Speaking of which, none of the others were anywhere in sight.

Ella looked exasperated. While John dressed like he'd been interrupted on his way to a board meeting, Ella might have been called out of giving her tile a good grouting: blue jeans, a sloppy T-shirt, a flowered Hawaiian-style shirt over that. She had graying, coarse hair that looked windblown.

They both turned toward me when I knocked, and Ella's mouth fell open. "Jo!" she yelled at ear-bleeding volume, dashed for the door, and knocked it back with a nudge of her Nike-clad foot. Before I could say "El!" she had me in a warm, soft hug, and then was dragging me over the threshold into the office.

Which was a wreck, too. Not as much as the door, but definitely not in the best of shape. Computers tossed around, papers lying everywhere, chairs overturned. The filing cabinets had tipped over, and the big metal drawers were out, their contents spilling in waterfalls of folders to the floor. Everything looked thoroughly bashed and dented.

"Love what you've done with the place. Sort of *Extreme Makeover* meets *Robot Wars*," I said. John—middle-aged, fit, graying at the temples in fine patriarchal style—smiled at me, but his heart wasn't in it. He looked strained and a little sick. "Okay, that was lame, I admit it. What happened?"

"We're trying to figure that out," John said, and extended his hand. "Sorry, Joanne. Good to see you, but as you can see, we're having a little bit of a crisis."

"Paul was trying to raise you on the phone and couldn't

get an answer. He sent me to check up." I looked around, eyebrows raised. "Robbery?"

"I doubt it," Ella said, and kicked a destroyed flat-screen monitor moodily. "They didn't take the electronics, and there wasn't any cash here. Maybe it was kids, smashing things up."

"You're not going to say *kids today,* are you? Because I never really thought of you as grandmotherly, despite the hair."

That earned me a filthy look.

John sighed and put his hands in his trouser pockets, watching me. "We're fine, thanks. Tell Paul I'm sorry. My cell battery ran down hours ago. How are you?" He sounded guarded, which wasn't unexpected. I realized, from the wary light in his eyes, that my arrival was looking more and more suspicious. I mean, he'd taken me for a ride and practically accused me of corruption, and here we were, standing in his wrecked offices, and I was saying I'd been sent by the boss.

I could see how it could be misinterpreted.

"I didn't do this," I said. "You know me better than that, John."

John and Ella exchanged looks. "Yeah," Ella agreed. "We do." John didn't say anything. He kept his arms folded.

I took a deep breath and plunged in over my head. "Any trouble with the Djinn on your end?"

"What?" John frowned. "No. Of course not." He had a Djinn, of course. Ella, so far as I knew, didn't. Only four Wardens in Florida were equipped with magical assistants and, by last count, only about two hundred in all of North and South America. It was an alarmingly low number, until you considered two hundred Djinn who might decide to kill off Wardens, in which case it was alarmingly high. "What are you talking about? What kind of trouble?"

"Some of the Djinn are breaking free of their masters. You haven't heard?"

Another look between the two of them. Silent communication, and me without my decoder ring. "No," John finally said. "Not about that."

"But you heard about some of the Wardens going rogue."

He looked grimmer. "Yes. And that's a subject I don't think we should be discussing with you."

A not-so-subtle reminder that I wasn't in the Warden business anymore, and therefore not privy to the fun, interesting politics. I changed the subject with a wave around the trashed office. "Think this is related?"

"I doubt it."

"Yeah? You get this kind of thing often around here?"

"Never," Ella put in. "I guess it *could* be kids, though the timing's odd. But Djinn wouldn't have a reason to do this, and if a Warden did it, well, there must have been a reason."

"Were they out to steal records? Destroy them?" I asked.

Oh, boy. Another significant glance.

"Again," John said, "I think we're on a subject that's off limits. Look, you did what Paul asked, you checked. We're fine. I think you should go now."

It hurt. I'd worked for John for a long time, and we'd been friends. Not bosom-buddy friends, but strong acquaintances, good to get together for the occasional drink, chat about family and friends, exchange Christmas presents. I'd trusted him with my life. I couldn't believe that had changed overnight.

But maybe I should have known, considering how many things were changing overnight these days.

"Jo, don't take it personally. You did quit, you know," Ella said. "And I'm still finding that hard to believe, sunshine. You're the most dedicated Warden I've ever met."

"I *was* the most dedicated Warden you ever met," I said. "Trust me, I had reasons."

"Well, if you quit over some dumb disagreement, it's a bad time for it," she said. "Bad Bob is gone and we've down three Wardens around here. From what I've heard, half the senior members of the organization are dead or disabled, and the other half can't decide what to do about it. We're barely holding together."

I hadn't come to listen to the we-need-you-back speech, but something Ella had said stopped me. "Three team members?" I asked. "Me, Bad Bob . . . who else?"

"Ella," John warned. She ignored him and kept talking.

"We lost another Weather Warden two nights ago," Ella said. "Carol Shearer. Car accident."

Another Djinn casualty, probably. They used natural forces to do the dirty work, not their own hands. They hit hard and fast, before a Warden could react to give their Djinn commands, and if the Djinn wasn't commanded to be proactive, or wasn't in the mood, then Ashan was the winner. Maybe he was systematically working his way through the ranks, testing.

Maybe John had already been targeted for death, but his Djinn had protected him without orders. The two of them had always seemed to enjoy a good professional relationship.

"I'm sorry to hear about Carol," I said. "But I can't come back right now even if you'd have me. And frankly, I wouldn't be any good to you if I did. I've got some, ah, issues."

John gave me the unfocused, faraway look of someone using Oversight. Whatever he saw, he went a shade graver and nodded. No comments. He'd seen the damage that had been done to me.

"Thanks for the offer, anyway," he said. Not that I'd really made one.

"Let me help you clean up. Least I can do, after all the chaos I've caused over the years."

John hesitated, but hell, he was shorthanded. I called Paul and reassured him all was well. While I was doing that, John called up his Djinn—who was a sweet-faced young man with glittering white-diamond eyes—and got the worst of the big damage repaired with a few murmured commands. I kept an eagle eye on *that,* believe me . . . but I didn't see any indication of an impending rebellion. He and his Djinn got on well. Always had. I sensed a certain restrained fondness between them—not love, and not even friendship, but a good partnership. In many ways, John Foster was the poster child for what a Warden ought to be.

It depressed me. It reminded me of just how much I wasn't, even when I was at my best. I was a messy, sloppy, emotional maverick. I couldn't color inside the lines even when I wanted to.

I helped Ella with the grunt work of restoring files to the cabinets, and as I did, I realized that most of the folders had to do with personnel. Detailed records of everything that we'd done, throughout our tenure with the Wardens. Ah, so *this* was where all those reports went to die . . . nice to know that all those hours spent typing on a keyboard actually had some kind of effect. I'd half suspected all my hard work just disappeared into the aetheric, where it got eaten by hungry demons. Or malicious Free Djinn.

About the fifteenth folder I picked up—and it was huge, papers spilling everywhere—had my name on it. I paused, startled, and flipped it open. The clips that held reports in the file were missing, and everything was crammed in at odd angles, as if it had been gone through fast.

The memo on top was signed by Paul Giancarlo, National Warden Pro Tem. It was an order to keep me under close surveillance for any suspicious activities related to fraud, blackmail, and illegal trading in weather control.

I felt a wave of cold rush over me, and in its backwash came another one of heat, burning down from the top of my head and taking up residence somewhere in my gullet. In the memo, Paul practically accused me of collusion with two other Wardens—one of them Bad Bob—in carrying out a scheme to steer tropical storms, hurricanes, and tornadoes toward certain areas of the coastline, where an outfit named Paradise Kingdom seemed to be making a business of building expensive resorts and condominiums, only to have them destroyed before opening by bad weather.

For the insurance money.

The score so far: storms four, Paradise Kingdom zero. They'd never actually opened a single property.

Paradise Kingdom. I remembered that name, and it came back with a jolt . . . the drive out along the coast. A dead dad and kids. Tornadoes twisting the under-construction hotel to wreckage.

I flipped pages. The photos showed shoddy construction, with detailed notes. Substandard parts. Bad wiring. Reused materials. If the buildings had ever actually opened, they'd have been deathtraps—but the insurance records showed payouts as if the construction had been to the finest possible standards.

I'd never even *heard* of Paradise Kingdom, but I was starting to shake with fury and a little bit of fear.

The folder was snatched out of my hands and slapped shut. John frowned at me, handed it to Ella, who mutely began straightening up the papers inside it.

"Let me guess," I said. "I wasn't supposed to see that." Except Ella must have thought differently; she'd pointedly ignored the folder lying all by itself, and left it to me to pick up.

"You know I can't talk to you about it."

"Don't I have the right to at least try to clear my name?"

"Nobody's blackened your name," he said, and crossed his arms. He looked tired. There was more gray in his hair than I remembered. "Look, yes, there's talk; there has been talk ever since Bad Bob died. Lots of people think you killed him to shut him up."

"It was self-defense!" I practically yelled it. He nodded, arms folded; the body language of rejection. "Dammit, John, don't you believe me? You knew that old bastard! He was a corrupt, scary old man—"

"He was a legend," John said softly. "You killed a legend. You have to understand that no matter what he was, what bad things he did, nobody's going to remember that now. What they remember are his accomplishments, not his flaws."

He stuck a demon down my throat! I wanted to scream, but I couldn't. And it didn't matter. John was right, Bad Bob was an untouchable saint, and I was the evil, scheming bitch who'd slaughtered a helpless old guy in his own home. No doubt the Paradise Kingdom scheme had been all his; it had all the hallmarks of his style. He'd probably involved a few other Wardens in it, for profit, but he hadn't included me. He'd known that I would have busted him.

I could practically hear him laughing, out there in hell. I hoped it was extra hot and he was drinking Tabasco sauce to cool off.

"I don't know anything about this," I said. John gave me a funny look, then turned to Ella. She shot him another glance back, raised her eyebrows, and nodded toward the other side of the room. John walked silently away. His Djinn was standing there, fixing up a shattered desk with long, smooth strokes of his fingers over wood. Where it had splintered, it fused together seamlessly.

"John can't say anything about this," Ella said, "but I've only got a couple of years to retirement; I couldn't give a shit what the Wardens do to me. Petal, claiming ignorance about Paradise Kingdom isn't going to do you any good. You'd better come up with another story, fast."

"What? Why?"

She straightened more papers in my file, reached for a bracket, and pushed it through the holes of the folder. Began systematically attaching reports to it. "Paradise Kingdom's owned by your boss, Marvin McLarty. Marvelous Marvin. You know, the 'weatherman.'" She paused to give it air quotes and an eyeroll. "So you can't exactly claim that you don't have a connection to it. He hired you without an interview. You must have known him before you took the job."

That bastard. That *snake.* That . . . horny, no-good little poodle! I couldn't believe it. He was too *stupid* to be venal. Right? Marvelous Marvin, investing in property fraud schemes with *Wardens*? That meant he knew about them, in the first place . . . and she was right, I'd sent in a resume, and Marvin had hired me after giving me one look. I'd thought it was, well, for the cheesecake value, and I'm sure that made the deal sweeter for him. But it must have been something more.

Somebody must have told him to do it. Somebody, maybe, who wanted a convenient scapegoat if things got scary for them. Because on paper, I damn sure *looked* guilty.

If Marvin was involved with Bad Bob, that explained a lot. His percent accuracy rate, for one thing, which would have been a source of amusement to somebody like Bad Bob. He'd have been able to pull it off, too, without attracting Warden notice. Bad Bob's rating had been far higher than John Foster's, and besides, he was a legend. Who questioned a legend?

Bad Bob Biringanine had been willing to sell his ethics and reputation for a nice house, a tidy bank account, and all the comforts of organized crime. But . . . *Marvelous Marvin*? Who could take him seriously as a bad guy? And maybe that was precisely the point.

Ella was watching me, waiting for an answer. I didn't have one.

"Don't you believe I'm innocent?" I asked her.

"Of course I do, honey. Don't be ridiculous!" I saw her eyes stay fixed and steady on me, in a way that only happens when the answer is a flat-out lie. "Even if you did do it, hell, the whole organization's falling apart. It's pretty much every woman for herself right now." She kept staring at me.

And I realized something fairly significant. There was still weather manipulation going on, even with Bad Bob dead. If I took myself out of the equation, there was a pretty limited pool of suspects.

Not John. I shifted my stare to him, watching the way he talked with his Djinn, the way he listened attentively, the way the Djinn moved in such an open, easy fashion.

No fear, no guarding, no resistance. John was one of the good guys; I knew it in my heart.

Carol Shearer, whom I hadn't known well, might have been in it, but I'd never know, would I? Because she was dead, killed in a car accident.

If it hadn't been Carol . . .

Why was Ella still looking at me?

"Does John know?" I asked her.

"About . . . ?"

"Marvin."

"Oh, sure. That's why he won't talk to you. It's killing him, you know; he wants to believe in you, but . . . ah, hell, honey, he's an idealist. You know how John can get. No sense of the real world."

I decided to jump in the alligator pond. "Well," I said, lowering my voice to a just-us-girls whisper, "confidentially, I wasn't in on it. But you know that, right? I mean, Bad Bob told me about it that morning, and I was thinking it over, but I had no idea it was still going on. It *is* still going on, though. Right?"

She blinked and said, "You don't think *I* have anything to do with it, do you?"

I raised my eyebrows.

And, after a split second, she lowered her eyelids and whispered, "Not while he's here."

I'm glad I wasn't quite looking at her; she probably would have read the heartbreak in my eyes. But she didn't notice. She turned away and finished putting the papers of my file in order, and bent the brackets to hold everything inside, nice and neat. I noticed there were some papers she hadn't put back. She shifted the stack in my direction with an unmistakable take-them nod.

I felt sick, but managed to hold on to my smile. I collected the papers and stuck them into my purse, trying to look casual about it. Ella watched me with a strange little smile, then winked and turned away to grub in folders again.

We were collaborating.

I pulled in a deep breath and walked over to John and

his Djinn. The Djinn focused on me, swept those white-fire eyes over me, and did such an obvious double take it was almost funny. I knew it wasn't my outfit—it wasn't *that* bad—and after the initial confusion I figured out what he was focusing so intently on.

I put a hand over my lower stomach, instinctively, as if I could somehow shield my unborn Djinn child from his stare.

He yanked his gaze back up, and I lifted my chin and dared him to say something.

He just lifted an eyebrow so dryly it almost made me laugh, then turned to John and said, "Will that be all, John?" He had an English accent, very butler-y. John thanked him politely and poof, we were Djinn free. I wondered what the Djinn's name was, but it was impolite to ask. When you met a Warden and a Djinn together, you weren't supposed to even acknowledge the Djinn.

I don't think that was etiquette invented by the Djinn.

"I'm sorry, John, but I need to get going," I said. He nodded and extended a hand for me to shake; I did, and then held on to it. I leaned forward and brushed a kiss across his cheek. He smelled of a dry, astringent cologne and a wisp of tobacco. "Take care," I said, and dropped my voice to a whisper while I was next to his ear. "Don't trust anyone. *Anyone.*"

I didn't want to point the finger at Ella specifically, not yet, but a general warning never did anyone any harm. He pulled back, frowning, and then composed himself and gave me a placid nod. "You take care, now."

"You, too," I said, and made my way through the still-messy room to the Djinn-repaired door.

It hadn't been a robbery. Somebody had come in here looking for records, and they'd gone through my file like a fine-toothed comb.

It looked like everybody wanted to keep track of me—good guys, bad guys, people I didn't even recognize as being on one side or the other. Who the hell knew.

I was seriously considering grabbing David's bottle and my sister, and fleeing the country.

INTERLUDE

On the island, the storm strips hundred-year-old trees bare, then snaps the trunks and throws them with lethal force into every man-made structure in the way. Walls disintegrate. Roofs disappear into a blizzard of broken wood and tile. Even palm fronds become deadly cutting instruments, driven by winds of unimaginable force.

The storm stops, turns, and begins to feed.

Death comes mostly from the storm surge, which creeps up over the land not in a wave but with the constant pace of a pail poured into a tub. Water rises to fill houses in minutes, drowning frantic occupants who can't flee into the killing winds. Some structures, farther from the shore, begin to shudder and breathe with the storm, walls collapsing outward, then pulling upright again, each vibration shattering more of the foundations.

Men, women, children, and animals are pulled from shelter and swept into the fury, where they're stripped first of clothes, then of flesh, then shattered into ragged bits.

The carnage is constant and merciless, and the storm feeds, and feeds, and feeds. It has no will to move on from the feast. Even when the island is stripped bare, to the rocks, the winds and waves continue to lash and lick the last fragments of life.

The exposed bedrock blackens. Even the algae die.

When the storm has sucked every breath from a land that once held millions, it buries it under the sea and moves on, searching for its next victim.

This is where I come in.

SEVEN

As above, so below. The old saying was holding true today. I got to the security doors of the lobby just as the clouds cut loose and the rain began.

Florida rain is like a faucet—two speeds, flood and stop. The setting was definitely on flood this morning. I stood at the glass and looked out at the thick gray wall of water—couldn't really make out the parking lot behind it—and looked down at my shoes. They weren't rain-appropriate, but then the rest of the outfit wasn't exactly going to be repelling a lot of water, either.

At least it's just rain, I told myself. Could be worse . . .

And right on cue, a white stab of lightning split the sky outside, close enough that I didn't need Warden senses to register the power jolt. I felt it sweep over my skin and draw every tiny hair to shivering attention.

The thunder that followed shook the glass and set off a howling chorus of car alarms.

The next strike was about fifty feet away from me, right outside in the parking lot, and it came as a fork of blue-white light reaching down and grounding itself in one of the cars. *What the hell . . . ?* It shouldn't have done that. There were lots of taller objects to draw it, but then lightning was whimsical that way. And vicious.

I jumped back from the glass and slapped my hands over my ears as the thunder exploded, and couldn't see a damn thing for the overloaded white-hot afterburn on my retinas. I blinked fiercely as I waited for my eyes to

return to normal and cursed my lack of strength as oversight would have been a real asset at the moment. Except
that I was too weak to get to it, and it was only as
the thunder died to an ominous, continuing growl that I
realized the car that had taken the brunt of that lightning
bolt had been midnight blue, lean, and sleek.

In other words, it had been Mona. *My* car.

"Oh, damn," I whispered, and blinked faster. Not that
I could really see anything through the incredibly dense
rain out there. No, wait, I could. There was something
flickering orange out there, barely visible . . .

My car was on freaking *fire*.

"Joanne!" John Foster, breathless, came pelting up behind me, grabbed me, and threw me to the floor. He
landed on top of me, and while I was busy registering
the unique ways a marble floor didn't make for a comfortable landing area, something outside exploded.

Not lightning. Something more man-made.

The explosion blew in the windows in a bright-edged
shower, and the rain followed, pounding in before the
glass even hit the marble. I smelled burning plastic and
metal and tried to get up, but John held me down with
an elbow across my shoulders. He was breathing hard. I
could feel his heart pounding against my back.

"Let go!" I yelled. "Dammit! John! Let go!"

He finally did, rolling off in a crunch of glass, and as
I flipped over I saw that he'd sustained some cuts, but
not a lot. So far, we'd been lucky.

"You all right?" he asked. I nodded. "Come with me."

He scrambled up to his feet and held out his hand. I
looked back at the parking lot, or at least what I could
see of it; there was an unholy bonfire out there, consum-
ing at least three cars.

The center of it was the blackened shell of the Viper
formerly known as Mona, who wouldn't be taking me on
any more fast drives, ever again. I gulped and clutched
my purse tight and took John's hand.

He led me out of the lobby, past the arriving cluster
of alarmed tenants and late-breaking security personnel,

to the stairwell. He hit the stairs running, tasseled loafers pounding, and I had to hustle to keep up. John had been working out, or else adrenaline was a wonderful fitness drug.

We ran full speed up seven floors, all the way to the top of the building, to the door that was marked ROOF ACCESS, AUTHORIZED PERSONNEL ONLY. And I was very thankful when we slowed down at the top, because my shoes were not of the cross-training persuasion, but then he grabbed me and towed me toward the exit.

"John!" I yelled, and yanked him to a stop before he could stiff-arm the ALARM WILL SOUND crossbar. "John, wait! What's going on?"

"You were right about the Djinn!" he yelled back. "We have to go, *now*! They're coming!"

Oh, crap.

He broke free and hit the door release. An alarm added its shriek to the general confusion—the fire alarms were going off, too, and I wondered if the fire had spread somehow from the parking lot to the building—and as the door opened out onto the roof, rain and wind shouldered through the opening to hit us like linebackers. I staggered, but John reached back and grabbed my wrist and dragged me outside into the chaos of the downpour.

"John!" I screamed, over the continuing roll of thunder. "It's not safe out here! The lightning—"

"Shut up; I'll take care of the lightning!" And he could. John was a highly competent Weather Warden in his own right. Even as he finished saying it, I felt a ripple over my skin, and my blunted Warden senses registered something whipping through the aetheric at us like a striking snake. . . .

John let go of me, turned, and focused his attention on a thick silver stanchion fixed to a corner of the roof.

Lightning hissed down. I could feel it struggling to reach us, fighting . . .

And then turning to hit the stanchion. The building's lightning protection system bled it off into the ground through a network of inlaid wiring. I could feel the heat of it blast over me from where I stood.

But I also felt how close it had been. Something was directing that lightning. Controlling it. Something a great deal stronger than John Foster.

He knew it, too; I saw it in the fixed, desperate set of his expression. "Come on!" John was tugging me onward, to a second concrete bunker on top of the roof. The door was propped open. He grabbed it just as another flash of lightning came out of nowhere, streaking for us. John wasn't ready, I knew it—he'd just spent a tremendous amount of energy redirecting that first bolt, and this one was just as big, if not bigger. And it was obviously bent on getting us.

What I had to throw into the pot barely qualified as power at all, but I did it, reaching out and trying to grab hold of the enormous burst of energy that was coming toward us. Electrons were shifting, jittering, realigning into polarities to create a path. All I had to do was snap a few . . . and I couldn't do it. As fast as I broke the chain, it whipped back at us, those tiny molecular polarities spinning and locking faster than I could even read their force structure. Rain lashed, and a gust of wind howled over us in a scream of rage. I felt John desperately working to save us, and more power pouring in from outside trying to save us, but it was no good. The bolt was going to hit us dead on, and we were out of time. Whatever had hold of this storm wasn't going to be denied.

I dived one way, knowing it wouldn't do any good; John dived the other.

I hit and rolled, and saw the lightning spear straight into John's chest.

"No!" Maybe I screamed it, maybe I didn't; whatever sound I made was lost in the massive rush of energy that slammed into his flesh. In its burst of brilliant light, I saw John's diamond-eyed Djinn standing nearby in the shadows, still and quiet, watching his master die. No expression on his face at all.

He didn't move to help.

John, cut off from the Wardens network, had never heard the instructions to give his Djinn a preemptive command to defend him. He'd never really understood the danger. And if he had, he probably wouldn't have believed it.

John dropped without a sound the second the lightning crackled and sizzled out. I couldn't see for long, agonizing seconds, so I fumbled my way over gravel and tar to take him in my arms. He was burning hot. As my vision cleared I saw that there were black burns at the top of his head, on the palms of his hands, and that his pants were riddled with sizzling, smoking holes. His shoes were melted to his feet.

I burned my fingers trying to check his pulse, but it was silent. His heart had taken a full jolt, and his nervous system was fried beyond repair.

The Djinn left the shadows and walked over to where I was huddled in the cold, pounding rain with John's weight across my lap.

"You could have done something," I said numbly. "Why didn't you do something? *He was your friend!*"

He looked down at me. Rain didn't touch him, just misted away an inch from his form. He was changing already, shifting from that quiet, unassuming young man John's will had imposed on him to a larger, stronger body. His hair lightened from brown to white, rippling with subtle undertones of color like an opal. Albino-pale skin. The down-home shirt and blue jeans transformed to rich, pale silk and velvet. He looked elegant and merciless and slightly barbaric.

"He wasn't my friend," the Djinn said. "A master can't be friends with a slave. There's no trust without equality."

I choked on the taste of cold rain and burned flesh in my mouth. I wanted to weep, because the Djinn was right. No equality. Just because we were fond of the Djinn didn't make them friends. Just because we loved them . . .

What had I done when I'd taken David as my servant? Had it destroyed the trust we'd had? How long would it take for that betrayal to soak into him, to erode his love for me, to turn it toxic?

Maybe the flaws that made him an Ifrit had started here, in me.

"You're free now," said a voice from behind me. I gasped and turned, blinking rain out of my eyes. It sounded like Ashan, and yes, it *was* Ashan, natty and businessman-perfect in his gray suit and chilly tie. His eyes had gone the color of the storm. Not a drop was touching him, of course. He walked forward, and where he walked, the rain just . . . vanished. He came to a halt a few feet from me, but he wasn't paying the least attention to me, or the dead man in my arms. His focus was all on the other Djinn.

"You bastard," I said, and his eyes cut to me and shut me up. Instantly. With the unmistakable impression that I was one single heartbeat away from joining John in the heavenly choir.

"I'm not talking to you," he said. "Shut up, meat."

"Are you addressing me?" the other Djinn asked. He still had a British accent, clipped and precise and very old-school, which went very oddly with the barbaric splendor of his albino rock-star look.

"Of course. I came to give you the opportunity to join us."

"Fortuitous timing."

Ashan's smile was cold and heartless. "Isn't it just?"

The other Djinn smiled in return. Not a comforting sight. "I find myself free for the first time in memory. Why should I give up that freedom to another master, even one so . . . important as you?"

Ashan nudged John's body carefully with the toe of his elegantly polished shoe. No giveaway misting at the knees for Ashan. He was the Dress For Success poster child of the new age.

"Well, first, I'm the one who granted you freedom by killing *this*," he said.

"It's not freedom if I exchange one form of slavery for another." The Djinn shrugged. "Not very appealing, I must say. And what would Jonathan think about it?"

"Jonathan?" Ashan put all his contempt into it. "Do you really want to be on the side of the one who made us slaves in the first place?"

I was shivering, cold, drenched, and numbed, but that still made me blink. "What?" I didn't meant to say it out loud, but when you hear something like that, well, the question naturally blurts itself out.

This time, Ashan decided I was worthy of an answer. "You didn't think this master-slave relationship was the natural order, did you? Did you really believe that *humans* rank higher than Djinn? Things are perverted in this world, little girl, and they have been ever since *Jonathan* gave the Wardens power over us."

"When—how long—"

"Yesterday," the other Djinn said quietly. "To us, it was yesterday."

I wasn't going to get an answer to that one, I could tell; Ashan had made his point, and I was no longer relevant except as something to nod toward when he wanted to drive home contempt.

"You can't want to follow Jonathan," Ashan said. The other Djinn met his eyes. Thunder rolled overhead, and they both waited out the roar. "If you follow me, you can free others."

"You mean kill," the Djinn said calmly. "Kill Wardens."

"Exactly." A full, sharp-toothed wolf's smile. "Come on, don't tell me you don't want to. You can start with this one, if you're interested. Believe me, she's got it coming."

The Djinn turned diamond-white eyes to stare at me. I gulped air and frantically rummaged the cupboards of my bare inner storehouse for power, *any* power, that might be strong enough to defend me against him. What Jonathan had gifted me with was definitely burning down to its embers. I'd used up everything I had, except for what I was living on, and that couldn't last.

The Djinn shook his head, smiled a little, and said, "I won't fight for Jonathan. But I won't kill for you, Ashan; like us, the Wardens exist for a reason."

"So you'll do what? Live as a rogue? An outcast?" Ashan sneered at the whole idea, and took a step forward. I felt tension snap tight between them. "Better off dead, I'd say."

Behind him, the stairwell door swung open. Silently. Nobody was touching it. A flash of lightning revealed a man standing there, tall and lean, hands at his sides.

Lewis's face was hard, expressionless, and *very* frightening.

"Leave him alone," he said, and stepped out into the rain. Unlike the Djinn, he didn't try to hide from it, and he didn't do any flashy redirection of energy. The water pounded over him, soaking his hair flat to his head, saturating his flannel shirt, T-shirt, and jeans in seconds.

He just didn't care.

Ashan turned to face him. I felt the crackle of power notch up—not like lightning. This was something else. Something . . . bigger. A little like the resonance that occurred between me and Lewis when things got a little close, only this was dissonance, disharmony, a jagged and cutting chaos.

"He has a choice," Lewis said. "He can join you, he can join Jonathan, or he can help the Ma'at put all this right again. Restore the balance of things. Stop the violence and the killing. Because this has to stop, Ashan, before everything goes to hell."

"You mean, everything in the human world."

"No. I mean *everything*. Djinn live here, too. And up there." Lewis indicated the aetheric, somehow, with a jerk of his chin. "If you're in this world, you're part of it. There's no escaping it. Maybe you think you're here to be gods, but you're not, no more than we are. We're all subordinate to something else."

"Well, maybe you are," Ashan said, and checked the line of his suit jacket with a casual flick of his fingers. "I have to tell you, I don't intend to be subordinate to anything or anyone. Ever again."

"That includes Jonathan, I suppose."

"It definitely includes Jonathan."

"Have you happened to mention that to him? Because I don't see the scars. I think you've been avoiding him since you decided on this little rebellion of yours."

Ashan's smile was thin, bloodless, and unamused. "I didn't come here to trade witty remarks with *you*, human. Go away."

"Fine. All us humans will just—"

"Not this one. This one's *mine*." Ashan reached out and grabbed me by the shoulder, and boy, it *hurt*. First of all, his hands were like forged iron. Second, they weren't really flesh, not as I could understand it—not the kind of flesh that David always wore, or even Jonathan. Ashan was just an illusion, and what was underneath was sharp and hurtful and cold.

I wanted him to stop touching me, but when I tried to yank away, it was like trying to pull back from an industrial vise.

Lewis went very, very still. *Oh, boy.* This wasn't going to end well, and I really didn't want to be in the middle. Lewis had tons of power, rarely used; Earth was his weakest, Weather his strongest. He hadn't been able to work miracles against tons of sand and a dying boy, but here, on this playing field . . .

He just might be equal to a Djinn.

"Let go," Lewis said.

Ashan actually grinned. It wasn't his best expression, but it was certainly one of the most human I'd ever seen on him. Not to mention one of the scariest. The rain hitting me turned from ice-cold to blood-warm to scalding-hot in seconds, thanks to the sudden ramp-up of power igniting the air around us.

"Lewis—" I didn't get the chance to finish the warning

because Ashan, without the slightest hint he was going to act, tried to set Lewis on fire.

Lewis batted away the attack without effort. I'd been burning the last of my power to reach Oversight when it happened, so I'd seen it . . . a white-hot burst of power arrowing for him, encircling him in a bubble of energy, pressing inward . . . and dissolving at a single touch of his hand. The energy went chaotic, bouncing back at Ashan, vectoring away to slam into other things, like the swirling fury of the storm, which sucked it up and let loose with another fusillade of lightning bolts overhead.

Lewis had barely even *moved*. Because he was always so careful with his power, such a good steward of it, it was easy to forget that he was, without question, the most powerful Warden breathing. He rarely lost his temper or acted without thought for the consequences . . . unlike me. But when he did . . .

"Ashan," he said, and his voice had gone into a velvet-deep growl range that made me shiver deep inside, "the next Warden you hurt gets you destroyed so completely that no one will remember you ever existed. And I mean that."

Ashan stared at him. Lewis stared back, unmoving, dripping with rain and fiercely elemental.

As if he was made of the elements he controlled.

"You aren't eternal," Lewis said, and there was something in his words that sounded not quite human in its depth and power. "You were born into this world, and you can die in it. You've got no place to run."

"A human can't threaten . . ."

"I'm talking to you as someone who can hear the whisper of the Mother as she sleeps. Do you really think that makes me *human*?"

Ashan's teal eyes flared gray for a second, then darkened again. Not quite under control.

"The Mother doesn't talk to meat."

"She talks to Wardens like me. Wardens who hold all the keys to power. You should remember that. You were around when Jonathan died as a human."

Ashan's iron-cold grip on me suddenly relaxed, and I overbalanced pulling away from him. Lewis helped me up. I felt cold and shaky and unreasonably weak, as if the Djinn had been sucking something out of me I couldn't afford to lose. Strength. Independence. Hope.

Lewis's touch brought all of that rushing back. Especially the independence part, which made me immediately pull away from his support. "I'm fine," I said. His dark eyes flicked to me and were momentarily just a man's again, harassed and short-tempered. "I can take care of myself."

"I know," he said. "Go. Somebody will meet you downstairs."

I couldn't seem to make myself move. Raindrops were pattering and pooling in John Foster's open eyes. "Ashan killed John. Why?"

"Because he could," Lewis said grimly. "Because John had something he wanted."

For a blind second I thought he meant me, but Lewis was looking past me, at the albino, opal-haired rock-'n'-roll Djinn.

"Recruits," Lewis finished. "Right, Ashan? You need cannon fodder. Djinn to toss into Jonathan's path to slow him down, because he's coming for you, and when he finds you it's not going to be a pretty sight."

The other Djinn looked at Ashan and tilted his head to one side. No expression on his face, but I had the sense of a razor-sharp mind at work. Ashan was a user, no question of that. And surely the other Djinn, who had a lot more experience of him than I did, had to know it.

"Go downstairs," Lewis said to me.

"Not without you."

Lewis let out a breathless, near-silent laugh. "Believe me, I'm right behind you. Most of that was bluff."

The albino Djinn took a sudden, pantherlike step forward, hand raised. Ashan fell back, assuming a defensive position.

Lewis urged me in the direction of the stairwell. "Don't

wait. Get out of the building. I can't guarantee it won't come down if this turns violent."

"Lewis—"

He didn't waste time arguing, just extended his hand toward me. I felt a burst of wind hit me, precisely in my midsection, knocking me back five steps to bounce against the stairwell railing, and the door slammed to cut us off.

Something hit the roof outside with enough force to shudder the whole building. I saw dust sift down from the ceiling and heard an inhuman groan go through the place as concrete and steel shifted.

I kicked off my shoes, stuck them in the purse still hanging from my shoulder, and began running down the steps as fast as I could go. On the fifth floor I ran into refugees. *Shit.* There were tenants still in the building. I abandoned my escape attempt and banged through the fire door, running from office to office rattling doorknobs and yelling for people to get the hell out. A cube farm on the fourth floor yielded up four people wearing headphones, oblivious to everything; I yanked them bodily out of their ergonomic chairs and sent them running for the stairwell. I interrupted a courting couple in a supply closet on the third floor; they ran for the exits still fastening up clothes.

Ella was nowhere to be found. I wondered if she'd had advance warning of the attack, and if so, whose side she was on. If she'd left John to die, it damn sure wasn't my side.

The cops were just pulling up in the parking lot, along with the fire department, when the evacuees began pouring screaming out of the building. Chaos. I left with them, got into the parking lot, and whirled to shield my eyes from the rain and get a look at what was happening on the roof.

The roof was on fire. Figures struggling in the flames. One hell of a fight going on up there, and a continuous roar of thunder as lightning struck again, and again, and again . . .

As I watched, the roof collapsed into the seventh floor and a huge roar of hissing flames shot up into the sky.

"No!" I screamed and lunged for the door. Arms wrapped around me from behind and held me still. I kicked and struggled, but they were strong arms, and besides, I wasn't at my best. I twisted enough to catch a glimpse of who was holding me, and felt the fight go out of my tense muscles.

I didn't know the burly guy who was giving me the modified Heimlich, but I knew the natty old man standing next to him, neatly covered from the rain by a black umbrella. His name was Charles Ashworth II, and he was one of the senior members of the Ma'at. He was flawlessly dressed in a gray Italian suit, a fine white shirt, a blue silk tie. Conservative, that was Ashworth . . . he reminded me of a bitter, old version of Ashan, actually. He still had an I-smell-something-rotten expression that betrayed exactly what he thought about the world in general, and me in particular.

"Let go," he ordered, and Burly Guy loosened his arms. "Don't be stupid, woman. You're not a Fire Warden. You can't run into a burning building. Lewis, on the other hand, can no doubt stroll out without any problem at all."

He had a point. I resented it. "What are you doing here?"

Ashworth nodded toward the building. "Helping him."

"Helping him do what, exactly?"

"None of your concern." Ashworth tapped his black-and-silver cane on the pavement for emphasis. "You're neither needed nor wanted here, Miss Baldwin. I suggest you go back to your duties, presuming you have them. The Wardens seem to need all the help they can get these days."

He sounded pretty smug about it. I wanted to slug him, remembering John Foster's simple, quiet commitment to the work. His courage. His grace under fire.

Before I could suggest any anatomically impossible sexual actions to him, a figure came walking out of the billowing chaos of the side fire escape door. Lewis looked smoke-stained, but fine. I took a few steps toward him, winced at the bite of broken glass on my bare feet, and paused to brush them more or less clean and jam on my shoes. When my balance wavered, Lewis was there, a hand steadying my elbow even while his attention was fixed on Ashworth.

Overhead, the rain slacked off noticeably. Lewis again, setting balances. He wouldn't just get rid of it, he'd let it wind itself down. I couldn't feel the energy currents, but I imagined he was grounding it seamlessly through every available safe avenue. He was thorough that way.

"I couldn't get to them in time," he said. "Foster was already dead."

"And the Djinn?" Ashworth asked.

Lewis shook his head. "I don't know. At best, he was badly wounded. But I don't think he's joining Ashan." Ashworth's lips tightened and he turned away, cane tapping, to join a knot of umbrellas standing near the fire engine. The Ma'at had come in force, looked like. Not that they'd be a lot of help in a fight. None of them were Wardens, per se, except Lewis; they had power, but it wasn't on the level of someone like John Foster, or even me. Training, not talent.

Well, maybe today, they were on the level with little old whipped-puppy me. Which didn't make me feel any better.

"All right?" Lewis was asking me. I looked up to see his dark eyes focused on me.

"Peachy," I assured him. There was a quaver in my voice. "What the *hell* are you doing here?"

"Trying to stop the war," he said, and took advantage of his hold on my elbow to steer me out of the way of some firefighters unrolling more hose. The building was still burning, but not nearly as briskly. I could sense a distant, low thrum of power—Lewis was keeping the blaze tamped down, making it manageable. He could have killed it, I was sure, but Lewis was a subscriber to the philosophy of Ma'at. Everything in balance. He would be working to put all of the power that had just been expended back into some kind of order.

"What? You're going to stop the war singlehandedly?"

"Obviously not." Lewis got me into a neutral territory, somewhere between the firefighters, the cops, and the Ma'at, and turned me to face him. "Jo, I need you to promise me that you'll go back to your apartment, pack your bags, and get out of here. Today."

"I can't promise that." Even though I'd been thinking about it, before my car had been blown up.

"I need you to do this for me." His eyes searched my face. "I can't be worrying about where you are, what's happening to you."

And that lit a fuse on my temper. "I didn't ask you to be my babysitter, Lewis! I can take care of myself, I always have!"

"And if you weren't drained so far that you barely register as a Warden on the aetheric, I'd accept that," he shot back. "Did David do this to you?"

I met his eyes and didn't answer. He shook his head, anger sparking in his eyes, and deliberately looked away.

"Fine," he said. "But you can't let him feed off you like this. He'll kill both of you."

"I know."

"I'm serious. You need to let him go. You need to break the bottle."

"*I know!* Jonathan already made it clear, believe me." I didn't mention Rahel's counterargument. I wasn't sure I wanted him to know I hadn't decided. "I'm fine, dammit. Don't worry about me."

He let go, reluctantly, and turned away to talk to the Ma'at, who were already signaling him impatiently for a confab.

That's when I saw Jonathan standing at the fringes of the crowd, arms folded.

Jonathan himself, Master of the Djinn Universe, in the flesh. Commander in chief of one side of what might turn out to be a world-ending civil war.

He was disguised as a regular guy, dressed in black

jeans and heavy boots and a brown leather jacket, ball cap pulled down low over his eyes. As with Ashan, the rain bent around him. I didn't think anybody but me would notice; I doubted anybody but me could see him.

He was a hundred feet away, and there were dozens of people between us, but I felt the shock as his eyes locked onto me. I felt a burn inside, nothing comfortable, nothing like the connection I felt with David, or the purely heat-driven fizz between me and Lewis.

It was as if Jonathan *owned* me, the way I owned David. Was this how it felt for David? Invasive and sickening? As if his every breath depended on mine?

"I warned you," Jonathan said, and the bill of that ball cap dipped just a fraction.

Time stopped. Raindrops froze into glittering silver threads around me.

I was in Jonathan's world now.

He walked through the silent landscape, moving around statues of humans in his way, breaking rain into fragments against that invisible shield he carried with him.

"I can't do what you want," I said when he stopped just three steps away. My words sounded weirdly flat in the still, dead air. "If I let him go, he'll come after you, and that'll be the end, won't it? The end of everything. You're important. That's what Rahel's been trying to tell me from the first time I met you. You're the key to everything. Without you—"

He cut me off by sticking an accusatory finger in my face. "I told you what would happen. I *told* you, Joanne. Is this a habit with you, courting death? Because it's getting old. You're carrying around a kid, you know. Could devote a little thought to that while you're walking over the cliff and mooning about your undying love."

"It's not about me. It's you. I can't let David come after you, and he will if I break the bottle."

"Dammit!" His flare of fury was scary. It evaporated rain in a pulsing circle for about fifty feet in every direction. I felt my skin take on an instant burn. "Are you always this stupid, or is it a special feature just for me? *Break the damn bottle, Joanne!"*

"No."

"Not even to save yourself and the kid."

"No."

"Not even to save David."

Because that's what all this was about, I suddenly realized. Not the world, not the war, not me. David. His constant and pure devotion to David, who'd been his friend since the world was younger than I could even imagine.

Who'd died in his arms, as a human.

"Because I can save him," Jonathan said. "I know how."

"Yeah," I said, and locked stares with him. "I know, too. You die, he lives. And where does that leave the rest of us?"

Galaxies in his eyes. A vast and endless power, but it wasn't his own. He was a conduit. A window to something larger than any of us, Djinn or human.

"He takes my place," Jonathan said. "He lives. You live. The baby lives. He's strong enough to take Ashan. I'm too damn tired for this; I've been running the show for too long. I've made too many mistakes, and we need a fresh start."

Oh, God. It wasn't Ashan suddenly deciding to rebel on his own . . . Ashan had just picked up on something else: Jonathan's weakness, if you could describe somebody like him as weak. He just didn't want to go on anymore.

"No," I said again. "You can't do this. I'm sorry, but you're just going to have to gut it out and stop Ashan and put everything back the way it was. I'm not helping you commit suicide by David."

He looked at me for a long time, in that still silent place where time didn't exist. And I felt something like a shiver run through the world.

He raised his head toward the sky for a second, listening, and then shook his head again.

"That your final answer?" he asked.

Something about his expression almost made me change my mind, but I couldn't, I just couldn't let his need and his despair drive the game. This was too important.

"That's it," I said. "I'm not letting David go."

"You'll kill him. And he'll destroy you."

"So be it. Now go do your job and get things done. The world's more important than me and David, and dammit, it's more important than your death wish!"

He hated me. I felt it, strong as acid poured in an open wound.

"All I have to do is kill you," he said. It was barely a whisper. "You know that, right? You die, the baby dies, and I can still do exactly what I want. Everybody wins but you."

For a breathless second I thought he was going to do it. I could feel the impulse firing in him, could see the way it would happen—his hands around my head, turning with shocking strength, my spine snapping with the crisp sound of crumpled paper. The work of less than a second.

I remembered Quinn, helpless on the ground, coughing up blood. Terror in his eyes, at the end. Jonathan hadn't even hesitated.

"I know," I said. "Butch up and do it, if you're going to. Don't keep me in suspense."

He stared at me for a second, eyes wild and dark, and then smiled.

Smiled.

He reached out, pulled a fingertip slowly down the line of my cheek, and walked away. Hands in his pockets. Raindrops shattering in his wake.

And then time slammed back in a fevered rush, and the world *moved*.

He was gone.

And something was very, very, *very* wrong with me.

I cried out, wrapped my hands over my stomach, and felt the sudden emptiness inside. The spark was gone, the potential, the *child* that David had put inside of me.

I felt the last of the energy Jonathan had given me leak out. My vision went gray and blurry, and I felt my knees give way.

Falling.

Too much effort to breathe. Nothing left inside to live on. I was a black hole, empty and alone and dying in the rain.

David. I couldn't even call him. And if he came, it would only be more death, faster death, no comfort and no love in it.

Warm arms scooped me up. Fingers slid from my arm down to clasp my limp hand, and as the world telescoped to a black pinpoint I felt a warm pulse of power go through my skin, my bones, my body. Hot as the sun, liquid and silky and rich.

It wasn't enough.

My eyes were still open, and a little color swam out of the gray, but I couldn't focus, couldn't blink. Lewis was bent over me. He looked pale and desperate. He cupped my face in his hands, watching my eyes, and then ripped open my shirt and put his hands on my stomach, right where the worst of the emptiness hid itself.

That sensation came again, a slow and deliberate wave rippling through me to pool like hot molten gold somewhere just below my navel.

It drained away.

I was going, just . . . going.

"Oh no you don't," Lewis grated, and I felt him breathing into my open mouth, his life pouring into mine with such power and fury that the emptiness couldn't keep up with it. That was David, that emptiness. That was how I would die, sucked into that darkness, and he'd still be trapped and alone, forever a creature driven by hunger and unable to stop feeding. . . .

I didn't want this to end in nightmare.

I couldn't let it end that way.

I breathed.

Lewis was still bent over me, panting, shaking, and I

saw the golden light still spilling out of his fingers into
my stomach. A thick stream of life.

I knocked his hand away, and he leaned back and
braced himself unsteadily on wet pavement. Head down.
Gasping for air as if he'd been drowning.

I was almost sure he had been. I'd nearly taken him
down with me.

"Dammit," he said furiously. "What *is* it with you and
dying, anyway? Can't you get a new hobby?"

"Shut up." I meant it to be defiant, but it came out a
bare, shaken whisper. I curled on my side, pummeled by
rain, chilled to the bone, but with a rich, golden warmth
somewhere deep inside to sustain me. His gift, like Jona
than's, but unlike Jonathan's it was a human sort of
power, and my body was already accepting it. Re-
newing itself.

I let my breath slide out in a sigh, staring at him, and
saw Lewis's narrow pupils expand into huge, black rings.

Felt the feedback begin to build between us.

The pulse beat faster, pulling me like the tide.

I closed my eyes and drifted up to the aetheric. It felt
effortless and elegant and perfectly controlled.

"What happened?" Lewis asked.

"Jonathan," I murmured. *He kidnapped my child.* I
couldn't say it out loud, couldn't begin to explain all of
what I'd realized while lying here in the rain, and certainly not to Lewis. "He's not going to fight. Ashan's
going to win."

Lewis sucked in a very sharp breath, as if he knew
implications to that I couldn't imagine. "That can't happen."

"Well, it's going to happen, so you'd better make a
plan."

"Joanne, there *is* no plan for that." He looked miserable, suddenly—tired, soaked to the bone, chilled. "If we
lose Jonathan, we lose everything. He's like the keystone
in the arch. Take him away—"

"Everything collapses," I finished, and slowly found

the strength to sit up, then mutely extended my hand to him. He brought me to my feet. All my parts seemed to be working more or less correctly. "You told me to go. Where can I go that will be safe from that?"

His cold lips pressed against my forehead for a second. "Nowhere. Just—I don't know. I'll try to find him, talk to him. Meanwhile, just go home. Use what I gave you for defense only. Your body needs time to replenish itself." His voice sounded rough and silken, and I tried to keep my breathing slow. Nothing I could do about my heartrate, which spiked like crazy. "Stay alive for me."

"I'll try," I said. My own voice sounded about half an octave lower than normal. I cleared my throat and opened my eyes to look at him. "Thank you."

He half turned, then whipped back, grabbed me, and kissed me.

I mean, *kissed* me. This wasn't some peck-on-the-cheek, let's-be-friends gesture, this was hot and damp and desperate, and *wow*. After the first shocked instant I came to my senses and put hands on his chest to shove hard enough to break the suction and back him off a couple of steps.

We didn't say anything. There really wasn't anything we could say. He wasn't going to apologize.

I wasn't sure I wanted him to try. It was a kind of good-bye, and both of us knew it.

That, more than anything else, told me how near to the end of the world we were coming.

He walked over to the Ma'at and bent his head to listen to what Charles Ashworth had to say to him, which looked like plenty, most of it probably having to do with the inadvisability of getting involved with me. So I walked over to join them.

"Seeing as the lightning kind of trashed my ride, I need transportation," I said. "Or at least the loan of a car."

Ashworth, who probably had a fleet of them, frowned at me, then nodded to one of his flunkies, a crew-cut young woman dressed in a sharp-looking tailored suit and shoes I was almost certain were from Stuart Weitz-man's new fall collection. I was surprised to see he was hiring the fashion-enabled. He didn't really seem all that hip to me.

She tossed over a set of keys, looking grumpy. "Don't dent it," she said.

"I'm offended." I scanned the undamaged cars in the lot. I was hoping for the honey of a BMW sport coupe parked near the street, but her ride turned out to be something else.

Oh, dear God.

Even considering the hell my life had descended to, I didn't think I was really prepared, at this point in my life, to be driving a minivan.

Jonathan had left me for dead. That meant he probably wouldn't be coming back at me, looking for revenge—at least, not for a while. And I didn't get the sense that it was cruelty on his part . . . just an iron-hard kind of indifference. I'd ceased to be useful to him for what mattered, and he wasn't going to waste his time.

I climbed in the minivan, which was exactly the size of a small yacht, and started it up. Not a high-performance engine. I sat back in the captain's chair and let cool air blow on my face and dripping hair for a minute while I tried hard not to think about what had happened on the roof.

I fished my cell phone out of my purse and speed-dialed Paul Giancarlo. He didn't answer. I left a voice-mail, reporting John's death in as much detail as I dared, and then put in a call to the Wardens Crisis Center and reported that they were officially short a regional officer. The girl on the other end—God, she sounded young—was curt and scared, and I wondered how many calls she'd already had like this. They were clearly in emergency mode already, because the disasters would be coming as storms and earthquakes and wildfires erupted, and there were no high-level, Djinn-armed Wardens to combat them. In fact, today might mark the beginning of the kind of disaster that hadn't been seen on Earth since the Great Flood. These things built on each other, fed on the energy of each other.

"Dammit," I whispered, and tossed the cell phone into the passenger seat. The fire department was winding up the emergency, although I was sure that the fire had gone out thanks to Lewis's intervention and not the hose-and-ladder brigade. Lewis and the Ma'at were convened in a group near the corner of the parking lot, having some kind of serious huddle. The building's tenants milled around, looking lost and smoke-stained, a few sucking on oxygen masks, but all in all it was remarkably little destruction.

John was the only casualty.

I didn't want to think about how close it had come on the roof to being two bodies instead of one. I turned my attention to my brand-new (borrowed) ride instead. The van was so clean it might have been a rental, except for a few lived-in touches like a custom CD holder on the driver's side.

The mirror showed me an exhausted-looking drowned-rat woman, with dark circles under her eyes and lank, unattractive hair. I wasted a spark of power to dry my hair and clothes. I looked as though I could win a Morticia Addams look-alike contest, but, for once in my life, there were bigger issues than my personal vanity.

I grabbed a Modest Mouse CD from the selection on the visor. The van wasn't exactly the signature style of Joanne Baldwin, Speed Freak, but at least it was wheels and it would get me back home. I desperately wanted to be home. Maybe David was an Ifrit, maybe my sister was by turns nuts and annoying, but at least it was . . . home.

It's all going to be gone soon, something in me whispered. *All this around you. The city, the people, the life you know. When Jonathan goes, everything goes. Are you ready for that? Are you ready to stand by and let it happen?*

Jonathan was offering to die for David. I was aware that there was some core of stubborn jealousy in me,

and that it wasn't very honorable, but it was more than
that holding me back from his solution to the problem.
If I released David, if David went after Jonathan and
killed him—and by Rahel's assessment, that was almost
certain to happen—then I lost David three times over.
First, to being an Ifrit; second, to being the killer of his
friend and brother. Last, to becoming what Jonathan
was . . . and I didn't think that left any room for me.

Well, it's all about you, isn't it?

No, it wasn't, but I had a stake in it. And I couldn't
shake that off.

Jonathan had taken my Djinn-child. I'd thought that
was just because he was a cruel bastard, but thinking
back on it, maybe he'd just been trying to preserve something of David. Even something of me. He'd known that
if I refused to give up David's bottle, I'd die, and David
would be lost to him.

*Please, let her be with him. Existing, somehow. Not
just . . .*

Not just gone.

In the shelter of the minivan, where nobody could see
it happen, I fell apart. All the fury, all the fear, all the
pain came out in sudden, wrenching sobs, in pounding
on the steering wheel, in outright screams of rage. This
wasn't right, and it shouldn't be this way—I hadn't come
this far just to see the world die around me. Or to let
David slip into darkness.

Or to lose a child I barely knew.

There's an answer, I told myself, hands pressing hard
enough against my eyes to create white sparks, tears
slicking my cheeks in cold sheets. *There's a goddamn
answer to this, there has to be.*

Lightning shivered overhead, raw and uncontrolled. It
hit a transformer across the city and blew it into a blue-
white shower of sparks. Several square blocks of lights
went out, and overhead, the clouds swirled in from the
ocean, carrying the smell of rain and the promise of worse.

I had to get home.

*   *   *

By the time I trudged up the steps to my apartment I was exhausted, stinky, smoke-stained, and dispirited. Now that I was full of borrowed power again, I could sense the incredible roiling of the aetheric, mirrored by the wild fury of the sky overhead. The rain was the least of what was coming. I wondered what Marvelous Marvin would be making of it. Probably churning out revised predictions and ordering Ella to make it happen—not that Ella could, at this stage. Things were far too chaotic for any one Warden to try to influence them.

With John Foster dead, and Ella's loyalties questionable at best, it left this part of Florida lightly protected. The same was probably true up and down the Eastern seaboard. The Wardens were falling apart, and the Djinn didn't care about the consequences. And the regular people, the ones the Wardens were sworn to protect? No clue what was coming.

At least I could protect Sarah. That was something, anyway.

I dug my key out of my purse, unlocked the front door, and walked into . . .

. . . a stranger's apartment.

For a brief, surreal moment, I thought I really *had* walked into the wrong apartment, proving that urban legend that apartment keys work on every lock in the building . . . but then I recognized little, familiar things. The ding on the wall next to the TV—which was now plasma flat-screen, and the size of a small theater. The pictures on the coffee table of Mom, Sarah, an ancient one of our grandparents—although they were encased in new silver frames, all matching. One of the rugs on the floor looked familiar. It even had a coffee stain on it from when I'd tripped one morning, half-asleep.

Apart from those touchstones, it was a whole new place.

I stood frozen in shock, eyes wide, and Sarah came bustling breathlessly around the corner, wiping her hands on a towel.

"There you are!" she cried, and threw her arms around me. Then immediately withdrew. "Ugh! You smell awful; where have you been?"

"In a fire," I said absently. "What the hell . . . ?"

In typical Sarah fashion, she skipped right over that, whirled away and did an honest-to-God Mary Tyler Moore pirouette in the middle of the living room. "You like it? Tell me you like it!"

I stared at her, trying to work out what she was talking about. None of this was making sense. "Um—"

She beamed. "I had to do something to make up for the burden I've been on you. Honestly, you've been such a saint these past few days, and I've done nothing but mooch off of you." She looked so bright and shiny, so thrilled. "Chrêtien finally came through with an alimony check; it showed up this morning—of course, the stupid bank won't cash it, they have to hold it until it clears, but Eamon let me have the cash in the meantime. So I decided to give you a makeover!"

Makeover? I blinked. Not that I was unwilling to go be pampered somewhere, but in the middle of an approaching apocalypse probably wasn't the best possible time . . .

Oh. She was talking about the furniture.

"Isn't it gorgeous? Look, there's a new sofa, and chairs, and the TV of course, Eamon helped pick that one out—" She grabbed my hand and pulled me through to the bedrooms. Threw open her door. "I got rid of that terrible French Provincial and went for a nice maple. . . . You know, I've been watching those home improvement shows on BBC America, they have all the best ideas, don't you think? It's just so much fun. Look, see how the maroon pillows complement the sponging on the wall . . ."

It was all dissolving into nonsense word balloons. Obviously, Sarah had gotten in money, and obviously, she'd been shopping. Her bedroom looked like a showroom in a furniture store, with gleaming, highly polished wood and a lace bedspread over some kind of silky throw. Every detail excruciatingly precise. She must have spent hours with a Feng Shui manual.

"Nice," I said numbly. "Right, it's great. Look, I just need to take a shower and lie down for a while . . ."

"Wait! I'm not done!"

She towed me next door.

My room was . . . gone. Gutted. There was a new bed, sleek black lacquer and inlaid mother-of-pearl on the headboard in geometric designs. The dumpy dresser was MIA, replaced by something that looked like a giant Chinese apothecary cabinet in the same black lacquer with brass accents. My knickknacks—not that there had been many—were gone, replaced by red temple dogs and jade goddesses. Very elegant and expensive-looking.

I took it in slowly. My brain had handled too many shocks today. I wasn't prepared for being the victim on the guerilla warfare version of *Trading Spaces*. I'd just been nearly killed *twice*, for God's sake. I wasn't ready for redecorating.

"Well?" Sarah asked anxiously. "I know the walls still look plain, but I thought later this week we could go to one of those home stores and get something to sponge-paint with in here—maybe metallic gold, what do you think? And some throw pillows. I didn't get enough throw pillows."

My eyes wandered to the bedside table.

It was gone.

Gone.

In its place was a black lacquer stand with one delicate-looking drawer instead of the two large ones I'd had before.

My paralysis broke. I yanked free of Sarah's hold and lunged for the nightstand, pulled open the drawer and found the familiar collection of junk that tended to congregate in such places. Books. Magazines. A zippered cosmetic case I sincerely hoped she hadn't opened.

A few things were missing. Some half-empty tubes of hand lotion, for instance. Some out-of-date sale catalogs.

The case containing David's bottle.

I turned and looked at her, and whatever was in my expression caused her to fall back a step.

"Where's the padded case?" I asked.

"What?" She took another step back. I followed, well aware I must have looked dangerous and not caring at all.

"Sarah, I'm not going to ask you again. *Where's the padded case with the damn bottle in it?*" I screamed it, lunged at her and shoved her back against the apothecary cabinet. Temple dogs and goddesses rattled nervously behind her. Sarah's eyes went wide with panic.

"Case . . . there's a case still in there . . . ?"

"THE OTHER ONE!" I didn't know I could yell that loudly. Even my own eardrums hurt.

Sarah looked entirely terrified. "Well, um . . . yes . . . there *was* another case . . . isn't it in there? You had—um—empty bottles of lotion and stuff—and—did you want to keep them? Why would you want to keep them? Jo, I don't understand! They weren't special formulas or anything!"

I wanted to kill her. I found myself hyperventilating, saw spots, and let go before I could act on the impulse. Fought for control.

"Sarah," I said with utter, merciless precision, "what did you do with *the zippered case that was in the bedside table and had a bottle in it*?"

She went pale as milk. "I don't know. Is it important?"

"Yes!"

"Well, I—I—it should be in there, I thought I took everything out . . . maybe, um, maybe I left it in the old nightstand."

I didn't have time. "Where did you put the old furniture?"

She bit her lip. Her hands were twisting each other anxiously. "Um . . . the furniture guys hauled it off. I paid them extra to take everything to the dump."

Any second now, I was going to lose control. I reeled unsteadily and ended up sitting on the edge of the bed.

It gave with an ease and firmness that spoke of memory foam somewhere in the construction. Sarah had gone all out to make me happy. Except that she'd done the one thing guaranteed to destroy my life.

Maybe the life of every person on the planet, if I stretched things out to their logical conclusion.

I put my head down and forced myself to focus, to be still and calm.

"What did I do?" she asked in a meek, little-girl voice. "Jo, just tell me, what did I do?"

I couldn't exactly explain that she'd just tossed away the love of my life in a garbage truck. *Oh God, David . . .* This was surreal, it was so ridiculous.

Sarah, of course, came to exactly the wrong conclusion. She clapped both hands over her mouth, tears forming in her eyes, and then ventured, "Oh God, Jo . . . Was it drugs? Are you on drugs? Did I throw away your stash?"

I laughed. I couldn't help it. It came out as a kind of mad, despairing burst of sound, and I covered my face with my hands and stood there for a moment, shaking. Dragging in one gulp of air after another.

Sarah's hand fell on my shoulder, warm but tentative.

"I screwed up," she said. "I get it. I'm sorry. Look, I'll do whatever I have to do to get it back for you. I'm sorry, believe me, I thought—we thought we were doing something good for you—"

Oh yeah, it was good. I had an apartment full of furniture I didn't want, the Djinn were at war, Wardens were dying, and my boyfriend had gone out with the trash.

I stood up and walked to the closet.

"Jo? Where—where are you going?"

I didn't even look back as I pulled out industrial-strength jeans and tossed my hiking boots onto the brand-new bed.

"We," I corrected her. "We are going dump-diving. Get dressed."

I don't know if you've ever been to a big-city dump at twilight, but it's definitely an adventure. I'd come prepared for the worst—my trashed-out blue jeans, thick, long-sleeved tee, hiking boots, hair twisted up in a knot, face mask and gloves. Sarah wore brand-new jeans, a delicate pink top, and old tennis shoes. After some top-of-my-voice persuasion, she'd decided against the new, expensive footwear.

At least the rain had stopped. If it had been storming, I don't think even I could have bullied her into it.

Armed with the name of the furniture company, we arrived at the dump an hour before closing, and tracked the delivery to a huge pit that was earmarked for furniture, appliances, and other large junk. Trucks were still arriving. As we pulled up in the minivan, a commercial truck backed up to the dropoff, sounded a beeping alarm, and tilted its bed slowly into the air.

An avalanche of twisted metal, old, splintered furniture, and busted TVs joined the mass grave.

Sarah was fidgeting before we'd parked the mommy-van. "Oh, my God! Jo, it *smells* out here!"

"Yes," I said, and handed her a face mask and gloves. "You're sure you left it in the drawer of the nightstand?"

"Yes, why?"

"Because otherwise we're in the other pit. The one with the biodegradable garbage like rotten food and old diapers. And believe me, you'll like this better."

She shuddered, pinching her nose shut. "I'm dure." She sounded like a wacky 1940s comedienne. "Thid id awful!"

"Yeah, no shit. Watch out for rats."

"Rats?" she squeaked.

"Rats." I'd had a friend once whose boss had sent her to the dump to retrieve legal papers from a trash bag. I decided not to tell Sarah about the scary cockroaches. "Take the flashlight. It may be dark down there."

"Dark?" Sarah's commitment to make things right was rapidly eroding and gaining qualifiers like *so long as it's convenient* and *so long as I don't get my hands dirty*.

I ignored her, popped the door, and got out. The newer arrivals seemed to be dumped toward the right-hand side, and I scanned the mass of crap to try to spot something familiar. It was like trying to identify pieces of your life after a tornado, the familiar pureed into rubbish. I gulped down a choking sense of panic and kept systematically looking. According to the map they'd given me, the furniture company had dumped in grid E-7. Of course, a map in a dump lacked landmarks, but since the cheerful, flannel-clad guy on duty had said they were currently dumping in E-12, I had a pretty good general range. I scanned junk, which all looked, well, the same, and finally caught a flash of white among all of the gray and brown.

I jumped down from the packed earth ledge into the pit, braced myself with one hand on the wall, and started carefully picking my way over the junk pile. It was dangerous. Sharp corners and nails and jagged metal. Glass. Broken mirrors. The place was a tetanus shot waiting to happen.

Even though I was completely focused on the mission at hand, my eyes kept focusing on interesting bits of garbage. A broken, tiger-maple chest that looked antique. A massive, carved teak table that was magnificently in one piece and probably would be until the sun consumed the earth, as hard as teak was—I couldn't believe somebody had actually moved it in the first place. It made me exhausted just looking at it.

I tripped over a big, dented brass pot and nearly fell into a steel cabinet, but managed to brace myself. I looked over my shoulder to make sure Sarah was okay. She was picking her way slowly behind me, testing every step twice before putting her weight on anything, one hand always outstretched to catch herself. The other held a flashlight in a death grip, not that she really needed it yet.

The face mask and cherry pink top made quite a fashion statement.

I climbed a small, slippery hill of appliances—somebody had thrown out a gigantic Maytag washer—and saw something that might have been the leg of a

French Provincial nightstand. I reached for it and yanked; it was a slender, delicately curved leg, freshly broken off, with faded gilt on white.

Definitely from Sarah's room. Or, okay, somebody else with the bad taste to have French Provincial bedroom furniture. But I doubted there'd be two of us contributing to the city dump on the same afternoon.

"It's somewhere around here!" I yelled. She nodded breathlessly and climbed up to join me. She found the first piece of my bedroom suite—the headboard—and yelled in triumph as if she'd discovered King Tut's tomb. I scrambled over to haul it to the side. Underneath was a broken drawer from my dresser. Empty.

We worked silently, panting, sweating, as night brushed closer and darker. Alarms sounded the *everybody out,* along with loudspeaker announcements. Floodlights snapped on, harsh and white, throwing everything into alien relief.

"We'll never find it!" Sarah wailed. She straightened up, yanked down her mask, and wiped her streaming forehead with the back of her forearm. Dirt smudged her face in a circle around the mask, and her normally cute hair was plastered lankly around her skull. Her desire to please had ebbed into pure, disgusted exhaustion. "Dammit, Jo, just forget about it, would you? What was it, cocaine? Jesus! Bill me for it!"

I yanked a shattered television aside—yes, that was mine; I remembered it with a lurch of affection because I'd bought that crappy little thing with my own hard-earned money at a yard sale—and uncovered another dresser drawer. Blank, except for a coating of liner paper. I kicked it out of the way with unnecessary violence.

"It wasn't *cocaine,* you idiot!" I yelled back, and felt my hands curling into fists at my sides. "Maybe that's your lifestyle of the rich and blameless, but—"

"Hey! I'm hip-deep in garbage trying to help you, you know—"

"Excuse me, but you showed up begging *me* for help,

if I remember! And all you've done is cost me money and fuck up my life!"

I didn't mean to say that . . . exactly. But it was true. I watched Sarah's flushed face drain of color and bit back an impulse to apologize.

"Fine," she said, with unnatural control. "I thought I was doing something nice for you, Joanne. I took the little bit of money I got from my deadbeat bastard of an abusive husband and I spent it on you to make up for imposing on you. I'm sorry that it interfered with your *stupid bottle collection*!"

She turned and scrambled away, graceless and angry.

"Hey!" I yelled.

"Fuck off!" she yelled back, and kept going. "Find it yourself!"

Fine. Whatever. My back hurt, my head ached, I was sweaty and exhausted and I could hear—and feel—a black ugly mutter of thunder out to sea. The vultures were coming home to roost.

And I had to find David's bottle. I just had to. It couldn't end this way.

I uncovered the shattered shell of my dresser. It was too big to move. I cried for a little while, tears soaking into the gauze mask, and then grabbed hold and kicked the damn thing with my hiking boots until it splintered into pieces small enough to drag out of the way.

As the last one came free, I saw the nightstand, and it was all in one piece.

I gave a wordless, breathless yell, and hauled it out of the heap of junk it was buried in, leaned it against a rusted-out harvest gold washing machine, and slowly opened the drawer.

It was full of stuff. Old lotion bottles with half a handful left in each one. My out-of-date sale catalogs.

A zippered bag full of foam cushioning.

I grabbed it, hugged it like a little girl reunited with her favorite stuffed animal, and unzipped it with shaking gloved fingers.

There was nothing inside.

Nothing.

I screamed, bit my lip, and forced myself to do things slowly. One piece at a time, taken out, examined, and tossed aside. Foam padding last.

It wasn't there.

David's bottle wasn't fucking there.

In the dark, under the glare of the floodlights, I saw the cold green gleam of eyes out in the dark. Rats? Cats? They winked on and off in the shadows, too cautious to come near me, but too close for comfort.

One of those legendary giant cockroaches crawled out of the heap and began trundling like a shiny brown bus over heaps of metal.

The bottle wasn't in the drawer, and it wasn't in the bag where it was supposed to be. Night was falling. I couldn't do this once the floodlights shut off, and tomorrow another layer of junk would arrive and bury any chance I had . . .

I had to do it. "David," I said, and closed my eyes. "David, come to me. David, come to me. David, *come to me.*" Rule of three. Even if he'd wanted to, he couldn't refuse to obey that, not even as an Ifrit, so long as he was bound to a bottle. I had to know if the bottle was intact, at least. If David was still bound.

Out in the shadows, something moved. It was unsettlingly like that giant cockroach, the way it caught the floodlights in shiny angles and sharp points. Skin like coal. Nothing human about it.

"David?" I whispered.

The Ifrit stood there, motionless. I got nothing from it. No sense of connection, no sense of it even existing beyond the evidence of my eyes.

If he'd come when I called, he was still bound to the bottle. Worst possible news. I felt tears burning in my eyes again. "God, no. David, I'm so sorry. I'm going to find you. There's got to be a way to make this right, to make this—"

He *moved.* Quicker than a Djinn, scarier, he was touching-close in less time than it took my nerves to fire an impulse to scream. His black-clawed hands slashed through me and plunged into . . .

. . . into that golden reservoir of power that Lewis had given me.

Why? How? Ifrits couldn't feed on humans, not even Wardens, they couldn't . . .

He was. "No!" I screamed, and tried to back up. I tripped and went down, felt something slash my shoulder, took a sharp angle hard in the back. The impact stunned the breath out of me and made me go momentarily hazy.

He didn't let go. When I opened my eyes he was crouched on top of me; black edges and angles, hunger and an absence of everything I knew as human, a Djinn emptied of all that made him part of the world. . . .

And then, he flickered and became flesh, bone, blood, heartbeat, *real*. Djinn in human form. Copper-bright hair, burning eyes, skin like burnished gold.

"Oh, God," he murmured, and staggered back from me, clothes forming around him—blue jeans, open flannel shirt, his olive drab coat. "I didn't mean to—Jo—"

"Where are you?" It was all I could do to form the words; he'd taken so much energy from me that I felt oddly slow, as if there wasn't enough current left in my cells to drive the process of life and thought again. "Tell me."

He reached down and lifted me in his arms, buried his face in the curve of my neck. He felt blazing hot, powered by my stolen life. I felt his agonized scream shiver through me. I stilled him by clumsily putting a hand on his face. "David, tell me where you are."

He was weeping. *Weeping.* Human tears from inhuman eyes, a kind of despair I'd never seen in him before, a trapped and hunted fury. "I can't," he said. "I'm sorry. I'm so sorry. I told you to stop me, I told you—"

"Hey! Put her down!"

I blinked and saw the dump whirl around me as David turned, still holding me. Sarah was standing about ten feet away, holding—what the hell was that? A frying pan? Yep, a huge iron skillet. It must have weighed twenty pounds. Her arms were trembling with the effort of keeping it held at threat level.

"I mean it!" she yelled, and took another step toward us. "Put my sister down *right now* or it's batter up!"

"It's okay," I said, and felt the world start to gray out. I held on with an effort. "Sarah, no. This is David."

She looked confused. Her knuckles whitened around the skillet.

"Boyfriend," I managed.

"Oh." She swallowed, dropped the skillet with a clang of metal, and scrubbed her fingers against her filthy blue jeans. "Um, sorry. But—Jo? Are you okay?"

"She fell," David said. He sounded shaken. When I looked up at him I saw that he'd formed glasses, and his eyes were fading to human brown. He still looked way too gorgeous to be real, but maybe that was just my prejudice. "I'll carry her out."

"Sorry," I whispered, and put my arms around his neck. His strength and warmth folded around me, sheltering and protecting. "I love you. I love you. I love you."

"I know." He touched his lips to my hair, then my forehead. "I wish you didn't. I wish I could make this— stop. If I didn't love you, wasn't part of you, I couldn't do this to you . . ."

"David, *tell me where you are!*"

He tried to tell me. His mouth opened, but nothing came out. He shook his head in frustration and tightened his hold on me as he made his way over the mountains of sharp metal and broken furniture, heading for the metal steps back up to the parking lot.

"Please. No, wait—I need to get your bottle, we can't just leave it here—David, I'm *ordering* you, tell me where it is!"

He brushed my lips with a kiss, something gentle and very sad. "It won't work," he said. "You're not my master anymore."

And that was when I realized that I didn't feel the draw anymore—the connection of master to Djinn.

Somebody else had his bottle.

"Who—"

Overhead, black clouds rumbled. I felt a breeze ruffle my hair. David moved faster, effortlessly graceful. No longer trying to look all that human. I remembered how he'd been on the overpass, all that unnatural balance and weird, fey control. He took the metal steps two at a time.

Sarah was still struggling along in his wake.

David carried me to the minivan and put me in the passenger seat, one hand dragging warm down the curve of my cheek as he settled my head against the cushions. A flash of lightning lit him blue on one side while the floodlights washed him white on the other.

"Don't look for me," he said. "It's better that you don't. You're not safe with me now."

He kissed me. Baby-soft lips, damp and silken and hot. I tasted peaches and cinnamon and power.

When he tried to pull back, I held on, holding the kiss, deepening it, demanding. Drinking a little bit of my power back from him.

Enough to make me a Warden again, even though not much of one.

He faded and cooled as I did it, but not quite enough to slide back into Ifrit-state. But he would. As the power faded, he'd revert.

But for now, at least, we were balanced. The connection—and it was a different one than we'd had as master and Djinn—worked both ways.

"You didn't have to answer when I called," I said, and touched the side of his face, then tangled my hands in the soft strands of his hair. "If I'm not your master—"

"I'll always be yours," he interrupted. "Always. The bottle doesn't matter." His forehead pressed against mine, and his breath pulsed warm on my skin. "Don't you understand that yet?"

Another flash of lightning blinded me. When I opened my eyes, my hands were empty, and David was gone. I didn't cry. I felt too numbed and empty to cry. Sarah lunged over the top of the metal steps from the junkpile, panting, flushed, thoroughly filthy. She grabbed the open door and looked inside, then met my eyes. Hers were anime-wide.

"Where'd he come from? Wait . . . where'd he go?"

I just shook my head. Sarah stared at me for a long, considered second, and then shut the door and climbed into the driver's seat. The engine started with a roar, and she began piloting the Good Ship Minivan out of the dump.

"He's a Djinn," I said wearily, and leaned my head against the glass. "Magic's real. I control the weather. He's an immortal creature made out of fire, and he grants wishes. I was getting around to telling you."

Silence. Sarah hit the brakes hard enough to jerk, and for a few long seconds we just sat there, idling, until the first fat drops of rain began pelting the van with hard, resonant thumps.

"Well," she finally said, "at least he's cute. Are you insane?"

I sighed. "Oh, I *so* wish I was."

We drove home. I felt exhausted and sick and sore, and refused Sarah's multiple offers of visits to the local emergency room or mental health center, no matter how rich, cute, and single the doctors might be. I showered away the dump under the new high-pressure massaging bath nozzle—not all of Sarah's upgrades were objectionable—and crawled into my brand-new bed, too tired to wonder what I was going to do in the morning about all my various enemies, crises, and wars.

David was, at least, not buried under half a ton of garbage at the dump, or at least I didn't think he was. That was about as much of a victory as I could aspire to for one day.

In retrospect, if I'd had half a brain in my head, I'd have never shut my eyes.

INTERLUDE

As the storm destroys the island that men called Atlantis, as it strips it bare and devours every fragment of life before sinking the bare rocks under the waves—something strange happens. The explosion of death-energy from the destruction is so huge that, to balance the scales, five hundred Djinn snap into existence, each holding some small measure of the life of that lost, beautiful land. Lost and alone, newborn.

Powerful, and afraid.

The storm doesn't see them as fuel for its fires, and turns north, toward a rich, green land full of energy, full of life, full of fragile things that it can grind apart in its fury.

And this is when it becomes my story, and my mistake. I can't stop it. The Djinn can't stop it, even with the addition of the Five Hundred; the storm is a natural thing, and we can't fight manifestations of the Mother nearly so well as we fight each other, or things in the world of man.

The end of the world is on us. We argue, the Djinn. Some of us try to turn the storm aside, but it's too much for us.

I realize there is no way for Djinn to help mankind, and no way for mankind to save itself, without making an irrevocable choice.

So I pull from the Mother and give power to humans to make them Wardens. And I give them the means to enslave the Djinn. By binding the Djinn, the Wardens can direct us, and we can tap the power pooled inside of humanity and amplify it, creating a web of intent and potential large enough to contain and weaken the storm.

The moment when we join together, humans and Djinn, and defeat the storm at the end of the world . . . it is, for a moment, the unity of all things. A perfect peace. But perfect peace can't last, and when it comes time for the Wardens to give up the power I've granted them over the Djinn, they refuse.

Should have seen that coming.

Ashan and the others are breaking the deal I made, all those millennia ago. They're doing what I never had the courage to do: They're taking back their freedom.

And I don't blame them. I blame myself.

It's time for things to be clean again. Scrubbed raw, like the rocks of Atlantis. Maybe what comes out of this will be better. I've wanted freedom for the Djinn for a long time, but I've never actually been faced with seeing it happen before. Choosing it.

But it's the right choice.

If David were here, he'd tell me I'm crazy.

But he's not here. For the first time in my life, human or Djinn, he's not here to help me. I'm at the end of the road, and it's all dark out there, and I don't know that there's any right answer to anything, in the end.

Only choices.

So I think I'll sit here on the beach, with the waves spraying the sky, watching as that long-ago storm swirls itself back into life again, finishing what it started. The Wardens have been fighting this same storm for thousands of years, whether they know it or not. I always feel something about it, something familiar, when it manages to put on its cloak of clouds and come back for another round.

I can't stop it alone. Neither can the Wardens. And the Djinn . . . the Djinn have had enough of sacrifice.

I watch as the storm's heart turns black and furious, and I wish it didn't have to end this way.

But I don't know of any other way for it to happen.

EIGHT

No surprise: I woke up feeling like I'd had the hell beaten out of me by the Jolly Green Giant. Definitely not one of my better mornings. I tried to get out of bed, ended up more or less leaning on the wall, staring down at my naked body. I'd washed away the dump stains, but the bruises were pretty spectacular. Couldn't see the really painful one, which was in the small of my back; I shuffled into the bathroom, dragged messy hair out of my eyes, and used an awkwardly angled hand mirror to take an appraisal of the damage. It didn't look as bad as it felt, but then, it felt awful. The bruise was black and blue, the size of a fist. Swollen, too. Ow.

I took another shower, because what the hell . . . massaging showerhead . . . and dried my hair into a more or less glorious shower of curls that didn't frizz too much, and put on makeup. Why? Hell if I know, except that the worse I feel, the better I want to look. After applying all the disguise, I put on a light bra and a kickin' peau de soie blouse, and contemplated my choices for things that wouldn't press agonizingly against the bruise on my back. The low-rise panties and blue jeans seemed the only possible choice, other than walking around half-naked. . . .

I flipped on the sleek little flat-screen TV that had come with my new bedroom suite, a luxury I'd never even considered before, and tuned to WXTV. Just to see. They were finishing up the news portion of the morning show and moving to the weather. They had a new Weather Girl, I saw immediately, and hey, I felt just a little bit bitter about it for a second, because she was stunningly pretty and had a lovely smile and was well dressed in a blue jacket and silk blouse and tailored slacks, and *what the hell?*

The anchors were laughing. She was forecasting a storm for later today.

The camera pulled back, and back . . .

. . . and there was Marvin. Squeezed into a foam rubber cloud suit, with little silver drops hanging off of him, sweating like a pig and glaring like a pit bull. Red with fury.

"Sorry," the new Weather Girl said, "but you out there know that Marvin always puts his integrity first, and today, he's paying off a bet to Joanne, our former meteorological assistant. Love the outfit, Marv. So what's today going to be like out there?"

"Cloudy," he snapped. "Severe storms. And—"

Water. Lots of it. Dumped from way up high. He gasped, jumped, and they cut his mike before he got more than the first syllable of the curse out, but the camera itself was shaking from the force of the laughter on the set.

Son of a bitch.

It was probably evil of me to feel so good about watching him dance around dripping and cursing, but, well . . . I was at peace with it.

I was feeling almost happy when I walked out into the living room, heading for the kitchen. It was still dark outside—cloudy, with muttering and lightning continuing over the ocean—so I didn't immediately see my sister's new boyfriend until he flicked on the light next to the couch.

He was sitting on one end, sprawled gracefully, head leaning back against the thick leather tufted back. Sarah was curled on her side with her head resting on his thigh. She was wrapped in a thick terrycloth robe that gaped at the top, showing the inside slopes of her breasts. She looked exhausted and vulnerable, and he looked down at her with a careful expression, and touched her very gently. Fingertips tracing her cheek.

I knew that touch. That was the way David touched me. That was regret, and love.

She didn't move, even with the light blazing down, and continued to breathe deeply and steadily. Deeply asleep. Eamon's long, elegant fingers threaded through her frosted hair and stroked the curve of her head in long, soothing motions, as if he couldn't bear to stop touching her.

I wondered for a second if he even knew I was there, and then he said, "Good morning." He looked up. "Did you enjoy the new bed?"

"Yeah." I paused, watching him, trying to figure out how they'd ended up on the couch like this when Sarah should have gone straight to her room, tired as she was. Also, when and how Eamon had found his way into the apartment. Sarah had probably given him a key already. She was like that. "Did you guys sleep out here?"

"I haven't slept at all," he said, and it struck me that he was speaking in a normal tone of voice, not keeping his voice down. That was odd.

Then he shifted a little, and Sarah's head rolled off his leg, limp as a rag doll.

Too limp. Her eyelids didn't even flutter.

"Sarah?" I asked. No reaction. "Oh my God, what's wrong with her?"

Eamon didn't answer. He readjusted her to put her head back in his lap, stroking her hair, the curve of her face. A lover's slow, steady touch.

I could not understand what I was seeing in his expression. "Eamon? Is there something wrong with her?"

"No," he said. "Nothing that won't wear off in a few hours. She may have a few side effects; most likely some mild nausea and a dull headache." His eyes remained fixed on me.

I couldn't believe it. Couldn't honestly *fathom* it. "What are you saying?"

"I'm saying that I injected your sister with a drug—nothing too addictive, don't worry—and I put her to sleep for a while." His tone was changing, moving away from the kind, slow, gentle cadence I was used to and toward something more clipped and cold. Not the eyes, though. Or the caresses of Sarah's skin. Those stayed gentle. "Don't fuss, Joanne, it's not the first time. I like my women a little less talkative and more compliant, in general. Sarah thought it was a bit strange, too, when I asked, but she's willing to try new things. I find that truly sexy, don't you? She's exceptional, your sister."

I took a step toward him, bruises forgotten. I was going to *kill* this son of a bitch.

His hand instantly slid from stroking her hair to fasten around the pale white column of her throat. "I wouldn't," he said. Now there was a feverish hint of cruelty in his face. "It only takes about one second to crush a trachea. I'd rather not do it. I honestly do like her. So relax. Let's be friends. We've been friends up till now; there's no reason we can't go on being civil to one another."

I knew nothing about crushing tracheas, except that it would kill her and there was nothing I could do to stop it. I froze where I was. His hands, although long and soft and elegant, also looked strong and very capable.

And the expression in his eyes was deadly serious now.

"Go on," he invited. "I know you want to ask questions. I'll oblige."

"Fine. What do you want, Eamon? If that's even your name."

"It is, actually." He didn't move his hand from her throat, but he let it relax a little. His fingertips trailed over her skin in a random, soothing pattern. I wasn't sure he even knew he was doing it. "I didn't lie about that, although of course the last name isn't the one on my passport. Then again, the one on my passport may not be right, either. You follow?"

"You're a criminal."

"Good girl. I'm a criminal. I'm a bad, evil man, and I

came here for one reason. Not your sister, although I have to say that I'd never have imagined meeting someone so . . . lovely. It's quite a benefit." Those fingers strayed, curving over the skin revealed by the parted terrycloth robe. I shivered all over with the urge to kill him really, really dead, but those eyes were constantly focused on me, assessing. Too careful. "I came here for you, Joanne."

"Get your hands off her."

"I don't think I can." His smile was gentle and sad, a little-boy smile begging to be understood and forgiven, no matter what he did. Women probably forgave him anything. Gave him everything. Even now, sitting there staring at me, I couldn't wrap my head around the unmistakable fact that he was a very, very bad man, because very, very bad men don't have such a soothing, gentle touch, do they?

Sarah loved him. Oh, God, Sarah loved him. That turned my stomach.

I must have let my revulsion show, because he lost the smile, and his eyes turned colder. "Are you afraid I'll molest her in front of you?"

"You *are* molesting her in front of me, asshole!"

"No." There was now no trace at all of warmth in his tone, and even his hands had gone still. "Not yet. Why, do you want me to? You'll have to ask nicely, in that case."

"Keep your fucking hands off my sister!"

He lost that last tinge of humor, and without it, Eamon was something very different indeed. Very cold and focused and scary. "Don't tell me what to do, petal. I don't care for it. And every time you do it, I'm going to leave a mark on Sarah, to remind you."

He pinched her inner thigh in a sudden, vicious movement. She didn't move, didn't react, but it was shocking enough that I flinched and involuntarily took another step toward him. His hand moved back to her throat and squeezed in unmistakable warning.

I stopped. Neither one of us made a sound.

The place he'd pinched her flushed a bright, angry red. He'd really hurt her; that hadn't been just show. *Son of a bitch* . . .

"Do we understand each other?" he asked. "I'm only using my hands. I do have other methods."

I was a Warden, dammit. I could command storms and call lightning. I shouldn't have been *helpless*.

I rubbed my fingertips together and concentrated. Got a crackle of power, maybe enough to administer a good sharp shock . . . but not enough to knock him out from a distance. I didn't have enough power to manipulate the air, either. What I had might be good enough for one shot, but I had to make it count, and Eamon's hand was one motion away from killing my sister.

"I'm listening," I said. "Just tell me what you want."

He nodded and relaxed a bit again. "My business associate—I think you're acquainted with him, Thomas Quinn, sometimes known as Orry—was in the midst of a transaction when he—disappeared. He'd acquired several dozen bottles of a unique nature, which disappeared along with him. I understand that you might have been there to see what happened to them."

"Who told you that?"

"Quinn's detective partner, Detective Rodriguez? I believe you know him as well, as he's spent several days down there in your parking lot spying on you. I had to go ask him some questions yesterday. He really wasn't forthcoming, until I got out the knife. You won't make me get out the knife, will you, love? The furniture's new. I'd hate to bloody it." I was watching Eamon's personality change right before my eyes, and it was completely *terrifying*.

The worst part? The look in his eyes. He still, even now, looked as if he were genuinely sorry he had to do this.

But nowhere near sorry enough to stop.

I backed up and sank into a chair, unable to stand any more; my knees were shaking, and my back was on fire. Son of a *bitch*. There were two possibilities to what he'd just said, neither of them good: one, I'd totally misread Rodriguez and he'd been in this from the beginning with Eamon; or two, Eamon had somehow gotten the drop on him yesterday and Rodriguez was . . .

"Is he dead?" I asked.

Eamon put his right hand—the one he wasn't using on my sister's throat—palm up. "No idea, really. By the time he decides to recover enough to talk, if he can, I'll be long gone, so I can't see that it really matters. Of course, you'll be the person who was last seen having words with him. That might be a problem for you, seeing as he's some sort of policeman. The plods do not like one of their own being maimed, in my experience. They might not ask too many questions. Might even get a bit overzealous when they come to take you in, as well." He glanced down at the mark on Sarah's thigh. "You fair-skinned girls bruise so easily."

I didn't take the bait. He raised his eyebrows and sank even lower against the leather couch. I remembered all his gentleness, his smiles, his courtesy. I wondered which Eamon was real, or if it all was . . . maybe he was capable of all of this, from passion and friendship to cold-blooded menace, all of it real.

Maybe the regard he felt for Sarah was real. Even now, the way he touched her was . . . odd. Gentle. As if he could force himself to be cruel, but it wasn't his first choice.

My mouth was so dry. I tried to swallow and deliberately unclenched my fists. "All right," I said, trying to keep it calm and even. "What exactly is it you want?"

"I want the bottles," he said. "I want them back. It's not personal, love, it's business. My client paid Quinn a great fucking pile of money for them, and he's none too happy about seeing neither merchandise nor refund. And as I have no refund for him . . ."

"Eamon, there *are* no bottles. Quinn's SUV exploded in the desert. The bottles were inside. They were destroyed."

"So the Djinn were set free," he said quietly. "Correct?"

I deliberately played stupid. "Gin? You're threatening to kill my sister over bottles of martini juice?"

That got a genuine, charming smile. "I knew I liked you, love, you're quick. Nice try, but I'm afraid I've known about the Djinn for a long time now. Magic, bottles, controlling the weather . . . does it sound familiar? Because Quinn was very informative on the subject. He was positively obsessed."

"Quinn was insane."

"Well, yes, I'd have thought so, too, until I met a few more of your friends. Like, for instance, your friend Ella, you remember her. You were talking with her earlier today before that messy business at the office building. I took her back to her house for a chat. Reminds me of my mum, Ella—not very bright, and likes money, though I'm not sure she'd do street trade for it, so perhaps she's not that much like Mum at all." He rolled his head slightly to one side and let his eyelids drop to half mast, watching me. I wasn't fool enough to think he'd let down his guard. "Ella really can control the weather. I've seen it. So don't try to give me any bollocks about it not working. She's done a nice job of it for your weatherman boss these past couple of years, she told me. And she's made some tidy sums off of it. I believe her on that score. She tried to give me some of it to leave her alone."

I'd wondered what had happened to Ella during the chaos at the offices. She'd just . . . vanished. Eamon was the answer. Eamon had followed me. Eamon had grabbed her and hustled her off without anyone noticing, in the chaos.

"Is she still alive?" I asked.

"Repetitive question. Same answer." His eyes were taking on an almost metallic shine. "Amusing as all this is, I'm running out of patience, love. So let's get back to the subject."

"I told you, I don't have the ones Quinn stole."

"Oh, yes, I understand that. Those are gone, never to return. I hope you understand; this gentleman Quinn took money from, this lovely gentleman in South America with whom he had a preexisting drug business, he won't be very happy with that. But that's really not my affair, as I was fortunately a very quiet partner, and the South American gentleman doesn't know my name any more than you do. But if he locates me, I'm afraid I'll have to tell him exactly what *yours* is."

"I—" I hated to admit anything to him. "I don't understand. What the hell do you want?"

"Well, I came here to recover property for my client," he said, as if it was a normal business arrangement and he was more than a little surprised that I wasn't following. "There's no property to be recovered—and I do believe you about that, by the way—but I still have expenses. You can, in fact, be rid of me very cheaply. All I'm asking for is my commission." He paused and looked down at my sister's slack, unconscious face. Ran a contemplative thumb over her parted lips and tilted his head, considering her. Enraptured. When his voice came again, it had lost its briskness and sounded more like the old Eamon, slow and warm. "All I want is one. Even trade, one sister for one Djinn."

I felt my breath lock up tight in my chest, but managed to loosen enough to get the words out. They sounded tight and furious. "You're deluded. That's one Djinn more than I have to give you, you asshole."

For answer, he picked up the remote control from the coffee table and flicked on the big-screen plasma TV on the wall. I turned to look at it. CNNfn was playing, giving a report on falling stocks; he pressed buttons, and a recording began to play. It was at an odd angle, but the focus was sharp enough.

It was my bedroom. My *old* bedroom. As I watched, the door banged open and I came backing into the room, David with me, both of us feverishly touching each other, devouring each other . . .

"Stop it," I whispered.

My on-screen image fell backward onto the bed. David stood looking down at her, and he looked inhuman, beautiful and unsettling, and incredibly . . .

"Stop it!"

Eamon hit PAUSE. "As pornography goes, it isn't bad," he said. "Although personally I prefer my women a little less vocal, as you know. I've had your apartment bugged for weeks, love. I had to get to know you before I got to know you, if you follow me. Your sister's arrival was a complication, but I was able to . . . improvise."

I was so angry I was seeing red spots, and had to breathe hard to try to keep from leaping out of the chair and throttling the man dead. He must have known it. He clicked the power off and dropped the remote back to the coffee table.

"You've got a Djinn," he said. "Obviously. And although I hate to break up a grand love affair, well, sorry, but maybe you can have him back when I'm done with him."

"No. I can't. I don't have him."

"Lying to me will cost your sister another injury, love. I know you have him. I'm not being unreasonable about this, but I'm not going to be lied to." He put those fingers on the creamy-pale skin of the swell of Sarah's breast that was exposed in the gap of her robe. "You know I'm not bluffing."

"*I don't have him!* Look, Sarah and I spent last night at the dump, all right? We were looking for David's bottle, his Djinn bottle! She threw it out during the—the— the big makeover! *The one you helped her with!*" I gestured compulsively around at the designer's showroom of an apartment.

He stared at me for a second, astonished, and then laughed. Really laughed, a genuinely amused guffaw. He moved his hand away from Sarah's throat to stroke her hair, then grabbed it and wrenched her head back to a dangerous angle.

I came up out of the chair. "Leave her alone!"

"Or?" Eamon didn't even look at me. He no longer seemed amused, or casual. There was something dark and tense in him now, and I could see a compulsively cruel streak in him that was very unsettling. He *liked* doing this to her. Almost couldn't resist it. *It's hardly the first time* . . . I wondered what he'd done to her at night, when she'd been lying in that bed with him, zoned out on whatever drug he'd given her. Oh dear *God*. I had to stop this.

"Stop it or I'll kill you," I said. I meant it.

He looked up then, the nightmare still in his avid eyes, the hungry set of his lips. "I live on borrowed time with a very scary set of characters as company. Threats from you are like being threatened by a sprog on the playground, love. But do go on. It's amusing."

I changed tacks. "Is that why you want to get a Djinn? To save your skin? Make you invincible?"

He was thinking over what I'd said, clicking it over in his brain. It was easy to see that he was brilliant. His transparency was part of what made him so damn frightening. "Invincibility," he said. "No. Although that would be nice, wouldn't it, invincibility? But I can take care of myself, always have. Not interested, really."

"Why do you need a Djinn, then?"

"For someone else."

"You don't strike me as the type who thinks of others."

I got a hot flash of temper, the first I'd really seen. "I haven't *struck* you at all, pet. But if you insult me, I may have to take my fit of pique out on someone more ready to hand. Here's what I want from you, and it's not negotiable: be a good little bitch and go out and find me a Djinn. Any Djinn. I don't care what it looks like, because unlike you I won't be fucking it."

"I'm not leaving you here with Sarah!"

The flare of temper I'd spotted was nothing compared to the full-throated roar that erupted out of him. "I'm not giving you a bloody choice!" He took Sarah's limp left arm, skimmed the sleeve back, and held her forearm in both hands.

Prepared to snap it.

His eyes dared me to test him.

I swallowed hard and said, "If you hurt her, you have no idea how much I'll make you suffer before you die."

"You're repeating yourself, and as there's only one of the three of us who's sustained any injury at all, you might think hard about the trend." He tightened his hold on her fragile, limp arm. "You have exactly two hours before I start breaking things, working up from the bottom. If I go slowly enough, she'll wake up before I'm finished. Oh, and love, just in case you have any brilliant ideas about calling the police, I'm taking her with me. I'll call and tell you where to meet me with the Djinn. One life for another. I'm not unreasonable, but I am very, very determined."

I stood, tense and agonized, as he rose and effortlessly lifted Sarah's limp body in his arms. It was a parody of a romantic picture, her hair tousled, her head cradled against his chest. Arm draped loosely around his neck. I remembered seeing them asleep in bed together, curled into each others' warmth.

It made me sick.

"If you try to stop me leaving, I'll toss her down the stairs," he said, and walked to the door. "I can assure you she'll break her neck at the very least. Maybe if you're lucky she'll only be paralyzed and you can be changing her bedpans and apologizing to her the rest of your life."

I swallowed and somehow managed to get myself to stand still. He looked back on his way out, warning clear in his eyes.

"Two hours, Joanne. No excuses."

I let him go. Partly, I just didn't see a way to stop him without risking Sarah's life; partly, I was just too stunned to cope. It was too much. Just . . . too much.

I slid back the patio door and walked out into the cool predawn breeze. Cotton-thick clouds formed a black shield and blotted out every evidence of approaching morning. It was as dark as midnight out here.

The security lights in the parking lot showed Eamon

walking calmly to his car. Sarah looked fragile and small and vulnerable in his arms. He put her in the passenger seat, strapped her in with no evidence of anything but gentleness, and shut the door. He even hesitated to be sure her robe was inside the car first.

He looked up at me for a moment, with no expression that I could read, and then got in and drove away.

I wanted a Djinn, all right.

And when I got my hands on one, Eamon was going to understand just how dangerous screwing with me could be.

I wouldn't have followed him even if I'd had the skills, mainly because there was no way he wouldn't notice the great white whale of the minivan trailing him through early-morning traffic. And Eamon, I already knew, had a criminal's perception about danger. No point in giving him a reason to carry through on threats I was pretty sure he meant.

I needed serious help. With John Foster gone, there was no Warden in town I could turn to for help, and I didn't have time to apply for any outside assistance. Two hours wouldn't get anything from Paul. Even if Marion had been inclined to lend a hand, she was out of the picture, recovering in some hospital from what must have been a near-death experience with one of Ashan's militant Djinn.

My allies—never plentiful—were MIA. I tried making calls, but Lewis wasn't answering his cell, Rahel didn't seem inclined to show up at my beck and call, and I knew better than to count on anything but the back of Jonathan's hand at this point.

David . . . no. I couldn't rely on David at all.

It was just me, and time wasn't on my side. Neither was power. I had enough power to get by, not enough to stage a major confrontation. It would take more than vitamins and protein shakes to bring me back from the kind of energy devastation I'd been through recently . . .

it was going to take time, and rest. Neither of which I'd
had, or was likely to get.

I stood on the balcony, watching the horizon. There
was something out there, something big and badass and
coming this way, and I could feel it like a storm of needles over my skin. It wasn't supposed to be there, hadn't
been forecast by any of the normal weather models. It
was purely, aetherically magical.

Everything was out of balance, wobbling like a bent
wheel, and I didn't know if it could ever be fixed
again . . . or if it could, what that price would be.

I closed my eyes and went up to the higher plane.

The world dissolved into a map of shadows and lights
and fog. My apartment building turned featureless; nobody spent enough time in it to give it character. I soared
up, arms outstretched, and watched the city grow smaller
under me, consolidating itself into a flickering pattern
of energy.

I went higher, until the Earth curved away from me.
As high as Wardens could safely go. I felt the drag warning me to stop, and hovered there, staring down at the
world's giant, swirling mass. In Oversight, it wasn't blue
and green and peaceful; it was a mass of shifting colors,
bands of energy that moved and twisted, fought and shattered and reformed. That wasn't just human potential at
work. Part of it was Djinn. Part of it came from deeper,
stronger places.

The world was fighting. Struggling with itself.

The storm off the coast of Florida was a black hole, a
photonegative of a hurricane. Still tightly wound up,
clouds just starting to spiral out from that hard center.
It felt . . . *old. Ancient.* And powerful.

I tore my attention away from it and concentrated on
what else I could see. Djinn were hard to spot; they
registered as flickers in the corners of my eyes, if they
were bound to service, and as nothing at all if they were
Free Djinn and trying to keep out of sight, which most
of them would be. Wardens flared here and there like

fireworks. Lots of activity throughout North and South America. The intensity of the flares meant that substantial power was getting expended. I couldn't help but imagine what that meant. Wardens were being killed, or fighting for their lives at the very least. And there was nothing I could do about that, either. A lot of them would be friends, people I'd met or worked with. Lots of names going up on the memorial wall, if there was a world at the end of this to remember them at all.

I couldn't see anything that would help me. The closest Warden to me was in the Florida panhandle, and he or she was hard-pressed with some kind of tornadic activity. Besides, from the intensity of the flares, no Djinn were involved.

Somebody has you, I whispered into the fog. *Where are you, David? Who found you? Who took you?*

Something stirred, creating eddies of power that whispered warm on my skin. I couldn't see him, but I could feel him. David was still alive. Still barely qualifying as Djinn, hoarding the power he'd taken from me at the dump.

Just tell me, I begged him. *Tell me and I'll come get you.*

I wasn't prepared for something to hit me, but something did, hard, knocking me in a stunned loop on the aetheric. My insubstantial body wavered, and I started to fall back toward reality in an uncontrolled spin. The world spun into a blur, and *wham,* I hit flesh again with enough of a shock to cause my body to stagger and make painful acquaintance with the stucco wall.

Whoever had David didn't want me finding him.

I remembered, with a hard shock, that I'd actually seen someone with a Djinn just two nights before. On the beach. One of Shirl's wolfpack going toe-to-toe with Lewis had been packing a Djinn. The last I'd seen of them, they'd been taking to the hills, but if they were really serious about taking out Lewis . . .

. . . then, if I found Lewis, I'd find Shirl. And a Djinn. Right now, any Djinn would do. I wasn't about to be picky, and somehow, taking a Djinn away from that particular crowd didn't bother me nearly as much as it probably should have, but then, when it came to people trying to kill the people I loved, my ethics got a little bendy.

I went up on the aetheric level again, this time searching specifically for Lewis. A bright flare of power to the west, maybe an hour down the coast. Where other Wardens showed up in Roman candle spurts, Lewis was a steady, bright torch. He had the ability to disguise himself nearly as well as a Djinn, but he wasn't currently bothering.

I kept half of my attention in Oversight, grabbed minivan keys and purse, and banged out of the apartment. I didn't have a lot of time, and God knew the mommy-mobile was hardly power transportation. . . .

When I got to it, I realized that the land yacht was canting sideways, like a ship heeled over on a reef. Eamon had taken the trouble to slash two of my tires before he'd absconded with my sister. Probably had done it while I'd been sleeping. *Son of a bitch . . . !*

I grabbed my cell phone and hit speed dial, pacing the parking lot nervously while it rang, and rang, and rang . . .

Cherise's sleepy voice finally said, "Oh, you'd *better* be cute, male, and horny."

"Shut up. I need you," I said flatly. "Skip the gloss and get your ass over here."

A rustle of sheets. Cherise's voice sharpened into focus. "Jo? What's wrong?"

"I need a ride and a driver who's not afraid of the gas pedal. Are you up for it?"

"Um . . . okay . . ." She sounded cautious. I didn't blame her. She'd never heard me in full-on action mode before. "Give me thirty min—"

"I don't have thirty minutes. I don't care if you show up in a sheet and fuzzy slippers; for Christ's sake just *get here*. Five minutes, Cherise. I'm serious." I chewed my lip and finally added, "My sister could die if you don't."

I heard her intake of breath and had a bad moment,

wondering if she'd just quietly hang up and leave me stranded. But Cherise, when it came down to it, was made of sterner stuff than that.

"Five minutes," she promised, and I heard the phone clatter to the nightstand before it shut off.

It was six minutes, but I was impressed with her commitment; when Cherise's car screeched to a stop in front of me, she was wearing a pink crop top, tight sweat pants, and flip-flops. No makeup. Her hair was yanked back into a ponytail, still frizzy from the bed.

It was the most unpolished I'd ever seen her look, and I loved her for it.

I dived into the passenger door as she threw it open, and she hit the gas and scratched the Mustang's first gear as she accelerated back toward the road. I managed to get myself buckled in—that much, I figured, was necessary—and got myself up into Oversight. Just enough to keep an eye on Lewis's beacon.

"Get to the beach and head west," I said. Cherise threw me a look, blew past a yellow light, and scratched the gears again as she hit third. The car roared and threw itself into a flat-out run. "I owe you."

"Fuckin' A," she said, and checked her rearview mirror. No cops, so far. I didn't dare glance at the speedometer, but when Cherise made the turn onto the highway I felt the tires screaming and struggling to hold the road. She wasn't cutting it any slack. The Mustang got traction and fishtailed and broke into a full gallop on the open road. There was early-morning traffic, but it was light. Cherise pegged her speed at just under a hundred and maneuvered in and around the slower traffic with the kind of precision reserved for combat drivers and NASCAR professionals. I'd picked the right girl. She did love to drive.

"So," she said as we hit a clear stretch and the Mustang opened up to a low, feral growl in fifth, "maybe you'd better explain to me why I'm about to get my ass arrested, not to mention take a mug shot with bad hair and no makeup."

"Cute British Guy," I yelled, and held my whipping hair back from my face in the brutal wind. I'd forgotten how much of a beating it was to drive this speed in a convertible. "Turns out he's not so cute. He says he's going to kill Sarah if I don't turn over a ransom."

"What?" Cherise's eyes were all pupil in the dim wash of the headlights, her face zombie green from the dashboard lights. "No way. Cute British Guy? Dude, he was *fine*!"

"I'd tell you that you can't judge a book by its cover, but . . ."

"I know, first I'd have to have read one." Cherise sent me a faint, wind-whipped smile. "I'm not dumb, you know!"

"I never thought you were."

"I just like guys!"

"Yeah. I know."

"So he's bad? Really?"

I thought of him on the couch, smiling, a hand gripping Sarah's pale, slack throat. "The worst."

Cherise considered that for a few seconds in silence, and then nodded. "You going to pay him off?"

"I don't know."

She nodded again, as if everything I'd just said made perfect sense. "I'm glad we have a plan."

We blew past one hundred twenty miles an hour, still accelerating.

The winds started kicking up twenty minutes later. I shifted my view in Oversight and saw that the storm was picking up speed and rotation. From the color bands in the aetheric, the eyewall probably had already hit Force Three speeds, and it was just getting started. The clouds were unfurling like war banners out of its core. The rotation was going to be monstrous. It could cover the entire state, once it got to its full size.

I could *feel* it. This storm was old, and angry, and it wanted blood. The core of it was surrounded by a thick, black curtain that felt like death.

I swallowed hard as I dropped back into real-world time. Cherise was nervously eyeing the clouds.

"I think I'd better put the top up," she said.

"Do you have to stop to do it?" She sent me a wordless *Are you mental?* look. "We don't stop, not for anything."

"We'll get soaked!"

"I'll keep the rain off of us," I said. There wasn't any point in concealing anything now. "I can do that. Just worry about keeping us on the road."

The rain hit about five minutes later, a patter of thick drops that quickly turned into a flickering silver curtain. Cherise backed off on her speed, shivering, and I hardened the air in a bubble over the top of the car. Warmed it a little, too. Invisible hardtop.

The rain hit the hardened barrier and slid off, just like glass. Cherise nearly wrecked her Mustang trying to get a look at it. "What the hell . . . ?!"

"I can do that," I repeated. "Don't worry about it. Just keep going." If we survived all this, I'd be in big trouble, but trouble was a cute, fond memory, at this point. I'd settle for mere trouble. If the Wardens wanted to haul me in and dig out my powers with a spork, they were welcome to, but *after* I finished this. Anybody who got in my way today was going to get a very ugly surprise.

"Man, that's . . . *cool,*" Cherise murmured. She took one hand off the steering wheel, reached up, and flattened it against thin air. "My God, Jo. That's, like, the coolest thing I've ever seen. Or not seen. Whatever."

The rain slid off in a continuous stream about an inch above her hand. The Mustang hit a puddle of water and shivered, unsure of its footing; she slapped her hand back down on the steering wheel and fought the car's need to spin out. It took an endless two seconds, but she got it under control and never slacked off the gas. "Okay, that was close."

"No shit."

"Fun, eh?"

We blew past truckers and passenger buses and nervous morning travelers. No cops. I couldn't believe the luck, but I knew it wouldn't last . .

There was a sudden, white-hot bolt of lightning through the clouds, traveling in a straight line above our car.

Up on the aetheric, Lewis's beacon suddenly went out.

Chaos. There was a lot of it, and it was getting hard to tell what was significant from what wasn't; the storm towering up over the sea and moving relentlessly this way was filling the aetheric with energy and a kind of metaphysical static. On top of that, there was power being thrown around on a more Wardenish level, adding to the general blizzard of instability.

I could barely get my bearings up there. I hung on grimly, half aware of Cherise talking anxiously next to me, of the Mustang hurtling on through the darkness, and tried to remember where Lewis had been. Had he gotten Rahel to airlift him out? No, Lewis didn't own Rahel, and without that bond, she wouldn't have been able to blip him from one place to another. No Warden I knew—not even Lewis—could do that sort of thing on his own.

So he was still here. Somewhere. Moving, maybe, and concealing his presence from a magical perspective. Lewis was really good at it; he'd eluded the entire organization for years while continuing to do his own thing. That took guts and talent.

I didn't see Lewis, but I did see a distinctive red-hot flare of power that surged and faded like a vacuum tube about to blow. I fixed on it and waited.

Another flare, brighter. It was off to the west, almost directly parallel to the road we were traveling.

"Turn right!" I shouted.

"Where?"

"Anywhere!"

I felt the heavy physical impact of the Mustang taking the turn, and grabbed for a handhold to keep myself from being thrown against the safety straps. Kept my attention up on the aetheric, though. It was getting tougher. The thin-air hardtop I was maintaining over the moving car took a hell of a lot of concentration and control, not to mention draining that finite reserve of power I had from Lewis.

Another pulse of power, this one longer. A couple of answering spurts of gold, weaker and briefer.

"Where am I going?" Cherise asked. She was yelling again, with that edge to her voice that meant she'd asked the question at least once or twice already. "Yo! Jo! Out of the coma already!"

I blinked and dropped down enough to study the real world. Not that there was a lot to study. We'd turned off the main road onto a smaller two-lane blacktop, and apart from the hard, relentless shimmer of the rain and the floating hot gold of the road stripe, we might as well have been pioneering intergalactic travel. Nothing out here. Nothing with lights, anyway.

The Mustang growled up a long hill and, in the distance, I saw a flash of something that might have been lightning.

"There!" I pointed at the afterburn. "See them?"

Cars. Two cars, driving fast. Not as fast as we were, but then, not many people would even think of trying it, especially in the rain. Cherise nodded and concentrated on holding the Mustang on the wet road as it snaked and turned. In the backwash of the headlights, I could see the flapping green shadows of thick foliage and nodding, wind-whipped trees.

Jeez, I hoped there weren't any 'gators on the road.

We took a turn too fast but Cherise held it, in defiance of the laws of physics and gravity, and powered out to put us just about five car lengths behind the other two drivers. They were side by side, matching speeds—or, at least, the big black SUV was matching speeds and trying like hell to drive the smaller Jeep off the road. Every time it tried, it hit some kind of cushion and was shoved back. No grinding of metal.

"Lewis," I said. Lewis was in the Jeep. I couldn't see or feel him, but he was the only one I could think of to be able to pull off that kind of thing while on the move *and* driving. Driving pretty damn well, too. He wasn't Cherise, but he was staying on the road, even at seventy miles per hour.

"What now?" Cherise asked. I didn't know. The SUV gleamed in our headlights like a wet black bug, nearly twice as large as the Jeep it was threatening. There were Wardens in there. Even if I'd wanted to, I couldn't just go into a straight-up fight—lives at risk, and maybe they were innocent lives, at that. Not to mention that the chaos swirling around us hardly needed another push.

I was coming to the conclusion that there wasn't a hell of a lot I *could* do until the two cars ahead of us resolved their dispute, one way or another, when I felt a surge of power and suddenly there was a presence in the backseat, moving at the corner of my eye, and two hands came down on my shoulders from behind and clamped down hard, holding me in place.

Diamond-sharp talons dressed up as sparkling neon fingernails pricked me in warning.

"Hold on!" Rahel yelled, and it all happened really, really fast.

The Jeep's flare of brakes.

A blur of green. I couldn't even see what it was, but it came out of the underbrush on the left-hand side; suddenly the SUV was *lifting,* soaring up engine-first into the air as if it had been shot out of a cannon, corkscrewing—

"Shit!" Cherise yelped, and hit the gas *hard*. The Mustang screamed on wet pavement and whipped around the Jeep. I felt the shadow pass over us and looked up to see the shiny black roof of the SUV tumble lazily across the sky, close enough to reach up and touch, and then the back bumper hit the road behind us with a world-shaking crunch.

When it stopped rolling, it was a featureless tangle of metal.

Cherise braked, too hard, fishtailed the Mustang to a

barely on-the-road stop, and Rahel's hands came away from my shoulders. It felt like there'd be bruises, later. I unbuckled my seat belt with shaking fingers and bailed out of the car to run back toward the wreckage.

I was halfway there, pelted by the cold rain, when the wreck blew apart in a fireball that knocked me flat and rolled me for ten painful feet. When I turned my head and got wet hair out of my eyes, I expected to see a Hollywood-style bonfire.

No. There was nothing much left to burn. Pieces of the SUV rained all over a hundred-foot area. A shredded tire smacked the pavement next to my outstretched hand, hot enough that I could feel its warmth; it was melted in places and sizzling in the rain.

Three people were standing in the road where the wreckage of the SUV had been. No—I corrected myself. Two people, one Djinn. I could see the flare of his yellow eyes even at this distance.

There was a heat shimmer coming off the other two, both in the real world and in the aetheric, that made me shiver in a sudden flood of memories. They were still wearing skin, but Shirl and the other Warden with her were just shells for something else. Something worse.

I remembered the feeling of the Demon Mark hatching under my skin, and had to control an impulse to run. *They're after Lewis.* They'd be irresistibly drawn to power that way.

I hadn't come to fight Lewis's battles for him. I needed a Djinn, and Shirl had one. Clearly, she'd kept the bottle on her, and it remained miraculously unbroken. Yep, all I had to do now was fight two Wardens with Demon Marks, liberate a Djinn, avoid explaining any of it to Lewis, and . . .

. . . and not die.

Simple.

I hadn't had any doubt that it was Lewis driving the Jeep, but I'd forgotten about Kevin; the kid exited the passenger door and ran to my side. He reached down to pull me up to a sitting position.

"Shit, you're alive," he said. He sounded surprised.

"Sorry about that. I'll try to do better next time."

Since I was getting up anyway, he gave me a strong yank and steadied me when I went a little soft on the upright part of standing. He didn't say anything else. His eyes were on the three facing us—or, actually, facing the Jeep.

Lewis stepped out of the driver's side, closed the door, and sent a quick glance toward me and Kevin. "Get them out of here," he said to Kevin. "Take the Mustang."

"I'm not going," I said. Lewis gave me the *look*, but he really didn't have time to argue because right then, the yellow-eyed Djinn came at him.

He wasn't fast enough to beat Rahel. The two met in midair, snarling and cutting at each other, and I felt the aetheric boiling and burning with the force of it. The Djinn was trying to move the Jeep, roll it over on Lewis. Lewis didn't move.

Neither did the Jeep.

"If you're staying," Lewis said, "do me a favor and hang on to my truck a minute."

He sounded utterly normal, like this was all in a day's work for him. Hell, maybe it was. Lewis's life was probably a lot more unexpected than mine. I didn't understand what he was saying for a second, and then I felt him shift his attention, and the Jeep started to shiver.

I hardened the air around it, holding it in place, as Lewis walked forward to within ten feet of where the other two Wardens were standing. Shirl—punk-ass Shirl, with her black goth clothes and bad attitude—was looking pretty rough these days. Lank, greasy hair; dark shadows around her eyes that weren't so much affectation as exhaustion. Her skin was an unhealthy shade of pale, so thin I could see blue veins under her skin. The shimmer in her eyes was full of pain and rage and something else, something inhuman.

"Lewis," I warned. He stopped me with an out-

...retched hand. He knew the danger of Demon Marks as well as I did, maybe better. The thing inside Shirl would do anything to get into him, to have access to that huge lake of power.

"I can help you," he said to her. "Let me help you."

I wanted to yell *No* or, more appropriately, *Are you insane?* but that was Lewis, all right. His first impulse always had been to heal.

Shirl called up a two-handed fireball and slammed it straight into his chest. It hit, exploded, and spread over him like molten lava. Under normal circumstances, Lewis would have simply shaken it off—fire was one of his powers, of course, and he had a natural resistance to it— but this was demon-fueled, and a hell of a lot stronger than usual.

It dug deep into his skin. I saw him stagger, concentrate, and manage to clear it off, but it left blackened holes in his clothes and angry red marks on his skin that looked raw and painful. Before he could do more than take a breath, the other Warden called up the Earth, and I felt the ground shudder as a huge tree toppled, straight toward Lewis. Lewis managed to move, jumping forward, almost close enough to go toe-to-toe with the two fighting him.

Shirl slammed him again, a dazzling orange curtain of flames, and he staggered and fell. Vines whipped out of the underbrush and fastened around his ankles, snaking around his calves, pulling him flat. Before he could focus on fighting them, Shirl was on him again, leaping like a tiger, fireball at the ready.

I hit her with wind and tossed her a dozen feet down the road. "Do something!" I yelled at Kevin. He looked torn, and more than a little scared; I remembered that he'd already been in a dogfight with Shirl and her crew, and come out near death. *Dammit.* I couldn't blame the kid.

"No, Kevin! Stay out of it!" Lewis yelled, countermanding me, and the vines holding his ankles shriveled and he rolled up to his feet . . .

. . . just in time for Shirl to throw another fireball.

This time, he caught it. One-handed, a neat, graceful capture, and he juggled the hell-ball from one hand to the other as he watched Shirl approach. The other Warden was up and moving, too. Both stalking him.

"Dammit, Lewis—" I said.

"Nag me later."

One of the two Wardens must own the Djinn, and I was pretty sure it wasn't Shirl. That meant the other guy—the one who had the clever, off-kilter face and Canadian accent that I remembered from back on the beach—was the proud owner. One of Shirl's running buddies.

One I needed to take down.

I shook free of Kevin and moved right. Shirl watched me with bright-glimmering eyes. I was more powerful than she was, and that meant the Demon would want to jump to me . . . but then again, Lewis was the most powerful guy in the world. No way it would pass him up for me.

Unless, of course, it didn't mind doing a little hopscotching. I watched her carefully as I spiraled in closer to the other Warden.

"So," I said to him, "I don't think we've been properly introduced. Joanne Baldwin. Weather. You are . . . ?"

Pissed off, apparently. Because we were on an asphalt road, he couldn't do Marion Bearheart's favorite trick of softening the sand beneath my feet, but he had plenty of other stuff to work with. The area wasn't exactly denuded of life.

Sure enough, he found something. Something that sailed out of the dark and landed on the road with a raw growl, and padded into the glow of the headlights.

It was a cougar. Its long, lean body gleamed in the rain, and it had the most gorgeous green eyes I'd ever seen, large and liquid and pure animal power. It paced toward me with unnatural focus, and I could see its back legs tensing for a jump. Oh, yeah, that would keep me busy.

"Um . . . nice . . . kitty . . ." I took a step back, trying to figure out what I had in my arsenal, short of lightning bolts, that was likely to stop a predatory feline.

Nope. I had nothing.

There was a flare of fire, and Lewis was abruptly too busy to help—I felt the heat blaze over my skin, harsh enough to singe my hair. That left me, the cougar, and the Earth Warden.

"No fair, using endangered species," I said, and swallowed hard as the cat began to growl. It was watching me with fixed, hungry, empty eyes. "Seriously. Not good, man."

The cat jumped. I yelped and ducked and called for wind, which was a mistake because the intense fire being summoned up between Lewis and Shirl created updrafts and unpredictable wind shears and, instead of tossing the cat safely off to the side, it landed right on me and knocked me flat on the pavement.

Heavy as a man, warmer than one, smelling of wet fur and fury and blood, claws already digging into the soft flesh of my stomach and *oh God* . . .

I sucked the air out of its lungs. Just like that, faster than thought—I admit, I wasn't worried about doing it nicely. The cat choked, opened its mouth, and gagged for air, but it couldn't find any. I rolled. It scrabbled for balance, digging bloody furrows in my flesh. I called another gust of wind. This time, it cooperated, and knocked the big cat off of me onto its side. It rolled up immediately, gagging, head down, shaking in confusion.

"Sorry," I whispered, and swiped bloody hands across my face to drag my wet hair back. I didn't dare take too close a look at my body. The bottom part of my torso felt suspiciously warm and numb. At least my guts weren't falling out. I was counting my blessings.

I couldn't kill the cougar—evil people, yeah, okay, but not cats who were just doing their survival job—so I only had a few minutes at most to get rid of the one controlling it.

And he already had something else lined up. I caught the blur of motion out of the corner of my eye. There was no way I could move in time, and my brain snap-shotted a snake—a big, unhappy-looking snake—striking for me with enormous fangs in a flat, triangular shaped head as big as my hand.

Rahel caught it in midstrike, thumped its head with one neon-polished fingernail, and the snake went limp in her hands. She looked perfectly well groomed. There was no sign she'd been in any kind of a fight, and I didn't see the other Djinn anywhere.

"You should be more careful," she said—to the snake—and set him down in the underbrush. He crawled away with fast convulsions of his body and disappeared in seconds.

Rahel turned her eerie, hawk gold eyes on the Earth Warden, and smiled. Not the kind of smile you'd want to get on your worst day, believe me.

The Earth Warden took a giant step back.

"Djinn are killing Wardens," she said. Again, it might have been a comment to me . . . or not. "I don't alto-gether find this distressing."

"Good thing for me that I'm not a Warden anymore, then," I said. "Busy?"

"Not especially."

"Don't need to, ah, help Lewis . . . ?"

Her eyes flicked briefly to the enormous fireball that surrounded the other two. Inside of it, it looked as though Lewis had Shirl in a choke hold. "I don't believe that will be necessary."

"Then would you mind—?"

"Not at all."

The Earth Warden's nerve failed and he bolted. Rahel took him down with one neat jump, carrying him down to the shining, wet pavement, and shoved him flat with a knee in the small of his back. He flailed. It didn't much matter.

"You can let the cougar go now," she called back to me. "It won't harm you."

Oh, right, easy for her to say . . . I removed the vac-uum from around the cat, and it choked in a fast breath, then another, and bounded up and away. Following the path of the snake. I wished them both luck.

Speaking of which . . . I skinned up my shirt and traced the wounds in my stomach with my fingertips. Blood sheeted wetly down, pink in the rain, but it looked pretty superficial. No guts poking out. Some prime scar material, though. I gulped damp air and tried not to think how close I'd come to being cat chow, and then moved to where Rahel had the Warden in a position of utter helplessness.

I got down on one knee, which was painful, and he turned his head to stare at me. Yep, there was a definite component of demon-shimmer in his eyes. I didn't know if anyone else could have seen it; I was a pretty unique case, having had the Demon Mark and Djinn experiences. It looked like he was in the early stages. Probably wasn't even aware yet how the creature growing inside of him under that mark would be influencing his actions, compromising his judgment.

Eating his power even as it stoked the fire and made him feel more in control.

I couldn't help him with that. He had to help himself, and I was about to take away his only way to do that.

"Hold him," I said to Rahel. She shifted her weight off the man, but kept him flat with one hand between his shoulder blades.

"Let go!" he yelled. I ignored him and stuck my hand in his right coat pocket. Nothing. The left held a ring of keys. I dropped them on the ground.

"Roll him over," I said. The Djinn took one arm and flipped him like a pancake, and this time held him down with her palm on his forehead. Paralyzed. She flicked me a look, and I read unease in it. She reached over and sliced open his shirt with one taloned finger, and folded the cloth back to show me the black, slow-moving tattoo of the Demon Mark.

He started screaming. Whatever she was doing to hold him down, the demon didn't like it. His whole body arched in pain, and Rahel's face went blank with concentration.

I ransacked his pants pockets and came up with—of all things—one of those cheap leather lipstick cases, the stiff kind exported from India or China that snap open and have a mirror built in for touchups. No lipstick inside of this one.

This one held some cotton batting and a small perfume sample bottle, open and empty. The plastic snap-in plug was lying next to it.

I reached in and grabbed the cool glass, and felt the world shift in that odd, indefinable way, as if gravity had suddenly taken a left turn.

A Djinn misted out of the dark, staring at me. It began forming into a new appearance, and I realized that I didn't want to see what effect my subconscious was going to have on it (please, God, don't let it look like David . . .). I folded it in my fist and said, "Back in the bottle."

It disappeared. I took the plug from the cotton in the lipstick case and slid it home in the mouth of the bottle, and felt that connection cut out, except for a low-level hum. Not nearly as strong as David, this one, but then it didn't really matter.

Rahel was watching me with a frown. It's not good when Djinn frown. In general, Djinn shouldn't be annoyed.

"I thought you didn't believe in slavery," she said. Her cornrows rustled as she cocked her head, and I heard the cold click of beads even over the continuing pounding rain. "Ah. Unless, of course, it's expedient. How human of you."

"Shut up," I said. "And thanks for saving my life."

She shrugged. "I haven't yet."

And she let go of the Earth Warden.

He came up fast and fighting, and we went back to work.

* * *

The aftermath was like a war zone, if war zones had spectator sections. The wrecked SUV still smoldered and belched smoke; the whole damn road was buckled and uneven and burned down to the gravel in places. There would be some serious repaving later.

The spectator section was composed of Cherise and Kevin and Rahel, who were over by the Mustang. Cherise and Kevin were sitting on the trunk, huddled together under a yellow rain poncho held like a tent. Rahel paced back and forth, oblivious to the rain, casting looks out to the east, toward the ocean. Her eyes were glowing so brightly that they were like miniature suns.

Shirl and the Earth Warden—I still didn't know his name—were unconscious in the Jeep, restrained with good old-fashioned duct tape. Lewis had also done some fancy Earth-power thing that lowered their metabolisms. He could keep them in a sleep state for hours, maybe days, if he didn't have better things to do.

Lewis and I were leaning against the Jeep, gasping for air and trying not to moan. Much.

"You okay?" he asked me at last, and put that warm hand on the back of my neck. I managed to nod. "No, you're not. You're too weak. Again."

"I'm all right."

"Bullshit." He looked like hell; he was one to talk. Burned, blistered, ragged, suffering in his eyes. And a bone-deep weariness, too. He'd been running hard for a long time, and today was just another one of those days. He didn't push the subject, though; he looked over at Rahel, then out toward the sea. "You feel that?"

"Yeah." I sucked in a deep breath. "It's bad. Maybe as bad as Andrew back in '92."

"Worse," he said succinctly. "This is bigger and stronger."

Worse than a Category Five. That wasn't good news, clearly. "So? What do we do?"

"*You* do nothing. Jo, you're like a wet rag; there's nothing you can contribute. You need to get the hell out of here, I told you before. Fighting will get you killed."

I swept him with a look. Burns, bloody wounds, and all. "Is this the last of them? The ones looking to take you out?"

"Probably not."

"And *who* should be running?"

He smiled. It was just a little smile, tired and sweet, but it went through me like an arrow. "How's David?"

I turned away, all the light going out inside. "I don't know. I don't know where he is. Things are . . ." I took a deep breath and said it, just said it. "I lost him. I lost the bottle." God, it hurt. I couldn't imagine that anything could ever hurt worse.

I could feel Lewis staring at the back of my head for a long few heartbeats, and then the Jeep's weight shifted as he pushed off.

When I turned, he was stalking through the pouring rain to where Cherise, Kevin, and Rahel were.

Okay, what did I say?

He grabbed Kevin by the collar and yanked him bodily out from under the plastic poncho. Cherise yelped and flinched, and Kevin yelled, and Lewis dragged him, stumbling, by the front of his greasy-looking T-shirt back over to me.

"Give it back," he said. Kevin flailed until Lewis shook him, hard. "I'm not fucking around with you, kid. *Give her back the bottle.*"

"What the hell . . . ?" I blurted, amazed, and then I remembered something Detective Rodriguez had said, in the surveillance van. *The kid who was in your apartment last night ripped off some cash from the flour jar in your kitchen.* Kevin had ransacked his way through the apartment, hadn't he? And if anybody knew about the value of Djinn bottles . . .

I'd never even thought about it. I was too stunned to be angry.

Kevin looked pale, panicked, and stubborn. "I don't know what you're talking about, man!"

Oh, wait, the stun was wearing off now. Yep, anger was coming on strong. I shoved Lewis out of the way and grabbed the kid's skinny, strong arms, shoving him back against the Jeep. "Don't bullshit me, Kevin! Did you call him out? Did you try to use him?" Kevin didn't say anything, just looked at me. Pale as skim milk, and just about as appetizing. "Dammit, *say something*! Is David all right?"

Kevin licked his already wet lips, averted his eyes, and mumbled, "Not my fault. He asked me to do it."

I felt shock slip over me in a cold wave. "Excuse me?"

"I was just looking around. He—he appeared in the room and he told me to take the bottle."

"He couldn't tell you *where it was,* you asshole!" Djinn rules, although I'd seen Jonathan break them once. I'd asked David point-blank where his bottle was, and he couldn't tell me . . .

. . . or, I realized with a sinking feeling close to despair, he didn't *want* to tell me.

"He didn't have to say anything," Kevin was explaining. "He just stood there, you know, next to the nightstand. It was kinda obvious."

I tried to say something—what, I don't know—but it didn't make sense when it got to my lips. I just stood there, staring at Kevin's blank eyes.

"Look, he didn't want you to get hurt anymore," Kevin said. "He thought—if I held on to the bottle for a while—maybe you could get stronger. I was supposed to give him back, later. When things got better."

I felt my knees go weak. My stomach hurt where the cat had clawed me, my head hurt, my knees hurt; God, my heart was breaking. "He wanted to leave me."

Lewis put his hands on my shoulders. "I think he was trying to save your life, Jo."

"Bullshit. *Bullshit!*" I was suddenly furious. "This is— you guys just—*men!* You don't make decisions for me, got it? I'm not some fragile little flower! I have a life, and it's *my* life, and if I want to—"

"Throw it away?" Lewis interjected helpfully.

Okay, he had a point. I didn't let it bother me. "Hey, I grubbed around at the *dump* looking for him! Hello! *Leave a damn note if you're stealing my boyfriend!*"

And I realized that Kevin hadn't answered my original question. His eyes were still frightened and blank.

"Oh God," I said. "Did you use him? Kevin, did you call him out of the bottle and use him?"

He nodded. Rain dripped in silver strings from his lank hair to patter onto his soaked T-shirt. He was shivering. We were all likely to get hypothermia out there if we weren't careful.

"Is he—"

"He's gone," Kevin said. It sounded hard and harsh, and I could tell he didn't want to say it. "Sorry, but it's like the bottle's empty. He's just—gone, he just screamed and he, you know . . . blipped out. I kept calling, but he wouldn't come back. He couldn't. I needed him, Jo, I'm sorry but I had to do it, Lewis was in trouble and—"

I knew. I'd done the same thing, hadn't I? I'd called David even when I knew it was killing both of us.

And now I knew why Kevin hadn't waded into the fight with his usual teen-angst enthusiasm. He couldn't. Like me, he'd been drained of power. And it hadn't been enough.

If he couldn't sense David in the bottle, it was because David was an Ifrit. Maybe he was in the bottle, maybe he wasn't; Kevin probably hadn't thought to order him back inside and seal it up. To him, David had just vanished without a trace.

I couldn't help but feel a sick certainty that this time he wouldn't be coming back.

I still had hopes, until Kevin dug the blue glass bottle out of his bag and put it into my hands, but it was no more mystical than grabbing an empty jar out of the kitchen cabinet. No sense of connection. It was an empty bottle, and *God,* I couldn't feel David's presence at all.

I couldn't even feel him draining me, and that had at least been something, before.

"Back in the bottle, David," I said, and waited a second before I slammed the rubber stopper home into the open mouth. I wrapped the bottle in a spare towel from the back of the Jeep, then buried it in my purse with the lipstick case and the Djinn sealed inside.

"Um," Kevin said hesitantly, "are we—are you—"

"Do I want to kill your punk ass? You betcha." My hands were shaking, and not from the chill. "I don't care what David said, you didn't have any right to do this. No *right*, do you understand?"

He nodded. He looked sullen and miserable, a combination only possible in teenagers.

"You *ever* touch anything I own again, and I swear to God, Kevin, you'll wish I'd torched your ass in Vegas."

"Like I don't wish it already," he muttered.

"What?"

"Nothing." He gave me a blank, militant stare. I threw Lewis a furious look.

He shrugged.

I growled in frustration. "I have to get back to Fort Lauderdale."

It wasn't like me to run out, not when the storm of the century was building up force out there off the coast and roaring our way. He raised his eyebrows. "I thought I'd have to get Rahel to haul you out of here kicking and screaming," he said. "And you didn't come chasing all the way out here to find me, flattering as it might be, did you? What's wrong?"

I told him about Eamon and Sarah, and watched his eyes go lightless and angry. If it had been me, I'd have dropped everything to go to his aid, but I knew not to expect the same in return. Lewis was a big-picture guy.

"I can't," he said finally. Regretfully. "I'm sorry. This thing—" He nodded out at the black void on the east horizon. "One life saved might mean thousands lost. I have to stay here."

"I know."

"Jo—"

"*I know.*" I swallowed hard and put my hand on his cold, wet, beard-roughened cheek. "Go do what you do. Eamon's just a guy, not a Warden. I can handle him."

I knew Lewis was thinking, *You've done a bang-up job of it so far,* but he was too much of a gentleman to say so.

"Yeah," Kevin snorted. "Like you've done such a good job so far."

Case in point.

I walked away, back to the Mustang, where Cherise was still sitting under her poncho. Shivering. Looking dazed and storm-tossed. Her high-gloss finish had been power-stripped, along with her self-confidence about her place in the world.

"Cher?" I said. She fastened a blank stare on me. "We can go back now."

"Uh-huh," she said, in a bright, almost normal tone, and slid off the trunk to go around to the driver's side. Sometime during the hysteria, I noticed she'd remembered to put the top up on the convertible. Her hand was shaking uncontrollably as she fumbled for the door handle.

I gently guided her back around the car and opened the passenger side for her. "My turn to drive," I said. It took her three tries to get in the car, even with help.

The interior was wet enough to squish. I sighed and hated myself for wasting the energy, but the truth was I was tired and cold and shaking too. I banished the moisture from the car and our hair and clothes, leaving a sharp, fresh ozone smell and, unfortunately, frizzed hair. Cherise didn't seem to notice. I turned on the car's heater and pointed all available vents in her direction.

I had to reach over and fasten her seat belt for her. She wasn't responding to suggestion.

The Mustang rumbled and growled as I backed it up and weaved it around the Jeep, catching Lewis and Kevin in the headlights. They looked fragile and bruised, far too small to go up against the fury of nature gathering out to sea. Lewis gave me a nod and a small, funny salute. Kevin's eyes were lingering not on me, but Cherise. I bumped the car over the uneven, buckled road until we were back at clean surface again, and then opened it up to a run. It drove tight and fast, hugging the road and responding to a touch like an eager lover.

I'd missed Mustangs.

Cherise said, "So you're, like, a witch, right?"

"What?"

"A good witch?" She didn't sound too sure of that. I sighed. "Yeah, kind of. I hope."

She nodded jerkily. "Okay, sure. That makes sense." Hollow words, and an empty, scared look in her eyes.

I'd forgotten what it must be like, to have your certainty in life taken away, to find all the science and order and logic taken away. To find out humankind wasn't the center of the universe, and things weren't simple and controllable.

It hurt. I knew it hurt.

"Cherise," I said. We rounded a curve and the headlights washed a riot of vegetation with color. I caught the glint of green eyes, quickly gone. "What you saw—that doesn't happen all the time, okay? It's not that the world is a lie you've been told. It's that there are some truths you haven't heard yet."

She shrugged. "I'm okay." The words were just as wrong as the movement, mechanical and dead. "So when you were working at the station, were you just—was it just some kind of game? Were you ever really—"

"This stuff doesn't pay the bills," I said gently. "Saving the world really isn't all that profitable. You'd be surprised how little you get paid for that kind of thing."

That won a smile of surprise.

"Not really," she said. "Crime pays better than virtue."

"You hear that on TV?"

"Read it," she said, and leaned her head against the window glass. "Damn, I'm freaked."

"Anybody would be. Take it easy, okay? Ask questions. I'll do my best to answer you."

She hesitated a second, then waved a hand out at the storm assembling over the ocean, like a million soldiers ready to attack. "Can't you stop that?"

"No."

"Just no?"

"When it's that big and mean? Yeah. Just no. Maybe Lewis can do it—"

"The old one or the young one?"

"What?"

"You know, the old guy in the flannel or the young one in black?"

Old guy? I threw her a look. "He's my age!"

"In your dreams."

"Not the young one, the—the—" I glared. "*Lewis* is my age. Kevin is the *punk-ass kid*."

"Well, the punk-ass kid was nice to me," she said, and shrugged. "What? It's not my fault I'm twenty-two and you're—not."

Oh, I was *so* going to get my own car.

We drove in silence for another ten minutes before I said, because I couldn't resist it, "I'm not old."

"Yeah," she agreed, and sighed, and put her head back against the upholstery. "You just keep telling yourself that."

I gunned the Mustang up to one hundred thirty on the way back through the storm.

Surprisingly, we didn't die in a fiery crash, but that was probably just God looking after fools and children, and as I blasted past the WELCOME TO FORT LAUDERDALE road sign and had to kill my speed to just under sixty, due to traffic, my cell phone rang. I fumbled for it and took the call.

"Eamon?"

"The same." That lovely voice sounded as calm and deceptively friendly as ever. "Got what I asked for?"

"Yes."

"Good. I'd hate for Sarah to suffer."

"Is she awake? I want to talk to her."

"What you want really doesn't concern me, love. As we seem to have a storm kicking up hell, I'd like to get this ended as soon as possible. No point in dying tonight, especially from something as stupid as fate."

My hand was clenched tight around the cell. I forced it to relax. Ahead on the road, some grandpa in an ancient Ford Fiesta swerved into my lane doing thirty-five; I instantly checked perimeters and glided into the left-hand passing lane to whip around him. Tractor trailer ahoy, lumbering like a brachiosaur. I managed to slip around him and behind a white Lamborghini that wasn't any more patient with the current traffic than I was. I drafted him as he negotiated his way to free airspace.

"Where?" I asked. Eamon's warm chuckle was unpleasantly intimate.

"Well, why don't you come to my place? Maybe we can enjoy a nice drink after we conclude our business. Possibly Sarah might be open-minded enough to . . ."

"Shut the hell up," I snapped. "I have a Djinn. Do you want it the nice way or the hard way? Because all I have to do is tell him to kill you, you know."

"I know." All of the needling humor dropped out of Eamon's voice, replaced by something hard and as chilly as winter's midnight. "But if you do that, you won't get your sister back. It took a lot of research—which was accomplished with a lot of screaming on the part of my research subjects—but I know the rules. I know what the Djinn can do, and what they can't. And you'd best not take a chance that I've been misled."

He was right. There were rules to the covenant with the Djinn. Responsibilities a master had to accept. Violating those rules had some serious blowback, and if he understood enough, he could have set it up to be sure Sarah died with him.

No, I couldn't take the chance. Not that I'd been willing to in the first place.

"Fine," I said. "Give me the address."

It was close to the beach, which wasn't an advantage right now; I hung up and checked the progress of the storm. The streetlights were blowing nearly sideways, and signs were fluttering like stiff metal flags in the relentless wind. Hurricane-force winds, and it was just the leading edge of the storm.

As I took the exit from the freeway heading for the beach, I caught sight of the ocean, and it made my guts knot up in fear. Those smooth, greasy-looking swells out toward the ocean, exploding into gigantic sails of spray when they hi shallow water . . . blow on a small bowl of water and look at the way the waves form, heading toward the edge. Concentric rings, mounting higher as force increases.

The storm surge was going to be horribly high. Houses at or near the beach were already doomed. My apartment complex was probably toast, too—so much for the new furniture.

Life was so fragile, so easily blown apart.

"Look out!" Cherise yelled, and threw out a hand to the right.

I barely had time to register something big coming from that direction, hit the brakes, send the car into a spin across two lanes of traffic—thankfully, unoccupied—and manage to get us straightened around in a lane by the time we came to a lurching stop.

A boat bounced in from the right and landed keel-first on the road, oars flying off like birds into the wind. It splintered into fiberglass junk. I watched, open-mouthed, as it rolled off in a tangle.

"Holy shit," Cherise whispered. "Um . . . shouldn't we, like, get somewhere? Maybe the hell out of Florida?"

Yeah. Good idea.

Eamon's building was a needle-thin avant-garde structure, the kind of place that, when they talk about building erection, they really mean the double entendre. I couldn't read the sign, but I decided the best possible name for it was Testosterone Towers, and it was someplace I intended never to live.

Even if Eamon wasn't there.

Cherise looked pale and scared, and I didn't blame her; the weather was getting worse, and this was exposed territory. Last place I wanted to be was in a high-rise . . . safe from the storm surge, sure, but way too much glass. I was thinking of something in a tasteful concrete bunker, up on a bluff. And as soon as I had Sarah back, we were going to find one.

"Should I stay here?" Cherise asked cautiously. I pulled the Mustang into the parking garage and went up to the next-to-highest level. It was the logical spot . . . not completely exposed, only one level could collapse on you, and it was higher than the likely storm surge. Bottom level would be safest from flying debris, but a collapse was possible, and drowning an added hazard.

"I think you'd better come with me," I said. "Just stay close."

We got out, and even in the shelter of the garage the scream of the wind was eerie. It ripped past me at gale speeds, pulling my hair and grabbing at my clothes. I braced myself and went around to take Cherise's hand. I had a little more height and weight than she did; she was too small and light for this kind of thing.

We made it to the stairs and found a hamster tunnel of plastic and lights leading from the parking garage to the building. It looked like being in the middle of a dishwasher on full spray, and I could hear an ominous creaking and cracking from the plastic. I tugged Cherise along at a trot. The concrete under our feet—padded by carpet—trembled and yawed. Leaks ran down the walls, and half the carpet was already soaked.

When we were three-quarters through it, I heard a sharp *crack* behind us, and turned to look back.

A huge metal road sign had impaled itself through the plastic and hung there, shuddering. It read SLIPPERY WHEN WET.

"Funny," I told Mother Nature. "Real funny."

The plastic shivered under the force of another brutal hit from the wind, and I saw stars forming around stress points. This little tunnel through the storm wasn't going to last.

I tugged Cherise the rest of the way. The big double doors were key-locked, but I was well beyond caring. My little theoretical addition to the practical chaos already swirling around wouldn't matter a damn, really; I focused and got hold of the running-on-empty power I had left, and found just about enough to fund a tiny lightning bolt to fry the electronic keypad.

The door clicked open.

Beyond that was a deserted, impersonal lobby, with a

long black couch with kidney-roll pillows running down one wall. It was very quiet. There was a large computer screen displaying names and numbers—almost all of the spaces were vacant. In fact, it looked as if the building was just opening up for renters.

Pity about the hamster-trail tunnel out there, in that case.

These kinds of places usually had security on duty, but there was a noticeable lack; I figured that the cops had already been around and instructed evacuation, and the security guy had scurried along with them.

I walked over to the touch screen and paged through the floors. Blank . . . blank . . . an import/export company . . . blank . . . blank . . . *Drake, Willoughby and Smythe*. Seventh floor. I took a look around the lobby. It was built for impressing visitors, not views, so there weren't many windows. That was good. I spotted a camouflaged door behind the empty security desk. When I tried the doorknob, it was locked; I braced myself and kicked half a dozen times before I got the lock to yield. It looks easier on TV, trust me.

The room behind was small, bare except for a cot, desk and chair. I sat Cherise down on the cot and took her hands. "Wait for me," I said. "Don't leave here unless you have to, okay? It's a windowless interior room; you're pretty safe here."

She nodded, pale and looking young enough to braid her hair and sell Girl Scout cookies. I couldn't help it; I hugged her. She hugged me back, fiercely.

"I won't let anything happen to you," I said. I felt her gulp for breath. "It's going to be fine, Cher. Who's the tough girl?"

"Me," she whispered.

"Damn right." I pulled away, gave her a smile, and watched her try to return it. She was scared to death. Had reason to be. I was trying not to indulge in a complete, total freakout myself.

I left her there, kicked off my shoes, and hit the stairs.

*   *   *

When I got to the seventh floor, I was wheezing and flushed and the place the cougar had slashed me was throbbing like a son of a bitch, but the bleeding was still minimal. Still, I was willing to bet that I was looking like a wrathful Amazon. Frizzy hair, bloody, ripped shirt, and I hadn't had the time or energy to shave my legs in days.

The mostly intact jeans were all that was saving me from complete embarrassment.

I gasped until I was sufficiently oxygenated, then adjusted the weight of my purse, dropped my shoes to the ground and stepped back into them. And yeah, okay, I straightened my hair. Because when you're going to confront someone like Eamon, every little bit helps.

The last thing I did was take the stopper from David's blue glass bottle. I left it buried in the bottom of my purse. *Now or never,* I told myself. I had no way to hedge this bet. I had to take some things on faith.

The frosted glass doors at the front advertised, in small, discreet type, the investment offices of Drake, Willoughby and Smythe. Lights on inside. I pulled on the ice-cold metal handle and the glass swung open with a well-balanced hiss.

Beyond was a reception area, all blond wood and silver, with a giant picture window at the back. The contrast was eerie and terrifying . . . the cool indifference of the interior design, the roiling primal fury of the storm outside, smearing the glass in sheets of rain. The glass was trembling, bowing in and out. There wasn't all that much time to waste.

There was a second set of glass doors, these clear instead of frosted. I shoved my way through them and into a hallway lined with a dozen offices.

Light spilled out the open door of the one at the end.

I walked down the expensively carpeted last mile, passing reproductions of old masters, framed documents, alcoves with statues. At the end of the hall I turned left and saw the name on the door.

EAMON DRAKE.

The office was a triangle of glass, and his desk sat at

the pointy end, sleek and black and empty of anything but a blotter, a penholder, and a single sheet of white paper. Very minimalist.

Sarah was lying on the black leather couch close to the left-hand wall. She was awake, but clearly not fully conscious; she was still wearing the bathrobe, and he hadn't bothered to fully close it. At least, I thought with a wave of sickness, he hadn't fully *opened* it. That was a little comfort.

Eamon was sitting on the arm of the couch, watching me. There was a gun in his hand.

It was pointed straight at Sarah's head.

"Let's not waste time," he said. "This storm could make our little, petty differences seem mild. Hand it over and we're finished, thanks, ta, bye."

I opened my purse and took out the lipstick case I'd taken from Shirl's demon-infected Warden friend. I flipped it open to show him the bottle.

"Open it and make him appear," Eamon said. "I hope you'll forgive me if I say that I don't want a free sample of Eternity for Men instead of what we agreed on."

I took the small perfume sample bottle out, unstopped it, and told the Djinn to appear. He obliged, not that he had much choice; he came out as a youngish-looking guy, dark-haired, with eyes the color of violets. Blank expression. I felt a resonance of connection, but nothing deep and certainly nothing strong. Djinn were, of course, powerful, but on a scale of one to ten, he was maybe a three.

"Back in the bottle," I told him, and he misted and vanished. I put the stopper back in and raised my eyebrows at Eamon. "Satisfied?"

He cocked his head, staring at me with those deceptively soft, innocent eyes. Oh, he was a clever one. He knew there was something wrong.

"I'm not a bad judge of people," he said. "And this is too easy, love. You're taking this too meekly."

"What do you want me to do? Scream? Cry? Get my sister killed?" I clenched my teeth and felt jaw muscles flutter as I tried to breathe through the surge of helpless fury. "*Take the fucking bottle, Eamon.* Otherwise we're all going to die in here."

He caressed Sarah's hair with the barrel of the gun. "Threats don't serve you."

"It's not a threat, you idiot! Look out there! We're in a goddamn Cuisinart if these windows go!"

He spared a glance for the storm, nodded, and held out his hand. Long, graceful fingers, well-manicured. He looked like a surgeon, a concert pianist, something brilliant and precise.

"Throw it," he said.

I pitched the bottle to him, underhanded. He plucked it effortlessly out of the air, and for a second I saw the awe in his eyes. He had what he wanted.

Now was the moment of risk, the moment when everything could go to hell. All he had to do was pull the trigger.

He looked at me, smiled, and thumbed the stopper out of the bottle. It rolled away, onto the carpet, and the Djinn misted out again. Subtly different, this time. Paler skin, eyes still violet but hair turning reddish, and cut in a longer style that made him look younger and prettier.

"Pity he isn't female," Eamon said critically. "What's your name?"

"Valentine."

"Valentine, can you keep these windows from breaking?"

The Djinn nodded. I opened my mouth to warn Eamon he was making a mistake phrasing it as a question, but he didn't need me to tell him that.

"Keep the windows from breaking," Eamon said, and the order clicked in. The glass stopped rattling. Outside, the storm continued to howl, but we were about as safe as it was possible to be. From broken glass, at least.

Eamon let out his breath in a trembling sigh, and I saw the hot spark in his eyes.

"You're only human," I told him. "You don't have

the reserves of power to fund him for anything more powerful than that. Don't be stupid."

"Oh, I'm not interested in the world, I assure you. One person at a time is my motto." He gave me another fevered, glittering smile. "You kept your bargain."

"Yes," I said. "I did."

"You know, I'm sorry I'm going to have to do this. Valentine, kill—"

"David," I said, "come out."

That was all it took.

A black blur that Eamon couldn't see, and suddenly Valentine was falling, screaming, ripping at the black shadow that formed over and around him. It was a nightmare to watch. David had changed into something more horrible than I could stand to see, and something that even my eyes wouldn't properly focus . . . I caught hints of sharp edges and teeth and claws, of insectile thrashing limbs. I stumbled off to the side, well away from them, until my hip banged painfully into Eamon's desk.

Eamon was thrown. "Valentine! Kill her!"

Valentine wasn't in any shape to obey commands. He was down flat on his face, screaming, and the Ifrit's claws were ripping him apart into mist.

Killing him.

Devouring him.

Eamon hadn't expected this, and for a long moment he was frozen, staring at his Djinn dying on the floor, bottle still held useless in his hand.

I called lightning and zapped him. Not fatally, because I didn't have it in me, but he screamed and jerked and slid bonelessly off the arm of the couch into a twisted pile on the carpet.

The bottle rolled free. The gun bounced under the couch.

The Ifrit finished its meal and began its transformation, taking on weight and shape and human form.

A trembling, naked human form.

David fell to his hands and knees, gagging, gasping, and collapsed on his side, his back to me. I stared at the beautiful long slide of his back and wanted so badly to run to him and stroke his hair, cover him in kisses, and hold him close and swear that I'd never let this happen again, never. . . .

He turned his head and looked at me, and what was in his eyes burned me to ash. Nobody, human or Djinn, should live with that kind of guilt and horror. That much longing.

"Let me go," he whispered. "I love you, but please, you have to *let me go*."

I knew he was right. And it was the only time possible I had left to do it.

I hardly felt the bottle shatter as I slammed it against the desktop. Even the slashes in my hand hardly registered. That kind of pain was nothing, it was insignificant against the bonfire burning in my soul.

I felt him leave me, a sudden cutting of the cord, an irrevocable loss that left me empty inside.

He stood up, clothing himself as he moved. Faded, loose khaki pants. A well-worn blue shirt. The olive drab coat swirling around him, brushing the tops of his boots.

He was warmth and fire and everything I had ever wanted in my life.

He fitted his large, square hands around my shoulders, slid them silently up to my face, and pulled me into a kiss. His breath shuddered into my mouth, and I felt his whole body trembling.

"I knew it had to be this way," he whispered. "I'm so sorry, Jo. I'm so—I can't stay in this form for long. I have to go."

"Go," I said. "I'll be fine."

One last kiss, this one fierce and devouring, and in the middle of it he turned to mist and faded away.

I cried out and lurched forward, reaching with a bloody hand for nothing.

At the other end of the room, a window blew out in a silver spray of glass, and buried shrapnel in the wall above the couch.

I gasped and lunged forward, nearly tripping over Eamon,

who was moving weakly, and grabbed Sarah to pull her upright. She couldn't walk, but she mumbled, something about Eamon; I slung her arm across my shoulder and half walked, half dragged her to the door.

As we reached the safety of the hall, another window let loose with the sound of a bomb exploding. *Oh God.* The whole building was shaking.

I dragged Sarah to the stairwell and leaned her against the wall, then ran back to get Eamon. I just couldn't leave him there, helpless, to get shredded, no matter what he'd done. He might deserve to die, but this would be a kind of death I wouldn't wish on anyone.

I pelted in and was blinded for a second by a blaze of lightning that hit close enough to make the hair on my arms tremble. Eamon was still slumped on the floor, bleeding already from a dozen deep cuts; I grabbed him under the arms and pulled, groaning with the strain in my back, across wet carpet and wedges of glittering glass. He twisted around, trying to help or fight; I screamed at him to stop and kept hauling.

Somehow, I wasn't really sure how, I got him into the stairwell and rolled him onto his bleeding back on the concrete. Sarah was on the steps, clinging to the railing, looking pale and vague-eyed and in danger of tumbling; I left Eamon there and jumped over him to catch her when she stumbled. "You're on your own!" I yelled back at him as he reached slowly for the handrail to pull himself up to a sitting position.

I put my arm around Sarah's waist to guide her down the steps.

It was a long, long, *long* way to the bottom. One torturous step at a time. Sarah's bare feet were scratched and bleeding by the time we made it, and she was more or less coherent.

Coherent enough to turn in my arms and look back up the stairs and mumble, "But Eamon . . ."

"Eamon can go to hell," I said grimly. "Come on. We need to get out of here."

She didn't want to, but I wasn't going to take any

crap from Sarah, not now. And not over her abusive psycho boyfriend.

We banged through the door to the stairs into the lobby . . .

. . . and into a group of men standing there looking at the touch screen, just the way I'd done earlier. *Rescue!* I thought in relief, just for a second, and then I realized that these guys weren't exactly dressed like they were public servants on patrol. Three of them looked tough as hell—tattooed, greasy, muscled up past any sensible point of no return.

The fourth one had on a Burberry trench coat that had gone from taupe to chocolate from the force of the rain, and under that a half-soaked hand-tailored suit with a silk tie. I felt sorry for the shoes, which surely looked Italian and not hurricane-safe. He had an expensive haircut even the rain couldn't dampen, a dark mustache, and a cruel twist to his mouth.

He took one look at me, nodded to his Muscle Squad, and they rushed me. Sarah went flying. One of them knotted a big, tattooed hand in her hair and dragged her upright; she wasn't medicated enough not to scream. I didn't fight. I knew I didn't have much of a chance, especially when the Suit pulled out a gun that looked remarkably similar to the one Eamon had been using upstairs. Apparently it was a model much favored by sleazebags.

I wasn't really scared anymore. The kind of day I'd had, adrenaline starts running low after a while. I just stared at him, dumbfounded, and he stared back with lightless dark eyes.

"You're the one," he said. "You're the one who killed Quinn. Drake said you'd be coming. Nice to know I don't have to cut his tongue out for lying to me."

Eamon had sold me out. I don't know why that didn't surprise me.

He walked up to me and shoved the gun under my chin. "I am Eladio Delgado, and you have something I want."

I shut my eyes and thought, *Here we go again.*

INTERLUDE

I'm still sitting on the beach when the storm makes land fall. It closes around me like a black fist, trying to crush me as it's crushing the things born of man all around me—boats shattered into splinters, buildings ripped from foundations, metal twisted and bones crushed.

It can't touch me.

I stand up and walk into the storm surge; it foams around my feet, then my knees, then my thighs . . . not that I have any of those things, really, they're just markers, symbols of what I am. Or was.

I stand in the storm and I listen to it, because it's talking. Not talking in mathematics and physics, the way the Wardens measure things, but in symbols and poetry and the music of a broken heart. It's the mourning of the Earth, this storm. It's the scream of a wounded creature that can't heal.

It's part of me.

As I'm standing there, listening, I feel David's presence slide into the world next to me, and a complex web of energy clicks together. Fulfilling me, and finishing me.

He says, "I don't want it to be this way. Jonathan, please, don't let it be this way."

"I don't have a choice," I tell him, and turn to look at him. She's done him damage, his human girl. Not really human anymore, although I guess she doesn't know that. David's barely Djinn anymore, sliding on that fragile slope back into the dark.

"*You have to stop this,*" he says. He's talking about the storm, of course. But he doesn't really know what he's talking about.

I shrug. "*I already stopped it once. Look how that turned out.*" In the distance, I can feel Ashan and the others waiting, hearing the song of the storm, responding to its call. They're coming for me, and together they're strong enough to take me. I know Rahel is coming, and Alice, and dozens more, and if they get here in time it'll be a pitched battle and the world will bleed. Not be destroyed, because the Earth is tougher than that, older, harder. But everything on it is, in one way or another, fragile.

Life is fragile.

David's eyes are flickering copper, then black, then copper, then black. He is trying desperately to hang on.

"*Jonathan, don't do this. You don't have to do this.*"

"*I do,*" I say, "*because I love you, brother.*"

And I turn and walk into the storm.

I feel him change, behind me, and even over the burning wail of the storm I hear his scream of mortal agony as he changes, as he loses control of who and what he is.

This is how it has to be, I think, just before the Ifrit sinks its talons into my back.

And it hurts just about as much as I expected it to.

NINE

Well, both Eamon and Detective Rodriguez had point-blank warned me that I'd better watch my back. Of course, Eamon had then proceeded to stick a knife in, but that was just his way. At least he'd warned me first.

The cold metal of the gun barrel under my chin made a pretty dramatic statement as to my new friend's intentions. He wasn't the subtle, sinister type like Eamon; he was more like me. Just state your business and get it done.

I respected that.

"I don't have Quinn's stash," I said flatly. No point in doing the I-don't-know-what-you're-talking-about tango. "It blew up with his truck out in the desert, and I've told this story about five times in the past week so excuse me if I don't go over it again except to say, sorry, you're out of luck."

I really was out of adrenaline. My pulse stayed steady, even when he jammed the gun harder into the soft skin under my throat. It made me want to gag. I opened my eyes and looked at him, and close up, he made Quinn look warm and puppy-friendly. Stone-cold killer, this guy. I could feel the lost lives crowding around him like smoke.

"Then I don't need you," he said, "and you need to be taught a lesson, bitch."

"You think you have time?" I shot back. "We're in a *tle bit of trouble here, in case you haven't noticed.

Unless you came in a Sherman tank, I think you may have a little trouble making your escape after—"

Windows blew at the far end of the lobby, and wind screamed in, flapping Delgado's coat in ways Burberry never intended. One of his musclemen rapped something out fast in Spanish, too fast for me to catch. I wanted to turn my head and see what was happening to Sarah, because she was quiet again, and I was worried.

"My friend reminds me that we have a plane to catch in Miami," Delgado said. "And the roads are very bad. So I don't have time for you or your bullshit. Do you have my stuff? Yes or no."

I kept holding the stare. "No."

"You have anything I might·be interested in?"

"No."

"Too bad." He shrugged and put the gun back in his pocket. "Take them outside. You know what to do."

His guys didn't hesitate. My feet scrabbled for purchase on the floor, but they just lifted me up by the elbows as he stepped away, and carried me like a paper doll toward the big, thick glass doors. There was some discussion about how to open them, given the wind pressure. They finally decided on the one on the right. When they opened it, the hurricane blast caught it, slammed it back, and shattered it into safety-glass fragments against the stone wall. The metal backstop had been ripped totally out of the concrete.

"Wait!" I screamed. It didn't matter, and in the next second the two men carrying me had me outside and whatever noise I made was drowned out by the piercing, constant shriek of the storm as it crept ashore.

We weren't anywhere near the worst of the storm yet, and the wreckage was awesome. The two musclemen were having a time of it, shuffling along hunched against the wind; they got to one of two giant palm trees that were bending and thrashing like rubber toys and threw me up against the rough trunk, facing out. I saw Sarah out of the corner of my watering eye, joining me. Our fingers instantly locked together.

Muscleman number one grabbed a roll of duct tape out of his jacket pocket and started wrapping it around me, Sarah, the tree trunk. Tough, sticky tape binding my hands together, then looping over my knees, my hips, my breasts, my shoulders, my neck.

Same with Sarah. We were duct-taped to the tree, facing the storm. The rain hit like needles, agonizing and unstoppable. I had no leverage, and I knew Sarah couldn't do anything, groggy as she was.

Muscleman grinned at us, wrinkling his tattoos, and he and his cronies shuffled off to join Big Boss Delgado inside his huge black Hummer. Which, if you didn't have a Sherman tank, was probably the best idea for a storm like this.

Delgado didn't even turn to look at us as they drove away. He was already on his cell phone, punching numbers. We were yesterday's to-do list.

I couldn't get my breath. The wind was pummeling us hard, in bruising gusts that were going to turn bone-breaking before long. My skin already felt as if it were being burned off with a soldering iron from the constant impact of the rain—water torture in fast-forward.

I screamed in rage and tried to draw power. I got a weak stir of response, but nothing that could counter the awesome power of this storm, nothing that could break duct tape. It was resistant to water. Over time, it might weaken enough for me to break free, but they'd done a damn good job of making sure I didn't have any stress points to work on.

I heard more windows blow out over the scream of the wind. I tasted salt and blood, gasped for breath, and closed my eyes against the relentless, pounding rain.

Sarah was screaming. I could hear her in the brief lulls before the next waves of gusts. Delgado hadn't wasted a bullet on us, but he'd executed us in fine style. If we were lucky, we'd pass out from the pain before debris tarted hitting us and slicing us apart, one piece at a time—or blown sand began to blast our skin off, layer by layer. We might suffocate from the pressure of the wind on our chests, since we couldn't move to relieve it.

But we were already dead. We were just going to take a long time getting to the end of it.

I summoned up enough breath to scream, "David!"

Because he'd come. He'd said he'd always come, and I needed him, God, I needed him right now more than I ever had. . . .

He didn't come. Nobody came.

I felt something sharp slice my cheek—blown metal, maybe, or maybe only a palm frond—and saw blood whip red in a stream into the wind.

I wasn't ready to die. I didn't want to die like this. Not like this. I'd faced it so many times already, and it was all bad, but *this* . . .

Please, I prayed.

A figure appeared out of the blur of the storm, leaning into the wind, grabbing hold of the trembling metal railing on the building ramp for stability, and when he turned his head toward me I saw that it was Eamon. Wind-bruised, streaming with rain. All his polish was gone, and what was left was frighteningly primal.

He lunged and caught hold of the duct tape around my waist, holding to it with those long, bloodied fingers.

For a frozen second, I couldn't say anything at all. He looked insane. Insane and oddly turned on.

"Ask me," he shouted. Even six inches away, the wind nearly ripped his words into nonsense. He tugged on the duct tape binding me. "Ask me!"

"Please," I screamed. "Please—"

He grinned, showing teeth, and reached into his pocket. Came up with a switchblade knife that he flicked open with a practiced twist of his hand. The blade was at least six inches long, and gleamed wetly in the dim light.

"Please what?" he asked, and put the knife to exposed skin just under the notch of my collarbone. "Articulate, my love. Speak up."

"Please save my sister!"

He froze, eyes blinking, and slowly took the knife away.

"Save my sister, you bastard. You owe me that."

Eamon Drake, bastard at large, stepped back, sliced through the duct tape, and dragged Sarah away from the tree. He tugged her flapping bathrobe back into place, yanked the knot tight, and hugged her in both arms to protect her from the wind.

And in that moment I knew, absolutely, that she wasn't just a means to an end to him. And maybe never had been.

He was still watching me, with a curious kind of light in his eyes.

"Beg," he shouted. I could barely catch the tattered rag of sound. A blast of wind nearly toppled him over and he braced himself with his knife hand against the tree, over my head. Leaning close.

"Fuck off!" I screamed back.

He grinned and leaned back, and drove the knife straight at me.

I jerked my head to one side, gasping, and felt the duct tape pull as he cut it barely a quarter inch from my neck. I felt the cold kiss of the knife drag down and bury itself shallowly in the skin of my shoulder.

He wasn't as careful in cutting the others. Quick, careless slashes. I felt the pinsparks of pain.

"You can beg me later, love," he said, and picked Sarah up with a sudden heave, dropping the knife to the ground. The wind skittered it away. He threw my sister's limp weight over his shoulder and staggered away toward the parking garage.

I fell forward, or tried to, but the storm held me up, anchoring me against the tree as firmly as the duct tape had. I managed to strip the remains of the restraints off, and staggered sideways, rubbing skin from my back against the harsh triangular scales of the tree, and when I turned the wind slammed me violently off balance, back toward the building.

Cherise was still inside.

I don't know how I made it back to the lobby—clawing the whole way, bleeding, nearly blind—and fell face-first on the glass-scattered, rain-slick marble. Shock was setting in. I felt distant and dreamy, and nothing seemed to matter much just now. Sarah was with Eamon, and that was bad, but at least she wasn't getting her skin abraded off out in the hurricane. *I'll fix it,* I promised myself. *I'll fix everything, soon.*

David hadn't come to save me. I tried not to think about that.

When I staggered to the closet and threw the door open, Cherise was huddled under the cot, wrapped in a blanket. All china-pale skin and huge, blue eyes.

"I stayed," she said in a small voice.

"Good job. And we're going," I said, and started to laugh. It wasn't a good kind of laugh. I choked it off and took her hand.

The less I say about making it from the building to the parking garage, the better. The tunnel was a shattered-open concrete bridge, a deathtrap only a complete idiot would attempt; we somehow made it by crawling across the open ground and made it into the relative shelter of the garage.

Stairs were a misery. I made it somehow, with Cherise tugging me this time.

I think I blacked out. When I came around again, Cherise was driving the Mustang out of the garage, chanting something under her breath that sounded like *please please please,* and the wind hit the car and shuddered it five feet to the left, violently, and I knew we weren't going to make it.

Something loomed out of the darkness to our right. I saw it at the same time as Cherise, and we both screamed.

Apparently Eladio Delgado's Hummer had caught a bad gust, and once it was on its side, it was like a giant sail. It was being shoved along at highway speeds, and it was heading straight for us.

It hit a broken chunk of concrete and flew into the

air, flipping uncontrollably. I covered my head, uselessly, and saw Cherise do the same . . .

The world stopped.

Breathless.

I felt Jonathan die, and it was a terrible thing, like every mouth in the world opening to scream. The fabric of things unraveled, and time twisted on its axis, and the sky went black and red and gold and green and a color that should only exist on the aetheric, but the aetheric was burning, everything was burning at levels that could never catch fire because *this shouldn't happen.* . . .

And the storm died with him.

Nothing just *stops,* of course; the wind kept blowing and the waves kept surging ahead of it, but I felt the sentient black anguish of that hurricane extinguish itself in a blaze of heart-destroying sorrow, and time skipped two beats for a period of mourning, and then . . .

. . . then Eladio Delgado's Hummer slammed to the ground two feet to the left of the Mustang, rolled, and exploded into flame so hot that I felt it on the passenger side of the car, through layers of steel and glass.

Cherise, screaming, hit the gas and got us the hell out. We skidded wildly, pushed around by the wind, but made it to the road.

I looked back and saw the windowless, shattered outline of the Testosterone Towers shivering and swaying in the wind. Not quite breaking, but almost.

Over the ocean, the black clouds slowed down their manic swirl, and while the rain kept lashing, the winds slowly decreased in speed.

Cherise drove too fast, skidding around debris and wrecks, trembling like a leaf. I didn't stop her. I was listening to the silence on the aetheric.

I'd never felt anything like this before, this . . . absence.

"Stop," I said suddenly. Cherise didn't seem to hear me. I lunged and grabbed for the steering wheel; she hit the brakes and fought me, but we somehow got the Mustang safely pulled over to the side of the road. Gale-force winds continued to shudder the car. "Stay here," I said, and got out.

My legs almost folded, but I found that inner core of strength David had always told me I had, and crossed the slick, hurricane-buckled surface of the road to what had once been the beach. More ocean than sand, now. Blue-white foam. Not really water, not really air; you could drown in it but never sink.

I'd lost my shoes somewhere. My feet sank deep into wet sand, and I kept walking, unsteady, wandering left and then right.

I saw the Djinn standing in the surf. Ashan, looking gray as death. Inhuman. Alice in her wet pinafore, with long golden hair whipped straight by the wind. Rahel, on her knees in the foam, staring out to sea.

Dozens of them.

Then hundreds, forming in whispers of mist and fog and ocean, all staring out to sea.

I felt the heat move through me, and went to my knees, too. Moaned and pitched forward on my hands, panting against the pressure.

Something was talking. Something huge. I couldn't understand it, only feel it, and humans weren't made to contain this kind of emotion. I wanted to scream, and laugh, and die. In a blinding rush I *knew;* I knew what it was all about, I knew love in its most intense, furious, burning form, and it was like nothing I had ever felt, even as a Djinn.

All around me, the Djinn were lifting up their heads, staring at the sky. Eyes closed. Drinking in the flood of light and love.

And then it ended, and I felt empty, so very empty.

Someone came walking out of the surf, naked and golden and beautiful, and he wasn't David anymore, not my David, he was something more.

On the aetheric, he was a white-hot star, and every-thing, *everything* linked to him. Every Djinn. Every War-

den. The network clicked into place and began to hum
with power, vast and intense.

Jonathan was dead.

And David had become the linchpin in his place.

He staggered and went down in the water, and Ashan
and Rahel leaped forward, taking his arms, dragging him
out onto the shore. I got to my feet but didn't move
toward them, because something in me told me . . . it
wasn't right. Not anymore.

When he got up, David was dressed and steady. He
looked the same as he always had, on the surface, but
what was underneath was hugely different.

As he looked at me, I saw eternity in his eyes. They
were black, swirling with galaxies and energy.

He came to me and crouched down. Not touching me,
except with the force of his emotion. "I'm sorry," he told
me softly. "I'm so sorry. I wish things were different, Jo."

All the Djinn turned to look at me, and I felt the force
of their stares. All those inhuman eyes. All that power,
back in their own hands.

Something was very, very wrong.

I heard that murmur again, echoing on a level that I
couldn't hear or understand, only feel.

David reached out, but his hand stopped a few inches
from my skin. There was a vast distance between us, a
gulf neither of us could reach across. "Tell the Wardens
that the Djinn can't be owned anymore. That agreement
died with Jonathan. It's a new world now."

I swallowed hard. I could feel the difference on the
aetheric, a silvery vibration that was growing stronger.
Like a gigantic, slow heartbeat.

"What's happening?"

He glanced up, as if he could see what I was feeling.
"She's coming awake."

"Who's coming awake?"

His black eyes came down to meet mine again. "The
Mother. *Our* Mother. *Your* Mother."

Earth.

"Is that . . ." I was really afraid to ask. "That's not good, is it."

"Not for you," he said. "I'm sorry. I love you, but I can't protect you, not from her."

Something changed in that whisper. A red thread of anger in the silver pulse. David's eyes swirled from black to crimson, then back again.

Rahel's, too.

And Ashan's.

"You need to tell the Wardens," David said. "You need to tell them that she's dreaming, but the dream is ending. She's going to be very—"

His eyes turned entirely red.

"Angry," he said. "She's already angry, even in her dreams. We don't have any choice. We belong to her now."

I stumbled back. He didn't move to attack. None of them did, but I could feel the pulse of menace, pounding faster.

"Run," David told me softly. "Tell the Wardens. Tell them they need to stop her. Stop us before it's too late. Before she wakes up all the way."

"How?" Because I had no idea, none at all, how any group of Wardens, no matter how powerful, could begin to fight the Djinn, much less the Earth itself. It was just . . . impossible. "David! *How?*"

"RUN!" he screamed.

I felt his control shatter with a sound like breaking crystal, and stumbled backward from what I saw in his eyes.

A hand closed around my arm and jerked me upright. Not David. Not Rahel. Not Ashan. I didn't know this Djinn. She had waist-length, glossy black hair falling in waves; she had burnished golden skin and eyes like the sun.

"Stop staring and *run*," she yelled, and shoved me to the car.

We ran. Behind us, hundreds of Djinn closed in on us like a silent, deadly pack of hounds. My savior practically threw me into the car, leaped in the passenger door and screamed at Cherise, *"DRIVE!"* When Cherise stared, uncomprehending, the Djinn gestured at the gas pedal.

We peeled out at an inhuman speed, leaving the storm-swept beach and the rest of the Djinn behind.

David came closest to catching us. I twisted to watch him disappearing in the back window, a tall figure standing in the road, coat blowing and belling in the wind.

"Are you all right?" the black-haired Djinn asked. I blinked at her. She looked familiar, but I had no idea why. "Hey! Can you hear me? Are you all right?"

I opened my mouth to tell her that I was, but something was happening in the back of my mind, something enormous and unbelievable. I knew something, but I couldn't think what it was.

She must have seen it in my eyes, the knowledge and the fear, because she smiled, and when I saw the smile, it all came into blinding clarity.

That was David's smile.

That was my *face*.

That was *my daughter*.

"Imara," I said. She closed her hand around mine, and her skin was hot and smooth and real. "Oh, my God. How . . ."

"Jonathan," she said, and the smile turned sad. "It takes death to make a Djinn. He told you."

I remembered him taking the spark of life from me and walking away. He'd known, even then, what he intended to do. Die. Put his power into David.

Give life to David's child.

I had a *child*. Okay, she was a six-foot Amazon goddess dressed in flawless, tailored black, but she was *my child*. And she wasn't like the others. She wasn't in thrall to the Earth, at least not completely; she could still think for herself, act for herself. Act against them.

And Jonathan must have known that, too. Maybe this was his way of apologizing.

Cherise gulped and said, "Jo? Is this some kind of alien thing? Are you really, like, from space and a thousand years old and going to take over the planet? Is this an invasion?" She was serious. But then, I supposed that explanation made more sense than the reality.

"You're kidding, right?" Imara asked, grinning. "Do we look like aliens to you?"

Cherise took her eyes off the road for so long I was afraid we were going to find out the crash-test rating of a Mustang. "Yeah," she said. "Well, *you* do. With the eyes and all."

Imara winked at her, and through the touch of her hand on mine she poured power into me, healing power, easing my various cuts and wounds and restoring some of my life energy.

"Maybe I am," she said. "You never know, right?"

Cherise was oddly cheered. "Nope," she said. "Jo? Where do you want me to go?"

I raised my eyebrows at Imara, who shrugged. So strange, seeing myself from the outside. Although I could see hints of David in the highlights of her hair, and the golden wash of her skin. Me, made exotic.

I couldn't feel anything yet, but I knew this was going to hit me later, in big, strange ways. Grief and love and terror and awareness of my own mortality, in ways I had never considered.

"New York," I said. "The Wardens need to get their act together, right now, if I have to kick every ass from here to Beijing. We can't afford to lose." Because if the Wardens folded, then there was nothing between the 6.5 billion people on the planet and Mother Earth in the grip of dreams, nightmares, and rage.

With the Djinn at her command.

David had told me, explicitly. *Tell them they need to stop her. Stop us.*

The Wardens were at war with the Djinn.

Track List

Music to read by (or at least, it really worked for me to write to . .)—and this time, it's a double album!

School	Supertramp
Paper in Fire	John Mellencamp
Larger Than Life	The Feelers
I Scare Myself	Thomas Dolby
Pain and Sorrow	Joe Bonamassa
Harder to Breathe	Maroon 5
Madonna	Jude Christadel
Let Go	Frou Frou
Tell Your Story Walking	Deb Talan
Travelin' Shoes	Ruthie Foster
A New Day Yesterday (Live)	Joe Bonamassa
Better	Brooke Fraser
Building a Mystery	Sarah McLachlan
Budapest by Blimp	Thomas Dolby
Serve Somebody	Bob Dylan
I'm Ready	Aerosmith
One Way	Amelia Royko
Lifeline	Brooke Fraser
Woke Up This Morning	A3
Highway Robbery	Amelia Royko
Cannonball	Supertramp
Crescent Heights Shuffle	Jude Christadel
Woke Up Dreaming	Joe Bonamassa

I Love You, Good-bye .... Thomas Dolby

Support these artists. Without your contributions, they can't continue to devote themselves to making music. And none of us want that.

And go buy *Had To Cry Today* by Joe Bonamassa. A special request from me . . . and a treat for you, too.

—Rachel Caine

A Public Service Announcement

Do you know what to do to prepare for most emergencies—especially those pesky weather-inspired ones? Follow this simple advice:

1. **Make a plan.** Create a list of important phone numbers, including an out-of-town contact. Agree on a meeting place with your family or loved ones in case you become separated. Keep your list of numbers and meeting places with you at all times.

2. **Get a kit together.** Assemble everything on the Ready Kit Checklist below, or pick up a Ready Kit at a local store. Keep it in a safe, dry place at home. This is a *recommended* list of items. You may want to add things to it, especially if you've got pets, small children, or elderly people depending on you.

3. **Be informed.** Know your local emergency plans, including those at your child's school. Participate in workplace emergency drills.

Here's your **Ready Kit Checklist:**

- Battery-powered flashlight
- Battery-powered radio
- Extra batteries
- Whistle

- First-Aid kit
- Dust mask or cotton T-shirt
- Three-day supply of food and water
- Wrench to turn off utilities
- Plastic sheeting
- Duct tape
- Moist towelettes
- Rain gear (ponchos and hats)
- Warm clothes
- Emergency blanket
- Container for extra water
- Extra doses of important medications
- Personal identification
- Leather gloves
- Garbage bags and ties
- Family communication plans
- Special needs items

Visit www.ready.gov to find out about different emergencies and how to prepare for them. *Always* listen to weather warnings from your local authorities, and seek shelter if bad weather approaches.

And please . . . leave stormchasing to the professionals.

Best wishes,

Rachel Caine

I was thinking that the Wardens needed a new motto. The old one, the one on the seals on my diploma, was *Defensor Hominem,* Latin for "Defender of Mankind," but sometime in the past twenty-four hours, I'd become convinced that I had a more appropriate one. *We're So Screwed.*

Yeah, that pretty much covered it.

That could have been the exhaustion talking, of course. After all, I'd been marked for death by virtually every group I'd come into contact with during the past couple of months, with the possible exception of the Girl Scouts, who only wanted to make me fat with their cookies. I'd been lied to, stalked, betrayed, attacked by Djinn, pummeled by South American drug dealers, and left to die in a hurricane, and my sister Sarah had been abducted— or possibly saved—by an evil lying British bastard who might have fallen in love with her.

And those were the good parts. I didn't even want to think about the low points, but that was all I'd been doing, really, through a really long, hellish drive from Florida to New York.

I was behind the wheel of Cherise's cherry red muscle car, and in the midst of all the bad news, that was a good thing. The Mustang purred around me like a contented tiger. Not the Mustang's fault that I was so tired I wanted to weep, or that my world was falling apart, or that I was headed for New York, in exactly the opposite direction from where I needed to be to find my sister.

Nope. Not the Mustang's fault. I liked the Mustang just fine.

The Mustang's actual owner—Cherise, in the passenger seat—stirred and smacked her lips the way people do when they wake up with monster morning breath. She blinked at the pastel wash of late-night lights as we came out of the Lincoln Tunnel, and stretched as we cruised to a halt at a stoplight. Guys in the cars all around us watched, even though Cherise wasn't at her well-groomed best at the moment. Some girls just have it. Cherise had so much of it, the rest of us needed time-shares to get by.

"Nurgh," she said, or something like it, then dry-rubbed her face and threw back her hair and tried again. "Whatimsit?" Or a mumble to that effect.

"Almost one a.m.," I said. Since we'd traveled directly up the Eastern seaboard, the Mustang's dashboard clock hadn't been fazed by our twelve-hundred-miles-in-just-under-one-day jaunt. I eyed it with the numbed disbelief of someone who couldn't quite fathom where all the hours had gone. Straight into my ass, it felt like. "Imara—"

I checked the backseat in the mirror, but it was in shadow, and I couldn't see anyone back there. The light turned green. As we passed in and out of the white-hot strobe of a streetlight, I saw that she wasn't just lying down; Imara was gone. The backseat was bare. "Great. She's missing again." Djinn did that. And Imara—my daughter Imara, by my beloved David—was certainly all Djinn, all the time, only oddly not subject to the same fever madness that had the rest of them just now. Funny, just two days before, I'd been on the maybe-someday side of motherhood, worried and nervous and not sure how all of this was going to happen. Or if it would at all. Today, my daughter was taller than I was, wore better clothes, and could blip around anywhere she pleased at the blink of an eye.

That's what happens when you get on any side—good or bad—of very powerful Djinn. I'd been on the good side of David. The bad side of Jonathan. And both of them had more or less conspired to make me a . . . mom.

Wasn't sure I liked it. I checked my readiness level. I was still a quart low, not that either of them had bothered to consult me about it . . . and now my daughter was out running around by herself. Adult and more capable of taking care of herself than I was, but still. I worried.

Maybe that came with the mom package.

"She's gone?" Cherise turned and peered over the leather seat. "Oh. Man, how does she *do* that?"

"Magic," I sighed.

"I think she beams up."

"Cher, she's not an alien."

"Right," she said. "Not an alien. Glowing eyes, disappears at the drop of a hat. But not from another planet, got it. So, tell me again where we're going?"

"You remember how I told you I control the weather? Well, there's an organization of people like me, and they have a headquarters here."

"Here in New York City."

"Midtown East, to be exact. First and Forty-sixth." She had a look of noncomprehension. "The UN Building."

Her expression didn't change.

"You have heard of the UN, right? United Nations? Bunch of guys who get together, talk about world peace . . . ?"

"Shut up! I know what the UN is!"

"Sorry."

"But . . . the UN controls the weather? Because I thought there was something about, you know, world peace."

"No, they don't control the weather. They lease office space to the Wardens, who do."

She didn't bother to say, "You're insane," but the expression on her face was pretty clear. She even edged a little bit more toward the passenger-side window. I was wishing that I'd dumped Cherise off at any of the various gas stations we'd visited along the way, but it would only take one unhappy phone call from her claiming I'd stolen her car to end my trip real quick. Hadn't seemed prudent, given the priorities.

I made the turns and parked in a public garage near Grand Central Station. There wasn't any parking at the UN for security reasons. I negotiated with the garage attendant, got a ticket, and grabbed hold of Cherise to steer her along. She didn't really want to move, and I could see why: The attendant was probably an aspiring model. He had that slightly starved look, frayed jeans that rode low on his hips, and a dreamy look in his eyes. I wasn't impressed, but Cherise looked tempted to take a bite out of the Big Apple.

"Walk," I told her sternly, and pointed her down Forty-second Street toward the intersection with First. Even this late, the foot traffic was still heavy, but it thinned dramatically when we turned onto First Avenue and headed for Forty-sixth. The UN building wasn't much to look at, architecturally speaking: just a medium-sized Lego of a building stuck in a big concrete block, dressed up with a lot of spotlit flags. The main entrance was up ahead, but I turned her left at the next block, heading for the back.

"You weren't kidding," Cherise said, studying the building as we got closer. "We really are going to the UN building. Is it even open?"

"Trust me, the Wardens never close." My feet hurt, and I really, really needed a shower. I'd scrubbed cleanish in a truck stop restroom six hours ago, because I just hadn't been able to stand it anymore, but I wasn't what you might call ready for a hot date. My eyes ached and watered from the glare of streetlights. I was grateful that at least it wasn't full daylight. That would have been much, much worse. "Come on, we have a special door."

"We do? Cool."

There was supposed to be a special guard on the spe-

cial door, too. There was certainly a special guardpost, a
tiny concrete hut next to the in-set, unmarked doorway,
and as far as I knew it was manned twenty-four/seven.
Only nobody was there. Maybe the guard had gone for
a call of nature, but I kind of doubted it. I tried the steel
door to the hut. Locked. Lights glowed on panels inside,
but the windows were covered with steel mesh. Cherise
and I were standing in a hot white wash of light, looking
suspicious. I looked around, and sure enough, there was
a camera. I waved, then turned to the door.

"There's no lock," Cherise said. "Don't they have to
open it from in there or something?"

"Or something."

I held up my hand and concentrated. A faint blue sparkle moved across it, lighting up the stylized sunburst that
was the symbol of the Wardens. It was magically tattooed
into my flesh, and it couldn't be faked.

The door didn't open. Evidently it wasn't keyed to the
manifestation of the symbol, either.

I waited, but nothing happened. If there'd been crick
ets around, they would have been chirping. I sighed,
looked at Cherise, and shook my head. I ran a hand
through my hair and pushed it back from my face, back
over my shoulders, and wondered what my chances were
of bluffing the regular UN guards into granting me
admittance.

Okay, I didn't wonder very long.

"Right," I said. "I guess we'll have to wait until . . ."

The door let loose with a thick metallic *chunk* and
swung open about a quarter of an inch.

". . . hey, right about now," I finished. I grabbed the
edge and moved it wider. It was heavy. Bombproof, most
likely. I ushered Cherise inside, grabbed the handle, and
pulled it tight behind me. The lock engaged with a snap
and hum of power. Not electrical power. The other kind.

"Um . . . Jo?" Cherise sounded spooked.

When I turned, there were two people standing in the
industrial concrete-block hallway facing us. Both were in
blue blazers with a logo on them—UN Security—but

with the additional graphic touch of the Wardens' symbol pinned to their lapels. Man and woman, both tall and capable-looking. I didn't know them.

I'd seen guns before, though, and they had two big ones, pointed right at us.

About the Author

Rachel Caine is the author of more than fifteen novels, including the Weather Warden series. She was born at White Sands Missile Range, which people who know her say explains a lot. She has been an accountant, a professional musician, and an insurance investigator, and still carries on a secret identity in the corporate world. She and her husband, fantasy artist R. Cat Conrad, live in Texas with their iguanas, Popeye and Darwin, a *mali uromastyx* named (appropriately) O'Malley, and a leopard tortoise named Shelley (for the poet, of course). Visit her Web site at www.rachelcaine.com.